THE
WICKED
LADY

BRENDA K. JERNIGAN

Zebra Books
Kensington Publishing Corp.
http://www.zebrabooks.com

IN MEMORY

This book is in memory of my mother Bonnie Dittman, who died much too young of breast cancer. A portion of the proceeds of this book will be donated to HOSPICE so they can help those who can't help themselves.

DEDICATION

Ken Bryan—this one is for you.

ZEBRA BOOKS are published by

Kensington Publishing Corp.
850 Third Avenue
New York, NY 10022

Zebra, the Z logo and Splendor Reg. U.S. Pat. & TM Off.

First Printing: March, 2000
10 9 8 7 6 5 4 3 2 1

Printed in the United States of America.

JUST ONE LITTLE KISS

That was all Trevor wanted. Then he'd be satisfied and could send Kristen on her way. Her lips were soft and wet as he moved his mouth over hers. It was a featherlike kiss, and then it was over.

" 'Twas nice." Her eyes were wide and clear, staring at him with unblinking innocence.

"Nice?" Trevor drew his brows together. Since when did a woman describe his kiss as merely nice. "Nice?" he repeated.

"I thought p'haps there would be more."

"Don't tell me you've never been kissed before."

"Nay, I have not."

"Then perhaps we should try again."

"What for?"

Trevor couldn't help but chuckle. "I would hate to leave you disappointed. There is a little more to a kiss than I've shown you."

His arms went around her, and he pressed her to him till she was molded to his body. Again his lips touched hers, softly at first, but this time the kiss was different and all her senses sprang to life as his mouth moved over hers. His tongue touched her lips, and she jerked away.

"Trust me," he whispered and pulled her back into his embrace. . . .

CHAPTER ONE

She hadn't meant to shoot the man!

Kristen Johnstone fled down the narrow, cobblestoned streets of London, trying to lose her pursuers. She glanced up at the eaves of the buildings she passed; gargoyles were laughing down at her.

Kristen knew she was doomed.

But the gargoyles didn't scare her half as much as the eyes of the man she'd just shot. The vivid blue still lingered in her mind: first the amused expression, followed by the irritated frown as he'd grabbed her in the act of picking his pocket, then the look of surprise when her gun went off.

She had to move faster!

She could go to jail for a very long time for what she'd done. Then who would take care of Hagan? Her five-year-old brother would have no one.

She had to hurry.

Stay close to the shadows of the buildings, she warned herself.

A tear slipped down her cheek as she rounded the next corner. What was the matter with her? She never cried. She hadn't wept once since her mother died, and now was no time to start.

She hadn't meant to hurt the man.

But what if she'd killed him?

Of course, it hadn't been entirely her fault. True, her hand had been in his pocket, but he'd grabbed her. That was when she smelled the liquor. All the horrible beatings she'd suffered from her stepfather came rushing back to torment her. Kristen had vowed then to die before she ever let anyone hit her again. So, she had simply reacted.

Turning to look over her shoulder, Kristen gasped.

The three men were gaining on her. Why couldn't she shake them? She knew the streets—every nook and cranny where one could hide—better than anyone. Two more turns, then down a small alley, and she'd be free.

Her lungs burned and her parched throat was dry and raw. She couldn't go much farther. Her heart pounded, and the lack of food made her weaker than normal. Not paying attention, she crashed into a trash heap, sending debris tumbling down the street as she fought to keep her footing.

"If ye'd just let me out of this one, Father," Kristen whispered as she glanced toward heaven. "I promise to repent."

Just then she tripped on a brick and went flying headfirst, landing in a heap on the cold cobblestones.

"Get up, girl," one of her pursuers said as he yanked her to her feet.

"I—I can't breathe," she managed to gasp.

"You're just winded." A big, burly man patted her on

the back. "Course, if ya hadn't run us to death this wouldn't have happened."

Kristen took a huge gasp of air. "I dinna mean to kill him. 'Twas an accident." Wide-eyed, she looked up at the bloke. This one was a giant with bulging muscles. "Ye don't really mean to turn me over now, do ye?" Kristen made sure she didn't break eye contact as she slipped his knife out of his pocket. The big ones were as dumb as the rest, she thought.

The other man found his voice, "My God, Robbie, she's a Scot. Ya know how Claremont hates all Scots."

"Yeah, I know." The one called Robbie nodded his head as if he might be thinking of letting her go. "The boss has been in a surly mood lately. She's only going to make it worse."

"And what might be wrong with a Scot? And who is this Claremont?" Kristen demanded.

"Come on, girl." Robbie grabbed her arm. "Claremont is the man you just shot. You'll meet him in good time." Robbie tugged, but she pulled back. "You've given us enough trouble for one day." This time he jerked her hard, and she fell against his chest. "I can see we're going to have to do this the hard way," he said, and tossed her over his shoulder like a sack. "I'm not going to turn you over to the authorities, girl. I'm taking you to Claremont."

"Put me down!" Kristen beat on his back. "I'll scream," she threatened when nothing else seemed to work.

Robbie swore. "Go ahead," he muttered. Then he chuckled.

Of course, Kristen didn't utter a sound. She knew no one could help her now, and she especially didn't want to attract a Bow Street officer. She was doomed at eighteen. And worse than that, who would take care of Hagan? He was too young to survive the streets alone.

Kristen could smell the saltwater and hear the rude comments of the dockworkers, letting her know she was nearing the river. All the blood had rushed to her head from hanging upside down and her temples pounded. She looked up to see her brother starting for them, and frantically waved him away.

"Let go of my sister." The sandy-haired child ran over and kicked the man following them.

"Run, Hagan! Run!"

"Now, what do we have here?" Robbie picked the child up by the collar. "A little scamp?"

"Leave my sister alone!" Hagan swung at Robbie, barely missing his nose.

"This gets more interesting all the time." Robbie tucked Hagan under his arm and started up the gangplank.

"No!" Kristen managed to scream in her upside-down position. "I—I can't swim." She started thrashing around, beating her hands on his back.

"Then I suggest you quit struggling," said a deep voice from someone she couldn't see, but was certain she'd not heard before. One that sent shivers down her spine.

She had to think fast. "Hagan, I told ye to stay home. Now look what's happened. Don't say a thing, ye hear?"

"Look, Kristen. 'Tis a ship," Hagan breathed. The child wasn't any more worried than a flea on a dog.

"I see you were successful, Robbie," said the same deep voice.

Kristen twisted to see the speaker, without success.

"Take the thief to my cabin. And what's this you have under your other arm?"

"Seems our thief has a brother, sir."

Kristen and Hagan were placed in a cabin. The big man called Robbie gave her a soulful look before he turned to leave. The light faded as the door closed and locked between them and freedom. She wondered how she'd ever get out of this one.

The room was large for a ship and very neat. A table commanded the middle, and a single bunk was built into the side. There was a desk in the far corner, and a sea chest in another. Kristen assumed this must be the captain's quarters.

"Gosh, Kristen. This is jolly good. Never been on a ship before."

" 'Tis not an adventure, Hagan. I could be in a lot of trouble."

"You'll get out of it, Kristen. You always do."

She could see complete faith in the child's big brown eyes. At the moment, he was the only one with confidence in her.

Suddenly, the door flew open, and Robbie and a man like no one she'd ever seen before filled every inch of the doorway. Kristen's legs trembled, but she struggled to hide her reaction. The man had unusual greenish-blue eyes. His jaw was rigid. A muscle worked below his cheekbone as he glared at her, and his left arm carried a crimson stain. Even though his stance was relaxed, it was clear he wasn't.

"Ye're not dead," she managed to whisper.

"Are you disappointed?" His scowl was hot enough to burn her.

"No." She swallowed hard. "I didna mean to shoot ye."

"So what do you call this?" He pointed to his injury with a cynical smile.

"A mistake," Kristen offered. "I did pull the trigger, but 'twas an accident."

He took a step closer, making Kristen feel smaller still. "And I suppose your hand in my pocket was an accident too?"

"Nay, that was on purpose," she admitted, and watched as the man smiled for the first time. He could almost be called handsome when he wasn't frowning and the coldness left his eyes. She noted his eyes had changed from the dark color they were a moment ago to a lighter blue. His hair was the color of dark wheat and a bit longer than stylish. He kept it tied back with a leather thong. Ah, but he was big—too big, she thought, now that she'd gotten a good look at him. Why hadn't she picked a smaller man's pocket?

Probably for the same reason she couldn't quit looking at the man now. He was a fine one.

"Well, at least you're an honest thief. Which surprises me since you're a *Scot.*" He took another step forward, and she took one backward, and then another when he didn't stop.

"Don't you hurt my sister!" Hagan drew back and kicked Claremont in the shin.

"Watch it!" Robbie's warning came a little too late. "The boy's got a nasty habit."

"Bloody hell," Trevor Claremont shouted as he snatched the child up by the scruff of the neck.

The child's brown eyes grew large, but he put on a brave front. "I'm not 'fraid of you," he blustered, reminding Claremont of a kitten spitting and hissing.

Trevor wanted to smile at the brave little boy who reminded him a lot of himself at that age, but he didn't. He admired the lad for taking up for his sister. The boy's hair was cut in a bob that hung to his eyebrows, and he looked as if he was peeking from beneath his bangs. A child this young shouldn't be on the streets. Then again, neither should his sister.

"I wasn't going to hurt your sister. I'm going to make sure she doesn't hurt me," Trevor explained in a very

THE WICKED LADY 11

level tone to the youngster. "Do you see this blood on my shoulder?"

"Aye." The child's head bobbed. "How did that happen?"

"Your sister shot me!" Trevor set the boy back on his feet.

The kid turned and looked at his sister. "What you do that for, Kristen?"

"Hush up, Hagan."

"No, go ahead." Trevor turned his attention back to the girl, who could be called pretty if she were properly dressed. He was surprised that she and her brother were fairly clean. Usually, such urchins had two layers of dirt on them. "Why did you shoot me when I've never done anything to you?"

"Ye had been drinkin' and when ye grabbed me—well, let's just say I didna want a beating."

"I only had one whiskey, and I'm not drunk. You would have found that out if you'd only asked first and shot later!"

Trevor had backed the girl to the bed where she couldn't go any further. He wondered how many beatings she'd suffered and by whose hand. He was sure she wouldn't tell him. But if she did, he'd make sure the man never struck her again.

Kristen. The boy had called her Kristen. He liked that name even if she was a bloody Scot. "You don't mind if I search you myself?" He held her with his gaze. "Just in case you're carrying another weapon." He placed his hand on her shoulders, and she jumped. "I don't need yet another hole in my body."

"Doesn't look like I can stop ye."

His hand moved slowly down arms that were much too thin. When he got to the end of her sleeve he felt something hard and carefully slid it out from beneath the thin material. "Ah, what's this, my lovely one?"

Robbie, who had been fairly quiet as he kept an eye on the child, shouted, "It's me bloody knife. When did she get that?"

Trevor threw it to his first mate. "You're lucky you don't have a hole in you too."

"I didn't suspect . . . didn't feel a thing."

"I know." Trevor said. "Take the boy and go get some bandages. I'm going to let the lady clean up the mess she has made of my arm."

"Kristen, you said we could get something to eat," Hagan said before he moved.

She was about to answer, but Trevor cut her off. "When was the last time you ate, son?"

"I had a piece of bread yesterday, but it was small."

"What's your name?"

"Hagan."

"Robbie, after you bring me the supplies, see to it that the child has something to eat."

"Aye," he said, and shut the door.

"We don't need yer charity," Kristen told him.

Trevor gave her a knowing look. "No, but you do need food." His eyes narrowed. "When was the last time you ate, Kristen?"

She didn't like the way he said her name in that soft manner of his. It kept her off guard. " 'Tis not important."

"Oh, but I think it is. I bet you didn't eat at all yesterday." He saw she was stubbornly not going to answer, and he wasn't sure why he cared, but he did.

What kind of hellcat did he have in front of him? Something told him she wasn't what she seemed. But just in case, he was going to make sure she didn't possess any more weapons. His hands crossed her breast, and she gasped, slapping them away.

"Yer wastin' yer time. I've nothing more."

"Then you don't mind if I make sure." Trevor's brow arched, yet he continued his search. He couldn't help noting what an exquisite body she had, and he admired her courage even if it involved doing wrong by stealing. He reached her waist. He could almost put his hands around her middle. She was much too small.

Farther down were shapely hips, perfect for babies. He frowned at where his thoughts were leading him.

The dress she wore was faded, the material badly worn, and it made him wonder how she'd come to be a common thief. Her legs, he bet, were free of silk stockings. He felt her shiver under his fingertips. When he finally reached her tiny feet, he realized that somewhere his thoughts had turned from angry to curious.

Standing back up, he looked at the girl. Even though her clothes were badly in need of replacing, they were fairly clean. The lamplight flickered across her hair, which hung in layers from her chin down to the middle of her back. He couldn't remember seeing hair exactly her color before. It was like a morning sunrise; the soft yellows and golds threatened to burst in an orange ball of color. Her face was delicate, not hard from years of rough treatment. And then, he made the mistake of looking into her eyes. They glittered like rare emeralds with a darker green in the middle. There was a mischievous sparkle that hadn't been diminished over the years of hardship she must have suffered.

He found himself completely entranced by a wharf rat with emerald eyes, and he didn't like it one bit. After all, she was a *Scot*.

"Can I go now?" Kristen asked softly.

"Not yet, my sweet." He smiled.

Kristen wasn't sure what this funny sensation was that made her skin feel as if needles were sticking her, but she needed to get away from this man.

His sheer size demanded respect. He was much too overpowering for her. When he touched her body, she'd ceased to think of anything else but the touch and feel of his strong hands. She'd glimpsed, if for only a moment, a look of tenderness, and her heart had skipped a beat. Yet he really hadn't tried anything improper, and that puzzled her. She'd never encountered anyone so intimidating, yet intriguing. She sensed he was a man who always got what he wanted. Evidently she wasn't one of those things, and she thanked her lucky stars.

"But I told ye it was an accident," she said.

"You were still trying to steal. I want some answers, but first I need my shoulder mended. And, seeing as you're the one that caused this"—he pointed to the red stain on his shirt—"you have the privilege of fixing it."

Robbie knocked, then entered the cabin and put down a leather satchel. "I'm going to take the lad with me. Seems he likes our ship."

"Thanks, Robbie." Trevor opened the bag and shoved it across the table to her. "This is everything you will need." He sat on the table so she could tend him better.

"Ye mean ye trust me to patch ye up? I could make it worse." She frankly couldn't believe he would want the likes of her touching him.

"I think you're smarter than that," he remarked casually. "Just a warning. If you try anything, one of my men will be outside the door to deal with you—that is, if I don't get to you first."

"I ain't afraid of ye." Kristen lifted her chin, hoping he didn't see the tremble that showed she was lying.

He reached over, took her chin, then brought her face so close to his that she could feel his breath on her cheek. For a slight moment, she thought he was going to kiss her. It was impossible to tear her gaze from him. He rubbed his thumb back and forth across her chin. "Well, you should be afraid, Kristen."

At that very moment she wanted to be kissed, something that had never occurred in her young eighteen years. She gazed into his eyes. She could see how intense he was, and she wondered if he had a wife and children. His eyes were not one color, but instead a mixture of blue-green with just a touch of brown specks in the middle. As they stood staring at each other, she could see how they darkened to a deep royal blue, and she wondered what he was contemplating.

Kristen couldn't read his eyes, so he must be good at keeping his emotions and thoughts to himself. His warning hadn't left her, though. She was no fool. She wouldn't push this man too far, and she'd pray he'd let her go. "I need to wash my hands before working on yer shoulder."

His eyes glittered with a reckless energy. He seemed a little hesitant to let her go, but he did, and she felt a stab of disappointment.

Gathering her wits, she found a metal basin and pitcher on a nearby stand. She poured water into the basin, then scrubbed her hands with lye soap.

When she came back to him she said, "I need to remove yer shirt so I can clean the wound."

She watched as he unbuttoned the white billowing shirt. He winced as he tried to remove the material off the damaged arm.

"Here, let me." Kristen gently moved her hand down his arm, and a fine arm it was too. He was very muscular, proving he'd done a bit of hard work. She loosened the material from the dried blood, not realizing she was rubbing her bust across his chest as she did so. Hearing his quick intake of breath, she looked sharply at him and asked, "Ye all right?"

"I think so." He scowled and his eyes darkened.

He didn't look all right, and he sounded a wee bit funny, but since he was quieter, she ignored him. With the shirt removed, she examined the nasty hole. She'd gotten used to taking care of unfortunates on the streets, so she was no longer squeamish. They all came to her with their bumps and bruises, but working on this one was very different. Her gaze went to the man's chest, and she breathed in the word "magnificent." Somehow she managed to keep a straight face. "Appears the bullet went straight through the meaty part of yer arm," she commented as she placed the dampened cloth on his wound.

He flinched.

"Sorry," she murmured, not liking the way he stared at her. It was as if he wanted to know all about her, yet she knew that was absurd. "I don't know yer full name," she realized out loud.

"Trevor Claremont." He paused. "And yours is Kristen—?"

"Johnstone."

"That figures," he said, and glowered.

"And what do ye mean by that?" She put her hands on her hips.

"I've no use for the Johnstones."

"Appears ye do at the moment," she answered tartly, and resumed her nursing. She couldn't help smiling at his frowning face.

"My da died a long time ago, so ye canna have known him." Gently, she cleaned his shoulder. Then she slid the box over and took some white salve and started applying it to the wound. His skin was warm, and his fragrance hadn't escaped her notice either. He smelled like the wind and the sea. A fresh scent she couldn't remember smelling on a man before.

She barely touched him, but each time she did, his muscles tightened. She wondered why her touch affected him so when she couldn't possibly be hurting him. This man was a puzzle to her. He seemed like gentry, yet he was different. The dandies, as she liked to call them, were such an indifferent lot who looked down their noses when they saw the likes of her.

She hadn't always been on the street. She had a vague memory of growing up in a big house, but the memory had dimmed so much over the years that she wasn't sure if her memory was genuine or a dream. She couldn't remember her real father, but sometimes in the wee hours of the morning she could hear his Scottish burr. "Kristen, my girl, yer goin' to be a real beauty someday." He would be disappointed that his prediction hadn't come true. When Kristen had questioned her mother about her da and what their life had been, she'd only received a blank look. The answer was always the same. "Why dredge up the past? This is your life now. Only you can make the best of it." Then two years ago, her mother had died of consumption, leaving Kristen with her stepfather and a three-year-old brother.

"Something tells me you've slipped away from me," Trevor whispered.

Kristen realized she'd finished his bandage, but she hadn't moved from between his legs. She'd been staring at his chest, lost in her thoughts. Now she looked up at him and saw that his expression had softened for the first time. "I—I think I've finished."

"Have you?" Trevor reached out and traced his finger

lazily along her jaw, marveling at how smooth her skin felt. He had no idea why he was feeling this odd attraction to the girl, but somehow he needed to touch her and, for just a moment, chase away the sadness he'd seen in her face. He found himself wanting her. He noted she hadn't jerked away from him. His hand slipped to the nape of her neck, and her silky hair seemed to wrap around his fingers while he pulled her ever so slowly to him.

Just one little kiss . . . that was all he wanted. Then he'd be satisfied and could send her on her way. Her lips were soft and wet as he moved his mouth over hers. It was a featherlike kiss, and then it was over.

" 'Twas nice." Her eyes were wide and clear, staring at him with unblinking innocence.

"Nice?" Trevor drew his brows together. Since when did a woman describe his kiss as merely nice. "Nice?" he repeated.

"I thought p'haps there would be more."

"Don't tell me you've never been kissed before."

"Nay, I have not."

"Then perhaps we should try again."

"What for?"

Trevor couldn't help but chuckle. "I would hate to leave you disappointed. There is a little more to a kiss than I've shown you."

Kristen had always wondered what a kiss would be like. Would it be magical? She sure hadn't felt any magic yet and, seeing as this man's teeth were not rotten like most of the lads she knew, she didn't see any harm in satisfying her curiosity. " 'Tis more, ye say?"

His arms went around her, and he pressed her to him till she was molded to his body. Again his lips touched hers, softly at first, but this time the kiss was different and all her senses sprang to life as his mouth moved over hers. His tongue touched her lips, and she jerked away.

"Trust me," he whispered and pulled her back into his embrace.

He touched her lips again, and she hesitantly opened her mouth to find a heaven she didn't know existed. Her arms slid up his chest and curved around his neck while she innocently pressed her breasts against his chest. Trevor's mouth was insistent, exploring, tasting, and a desire for something more burned within her.

Kristen trembled.

Trevor groaned.

Trevor's desire soared to red hot. She felt so good in his arms, and he sensed a passion lay buried deep within her. He ached inside. He was glad she wasn't experienced, or they would be in his bed in two seconds. Then it dawned on him what he was doing. He'd never been a seducer. His women had always been experienced and knew the rules. He took her by the arms and reluctantly moved her back.

The sudden shock from heaven to reality stunned Kristen for a moment. He seemed to be waiting for her to say something, so she said, " 'Twas better."

"I'm glad I could be your first teacher."

"I sense there is still more."

He chuckled and said, "There is, but that lesson would be better off taught at a later time. Maybe even by another man." As soon as he said it, he frowned at the picture of the girl in another man's arms.

"Now the question is what to do with you. I could turn you over to the constable or let you go." He chuckled. "Then, I suppose, you would just pick someone else's pocket."

"Ye should let me go," she answered solemnly.

Trevor stood and went over to a drawer. He pulled out another shirt and slipped it on. ''When was the last time you ate?''

''Ye asked that before,'' she challenged. ''Why do ye care?''

The defiance was back in her voice. Turning, he stared at her for a moment. ''I wish to God I knew.''

''I don't need yer charity. I've been doing the best I can for the last few months.''

Trevor looked at her skinny arms. He'd wager she'd not been eating very well. ''You don't have any family?''

She put the bandages back in the box. ''My mother died two years back, and I ran away from my stepfather.''

Trevor rubbed his chin. ''I see.''

Kristen eased toward the door. ''I'll just be collecting my brother, and we'll be out of yer hair.''

''I didn't say I was going to let you go.''

His brisk voice stopped her, and Kristen's breath caught. ''Why not? I've fixed yer arm and ye got yer coins back.''

''Maybe I want more.'' Trevor realized he wasn't too sure what he was thinking about doing was sane, but he couldn't seem to stop himself. It was possible he had the answer for one of his previous problems in this very room. ''If I turn you over to the authorities, you could rot in jail for a long time.''

''Aye.'' She nodded gravely and stared at him through wide emerald eyes.

Trevor knew he had to be insane, but he went on. ''What if I offered you a . . .'' He searched for the right word. ''A situation?''

''What kind of situation?''

''I have a small predicament that you can help me with, and in payment I won't turn you over to the authorities.'' He knew he was about to make a rash decision. It was something he normally didn't do, but he could see the answer to his problem right before him. He could solve everything quickly and with very little effort on his part.

"I can help ye?" Kristen started laughing. "I can barely help myself."

"I'm serious, Kristen. Please sit down." He waited until he had her attention again. "You see, my grandmère has decided it's time for me to marry and produce an heir. I wouldn't consider the thought, but she's been ill. Refusing her, I fear, might send her to an early grave. However, I don't care to attend every function the *ton* has to offer and fend off all the females looking for a rich husband."

"So what does that have to do with me?"

"If you agree to be my wife, Kristen, I won't have to be bothered with looking for one. I'll have a wife, and you'll be free to do what you like. As long as I approve, of course. And I'll have my freedom too."

"Are ye crazy? There is no way I could possibly fit into yer life."

"I agree you will need a little polishing and . . ." He wrinkled his nose. "Definitely some new clothes." He leaned closer. "But I think you're smart, Kristen. You'll learn quickly. What do you have to lose?"

Kristen shook her head, her eyes suddenly sad. "Ye should only marry for love."

"Don't be foolish. How many loving marriages have you seen?"

"To be truthful, none. But I do believe love is out there someplace."

He lifted her chin. "Well, maybe we'll find it. Stranger things have happened." He traced her soft skin with his thumb.

"Yer joking me?"

"No, Kristen. I'm serious. This is to be a business

arrangement. It will get you off the streets and hopefully into a better life.''

"I don't know." She shook her head again. This whole thing seemed like a wildly spinning dream. " 'Tis too fast. I need to think.''

"What is there to think about?'' Her cheeks flushed with her stubborn refusal, but Trevor pressed on. "You should think of your brother, if no one else. What will happen to him if he stays on the street? He doesn't have that hardness about him now, but he will." Trevor looked her straight in the eye, sensing the advantage. "Do you want him begging and stealing for the rest of his life? And what will happen to you? The next person whose pocket you pick might not let you off so easily. You'll end up in prison or as someone's whore.''

Kristen felt as though she'd been slapped, but he was right. "What you say is true." A sadness entered her eyes. "But I'll be *your* whore, so there's little difference.''

Trevor took her by the arms and pulled her to her feet, looking at her steadily. "No, Kristen. You'll be my wife, and I will not touch you unless you want it also. So you have nothing to lose.''

Nothing to lose. She frowned. She would be losing her freedom. However, her life hadn't been that wonderful in the past. And Claremont did say he wouldn't touch her unless she agreed. There was also Hagan. "Then I guess I agree. But life willna be easy.''

"I've no doubt." He chuckled. "There is one thing you must promise me.''

"And that being?''

"That you'll quit your thieving ways.''

"I don't know about that." She shook her head. The man was daft.

"That's part of the deal, Kristen. I'll have your promise now."

She hesitated. "Ye have my promise that I won't steal no more." She crossed her fingers behind her back, knowing she didn't mean a word of it. "I guess this means ye'll be wanting yer change purse back?"

Trevor patted his pocket. "How in the world did you do that?"

" 'Tis a secret." She smiled, knowing there was something special about this man. Something she liked.

"You're a wicked lady, Kristen Johnstone."

"Aye, that I am, Trevor Claremont."

CHAPTER TWO

Something tickled Kristen's nose.

She opened her eyes to find an eyelet ruffle on her pillowcase. Startled, she realized she couldn't remember having a pillow, much less a fancy case. She bolted straight up in bed, having no earthly idea where she was, but feeling certain it wasn't jail. Because if it was jail, it was a lot nicer than where she'd been living these last three years. "Think, Kristen. What happened to ye, girl?"

She shut her eyes, squeezing them tight as she thought back to yesterday. She remembered a man . . . a shooting . . . a capture. Then she recalled the captain of the ship. She'd made a deal with him so she wouldn't go to jail, but then she'd fallen asleep after they ate, and she didn't remember anything at all after that. Had she been drugged or was she just exhausted?

Her brother!

"Hagan!" Kristen shouted. Frantic, she tried to crush

the trepidation crawling over her as she listened for an answering call. She'd kill the man if he hurt her brother. When she didn't receive an immediate answer, she threw back the covers and sprang out of bed. That was when she realized she had on a soft cotton nightgown. One she didn't remember putting on herself.

"Hagan!"

"Kristen, in here." She heard a small voice from the other side of a door located near the far end of the bedroom. She scurried across the floor, barely feeling the smooth surface beneath her feet. Grasping the brass knob, she examined the finely polished metal, thinking what a price she could get for it on the streets.

She shook her head and pulled the door open. Kristen looked inside, spotting her brother in a huge bed surrounded by a mountain of covers. "Hagan, are ye all right?"

"Sure. But where are we?" He rubbed his eyes with the back of his hands. "Look at all the pillows." He patted one of the four fluffy pillows around him. "This bed sure is comfortable."

"Thank goodness ye're safe." She hugged her brother. "I dinna know where we are, but I'll find out." She looked around her. " 'Tis nice, wherever we are."

"Are you really going to marry the captain like you said?"

"Aye." She nodded her head. "And do ye approve?"

"Sure. He's fun once you get over being scared of him." Hagan crawled out from under the blankets, then sat back on his heels. "Does this mean we don't have to live at our place anymore and hide from Father?"

Kristen nodded. "That it does. Wasn't much of a home anyway. Now ye'll have a home or a ship. I think it will be better."

"I'm still a little sleepy," Hagan murmured, yawning and stretching his arms over his head.

A knock sounded on the door, and Kristen called, "Who is it?"

A young woman with short black hair entered the room. "Breakfast will be served in half an hour, mum."

"Where are we?" Kristen realized the question sounded stupid. How many people woke up not knowing where they were? But she couldn't figure out any other way to find out except ask.

"You are staying at His Grace's town house."

"His Grace?" Kristen frowned. "And who is His Grace?"

"Why everyone knows him, mum. He's very important." The maid's face turned red. "He's the one what brought you home last night. I really shouldn't say more, but I remember you and your brother were asleep when he carried you upstairs. His Grace is the Duke of Chatsworth."

"Duke?"

"I've said way too much, mum." She bobbed her white-capped head. "You'll have to ask His Grace the rest of your questions." With that she shut the door.

"What's a duke?" Hagan asked.

" 'Tis someone of great importance, so I've heard. Never met one close up before," Kristen mumbled while her mind whirled with explanations. She couldn't figure out how or why she was here ... wherever here was. She'd made a deal with the sea captain, or so she'd thought. Maybe the man had had second thoughts and sold her.

"Get dressed, Hagan. We'll find our answers downstairs! And mind ye, if I say run, ye don't stop to ask questions."

"We're not going to have to leave, are we?"

"I'm not sure." She had a nauseating feeling in the bottom of her stomach. "Now get dressed." She went back to her room and noticed the beautiful four-poster bed for the first time. She couldn't remember when she'd slept so well or in a real bed.

After hurrying to splash water on her face, she pinched her cheeks. Then she retrieved the only garment she had, praying her fingers wouldn't poke through the thin material.

Had Trevor sold her? Just who was this duke? She'd have her answers in a few minutes. One way or another.

She walked down the staircase holding onto Hagan's hand, and just for a moment another picture of a woman and a little girl moving down a staircase flashed through her mind. They both had hair the color of her own. She grasped the handrail and stopped. All her life she'd had these little flashes of what she assumed had been a life she couldn't remember, but she'd never made any sense of them.

"Why'd you stop?" Hagan asked.

"Huh?"

He stared at her, baffled. "What's wrong?"

"Nothing. Just felt a wee bit dizzy. Come on. Let's go find His Worship." At the bottom, she didn't have the slightest idea where they should go, and she almost tried to find the front door instead. But if she could give her brother a better kind of life, she'd wait and see what happened.

A maid of some sort came around the corner, so Kristen asked, "Can ye tell me where to get breakfast?"

The girl was pert, of medium height, with a short blond bob. She sparkled when she smiled. "You must be new around here."

"Aye, we are, and don't have the foggiest idea where we should go."

"I was the same way when I first came here, but the house is easy to learn." The girl pointed. "Just go through that door and down a hallway to the kitchen and they'll help you. My name is Rebecca, mum. I have to hurry now."

"Thank you." Kristen smiled as the cheerful young woman hurried off in a different direction.

Kristen and Hagan moved down the hall. She opened a huge wooden door, and the quietness of the house evaporated as the busy sounds of the kitchen surrounded them. There was a big hearth with a roaring fire and steaming pots. To her right stood a long table where several people sat eating and laughing.

"I'm hungry, Kristen." Hagan pulled at her hand. "Something sure smells good."

Kristen cleared her throat. "Is this where we eat?"

"If yer hungry, it is. Get two plates and have a seat, love." The largest woman motioned with a fork.

Kristen fixed Hagan some toast, and they settled down at the table listening to the girls gossip about the duke.

"He's a fine one. I wouldn't mind one bit if he looked in my direction."

"Don't you be dreaming, Fanny. Did you see Lady Bonnie? She looked crushed when His Grace said it was over between them. And before that it was Lady Sarah."

"She just knew—" The older woman stopped and looked at Hagan. "We should talk of something else since we've a lad present."

Fanny's face flushed. "Yer right. Are ye going to be an upstairs maid or a downstairs maid?"

Kristen set down her piece of toast. "I'm not sure. Ye see, I was on a ship yesterday, and this morning I find myself in a strange house. I haven't met His Lordship, so I canna say."

"Aye, a real big ship." Hagan held his hands wide.

The kitchen door opened and the woman Kristen had seen upstairs came in. "Lord have mercy. I've found you!"

Kristen jumped up. "I'm sorry, but ye're the one that told us we should have breakfast."

The woman came and stood in front of Kristen. "I've turned this house upside down looking for you both, and His Grace is now in a snit." She threw up her hands in disgust.

"Then we'll be leaving." Kristen grabbed Hagan's hand, but he refused to give up his toast, so she got a handful of jelly as she snatched him to his feet and started for the door, not taking time to wipe her hand.

"No, no!" The panic in the woman's voice grew. "He's upset because he thinks you've left. You are simply in the wrong room; please follow me."

Since the woman put it that way, Kristen decided to stick it out and thanked everyone at the table. She noticed they looked at her strangely, but they seemed a nice group of people anyway.

Still grasping her brother in one hand and trying to hide her other sticky hand, she followed the woman.

They entered a huge room that had a very long dining table and three chandeliers. Sitting at one end of the table was Trevor, only he looked very different.

When they entered, he placed his napkin on the table and came slowly to his feet. He wore cream-colored breeches, a dark blue coat, and gleaming Hessian boots that came to his knees. His hair was neatly combed and fell below his collar. He didn't resemble the carefree sea captain she'd met yesterday. Now, he looked arrogant, very rich, and a touch irritated. She hadn't missed that look. She wondered what role he had with the duke. Maybe he was an earl or one of those other titles she couldn't remember. Then she frowned. On second thought, he didn't fit any of the above.

"I see you've found them, Mrs. Ditchfield."

"I'm sorry, Yer Grace, seems there was a misunderstanding and they were in the kitchen. It won't happen again, sir. If you had only given us a little notice, I could have informed the staff of our guests' presence."

Trevor felt a moment of relief, followed by one of irritation. He'd thought the girl had run away, and he'd been ready to go out and search all of London for her. And he would have found her too. Nothing could have stopped him!

Then he had to ask himself, why? She was someone he barely knew, but someone he wanted to know better for whatever reason.

"Yes, I know how you like to be prepared, Mrs. Ditchfield, but this time I couldn't send you advance notice. Please have their breakfast served while it is hot."

Kristen breathed in a shallow, quick gasp. "Yer Grace?" She wrinkled her nose while she looked at him as if he had grown horns.

"At your service." He reached out and took her hand, but recoiled immediately. "What the—"

"Jelly," she replied.

"We have linen for wiping one's hand." He wiped his hand, then tried to hand her a napkin.

She ignored him. "Yer Grace," she repeated.

With a tip of his head, he motioned her to the chair beside him. "That's right, Kristen. Welcome to my home. At least, my London home."

"But I thought you were a captain," Hagan said with as much disappointment as his sister had shown. He climbed up in his chair. "I liked that ship."

Trevor had never met anyone who wasn't impressed by his title . . . now he had two very unimpressed people at his breakfast table. "That is my ship, young man, and I sail once or twice a year, but my main estate is on the

Scottish border. You will get to see my ship again. I promise."

"And yer a duke?" Kristen still had a strong look of distaste on her face.

"I'm afraid so." He nodded and chuckled at her. How refreshing! "You seem to have a problem with that small fact."

A woman appeared and placed two plates in front of her, one filled with fresh fruit and the other muffins and meat. She couldn't remember the last time she'd had fruit. "I don't know. Ye just didn't seem so high-and-mighty last night."

"If that was a compliment . . ." His brow rose a fraction. "Then thank you, but you shouldn't judge me by a title. I didn't judge—"

"Didn't ye now. Ye thought I was a thief."

He chuckled. "You are. Or were."

"Well, ye have me on that count, but ye thought I was a bad girl right away. And don't be botherin' to deny it. I could see the truth in yer eyes. Ye didn't even like my Scottish heritage." She shook a fork at him, and Trevor was quite thankful she didn't have a knife at the moment. "I can see ye don't need the likes of me."

"That's where you are wrong!" he stated very emphatically. "We had a bargain, and I intend to hold you to the agreement." He thought a moment, rubbing his chin. "Unless you've decided you would prefer jail to my company?"

"What's a bargain, Kristen?" Hagan asked, a purple ring of jelly very prevalent around his mouth.

She had forgotten her brother, who looked like a chipmunk with his pouches packed. "Don't talk with yer mouth full. A bargain is an agreement made between two people saying each will do what they promise."

"Is that what you do when you get married—make agreements?"

"That's exactly what a marriage is." Trevor smiled. "You are a very smart lad. With a bit of schooling you'll be brilliant when you're bigger."

"What's brilliant?"

"It means very, very smart. And that's enough questions," Kristen said, a little exasperated. "Now, back to our agreement. I canna possibly fit into yer world. Look around ye." She swept the room with her hand. "Then look at us. 'Tis quite evident we don't belong. Even yer staff thought I was a new servant."

"You belong where I say you belong," he stated firmly, and then softened his voice. "Sometimes it merely takes the right trappings to make someone fit in. We are going to remedy a lot of your problems today. We will visit Eva Marie, the dressmaker, and you'll be fitted with the finest clothes money can buy. I have also persuaded Eva to give you some lessons in the proper dos and don'ts."

"And who is Eva Marie?" Kristen asked.

"She owns a dress shop in London. Only the highest-born ladies can afford to shop there."

"What about me?" Hagan butted in with a child's impatience. "Can I come too?"

"You, young man, will accompany me while your sister is busy with Mistress Eva Marie."

"'Tis too much." Kristen stood. "I could never repay ye."

"You are going to repay me by becoming my wife." Trevor picked up a bell and rung it. Immediately, a lady in a white cap appeared.

"Yes, Your Grace?"

"Please take Master Hagan to his room for a bath and prepare him for our outing."

"What does Master mean? Everybody usually calls me Hagan."

Trevor chuckled. "I can see you're full of whats, but I must admit, it is a good way to learn."

"Yeah, you said I'm going to be brilliant, 'member?"

"That I did." Trevor stood, placing his napkin on the table. Hagan was a true gem, Trevor thought. And adorable, but strangely enough, he didn't resemble his sister at all.

"Miss Ruby will answer your questions while she takes you upstairs," Trevor said.

Just as they left the room Kristen heard Hagan say, "I don't like baths."

"His whats will try a saint." She turned her attention back to Claremont. "I don't understand why ye want us."

Obviously, she'd never studied her reflection, he realized. Even dressed in rags, she was beautiful, but that wasn't why he'd made the bargain. He really wasn't sure as to his reasons, and he didn't want to reflect on them at this time, but he had to tell her something.

"We've been through this before. I need a wife without a lot of fuss and bother. You need a home, and so does your brother. I don't usually take charity cases, but this is different. You owe me, and I have a hole in my shoulder to prove it. It's bad enough you were a thief, but do you know the penalty for the attempted murder of a duke?"

"I wasn't trying to murder ye," Kristen answered stubbornly. "The aim was much too high."

He moved closer, looking down at her intensely. "Would you like to debate the issue?"

"Nay."

"Then I suggest you drop the subject, and I don't want to hear anything more about our deal. I think you'll come to like our bargain."

"Your Grace." The young girl who had sent Kristen to the kitchen entered and curtsied. She stood waiting for Trevor to recognize her, but his gaze stayed on Kristen.

After a moment, he said, his eyes still on Kristen, "Rebecca, I would like you to meet Lady Kristen."

Kristen turned to face the girl.

"How do you do, mum?" Rebecca curtsied, and Kristen almost laughed, but she didn't want to embarrass the girl, whose face was as red as a newly fallen September apple.

"I would like you to be lady's maid to Lady Kristen," Trevor said. "I was told that you have been trained in such things."

"Yes, Your Grace, I have." Rebecca finally smiled. "I'd be honored to assist your lady."

"Good." He nodded. "Please prepare her bath. We are planning an outing today."

After Rebecca had left, Kristen couldn't hold her tongue any longer. "Are ye daft? I've been dressin' myself for the last fifteen years, and me mother dressed me before that. I don't need any assistance in getting in and out of my clothes."

"I can see you're going to argue every little thing, and at times will try my patience, as you're doing now." His eyes were dark and unfathomable as he moved until he stood right in front of her. "You *do* need a lady's maid. Every proper lady has one, and when we go later today to have garments made, you'll see a vast difference in your wardrobe with many hooks and buttons. And I've been hoping, perhaps praying, that Eva Marie can soften some of these hard edges of yours."

"Hard edges?" Her wide-eyed innocence looked out of place as her hands went to her hips. "Have ye just insulted me?"

He grinned. "Of course not. We are going to turn you into a very proper lady."

"I can picture me now sitting at some fancy table, having tea and crumpets. But I don't need a lady's maid when God gave me two good hands to work with," she continued primly.

"Damn, if you are not hardheaded. It isn't proper. You *do* need a maid. You might consider the fact that if you turn down Rebecca, she'll have no place to go and she won't be able to get a job when everyone hears the Duke of Chatsworth turned down her services."

" 'Tis a big head ye have." She grinned mischievously. "But since ye've put it that way, I'll keep her."

"Thank you," he answered dryly. Then he smiled in the way that made her knees weak. "Now run along and get ready. We've much to accomplish."

When Kristen went to her room, she found a large tub completely filled with steaming water and scented soap.

Rebecca flitted about the room, gathering bath sheets and soap. "Will your bags be coming later, mum?"

"Nay."

"Then they are already here?"

"Nay."

"I—I don't understand." Rebecca's brow creased into a frown.

"I only have the clothes I am wearing," Kristen admitted, but she noticed her new maid was still frowning, and she couldn't think of a nice way to tell her that she could be a maid herself. " 'Tis a long story. My clothes were lost," Kristen finally offered. She smiled as Rebecca accepted the lie.

"Here, let me help you undress." The maid moved toward her.

"Rebecca, I'd like to be honest. I'm goin' to have to get used to having a lady's maid."

Rebecca twisted her hands together, her distress showing in her face. "You're not going to send me away?"

"Nay, of course not." Kristen patted the girl's hand to reassure her.

After Kristen had removed her clothing, she slipped into the tub. "Saints be praised, this is heaven," she said with a sigh, gliding all the way under.

"Oh, mum, you're not hurt?" Rebecca's voice was horrified as she pulled Kristen back up by the hair.

Kristen gave a carefree laugh, thinking it was the first time she'd felt this way in a long, long time. "I think I've died and gone to heaven." She sighed, wiping the bubbles from her eyes.

"It's only a bath, mum."

"To ye maybe, but to me, 'tis heaven. Ye wouldn't believe how many cold baths I've taken. Would you help me wash my hair?"

"See, now you're getting the hang of it." Rebecca smiled for the first time, and finally that worried look she'd been displaying disappeared.

"I guess yer right."

As Rebecca lathered Kristen's hair, she said, "I want to thank you for not saying anything about me sending you to the kitchen."

"The way I see it"—Kristen reached over and took Rebecca's hand in hers—"we're going to be friends." Kristen squeezed Rebecca's arm. "I'll protect ye, and ye can protect me. Deal?"

"Deal."

"Ye know, I've never had a friend before."

Rebecca broke into an open, friendly smile. "Well, you have one now."

When the bath was finished—much to Kristen's disappointment—she sat patiently while Rebecca dried her hair in front of the fireplace. It was the end of March and the air still held the sting of cold. She felt guilty indulging in all this pampering. Quickly, she banished the thought. She was probably dreaming, and someone was bound to wake her up shortly.

"You have beautiful hair, mum."

"I don't like it. 'Tis much too thick and 'tisn't the same color like everyone else's. I wish it was a lovely brown or black."

"But that's what makes it so different. It shimmers like gold, yet it sparkles with fire. When we have more time, I'll arrange it in a different way for you."

"I guess I better get dressed so we can go out." Kristen stood up, dreading to put her old dress back on, but knowing she had no choice. "Have ye ever been to this place before?"

"Oh, no, mum." Rebecca rushed over to get Kristen's dress. "But I get to go with you today to help advise you." She held the dress up for Kristen. "I'm kind of excited to be going for an outing."

"It will be nice to have your company."

"Do you want to see yerself in the looking glass before we go?"

"Looking glass?"

"Yes, mum. To see how you look." Rebecca pointed to the mirror at the far end of the room. Kristen hadn't even noticed it this morning.

Rebecca's eyebrows raised inquiringly. "Surely you've seen your reflection before?"

Kristen felt her cheeks heat. "Actually, I've only seen myself in store windows. We never had need of such things."

Rebecca took Kristen's elbow and guided her to the long mirror. "Well, it is truly a shame because you are very beautiful."

Kristen stared at her reflection with the fascination of a child seeing something truly rare for the first time. Hesitantly, she reached up and touched her face. When had she grown up? The years all seemed a blur, and she didn't remember any of them being happy.

"Why do you look so sad?" Rebecca said, bringing Kristen out of her trance. "You have to be pleased with a face like yours."

"I know this sounds silly . . ." Kristen touched her cheeks. "But 'tis hard to believe 'tis really me." She turned to her new friend. "I've not lived a very normal life, I'm afraid."

The connecting door sprang open, and Hagan barged in. "Did you have to take a bath too, Kristen?"

Kristen's hand fell to her side, the mirror forgotten. "Aye, the tub, 'twas a big one."

"Aye. I told that Ruby lady that I could wash myself 'cause I'm a big boy."

"You are that." Rebecca smiled.

"Who are you?" Hagan's curiosity immediately registered in his eyes.

"I'm your sister's maid."

"Huh?"

"Sorry, Rebecca, but everythin' has to be explained to my brother." Kristen turned to Hagan. "She's going to help me with my clothes and hair and accompany me when I go places. She's called a lady's maid."

"You mean help you get dressed like you used to help me?" He giggled, truly enjoying himself.

"That's right," Kristen said, and waited for the next why.

"Why?"

"Hagan!" Her smile faded replaced with a frown. "Ye'd drive a person to drink with yer infernal questions, but the answer is because that's the way things are done."

"I hate it when you change your voice like that." He was crestfallen, and his smile faded for just a moment.

"Sometimes 'tis the only way to get through to ye."

Hagan stared at her a moment, then grinned. "If you need help, Kristen, you need help ... nothing to be ashamed of." At that he ran for the door, and was gone before she could catch him.

Kristen looked at a laughing Rebecca. "Do ye have brothers?"

"Afraid so." She nodded and held up two fingers. "Two of them."

"Ye poor lass. I feel sorry for ye."

They both laughed, then proceeded downstairs, prepared for the day's adventure.

CHAPTER THREE

Outside the three-storied brick town house, a carriage drawn by two black horses stood motionless while a footman held the horses' bridles. The sleek black carriage wasn't as fancy as some Kristen had seen. Perhaps, it was a clue to the mysterious duke's personality, she thought. So far she hadn't found Trevor Claremont a man to flaunt his wealth, but she knew absolutely nothing else about him. What was he really like? Then again, what difference did it really make? She probably wouldn't be with him that long. She thought of this arrangement as a temporary condition . . . one that would keep her out of jail.

A young, but somber, footman held the door open, his other hand extended to assist her into the carriage. Once inside, she found lush wine-colored cushions and drapes secured with gold cords at each window. The inside was much fancier than the outside. She wondered where the others were, but she didn't have long to wait for her answer.

Claremont entered and settled next to her. Next, Hagan and Rebecca made an appearance and sat across from them.

When the door closed, the carriage moved forward, and Kristen found the ride very smooth. She pulled back the curtain so she could see outside, marveling at the world as it passed. People walked down the sidewalks as if they had not a care in the world. The women's elaborate hats probably cost more than she'd seen in a lifetime. They rode through Hyde Park, passing several stylish carriages.

Here, no one darted across the street, trying to find a hiding place, in fear of his life. No one lounged in a doorway, sleeping off last night's supper of whiskey. And no one looked hungry or cold. These people were far removed from the "real" world. Kristen sighed. Could she somehow forget the place she'd come from? At the moment, she didn't have an answer to that question. She doubted she could ever forget some of the things she'd witnessed.

Hagan talked nonstop and Rebecca patiently answered all his "whys." The funny thing was how fast Hagan had adapted to their new situation. Maybe because he was so young, he would be able to put the past behind him.

"You're very quiet, Kristen," Trevor said. He leaned over and whispered, "Is something bothering you?"

His whispered question felt like a feather on the back of her neck, and she jumped as a chill ran over her. What was the matter with her? She couldn't let this man affect her this way. She barely knew him. Yet the minute he touched or looked at her, she couldn't seem to think straight.

Pulling back from the window, she looked at Trevor. "It's just that—" She searched for the right words, and hesitated when she saw his intense stare, as if he were truly worried about her. She wanted to reach out and touch his cheek, but knew she shouldn't. "I've never ridden in a carriage before."

Trevor smiled. When she stared at him again with that wide-eyed look, he saw her rare beauty. She'd bring any man to his knees. When she let down that guard of hers, the one she used so effectively to protect herself, she became a child-woman, and the combination fascinated him.

Kristen was as fresh as a sunny morning, not corrupted by the *ton* like so many of the others he'd known. Things he took for granted, she thought of as luxury. Had he grown so distant from the things around him that he'd truly become as cynical as the rest? Had he learned to accept all the things he despised about the *ton*? God, he hoped not. Maybe that was another reason he needed Kristen.

"I hope this will be the first of many things I will show you," he said as he leaned over so only she could hear. Her answering blush only heightened his desire and pleasure.

"I will escort you to Grafton House, and Rebecca will stay to assist you while I take Master Hagan to another shop for men."

"Us men have to have our own place." Hagan grinned at his sister. "We don't need that girl stuff."

Kristen reached over and patted Hagan on the knee. "Ye have a little growin' to do, young man, so mind yer manners."

"Ah, Kristen."

The sleek carriage came to a halt in front of a linen-draper's shop that didn't look very important at all. As they disembarked, two elegant ladies dressed in fancy velvets and silk were emerging from Grafton House, but they stopped suddenly when they saw Trevor step from the carriage.

"Your Grace." They both curtsied. One of the ladies tapped him on the arm. "It is so nice to have you back in town. You have been very naughty by ignoring us for so long," the younger lady said as she batted her eyes flirtatiously.

Kristen watched through the carriage window. The girl had the same coloring, and it was evident she was the grand lady's daughter. She smiled at Trevor. "Are you attending the Cranford bash? Everyone's bound to be there." She giggled nervously.

Since Trevor was occupied with the two women, the footman helped everyone else from the carriage and they started for the door of the small shop.

"I haven't made plans yet, ladies. It was good to see you." Trevor nodded, dismissing them both as if they were pesky flies. "If you'll excuse me."

He opened the shop door for Rebecca and Hagan, who entered the place, followed by Kristen, but not before she turned and said, "How can ye miss such a lovely invitation?" She batted her eyes as she'd seen the other lady do. Trevor gave her a smile that sent her pulse racing as he gently pushed her through the door.

"Who's Cranford going to hit?" Hagan whispered behind his hand to Trevor.

Trevor chuckled. "In this instance it doesn't mean hit. Bash means a party."

Hagan digested the information. "Really? Can I go?"

"May I," Trevor corrected automatically. "Afraid not. It's only for your elders."

Kristen smiled at the patience that Claremont displayed with her brother. He would probably make a good father someday. Then she shook that notion right out of her head. She didn't want to be attracted to this man. How many times did she have to remind herself? She needed to keep her wits about her, so when it came time for her and Hagan to leave, she could do so without any regrets. A marriage could not survive without love.

A lady appeared from the back. Her blond hair was streaked with strands of white and pulled up high into a chignon. Her *Teray* velvet dress was a rich brown with a standing collar.

"Your Grace, what a pleasure to have you once again in my shop. Word was sent that I am to be clothing your fiancée. Will she be coming shortly? I see she has sent her maids ahead."

"Rubbish." Kristen started for the door, but Trevor caught her by the elbow and brought her next to him. She thought about jabbing him in the ribs with her elbow, but he must have expected such a move, and held her firmly within his grasp.

"You are mistaken, Madam Marie." His brow raised. "This is Lady Kristen, my future wife."

Kristen watched the woman's face flush the color of a ripe apple, but she didn't question him. At the moment, she seemed at a loss for the right word.

"And I'm Master Hagan."

"As I was saying . . ." Trevor cut his eyes at Hagan with a warning. "Kristen is in need of a complete wardrobe as hers has been stolen. Plus the few lessons that I informed you about earlier. Kristen was raised in a convent and has been shut away from society."

Kristen looked sharply at Trevor. The man was daft!

"What's a convent?" Hagan chimed in.

"Not now, Hagan," Trevor warned.

Marie walked about Kristen with her hand propped beneath her chin as she studied every inch of the girl. "She has very unusual coloring, but if I pick just the right colors and accessories, you'll not recognize your future bride upon your return."

"I truly doubt that," he observed.

"Then let's say I'll make her so lovely you will not be able to take your eyes off her."

Trevor chuckled. "I would know Kristen across any room." And, he realized, what he said was true. In just this short time, he couldn't imagine not ever seeing her. And it frightened him to admit the fact. "Then, I shall leave her in your capable hands. When shall I return?"

"We have much to do." Madam Marie clicked her tongue and tapped her chin and considered. "I should think late in the afternoon," she said finally. She searched the pockets of her skirt. "Oh, dear. I seem to have misplaced my timepiece." Her brows drew together in puzzlement. "A moment please while I check the back." She scurried through the curtains.

Trevor looked at Kristen. She stared back at him with those guilty green eyes, never once batting her pretty eyelashes. "Rebecca, please escort Hagan to the carriage, and I will follow in just a moment."

When the door had shut, he simply turned to Kristen and held out his hand, a stern expression on his face.

"What?" She looked at him, trying to look puzzled but failing miserably.

He took her arm and pulled her to the side. Again he held out his hand, more insistently this time. Kristen sighed. Reluctantly, she reached into her pocket, pulled out the missing watch, and unwillingly placed it in the palm of his hand.

"You promised," he whispered with a vague hint of disapproval.

" 'Tis hard."

"Well, try!" Trevor slipped the watch back onto the

table, easing it under some papers just in the nick of time before Marie came through the curtains.

"I just don't know—I'm not usually so absentminded." She fumbled with the papers on her desk. "Here it is! I must apologize, Your Grace. Perhaps I'm getting feeble-minded in my old age."

Trevor looked at Kristen and, at least, she did have the grace to blush. Perhaps it was a small sign that she might have some kind of conscience. "We all misplace things, Madam Marie," he said. "I believe Kristen can attest to losing a few things herself."

"At least once," Kristen murmured.

"However, she is much better at finding things," Trevor teased.

"I'll keep that in mind." Madam Marie laughed. "Your Grace, you seem so different from the man who came to see me six months ago. Could it be love?"

Trevor stared at her, but didn't bother to respond.

Marie rushed on. "For a complete trousseau, I'm afraid, we will not be finished until five, and it will be quite expensive."

"Spare no expense." He moved over and kissed Kristen on the cheek, surprising himself at how natural it felt. "I'll fetch you sharply at five." He opened the door and Rebecca came in as he was leaving.

"Good-bye," Kristen said to Trevor as she touched her cheek. She hadn't expected the small display of affection. She figured he'd be angry at her for swiping the watch. The man surely puzzled her, and she wondered if there was more to this marriage business than he let on. No matter, 'twas better than being in the streets.

"This way, madam." Marie pulled the curtains back as Kristen and Rebecca followed to the back. "Is there a particular color that you like?"

"Color? I should like something truly different. Perhaps a lavender."

"I agree. Would go nicely with your complexion. I can also see you in russets, reds, golds, and rich greens," the older woman commented.

"I think an apple-green would look pretty on Kristen too," Rebecca said, voicing her opinion.

"Then I should like a green dress too." Kristen smiled at her maid. "Please help me decide and choose wisely."

The next few hours became a blur of satins, laces, gauze, and Indian muslins. There were buttons to choose and shoes and hats, and some of the softest fabrics she'd ever felt for undergarments. Kristen had never been pinched and prodded so much in her entire life, and she soon tired of all the fuss.

Every time a new material was wrapped about Kristen, Madam Marie exclaimed, "*Oui,* you are lovely. His Grace won't be able to take his eyes off you—not that he could when he was here earlier."

"Really?"

"*Oui,* I could see he is quite taken with you."

Kristen thought the lady was just imagining what she saw because Trevor didn't care for her in any way other than for his own purposes. Theirs was a business agreement—nothing more.

She stared at herself in the mirror. She couldn't believe how different she looked when she finally dressed in the gown that had been made last night for her, at Trevor's request. Evidently the seamstress had been up all night sewing.

The pelisse was of silk, its color a light shade of marguerite. The collar stood up to allow a white ruffle, and in the front, rich satin of the same hue ran down the middle in a swirling design.

Rebecca insisted Kristen's hair must be done to go with her new outfit. She pulled Kristen's hair up and twisted and fastened the long curls at the crown.

After Kristen dressed, she sat at a table with Marie, who began drilling the etiquette of the *ton* into her head. There were too many forks and too many glasses. They went over it again and again, and surprisingly, Kristen learned very quickly. It was like a game to her, and she was a master of games . . . a lesson she'd learned early in life.

Kristen felt almost like a lady, and she smiled under Madam Marie's praise. It was amazing how new clothes could make her feel so different, even though she knew she was the same person.

They finished a little earlier than expected, so they were escorted to the front lounge to wait until Trevor came to pick them up.

"If you ladies will make yourselves comfortable," Madam Marie said, "I need to give the seamstresses instructions, so you'll have your gowns in a few days. You're a very lucky lady."

"I know," Kristen agreed. "Thank you for all your help." She squeezed Marie's hand, deciding she liked the dressmaker.

Rebecca automatically relaxed upon the green velvet settee, but Kristen couldn't sit still. She paced, then stopped, stared out the window, and then began to pace again. She wasn't sure if what she was about to do was very smart, but she was going to do it anyway, and now was the perfect time before she changed her mind. She tugged at the neck of her gown, not used to wearing such a confining garment.

"Listen, Rebecca. Where I used to live isn't far from here." Kristen's mind was working furiously again. She could do this. She needed to.

"I don't recall any convents around here."

Kristen recalled Trevor's lie. "I'll explain about that later. I need to get a few things I cherish before they're stolen."

"But mum, it's after two," Rebecca said.

Kristen started at her maid a little dumbfounded. "What does the hour have to do with anything?"

"Ladies are not usually seen after two o'clock around here. They don't wish to be thought of as fast."

Kristen laughed at the absurdity. If Rebecca only knew that she'd been on the streets at every hour of the day, she would probably turn several shades of red. "I will not bump into anyone, so dinna fret."

Rebecca hesitated, blinking with surprise. "I'm sure His Grace will take you there, mum."

"No." Kristen shook her head. "Ye don't comprehend. Where I came from 'tisn't very nice, and I dinna want Trevor to go there. 'Tis bad enough he knows where I came from, but seeing the actual place is a different story." She bent down and picked up her empty purse. "If I hurry, I can get everything I need and be back here before he returns. Ye'll have to stall him if he happens to return early, but I'm sure he won't."

"No, mum! You can't go out alone." Rebecca got up with the intention of going too. "His Grace will have a royal fit."

"Rebecca, ye don't understand." Kristen grabbed the girl's arms. "I've been alone for years. One more time isn't going to hurt. I'm only dressed differently, but I am the same person I was yesterday and the day before." Kristen dropped her hands and smoothed her dress. "Now, ye stay here and stall His Worship in case he takes a notion to return early."

"But, mum . . ."

That was all Kristen heard. She shut the door and hurried down the street. She knew these alleys like the back of her hand, but she felt different walking the streets this time, and very much alone. Her heels clicking on the sidewalk sounded like a drum in her head.

A gentleman passing her doffed his hat, and she smiled, resisting the urge to see how much he had in his pocket.

It would be hard to mend her ways, but she'd try a little for Trevor's sake. However, she wasn't a fool. She'd be sure to fix a little nest egg for herself and Hagan.

She turned left at the corner and then a right, and finally she saw her old grimy neighborhood—just the way she'd left it. Her stomach clenched tight. Some things would never change.

A wave of apprehension swept through her, but she'd come this far and now wasn't the time to turn into a coward. Besides, it wasn't anything but a house—one she didn't have to stay in anymore.

Wasting little time, she entered the shack that she'd called home for as long as she could remember. She shivered the minute she was inside. Funny, she hadn't thought of the place as being dumpy when it was all she had. Now it looked small and dirty, and Kristen realized she was thankful to be out of the place, even if it might only be for a little while. Trevor had truly rescued her.

There wasn't time to stand around. She needed to get out of there. A brown box sat in one corner of the room, and Kristen went directly over to it. She searched through the wooden box until she found her mother's silver brush and mirror. Picking up the cold metal objects, she set them aside. They were too large for her purse. Then she looked for the old can where she'd stashed a few pounds for when she was in dire straits.

Taking a deep breath, she glanced around for the final

time without regrets. "Thank ye, Father, for giving us a chance," she prayed.

At least she could get back to the shop before Trevor, and he wouldn't have to know a thing. She hoped Rebecca hadn't pulled her hair out worrying.

Kristen had everything. It was time to go.

But when she turned, her smile faded. Standing between her and the door was her stepfather. He hadn't changed a bit. Ned Blume stood an inch taller than she, but he was much heavier. His big belly hung over his belt and his faded brown coat was wrinkled and dirty. It appeared he hadn't shaved in a week, to judge by the gray stubble on his chin.

"I knew if I kept looking, I'd find your ungrateful hide!" Ned Blume stood hunched over in the doorway, one hand propped on the doorjamb. "And look at ya!" He took a step forward. "All gussied up when the rest of us poor souls are starving."

Kristen tried to choke down the panic that sprang up in her throat. "Get out of my way."

"Not on your life, girly." He took two more steps and grabbed her by the shoulder. "Look at ya. Whose pockets ya been pickin' to buy clothes like this, or have ya finally wised up and started selling yaself?"

" 'Tisn't any of yer business." She shoved him hard, and he stumbled, grabbing at her dress.

Kristen heard her sleeve tear. She gasped. Ned had ruined the first new dress she'd ever had. She wondered how her mother could ever have loved such a man. Kristen was thankful he wasn't any of her blood.

"Ya haven't learned a damned thing, girl." He slapped her, and she stumbled backward, hitting her head on a shelf. "If ya think I'm going to let the likes of ya get away from me again, then girly, you're badly mistaken."

Kristen slowly got to her feet, feeling a little wobbly from the crack on her head. This couldn't be happening. Not now. Not when she'd been given a chance at something more. She touched her mouth and felt the sticky blood on her fingers. Bracing her head on the wall, she attempted to steady herself from the dizziness spinning in her head, and tried to keep her fragile control.

Ned's gaze swept the miserable interior of the shack. "Where's my boy?"

"Safe," she said in a choked voice. "Ye'll never get yer hands on him."

Ned started advancing on her again, and Kristen backed up, searching for anything to protect herself. He would not hit her again and get away with it!

"The boy's my flesh and blood, girl, but you, on the other hand—"

Kristen's fingers brushed against a knife lying on a small wooden table. She gripped the hilt and waited. Her stomach quivered. Silence loomed around them as her breath came in shallow, quick gasps. Kristen realized she was scared. She'd never taken a life before, but he wouldn't touch her again. She'd make sure of that.

A loud rattling sounded outside the half-open door. Ned turned as a man burst through the doorway.

"Who the hell are ya?" Ned shouted just before his body flew across the room, slamming against the far wall.

Kristen slumped down in the corner, her legs refusing to hold her up a moment longer. She turned around and saw Trevor reaching down to get her. He pulled her to his side, never saying a word as his gaze quickly scanned her body.

He pried the knife, which she'd forgotten she still held, from her hand, then urged her forward. She stumbled as he moved her toward the door, but Trevor merely tightened his grip on her waist to steady her.

"That's my girl you're taking with ya!"

Trevor stopped, looked down at Kristen, and calmly said, "Go to the carriage."

Kristen gathered the mirror and brush before she hurried out the door.

After she'd left, Trevor turned to the scum that had the nerve to call himself a father, much less a man. His sanity seemed to be returning now that he knew Kristen was safe. He'd been angry when he'd first arrived at the shop and found that she had left, but when the carriage had stopped a moment ago and he'd heard Kristen's muffled cry, his heart had jumped into his throat and he'd reacted out of instinct. "Kristen is your stepdaughter; therefore you have no rights to her."

"What about me boy?"

Trevor ignored the question. How could such a sweet child come from such trash? "What name do you go by?"

"Ned Blume." He stood a little straighter as if he was proud of who he was. And suddenly he got braver, sensing he just might have the upper hand. "What's it to ya?"

What Trevor wouldn't give to snuff out this miserable excuse, but Ned Blume was the child's father. "I would like the boy to live with me," Trevor said.

"I don't rightly think I can allow that, mate." He grinned, showing stained brown teeth. "He's me own flesh and blood."

"I see how well you've taken care of him in the past." Trevor sneered. His hand swept the room; then he looked at the man with disgust. "Name your price."

Greed sprang to his eyes. "Well, now, I'm not too sure—"

"How about a bag of gold guineas?"

"I can see ya are a very generous man." Ned grinned, then held out his dirty hand, waiting for payment.

Trevor placed a small brown pouch in it. "I don't expect to see you again!" He took a step toward the man to make sure he heard every word. "And don't *ever* touch Kristen or the boy again!"

After the coward had backed up against the wall, clutching his pouch in front of him, Trevor turned and left.

Outside by the carriage, he nodded to the driver to take his leave. Then he entered the carriage. Kristen was in the corner, hugging her sniffling brother next to her.

"Everything is all right, Hagan," Trevor said. He placed his hand on the boy's shoulder. "Sit with Rebecca, and let me take care of your sister."

The child did as instructed, then looked at Trevor with trembling lips. "Pa's not going to get us?"

"No, son." Trevor gave him a reassuring smile. "We're going home."

Trevor took a handkerchief out of his breast pocket and dabbed the blood off Kristen's mouth. He felt her tremble the moment he touched her, and he wondered how much abuse she had suffered in the past. He'd seen only her brave side up until now.

He pulled her next to him, and that was when he saw the silver brush and mirror. If that was what she'd gone back for, he could have bought her a dozen of them.

He knew he held a frightened young woman who really didn't deserve any of this. Something deep within him stirred, and he wasn't sure how to deal with the odd feeling. His pride and his passion were waging such a tug of war, he felt his insides were being wrenched from him.

Kristen turned her head toward him. "I'm sorry," she whispered, but to his surprise there were no tears in her eyes. She stared at him with a dull, haunting gaze that completely tore his heart out of his chest.

Trevor pulled her to him and wrapped his arms around her. "It's all right." He kissed the top of her head and said no more as he took a slow steady breath. He wasn't sure what he felt at the moment. He knew it was a sensation he'd never really experienced before, and that was the reason he couldn't describe such feelings.

But the one feeling he could identify was relief.

Relief that Kristen hadn't run away from him.

Relief that his little thief was safely in his arms.

CHAPTER FOUR

As they were pulling up in front of the town house, Kristen sighed with relief. She didn't know how to deal with this gentle version of Trevor she'd just seen.

She much preferred the demanding man ... the one she knew how to handle.

They had just entered the house when he stopped her by gripping her elbow. She turned to look at him quizzically.

Trevor took a deep breath, then said, "We need to talk in the library."

She really didn't understand why he wanted to talk to her, but she said nothing as he guided her down the long hallway. She assumed *the other* Trevor was about to reappear.

The room they entered was richly furnished with a cherry-wood desk and tall leather chairs. Bookcases stretched to the ceiling against every wall. A wooden ladder ran on a brass rail, making volumes on the higher shelves easy to reach. She wondered if Trevor had read all the tomes. She'd be happy if she could read just one, but education had never been high on her parents' list. "Common sense will get you by," her mother had told her several times.

Kristen glanced down at her hands. She still clutched the brush and mirror, the only things she truly owned . . . She didn't even own a simple book, she thought sadly, moving over to one of the chairs. She sat down. Trevor remained standing. He placed both hands on the back of a royal-blue couch as he stared at her.

"I should know better than to trust a bloody Scot," he said with a disgusted sigh.

Kristen stood. "I'm getting just a wee bit tired of ye callin' me a bloody Scot. 'Tis yerself to blame for suggesting this arrangement." She shook her finger at him. "What's this bloody thorn ye got in yer side anyway?"

"Sit down," he suggested firmly, and she decided to comply for now.

"Ian Johnstone killed my grandfather."

"What did yer grandfather do to him?" Kristen challenged.

"Not a thing."

"Really?" Kristen gave him a doubtful look. "Surely, he did something to provoke him."

"They had been business partners for years despite the differences between England and Scotland. There was a huge tract of land between their estates that they both coveted. And to make a very long story short, they quarreled, and when it was over my grandfather was dead."

"Did Johnstone shoot him?"

Trevor straightened and moved around to sit on the settee. "No, my grandfather's heart failed."

"Then ye can't blame Ian Johnstone for that. However,

none of this has a thing to do with me, now does it? I wasna even born then." She came to her feet again. "So why would ye be wanting to marry me at all since ye've got this thorn stuck so deep in yer pompous arse?"

"Watch your language," he warned as he stood. "We've been through this before. What I want to know is why you left the shop when I gave you strict orders to stay put."

Kristen laughed. "Have ye not noticed that I don't take orders very well? Ye need to get that through yer thick head."

Trevor took a step toward her. "You'll do well to follow my orders because the consequences could become severe," he warned. "Leaving the shop was a very foolish thing for you to do. You could have been killed in that part of town, dressed as you were."

" 'Twas not dangerous at all. I know those streets like the back of me hand." She held her hand up to emphasize her point. "But what I dinna expect was for Da to show up."

Trevor folded his arms across his chest. "Tell me about him."

" 'Tisn't much to say." Her voice seemed cold. Then she pressed her lips together in anger as she added, "He's a good-for-nothing, as I'm sure ye've noticed, and he was mean to my mother. I want nothing more to do with him ever again."

Trevor's shuttered expression suggested he was holding his emotions in check, and a muscle twitched in his cheek. "You won't have to worry about that, I promise. Did he beat you?"

"Aye." She nodded. "He did until about eight months ago when I took Hagan and ran away."

"Why didn't you leave sooner?"

"And go where?" she asked indignantly. "I had no

money. No home. No family. Not everyone lives like ye do.''

"What changed?" Trevor wasn't sure he wanted the answer, but for some reason he had to know. He didn't want to think about what horror had prompted her to run. God, had she been selling herself on the street?

'' 'Twasn't what ye think,'' Kristen answered stiffly as she lifted a brow at him. "I lifted a hefty purse." The corner of her mouth twitched.

Trevor relaxed with relief. On top of that, he felt a little guilty for thinking the worst. But her past wasn't the issue. What had happened earlier was. "What was so important that you couldn't wait for me to take you back to where you lived?"

Kristen tried to move past him, but he blocked her with his stiff arm. "I'd rather not say."

Trevor turned her back around to him and tilted her chin up so he could see her eyes. He seemed to be getting good at reading her thoughts. "I would rather that you did." He stood her in front of him, holding her lightly by the upper arms.

"I—I don't care a twit what ye'd rather."

"Kristen!" His grip tightened. "Have I treated you so badly that you can't trust me with a simple answer?"

"Nay," she said, shrugging him off. He hadn't treated her badly at all. So far he had rescued her and Hagan, fed them, and now clothed them, and she felt guilty. "I—I didn't want ye to see the filth I lived in before."

Trevor recognized the pride in her eyes, and something inside him twisted. "Kristen." This time her name was a whisper, a caress on his lips. He rubbed his thumb across her chin. Her skin felt like silk, and she was so incredibly beautiful he wanted to do more than just touch her. This woman was so unpredictable and unspoiled that she attracted him more than any of the sophisticated, flirtatious women he'd known.

"Yer getting off the topic," she whispered.

"I know." His lips brushed hers. "But for some strange reason I like doing this."

"Aye, ye do." She breathed softly and closed her eyes as he pulled her closer.

"There is something about you—" Trevor's mouth pressed feathering kisses across her cheeks, cutting off the rest of his words. Kristen felt so comfortable, so right, in his arms, yet he couldn't explain why. He'd held many women before and then calmly shoved them away when he lost interest. Why was this small, stubborn woman different from the rest?

He kissed her again, his touch confident, sure. The kiss exploded into an intoxicating drug. What surprised him most was what an adept student Kristen had become after one lesson. She was remembering very well how to kiss, and instead of him having control of the situation, it began to slip away as he drowned in a sea of pleasure.

Kristen liked this kissing stuff, and *she knew* she liked the way Trevor held her. It was amazing how fast he could drain the resistance she should be displaying. Instead, she felt a need and desire for something else deep inside her. She felt dizzy and opened her mouth to say so, but the words never came out because Trevor seized the opportunity to deepen the kiss. He filled her mouth at the same time his hands slid toward her breasts.

Kristen's heart pounded against her chest as he robbed her of all the reasons why she shouldn't be in his arms. When he touched her breast, she gave a startled whimper, but he was such an expert, her small protest was soon forgotten and replaced with liquid warmth that spilled over her body, making her feel as if she were on fire.

A loud knock sounded on the door, and they broke apart quickly as Frederick, the butler, and another gentleman Kristen had never seen entered the room. She quickly moved away from Trevor.

"Begging your pardon, Your Grace, but—"

"Frederick. You can't announce me when I'm already in the room," a tall gentleman with reddish hair and light green eyes commented, grinning at the ruffled butler.

"Sir, you are entirely improper."

"Yes, my man, I know." The gentleman patted the butler's shoulder, then turned to face Trevor. "What's this I hear about your taking the plunge?"

"It's good to see you too, Rodney," Trevor said wryly, and extended his hand to the Marquess of Middleton.

"That's all you have to say?" The man shook Trevor's extended hand, but his eyes were on Kristen. "And who, pray tell, is this lovely creature hiding behind you? Don't tell me she's the one that has everybody chattering about the Duke of Chatsworth."

"So word has gotten out, I see."

"What are people saying about me?" Kristen asked.

"My God, man." Rodney threw his hands up to his face in mock shock. "She's a Scot!"

Kristen let her exasperation show. "Does everyone ye know have the same problem with my heritage?"

Rodney held up a hand in defense. "Not me. But Trevor now, that's an entirely different story."

"The same thing I've told him," Kristen burst out, "but the man is extremely hardheaded."

"Perhaps I should introduce my fiancée before you two start carrying on the conversation without me," Trevor said. "Rodney Norman Brownwell, Marquess of Middleton. I'd like you to meet Kristen Johnstone."

"Johnstone?" Rodney's eyes widened. He glanced at

Trevor before turning back to Kristen. "Lovely lady, you have accomplished the inexplicable." Rodney gave her an exaggerated bow. "You have somehow taken the most notorious rake in all of London out of circulation and seemingly managed to do it overnight."

Kristen liked this man. At least this one smiled. Something she'd not seen Trevor do a lot. Trevor was far too serious. Rodney had the most unusual auburn hair and light green eyes, and he was very good-looking. Nearly as handsome as Trevor.

"Ye might say we struck a bargain that neither of us could refuse." She smiled at Rodney. "If ye'll excuse me, I need to go change. I've somehow managed to tear my dress."

"By all means. But I do expect a promise to dance with me at the Cranford bash."

She looked at Trevor before leaving the room. "Are we going?"

Rodney answered first. "Of course you are."

After Kristen had taken her leave, Rodney turned to Trevor. "I noticed her cheek was red and swollen. Did she have an accident?"

"You might say that." Trevor looked at his friend. "Where did you hear my good news?"

"I heard it from my current lady love. She said Lady Eleanor saw you coming into a dress shop. And you know the gossip that woman can spread."

"Afraid I do. I guess I better write Grandmère so she doesn't hear it from anyone else. I also need her to start making wedding plans. That should get her out of her bed and on her feet again." Trevor smiled.

"Until she meets the bride." Rodney raised a brow. "May I ask what possessed you to take a Scot for a bride? Wait a minute." Rodney held up his hand. "After seeing the lovely creature I know the answer. My God, she is a beauty!" Rodney sat down in one of the wing-back chairs.

"Yes, she is. But there is more to Kristen than meets the eye." Trevor grinned, deciding not to reveal his lady's background. That would be a secret between him and Kristen for now. "Tell me. Did you find out anymore about Grandmère's jewels?"

"Only that they have been scattered. The largest ruby is no longer in Scotland. It seems the Earl of Hayword purchased it for the then-love of his life, Lady Carolyn Newberry. When they broke up, Carolyn sold the bauble, and that is where I've lost trail of that one. But never fear, I have several men hot on the trail."

"With Grandmère's health failing, I would like to grant her last wish and have the stolen jewelry returned to her."

"Do you really think the Scot stole her jewels?"

"Not really. Grandmère blames everything on our neighbors. But the highwaymen were probably my own low-life Englishmen."

"Nothing worse than a thief. Too bad you don't know one. They could steal back all your possessions posthaste," Rodney suggested innocently.

Trevor had been about to take a swallow of whiskey but choked on his friend's comments.

"Are you all right?" Rodney asked.

When Trevor caught his breath, he grinned. "You know, you might have hit on the perfect solution."

Kristen hurried to her room. She couldn't let Trevor get under her skin, especially since he now knew he could get his way just by kissing her.

The man drove her to distraction. If he thought she was going to bow to his every whim, then he didn't know her very well. She'd seen how her mother had bowed and scraped to her stepfather, and he had treated her terribly. Kristen wanted no part of that.

She could play along with this masquerade as long as she remembered that was all it was. But she wasn't fooling herself that this lust she felt could last a lifetime. Only love lasted that long, and in her eighteen years, she'd never seen love, much less experienced it. She wasn't even sure it existed.

Sighing, she removed her torn dress and slipped on a simple yellow day dress that Madam Marie had sent. Wouldn't it be wonderful to be loved and cherished by a man who loved her and only her? She couldn't think of anything that would make her happier, and she had no idea how it would feel to have a family where she truly belonged. She had never felt that in the hodgepodge family she'd been living in.

Her bedroom door swung open, and she jumped, thinking it would be Trevor. Hagan bounced through, dressed in his new clothes.

"Look at you, young man." Kristen smiled. "You look very proper."

"Yeah. Trevor said the same thing." He strutted around for her and then frowned. "What about Pa?"

"He hasn't changed a bit. He still reeks of whiskey. I'm so glad Trevor saved us, or we'd be back in his clutches."

Hagan sat on the edge of the bed. "Did Pa hurt you, Kristen?"

"Just a wee bit." She rubbed her swollen cheek, feeling the sore spot. "We don't have to worry about that again."

"Trevor would never do such a thing." Hagan shook his head, but she could see he needed reassuring. "Would he?"

Kristen glanced at her brother's concerned frown, not

knowing exactly what to say this time since they were in such different surroundings where she had very little control over their situation. "I don't think so."

"I like Trevor. He bought me some clothes, and said I'd have something different for every day."

"Did he now?" Kristen smiled again. "I got a lot of nice things too. I guess we owe him a lot."

"Does this mean we have to pay him?" Hagan asked so innocently she wanted to cry.

"Not exactly," Kristen answered in a light voice. "I'll explain it someday."

"All right." Hagan jumped off the bed and moved over to the dresser, where he started examining the perfume bottles. Scrunching up his nose at the lovely fragrances and giving a disapproving frown, he said, "Trevor said I can start my schooling next week. Someone by the name of Master Benjamin is coming to teach me some things. He's called a tutor. What's a tutor?"

"I'm not sure." She shrugged. "It looks like ye'll have to teach me what ye learn."

Hagan swung around and looked at his sister. "Why don't you go to school with me?"

"Because I'm too old."

"But if you don't know nothing, how are you going to learn?"

"I'm not sure. But someday, I would like to be able to read." Maybe somehow she could learn how to read along with Hagan.

The next week when Mr. Benjamin came to teach Hagan, Kristen stood outside the open door to the schoolroom so she could hear what he was teaching. After all, she rarely saw much of Trevor because he was constantly working. Every time she went by his study, he had his head down, writing. Or some stranger would be standing in front of his desk.

She was listening so intently that she didn't notice Trevor had moved up behind her to see what she was doing.

Trevor smiled. So she wanted to learn. He'd never known a woman who was interested in anything but sewing and clothes. But each day with Kristen brought a new surprise. Boring . . . she definitely was not. He hated to admit it, but he admired her spirit and courage. Carefully, he placed a hand on her arm.

Kristen jumped.

"Saints above! Ye scared me." She took a deep breath and clutched at her chest. "I—I just wanted to see what Hagan was doing." She turned and blushed, making her even more appealing. "I guess I should be doing something, but there is nothing to do."

Trevor noticed how self-conscious she seemed. Then she caught herself and added, "And ye are busy working."

"I know what you were doing, and it's all right."

"I just told ye what I was doing," she stubbornly insisted.

"Kristen, I have learned to read your expressions very well. You can't read, can you?" He watched her defiant stance. She *did* care what people thought of her, and he was glad.

"Dinna make fun of me!"

"I'm not making fun of you." He folded his arms, taking a stubborn stance of his own. "I have no problem with your learning. If that is what you truly want." His brow lifted, giving her a chance to deny his offer. "From now on I'll have Mr. Benjamin teach you also, if that will make you happy."

Her shoulders slumped a little. "But I'm so old." She spoke with a soft bitterness.

Reaching out, he took her hand. "You're never too old to learn. I wager you'd like to read and write. Am I right?"

She nodded her head.

"Then you shall have your wish." He smiled and hesitated before he added, "There is one thing I would like you to do for me."

Kristen knew it was too good to be true. He would probably want to sleep with her, and she wasn't ready for that. She wanted to wait until they got married. Even then, she wasn't sure she would be ready for her wifely duties. But how could she refuse a man who had been so good to her?

"My grandmère's jewels were stolen by highwaymen about a year ago. I've been trying to track them down with the help of Rodney, whom you met earlier. I think one of the necklaces might show up at the Cranford ball."

Kristen didn't immediately answer. She was so relieved that his request wasn't what she'd thought. She moved over to a chair and placed her hand on the back before she spoke. "Did I hear ye right? Ye, the saint of goodness, want me to steal it back for ye?"

"No," he said quickly. "I know you have a knack for spotting such valuable items. I will describe the jewelry and when you see it, you can let me know. Then I can make an offer to buy the item back."

"Buy it back when it's rightfully yers? Ye gentry have a funny way of doing things."

"It's called honesty, Kristen."

"More like foolishness, if ye ask me," Kristen said as she left the room.

When Kristen descended the stairs, Trevor couldn't believe the vision in front of him. She had dressed in a gown of pale blue silver over a blue satin slip. Trevor wondered if she knew she wore the colors of Scotland.

Her hair was a glorious mass of curls pulled up from the sides and left to hang down her back. But by far her most dazzling quality was those shining emerald eyes that glowed at him with a radiance he couldn't ignore. She could say a lot with those eyes. He recalled how her skin felt, and he knew as he held her gaze with his that something was going on between them . . . something he liked.

"Anything wrong?" she asked when he failed to speak.

"No, sweetheart. I don't see a thing wrong with you."

"Then ye like my dress?"

"Yes, I would definitely say I like your dress." He nodded, then grinned. "You are magnificent!" It was amazing how she'd changed her appearance so quickly. Just putting on the new clothes seemed to have given her confidence. She now appeared aloof and regal, and he found himself very proud she belonged to him—well, almost belonged to him.

Magnificent, Kristen thought. She'd just learned that word the other day, and she now knew Trevor had, in fact, given her her first compliment. She beamed beneath his approval and then sternly reminded herself it really didn't matter.

Don't get attached, she warned herself. *You'll only get hurt.*

The ride to the party was short, and soon they were walking up the steps of a grand house surrounded by scores of carriages.

Kristen felt very much alone as they entered the ballroom. She didn't belong with these people, and she was afraid of embarrassing Trevor. They paused, and a footman dressed in black tails announced, "The Duke of Chatsworth and Lady Kristen Johnstone."

The room grew quiet, and Kristen felt as if every pair

of eyes were on her. Self-consciously, she straightened her posture. Then the chattering resumed at a faster pace than before. Now she really felt awkward as people turned to gape openly at her. "Everyone is staring," she whispered as she tugged on Trevor's arm.

Trevor leaned over and whispered, "They are staring at me, so relax." He patted her hand and gave her a reassuring smile.

"Why?" she asked.

"Because I am titled. I usually don't attend these events."

"Why?"

"Mothers are looking for titles for their daughters."

There were so many pretty ladies, she didn't know why Trevor wouldn't be flattered by their attention.

Kristen went over every detail of her appearance. She knew her dress was appropriate. She only hoped the rest of her held up and she didn't make a complete fool out of herself.

After tonight everyone would know she was Claremont's fiancée, and she was surprised at how proud that made her feel. Never in her wildest dreams had she imagined she'd end up marrying someone like Trevor. Come to think of it, she never thought she'd marry anyone. Now she wondered if fate had somehow pushed her to pick his pocket.

Trevor tried to guide her past the two ladies Kristen had seen leaving the dress shop that first day. The older woman had a different idea and stepped in their path.

"Your Grace, it's nice to see you here," Mrs. Clanton said. "My Elizabeth has yearned to dance with you. I told her tonight she'd get her chance."

"Mama!"

Elizabeth blushed, and Kristen felt sorry for the girl's embarrassing situation.

"I will be honored, Elizabeth." Trevor turned toward

Kristen. "That is, if my fiancée will not be overly jealous." He pulled Kristen close to him, placing his arm around her waist. "Ladies, I would like you to meet my future bride."

Kristen knew her soon-to-be husband was baiting her. "Of course I dinna mind if ye dance with Elizabeth. I'll dance with others also." Kristen smiled sweetly at Trevor, then turned her attention back to the young girl. "It's nice to meet ye." She smiled at Elizabeth, feeling very sorry for the girl, who seemed to have an overbearing mother.

"Yes," Mrs. Clanton commented, then added in a haughty tone, "Isn't this a bit sudden?" Her expression held a touch of mockery.

Trevor raised a brow. "You know what they say about true love." He pressed gently on Kristen's waist, and they moved away from the nosy old woman and on to another group.

Kristen smiled and listened, all the while thinking how shallow and boring these people were . . . and most were snobs.

How could Trevor like any of them? They were much too busy trying to impress everyone. That left very few who were truly themselves.

Kristen gazed out across the ballroom and marveled at the beautiful dresses in every color imaginable. For just a moment, she could see another ballroom with a lady who looked just like herself dancing with a very distinguished gentleman. They were a fine-looking couple, gazing lovingly into each other's eyes. Then a child of no more than three or four ran up to them and the couple swung her up into their arms.

She shivered and blinked several times. Why did she keep slipping back into this imaginary world she had created for herself—and at the most unexpected times? She had done it since she was a child. She could understand creating an escape world when she was on the streets, but now things were different, and the visions were happening more often. Perhaps she was a little touched in the head.

"Are you all right?" Trevor's expression showed his concern.

"Aye," she murmured, and followed him to a secluded nook of the ballroom.

Finally, when they were alone, Kristen whispered to Trevor, "Do you really like these people?"

He shrugged. "Perhaps a few. Why do you ask?"

"They are so bumptious." She knew her face must be very pink because she could feel the heat in her cheeks, but that didn't stop her from continuing. "If this is all ye have to call friends, no wonder ye came looking for me."

Trevor chuckled. "I didna come looking for you." He mocked her accent, and Kristen frowned at him. "If you recall, you found me."

" 'Tis true." She smiled. "Must have been fate. But yer the one who decided to keep me."

He looked deep into her eyes. All the humor had left his expression. "It's a decision that I haven't yet regretted." He lowered his head as if he was going to kiss her.

"We'll have none of that," Rodney said, walking up behind them. "It's bad enough you've shown up at the Cranford ball when you've not attended another function in the last six months. That in itself is enough to set the tongues wagging, but then you make an appearance with your future wife, which"—Rodney chuckled, then continued—"has sent many a young woman crying to her mother. And now you have the audacity to show everyone that you might care for this woman by kissing her in public and crushing what little hope the mothers had that Kristen was merely a passing fling." Rodney took a deep breath. "Just where is your decency?"

"Rodney, did anyone ever tell you that you talk far too much?" Trevor asked.

"Yes." Rodney grinned, adding, "On occasion."

"Good, because I didn't want to be the first." Trevor grinned. "Who are you here with?"

"No one," Rodney replied offhandedly, then reached over and grabbed Kristen's hand. "This way, I can be the first to dance with your lovely lady."

Kristen tried to suppress a giggle as Rodney led her onto the dance floor. She hadn't uttered a sound, but once they were in the middle of the crowd she found her voice. "I canna dance."

Rodney peered at her for a long minute. "You're serious, aren't you?"

"Very." She nodded her head.

"Then I shall teach you," he simply said. "Here. Put your hand on my shoulder and the other goes here." He took her hand in his. "Now don't be so stiff and watch me. Move when I move, and don't look down." He cautioned. "There is nothing to it."

Kristen concentrated hard. She even insisted they should stop several times, but Rodney wouldn't hear of it.

After stepping on Rodney's feet a couple of times and apologizing profusely, she seemed to catch on. Once she did, she liked the fluid movement.

"What is this dance called?"

"A waltz. Do you like it?"

" 'Tis fun once ye master the steps."

"You are a very good pupil. Watch this." He pulled her a little closer.

"What?" Kristen looked at him with a puzzled expression.

"Look over there at Trevor."

She turned her head. "He's frowning. So?" She looked at Rodney again. "Trevor frowns a lot. I dinna ken why."

"Because he's jealous of me holding you much too close. He hasn't taken his eyes off you since we started dancing."

"He canna be jealous." Kristen actually laughed. "He doesn't love me."

"But he's marrying you."

" 'Tis true, but it isn't love. 'Tis merely an agreement."

"Listen, sweetheart, I don't know what you mean by agreement, but Trevor would not be marrying you if he didn't feel something. No matter what he has told you. He seldom does things without a good reason."

"Ye sure about this?"

"Most definitely." he said with a significant lifting of his brow. "He never does anything he doesn't want to do."

"I'm not so sure." Awkwardly, she cleared her throat as the music faded away. "Thank ye for teaching me to dance."

"You're very welcome, Kristen. I hope you will think of me as a friend too," he leaned down and whispered as he took her back to Trevor.

Trevor stood staring at them with his arms folded across his chest. And he wasn't smiling. "It's about time you returned her." He couldn't believe this sudden irritation he felt. After all, someday he would give Kristen her freedom and then he'd have his. That was why he'd made the bargain in the first place—no demands would be made. But damn it, when he was around, he expected her undivided attention. They would have to have a long talk about what he expected of her once they were married.

"I thought perhaps you might like to dance, so I've graciously brought Kristen back to you," Rodney said lightly.

A satanic smile touched Trevor's lips. "Thank you for your permission."

The violins shifted to a new tune. Trevor swept Kristen

up into his arms, and they began to move around and around until she felt she was floating on a cloud. He was a much better dancer than Rodney, and Trevor held her much closer. She could feel the heat seeping through the material of her dress, and she realized she felt much too content with his arms around her.

His hand splayed across her lower back, and she couldn't catch her breath for a few minutes. She probably should be saying something, but all she could do was stare at his dark blue eyes. It was amazing how they could change from dark to light. What was he thinking? More important, how did he feel? He held her as if she was a most treasured prize, yet he never said a word. But then, what was she to expect? Theirs was a business arrangement.

Suddenly Trevor smiled at her. His smiles had the strangest effect on her, and Kristen wondered if she was so starved for attention that she jumped at the least little display.

"What are you thinking, my love?" he asked.

"That I like looking at ye." She blushed.

"Then that makes two of us. You know I like the way your cheeks turn soft pink when you are embarrassed."

"And what makes ye think I'm embarrassed? Perhaps I'm just a wee bit hot."

"And all the time I thought I was the reason." Trevor laughed, and then pulled her to him for a brief kiss.

"Ye canna be doing such in the middle of the dance floor. I'm sure 'tisn't proper."

"Merely kissing my future bride," he said as his lips brushed her forehead. He then led her over to another group of ladies. "I'll go and get us something to drink. Excuse me."

Kristen didn't try to fit into the conversation. Instead she politely listened to the boring ladies as best she could. She couldn't help noticing the beautiful, priceless jewelry each lady wore, and she was sure they wouldn't miss a few baubles. Thank goodness, she'd convinced the seamstress to make a slit in her skirt for a hidden pocket.

Carefully moving around the ladies, as if to change to a different view of the room, she successfully retrieved a bracelet, two brooches, and a ring. Good, she hadn't lost her touch.

"Kristen girl, ye should be ashamed." Her conscience decided to rear its ugly head, and that was the one thing she really didn't need. She had to survive. That was something the streets had taught her, so over the years her conscience had learned to be quiet. But now the voice was back louder than ever.

She pushed the thought to the back of her mind, but blushed nonetheless. Now was no time to develop a conscience. After all, she didn't really think of her skill as something bad. She merely robbed from the rich to give to the poor—mainly herself. These few items she'd keep as a nest egg, just in case.

When Kristen looked up, she noticed a new woman had joined the group. She was introduced as Ella. Ella had beautiful blond hair, but what Kristen noticed first was the exquisite necklace that Trevor had described to her earlier. The necklace was simple, yet elegant. A huge emerald about the size of a walnut hung at the end of a gold rope and rested just above the woman's breast.

This would be a challenge, Kristen thought as she made her way carefully around the group so she could stand beside her victim. At least the lady had her hair pulled up so the clasp could come easily undone.

While Kristen waited for the precise moment, she halfway joined in the conversation. "Excuse me, but it looks like you have torn your gown." She pointed to the bottom of Ella's gown.

Ella took the bait and murmured, "Oh, heavens."

They both bent over, and Kristen accidentally bumped Ella. The rest was a piece of cake. The poor woman never knew what happened, nor did she notice that her necklace had suddenly disappeared.

Kristen was just getting ready to leave the little group when Ella shrieked. "My necklace! Don't anyone move."

Kristen froze. *Oh, no.* She'd been caught.

"I probably dropped it on the floor when I bent over," Ella gasped as she felt across the top of her grown. "Help me look."

Kristen immediately let her breath out and stooped down and started searching the floor. "This is just terrible. Your clasp must have been very loose."

"It was. I have had trouble before."

Thank goodness. Kristen smiled to herself, then said, "Perhaps you lost it elsewhere. I don't remember seeing it on you when you came in here." Kristen immediately looked toward heaven. *Forgive me, Father.*

"Do the rest of you remember seeing it on me?" Ella asked the group, and they looked at each other, puzzled.

"Now that you mention it, no. Maybe Kristen is correct and you lost it in another part of the house. Here, let me help you retrace your steps," one of the older women offered.

"Thank you."

Trevor decided to join the group just then. "What's the trouble, ladies?"

"It seems Ella has dropped her necklace. We are helping her look for it," one of the ladies told him.

"Oh, really." Trevor immediately looked at Kristen.

"'Tis truly a shame," Kristen said, then added, "Wouldn't you agree?"

"Yes, I would." Trevor took Kristen's elbow without waiting for her to argue. "If you'll excuse us, we need to be going."

Once they were in the carriage, he looked at her but didn't say anything.

Kristen shifted in her seat, but remained silent as she straightened out her skirts so she wouldn't sit on the loot.

"I thought we had an agreement."

"Aye."

"Well?"

"Ye needed yer grandmère's necklace back. I simply found it." She opened her hand and produced the huge emerald.

Trevor didn't seem to notice. "I thought we agreed you wouldn't take it. You'd just let me know who was wearing the jewel; then I could buy it back." He waited for her to answer.

She didn't.

"Kristen!"

" 'Twas simple."

Trevor took both her arms. "I didn't want you stealing the piece."

"Well, it was yers. I simply retrieved it." She smiled.

He gritted his teeth. How could he get angry with her when she looked at him in that innocent way?

Because he knew she wasn't innocent by any means.

"Kristen." Trevor sighed, and then gave up and hugged her to him. "What ever am I going to do with you?"

"Marry me, I suppose."

"Yes, I'm going to do that, but how am I going to tame you?"

"It won't be easy."

CHAPTER FIVE

The sun hadn't even thought about peeking its head out when they loaded up the carriages and the lead vehicle pulled away from Trevor's town house.

They were headed to Chatsworth, Trevor's country estate, located on the Scottish border. He had informed her that was where they would be married, at his grandmother's insistence. Kristen wondered about the woman who seemed to hold so much power over Trevor. She couldn't imagine him ever bending to any woman's will.

Kristen felt awkward riding with Trevor . . . alone.

The others would be sent in another carriage that would follow theirs later in the day.

She looked at Trevor from beneath her lashes. A stranger! A perfectly good-looking, breathtaking stranger. But a stranger nonetheless.

Kristen realized she'd agreed to marry someone she

really didn't know and definitely had nothing in common with.

She bit the side of her mouth as she watched Trevor write on his tablet. It seemed the man worked constantly. She couldn't remember seeing him idle since they had met. He was either jotting something down in his book or issuing commands. And look how he frowned at what he was doing! That kind of burden couldn't be good for anyone.

But the man constantly worked.

He didn't seem to know how to do anything else, and Kristen realized he must have forgotten what enjoyment meant. How would she ever fit into his world? It was hard enough just to get him to talk, even though, she had to admit, he always made time for her if she needed him. But sometimes that wasn't enough.

He seemed to have built a wall around himself, and Kristen wondered why. Perhaps he'd always been that way, but she didn't think so. Maybe something awful had happened in his past that had made him so withdrawn. She sighed as something stirred deep within her. Somehow, some way, she wanted to help him change.

Kristen was sure, one day, she'd find all her answers.

Restlessly, she shifted her weight and crossed her legs for at least the tenth time. She still hadn't gotten a response, and sitting here staring at him, even if she did like looking at the man, wasn't going to do anything but give her a bad headache. If she didn't get Trevor talking soon, she'd be bored to tears.

"Do you always work?" Kristen's question came out sharper than she'd meant. At least she'd gotten results, because he laid the pad on his lap.

He looked at her as if she'd grown horns. "Most of the time."

"Why?"

"Because things needs to be done."

"All that work must be awful dull."

He didn't say anything; he just stared. How could she penetrate the deliberate blankness of his eyes?

"What do you do for enjoyment?" Kristen asked.

"Enjoyment?"

"Wonderful!" She felt the screams of frustration at the back of her throat. "Ye don't even know what the word means."

"You're wrong." She didn't fail to catch the note of sarcasm in his voice.

"I do know the meaning of the word, and I'm sure I've had some enjoyable moments," he said. He smiled, then continued. "I can think of a few since I've met you."

Kristen blushed.

"Someone has to run my shipping business, though I do admit I've turned a good portion of it over to a gentleman you've not yet met. But putting business aside, I also have three houses to run and somehow all the 'enjoyments of life' got swept away when I wasn't looking." He frowned as his own words seemed to sink into his head. Then he looked back at her. "I guess I haven't realized how much I work."

" 'Tis never too late." She bent her head and studied her hands before shyly looking back at him. "Maybe we can change ye." She saw the heartrending tenderness of his gaze, and her stomach tightened.

Trevor stretched his arm across the back of the seat and pushed his papers beside him. "Then you'd work a miracle."

"Aye. But I do believe in miracles," she whispered, knowing how easily he could draw her to him. It was the way he looked at her that made her whole body turn to jelly.

She blinked a couple of times, realizing the rocking of the carriage was making her sleepy. She tried to stifle a yawn.

"Would you like to sit beside me and perhaps use my shoulder for a pillow?" he asked.

She didn't hesitate a moment longer to take him up on the offer because she hadn't slept much at all last night. Trevor had been on her mind all night . . . especially those wondrous kisses that could make her forget everything else.

Moving beside him, she only meant to rest her head on his shoulder, but he draped an arm around her in a possessive gesture and leaned back himself. Evidently, he hadn't slept well either, she decided, and smiled. Good. She didn't want to be the only one who had suffered.

Kristen, strangely enough, felt secure and comfortable as she shut her eyes. Then it dawned on her that she felt much too comfortable. It would be so easy to get used to all this luxury, and perhaps also to this man. Every day he grew special to her in a way she'd never experienced before. The same question always came back to haunt her. How long?

She decided, just as she felt the edges of sleep touch her, she wouldn't worry about the problem any longer. She had lived by her wits all her life, taking one day at a time.

So her decision was now made . . .

She'd take one day at a time and deal with whatever came her way.

Her dreams were so pleasant she didn't want to open her eyes. She dreamed of Trevor and those wonderful kisses he'd taught her, and how they made her head spin and her heart flutter. There was so much between them that she didn't understand, and she didn't want to be attracted to him. Again, the image of him kissing her floated before her eyes. She could almost picture his face hovering above hers as he lifted his lips. Desire and love floated in his eyes.

Did he say something about love?

At that precise moment, Kristen came fully awake. Love would jar anyone awake, but that wasn't the case this time. Something was wrong with the carriage!

The carriage gave a sharp lunge, and she slid to the floor with a muffled cry.

"What the hell?" Trevor's voice boomed beside her.

"W—what's happening?" Kristen tried to stand, but stepped on her skirt, which sent her sailing back into Trevor's arms. He held her close while the vehicle teetered on two wheels, then righted itself.

The carriage finally came to a jolting halt and voices, more than she remembered, surrounded the vehicle.

"Come on and get out, Ye Grace."

Trevor took Kristen by the arms and held her from him. "Kristen, do as I say," Trevor cautioned her. "I think we are about to be held up."

"You mean thieves?"

Trevor looked at her and managed not to laugh at her put-out expression. "Isn't that the pot calling the kettle black?"

"I resent that." She huffed past him as if he'd offended her. " 'Tis not the same."

Trevor shook his head. If the situation wasn't so serious, he'd probably be laughing at her, he thought as he exited and put his feet on firm ground. But he was afraid the situation was very serious as he looked around at the group of thugs.

"I see we've had a bit of luck, fellows. Looks like His Lordship is traveling with his lady. She should be good for a few dozen fine pieces of jewels."

"Well, that's where yer bloody wrong," Kristen quickly informed him when she was out of the carriage, even though Trevor squeezed her arm in warning. "So ye best be leavin'."

"She's got a mouth on her, that one does," the man standing beside the leader quipped.

Trevor decided he'd better step in before Kristen riled the four men pointing guns at them. Hadn't she noticed they both were outnumbered? Maybe he could have handled one man, perhaps two, but not four.

"She does have a bit of a mouth," Trevor said, breaking the uneasy silence. "But the lady is correct. We are not traveling with valuables." He reached into his coat to grab his wallet. "Here is my money. We've nothing else."

"Isn't much." The leader spat. He was a good three inches shorter than Trevor. "Perhaps we'll just take the little lady for our troubles." The leader grinned. "I'm sure you can come up with more when we have the likes of her for collateral." He reached out, but Trevor shoved Kristen behind him.

"I don't think so," Trevor said much too calmly.

The bandit then made the mistake of striking Trevor, who responded with a quick right to the jaw. Kristen wasn't sure what happened next. Trevor grabbed the man and, in the process, shoved Kristen away. She fell against the carriage, bumping her head against the hard metal on the wheel.

A scuffle ensued all around her. The thuds of fists meeting with flesh echoed in her ears. She could see boots and dust. Men shouted, followed by an explosion that brought dead silence.

Kristen managed to get to her feet, pushing her long hair out of her face as she did so. When she finally got her bearings and looked around, she screamed.

Trevor lay on the ground.

He wasn't moving.

A bright red splotch on his right shoulder told her where the bullet had ended up.

My God, Trevor was dead!

Kristen didn't take time to think as she lunged herself at the bandit in front of her. "Ye bloody bastard, ye killed him." She became a whirling hellcat, and it took two men to pull her off their leader.

"You sure don't talk like no lady," the bloke managed to spit out. "But I bet someone would pay a nice sum to get you back."

"Then, ye should think again. I'm not worth two pence to anyone, and ye killed the only man who might have paid ye."

Her comment brought a resounding slap across the face.

Instead of collapsing in tears, the blow only made Kristen angrier. Earlier, she had filched a knife from one of the other men. In her scuffle, she grasped the handle and hurled it at their leader, landing it deep in the man's gun arm.

"You bitch!" he exploded, dropping the pistol to grab the blade sticking out of his arm. "I'll beat the life out of you for this!" Realizing a little too late that he'd dropped his weapon, he bent down to retrieve it, but when he did, he saw the gun was now pointed at his face.

"Unless you want to die first, I suggest you let the lady go." Trevor's deadly voice let everyone know that he meant what he said.

Even though the leader complied, he boldly said, "If you kill me, my men will kill her. So I still have the advantage."

"I think not." Trevor cocked the pistol and slowly came to his feet, his eyes never leaving the leader.

Thank God he wasn't dead, Kristen thought as she

watched him. He reminded Kristen of a cat stalking its prey.

Trevor's eyes flamed intently and his knuckles were white as he gripped the pistol. "I can always replace the lady, but you can't replace your life, now can you?"

That remark brought Kristen out of her stupor. She couldn't believe how casually Trevor could dismiss her. And she'd thought he might care just a little for her.

How could she have been so blind . . . so stupid? She'd even felt bad when she'd thought he had been mortally wounded. However, before she could voice her thoughts, the leader spoke again.

"But you love her. She's valuable to you."

Trevor placed the gun barrel to the tip of the man's nose, and cocked the trigger. "All women can be had."

The last statement enraged Kristen completely, and she completely forgot they were at the mercy of bandits. "So that's what ye bloody think of me!

"I should have thrown the knife at ye instead of him. The only thing that saved yer bloody hide was I thought ye were already dead." She jerked free of the men's loosened grip, but stumbled and fell over her skirt before she could reach Trevor.

That was all Trevor needed. He shot both men, causing their not-so-fearless leader and the fourth man to turn tail and run.

He gave a small sigh as his breathing returned to normal. Hearing the sounds of pounding hooves, he looked to his left and saw his second carriage rapidly approaching with a full guard, so he wouldn't have to worry about the thieves anymore. He realized a little too late that he should have had more guards traveling along. But he had hoped to make better time by traveling light.

He moved over, reached down, and pulled Kristen up

by the arm. However, she didn't come up peacefully. She swung at him, and he jerked back. She barely missed his nose.

"Wait a minute, my little hellcat." He stiffened as though she had struck him. "What, may I ask, has gotten into you?" He snapped out the words impatiently. "We were both just about killed."

"Ye bloody bastard. I don't know why I ever agreed to be seen with ye." She tried to jerk her arm free. "Well, I will not be seen with ye no more. Ye can damned well take me back to London, and get one of those other females ye boasted about to help yer sorry hide out of yer predicament." She raised her chin with a cool stare.

"Now I see what has you riled up." He laughed richly. "I don't want any of the other females." He loosened his grip. "I want you."

"That's not what ye just said. Ye said I wasn't no more than a piece of dirt to ye." She tried to hit him again, but he pinned her arms behind her back and stared down into her angry green eyes.

What spirit she had, Trevor thought. Her eyes glistened with fire, and he wondered if she would be just as passionate in his arms.

"If I had told them just how valuable you were to me," he stated softly, "then you would have been thrown across the saddle and hauled out of here posthaste." He watched the play of emotions on her face. "Perhaps you didn't notice that we were slightly outnumbered?"

"Aye, I did." She regarded him with a speculative, suspicious gaze. "However, the number didn't seem to bother ye none. Look how ye disposed of them."

He ignored her offhanded compliment. "Then maybe you've forgotten that I have been shot."

"Shot," Kristen almost whispered, realizing she had forgotten the wound during all the excitement. She'd even thought Trevor was dead a minute ago. She remembered the devastating hurt that had stabbed her chest when she thought she'd lost him. As she stared at him now, she realized she would have died if anything had happened to him. She reluctantly admitted that small fact to herself. Still—

She saw the light in his eyes reflecting a tenderness before he hid it from her again. She could feel his supple muscles tense.

"It would be very nice if you could stop the bleeding," he said. "Unless you want me to bleed to death."

"I thought they'd killed ye." Her voice cracked as she struggled with her emotions. She wanted to reach out and hug him to her as she did Hagan when he was hurt.

"Thought—or hoped?"

She frowned at him. He was fishing for some tenderness, but he wouldn't be getting what he desired. Better to let him think she didn't care. "Get back into the carriage so I can attend to yer wound."

The other vehicle had finally reached them, and Kristen could hear Hagan running toward them.

"What happened?" Hagan dashed up to his sister, followed by Rebecca.

"Are you all right, mum?" Rebecca asked.

The guards surrounded the carriages. One of them rode closer. "Should we go after them, Your Grace?"

"No, stay with the carriages," Trevor instructed. "The damage has been done."

"We were held up. One of the men shot Trevor," Kristen explained as she pushed the victim toward the carriage door.

"Well, you shot him too," Hagan quickly pointed out from behind her.

"Hagan!" Kristen's stern voice warned him. She didn't need to be reminded of what she'd done over and over again. "Go back to the carriage, so we can get out of here."

Trevor glanced back over his shoulder. "You're right, Hagan," Trevor said. "Being around your sister isn't good for my health." Trevor's gaze returned to Kristen. "If I can remember back a few weeks, my body was whole and without a scratch." He cupped her chin before entering the carriage. "You're dangerous, lady. Very dangerous."

"Aye." She smiled, then added, "We were looking to put some excitement into yer life. However, I dinna ken with putting more holes in yer body." The amusement died in her eyes, and she regarded him with searching gravity. "I truly am sorry. Perhaps yer right. I'm really not very good for ye."

Once they were in the carriage and it had begun to move again, he reached over and took her hand. "I'll be the judge of whether or not you're good for me. Now, if you'll kindly bandage my shoulder . . ."

Trevor was stretched out on the soft cushions of the vehicle, so it was easy to kneel down and look at his wound. She tore open his shirt and winced at the ugly hole in his right shoulder. "The bullet will have to be removed," she informed him needlessly. "But I don't think it has done much damage."

"Good. When we arrive at Chatsworth, Grandmère can summon the surgeon." He winced as Kristen placed a makeshift bandage torn from her slip against the hole. "I've instructed the driver to drive all night so we should arrive by midmorning."

"We can't get help sooner?"

"Afraid not, sweetheart. We're in the country now and don't have the conveniences of London."

This wasn't the first time he'd ever used an endearment,

but she knew he didn't mean anything by it, so she didn't bother to comment. Kristen tore long strips from her petticoat and started wrapping his shoulder. "I think I've stopped the bleeding for now."

"You are a very pretty nurse."

"Thank you." She smiled at him, thinking how helpless he looked just now with his head propped upon the cushions. However, she knew Trevor Claremont, Duke of Chatsworth, was anything but helpless. She'd seen just how dangerous he could be, but instead of being frightened, she found that the thought intrigued her instead. Unfortunately, she had an odd hankering for the man.

"What are you thinking?" he asked.

She chuckled, then decided to lie. "I was surprised at how well ye handled yerself back there. Most men of yer rank are nothing more than dandies. They would have probably fainted dead away."

"I'm not most men, Kristen."

Her eyes darted back to his as she heard him whisper her name like a caress. She felt that familiar warmth that she experienced when he was near her, and she barely whispered, "I know."

Trevor pulled her to him with his good arm and tasted her honey-sweet lips. How could this one small woman block out every sensible thought he had in his head until nothing was left but *her*? When he slept, he could smell her fragrance. He could remember her touch. Hear the sound of her very feminine voice. She seemed to be all around him.

He was used to women always wanting something from him—his title, his wealth, always something. But this woman wanted nothing from him but his protection, and that was only at his insistence. If it hadn't been for her brother and the threat of jail, he'd have lost her the minute he turned his back.

He felt as if he were holding a small bird in his hands, and if he opened his hands she might fly away. And that frightened him more than he'd like to admit. Was his small bargain becoming more than he'd first expected?

All his tumbling thoughts brought out a tenderness in him he didn't know he possessed as his mouth slanted over hers. His wounded arm moved painfully to slide around her waist, and he deepened the kiss, pressing her lips until she opened her mouth and he found what he sought.

Raw pleasure—pleasure he'd seldom known—coursed through his body, and he drew away from the temptation, hoping to see wariness in her expression. But that wasn't to be. What he saw was a lust that matched his own as she moistened her lips, and he lost what little sanity he had left.

Kristen wondered why he stopped. And why did he look at her in such an odd way? She liked this kissing stuff he'd taught her, yet she felt something was missing every time they ended up like this with him staring at her in that most peculiar way.

Sliding her hands up his chest, she brushed his lips again and stared down at his smoldering eyes, which appeared more gray than their usual bluish-green.

Again his lips molded to hers, and her head swam with a desire for something more as she innocently pressed her body closer to his. She needed to be near him. She needed more, even if she didn't know exactly what.

"Kristen, you'd drive a sane man crazy." The words tore from his throat.

His urgent whisper only made her body become more acutely alive, and she whispered back, "Aye."

His long, lingering kiss felt wonderful, and Kristen returned his passion with unrestrained enthusiasm as her hands roamed over his body, feeling every muscle that lay like steel beneath his fine linen shirt. When his lips started down her neck, pausing on her ear, she shivered and, only then, realized that she now lay on top of him.

Trevor must have perceived the same thing because he looked at her and whispered, "Not now, sweetheart. I want to wait until the time is right and I'm not so weak from a wound."

Embarrassed, Kristen had forgotten all about his wound, and quickly glanced down to see the bandage had turned a dark red. "I'm so sorry." She scrambled to get off him, feeling miserable. "You should have told me ye were in pain."

To her surprise, he grinned. "Oh, I was in pain, all right, but not from my wound."

She quickly removed herself and frowned at his unusual words, not quite sure what he meant. What other pain could he be experiencing? She sat down across from him.

"You're too far away." He held out a hand to her, reminding her of a child. "Come back and let me rest my head in your lap."

Kristen did as he instructed. As soon as his head was settled in her lap, he closed his eyes and went to sleep, leaving her to stare down at the most handsome man she'd ever met. In sleep he looked so different, so lovable. She trailed her hand through his tousled hair, and he snuggled closer to her, causing her to smile.

She didn't deserve him.

And she couldn't come to need him.

But just maybe, she would enjoy him . . . if only for a little while.

CHAPTER SIX

The sun had started to drop lower in the sky when the sleek black carriage made its way around a huge lake that shimmered like a looking glass. In the very middle, swimming with their heads held high, were a pair of black swans. And that was when Kristen first spotted Chatsworth. She wasn't prepared for the enormous size of the mansion. How could one family live in a place that could house hundreds? There must be dozens of servants to clean a place like this, and they would probably all laugh when she was introduced to them. They would see that she was an imposter who pretended to be something she wasn't.

From what she could tell, the house had at least seventy-five windows across the front. There were towers that seemed to reach to the sky, and she could count at least ten chimneys from her view.

Trevor slept with his cheek resting next to her stomach, and held the hand she had laid across his chest. Kristen looked down tenderly at him. She touched his forehead, and wondered if he'd developed a slight fever because his forehead was so much warmer than before. Squeezing his hand, she sighed. At least Trevor would have help soon. His grandmother would know what to do.

Kristen glanced back at the castle, spreading out before them nestled on perfect green lawns. Come to think of it, it was much too perfect. And too cold. She could not question Trevor's wealth now, and Kristen doubted that she'd ever fit into such a place. A few table manners and some new clothes didn't change the person she was.

As she stared at her new home, another large estate took its place, a house she'd seen many times in her daydreams. Instead of white, this house had a rusty hue that blended in with the rolling green of the highlands. But how could she know this? She'd never been here before and she'd never seen houses this large.

For a fleeting moment, she envisioned a child running across the grass, her streaming red hair waving like a flag behind her. And if Kristen listened closely, she could hear the child's laughter as she played.

Who was this strange child who kept appearing to her? It couldn't have been herself, for surely she'd remember such a grand place. And all she could recall were small houses and unhappy times.

The vehicle drew to a stop and brought her back to the present. She had arrived at Chatsworth. She was going to meet her new family. How would the dowager duchess feel about her? Would she welcome her with open arms? Kristen made a face. More likely, his grandmother would look down on her as just another piece of trash.

"Trevor. Wake up. We're home . . . er . . . rather, we've arrived at yer home."

Trevor's eyes fluttered open, and he blinked, the confu-

sion of an abrupt awakening on his flushed face. "H—
how long have I been sleeping?" He sat up. "Why didn't
you wake me before now?" He moaned and winced grog-
gily when he moved his shoulder. She wondered just how
much pain he was experiencing.

"I thought I'd let the sleeping beast lie," she told him
with a smile. "Sleep and a doctor are what ye need most."

The footman opened the carriage door and Trevor
descended first, then turned to lift a hand for Kristen, but
the sudden movement caused him to lose his balance and
he swayed drunkenly. Kristen scrambled out the best way
she could, and slipped an arm around his waist.

"Here, let me help you, mum," Rebecca said as she
rushed up from the second carriage, followed by Hagan.

"That will not be necessary," Trevor said, evidently
embarrassed that he couldn't make it without help.

However, Kristen wasn't fooled. "Lean on me," she whispered as they slowly made their way toward a most unusual
set of double doors. She stopped and waited for someone
to answer the knock. It gave her a chance to examine the
doors.

The broken pediment was surmounted by a lion and a
griffin. In the middle of the doorway, just above their
heads, was a carved shield that displayed a coat of arms.
Two large columns entwined with laurel leaves stood on
the side of the double doors.

Finally one of the doors swung open, and a tall, thin
man with white hair filled the space, blocking their
entrance. "Who should I say is calling?" His gaze raked
over Hagan and Rebecca.

"Why, His Grace, of course, Billingsly," Rebecca
informed him. "Where are your spectacles?"

"I—I beg your pardon," Billingsly stuttered, then
blinked, and looked past Rebecca.

"Billingsly, kindly get out of the way and fetch my grandmother posthaste," Trevor muttered, his voice demanding in spite of his pain.

The shocked butler instantly recognized the authoritative voice of his employer, and ran to do Trevor's bidding as fast as his seventy-plus years would let him.

"Billingsly is a bit nearsighted, or he'd have recognized my coach. He's also a tad old, as you can see, but insists on answering the door. This has been his job for the last forty years, and he's loath to give it up," Trevor explained while they stumbled into the house.

As they moved past the massive doors and into the main hallway, Kristen could only stare at the huge staircase that displayed portraits as large as she was. Everything was black and white, and except for the vivid oils in the portraits, there was very little color in the room.

Cold, she thought again. Much too cold.

"Ye actually lived here?" she whispered while supporting his weight the best she could.

"Most of the time. Don't you like it?" Trevor leaned against a table for support and to take some of his weight off Kristen.

"One couldn't help but like it, I suppose," Kristen answered, her voice betraying the doubt she tried to conceal. "How do ye keep from gettin' lost? I'm afraid I might take a wrong turn and never find ye again."

"Rest assured, sweetheart," Trevor said slowly, managing a low chuckle. "I'll always find you."

Kristen wasn't sure what he meant by that statement. Was he giving her a compliment or threatening her? However, she didn't have a chance to ask because a stout woman with white hair swept into the hallway. Kristen knew this had to be the dowager duchess by the regal way she carried herself. For her age, her skin was remarkably smooth, and her cheeks looked like rosy-red apples, but those crystal-blue eyes held no welcome as Kristen had hoped they would. The woman more or less glared at her; then a shrewd look entered her eyes before she looked away, dismissing Kristen as one would a servant.

"It's about time you made an appearance, Trevor. And what do you mean sending word to prepare for a wedding when I've not even met the bride?" She stopped in front of Trevor. "I do hope you chose well and she's from a good family."

"You sure do talk a lot," Hagan said, stating the obvious.

The duchess turned until her gaze rested on Hagan. "Mind your manners, young man. And who, pray tell, are you?"

"Grandmère," Trevor said, his tone conciliatory. "I see you are feeling much better. I feared you might still be in bed."

"I could hardly stay in bed after your announcement. And why are you draped across that young lady. Stand up." She motioned impatiently with her hand. "Haven't I taught you anything?"

"Grandmère, you have taught me so much." Trevor managed to tease her even though his face still mirrored his pain. "This young lady is my fiancée."

"I see," Constance Claremont said. Her white eyebrows rose a fraction of an inch.

She inspected Kristen as if she were buying a horse. Kristen wondered if the woman would ask her to open her mouth so she could check her teeth.

"She is a pretty little thing," Constance finally commented.

Trevor sagged a little further. His added weight forced

Kristen to finally speak. "Do ye mind if we get yer grandson to a bed? He's been shot."

"My God, she is Scottish. You're marrying a Scot!" Constance's tone sounded chilly. "And you've been shot!" Her eyes grew wide with horror and her face paled with revulsion just before she slumped to the floor in a dead faint.

" 'Tis not good." Kristen shook her head.

"Doesn't appear so." Trevor took a deep breath. "But actually, she took it very well." Trevor gave Kristen a grave smile before he turned slowly and called, his voice growing weaker, "Billingsly."

"Gracious me!" Billingsly exclaimed as he peered down at the duchess, a look of horror on his face as he wrung his hands together, uncertain of what he should do. "Yes, Your Grace."

"Please have someone fetch the physician and some smelling salts for Grandmère. Rebecca, if you'll look after my grandmother, I'm going to find a bed while I can still stand."

Suddenly the room filled with servants helping the duchess as Kristen and Trevor moved up the grand staircase. She could hear the duchess complaining to her servants.

"He's brought a bloody Scot home to marry! Claremont will roll over in his grave!" Grandmère declared.

"I don't think yer grandmother is very happy with me."

"Grandmère is always unhappy, for one reason or the other. Don't worry, she'll get used to you," Trevor answered.

"I'm not sure about that. Ye could always change yer mind about marrying me."

"I—I—" Trevor's voice cut off as he slumped halfway up the stairs, pulling Kristen down with him.

"Help!" Kristen screamed over the banister. "I need some help. Trevor has passed out."

"I'll help you," Hagan called out.

"Thanks, Hagan, but yer just a wee bit small." She managed to smile at him.

"We're coming." Several of the other servants hurried up the stairs, and managed to get Trevor up and moving again.

The upstairs maid threw open a door at the end of a long hall. "The master's room," she announced.

They entered Trevor's room, where they lowered him to the huge bed that commanded the room. Kristen didn't realize that Trevor had regained consciousness until he said, "I'm not going to change my mind, Kristen. You belong to me."

The man was stubborn even when wounded. Kristen smiled. She would have informed him that she wasn't one of his belongings, but when she looked up to speak her mind, she saw his face had lost the rest of its color. "Let's get ye settled in the bed."

The servants had left them alone, so she helped him remove his jacket and pulled the heavy embroidered spread over him, then placed a couple of pillows under his head. Kristen laid his jacket over a chair, then examined the room, unable to do anything else for Trevor until the doctor arrived. She noticed this room was definitely larger than the rooms in the London town house.

Two big windows graced one wall and let in plenty of light. The drapes were of Damask silk, flowered with gold. Kristen pulled the panels open and tied them back with a gold cord to let in more light. Turning, she saw a mahogany kneehole desk with matching wardrobe. Trevor's room seemed a little more inviting than the rest of the house, but still was very plain and impersonal.

Though Kristen knew there was an array of servants who could care for Trevor, she couldn't bring herself to leave him. Surprisingly, she wanted to care for him herself.

On a small washstand, she found a purple-flowered porcelain pitcher and bowl. She poured fresh water into the bowl, then picked up a cloth and carried everything back to Trevor's bedside.

Carefully, she removed his shirt. He managed a weak smile. "You're the prettiest nurse I've ever had."

"Thank you," she murmured as she let her gaze travel over his magnificent chest. He was so big. She swallowed and took a deep breath. "Now lie still so I can cleanse yer wound." She placed the damp rag gently over the ugly red hole.

"Ouch," Trevor said, and flinched.

"What are you doing to my grandson?" Constance Claremont entered the room without knocking.

"I see she's recovered from her 'Scot' attack," Kristen said softly as she straightened.

"Move aside," the old bat ordered, and Kristen had a good mind not to budge an inch, but Trevor was too sick for her to cause a scene, no matter how much she wanted to.

"What has she done to you?" Constance asked Trevor, her tone considerably more gentle than the one she'd used with Kristen.

"Grandmère." Trevor sighed and took her hand. "You need to calm yourself. Remember, you have a condition," he warned her gently. "Kristen has done nothing." He paused, as if mustering his strength. "We were set upon by highwaymen on our journey, and I seem to have gotten in the way of a bullet." He didn't bother to tell her about the other bullet hole, compliments of Kristen.

"And where, pray tell, were your guards?"

"With the second carriage. Really, Grandmère, I'm not up to this discussion at the moment. Where is Dr. Harrison?"

"Here I am, young man. Let me see what you've done to yourself." The old doctor went to the side of the bed and pushed Constance gently aside. "You need to sit over there, Constance. I can only handle one patient at a time."

"Don't be impertinent!" She glowered at him. "You forget whom you are speaking to, Harrison."

"You shouldn't forget who takes care of you," he shot back.

The duchess did have the grace to blush as she set her mouth in a thin, firm line, but she did make her way over to a chair. Evidently, no one usually talked back to her.

Kristen couldn't hold back the chuckle, and for that slip, she received a sharp look from the old bat.

"And who are you?" the doctor asked.

"I'm Trevor's fiancée."

"Well done, son." Harrison patted Trevor's hand. "It's about time you settled down." The doctor bent over his patient. "Now, let me see to this wound." His bushy brows drew together as he prodded the hole.

"Easy!" Trevor all but shouted.

"Not good." Harrison shook his head and sighed. "I'm going to have to take that bullet out, son."

Trevor's voice was absolutely emotionless when he spoke. "I was afraid you would say that."

"Constance, bring me a bottle of whiskey."

Surprisingly, she did as she was told. Though the old woman tried to hide them, Kristen saw the tears in her eyes. At least Constance did have a heart, though it seemed to be buried under a thick layer of ice.

"I think it's best you wait downstairs with that weak heart of yours," Dr. Harrison told her gently.

"Should I leave too?" Kristen asked.

"If you have a strong stomach, you may stay." He looked at her over his wire-rimmed spectacles. "I can use some help." He smiled a generous smile.

Kristen stepped forward. "What should I do?"

The doctor poured a second shot of whiskey and held it to Trevor's mouth. "I need fresh water and some bandages." He nodded to the whiskey in his hand. "A few more of these, and Trevor will be good and numb."

Kristen didn't waste any time getting everything they needed. She hated seeing the pain that dulled Trevor's eyes.

"Christ!" she heard Trevor swear.

"What happened?" Kristen asked.

"I disinfected his wound. Now . . ." The doctor looked her square in the eyes. "Can you hold him still?"

Kristen swallowed, then nodded.

"This won't be easy," Dr. Harrison warned one last time.

The odor of the liquor brought back too many ugly memories for Kristen, and she started to shake as the bile began to rise in her throat.

"Young woman, if you cannot handle this, I shall have to get someone else."

"No—no. I can do it." Kristen shook her head, forcing her stomach to behave. She knew she was being silly, letting all those old memories frighten her. This was Trevor. He'd never beaten her or hurt her in any way. She needed to push the old memories aside.

"Kristen." Trevor slurred her name as he held out his hand for her. His motion was jerky and sudden, so Kristen knew the whiskey was working. She grasped his hand, and he squeezed hers as if he were trying to reassure her when she should be the one comforting him.

"I'm ready, Doctor," Trevor said.

Harrison picked up his scalpel, and his eyes went again to Kristen. "Let go of his hand and hold him down."

The doctor poured liquor over his scalpel. Turning back to his patient, he pressed the point of the knife down into the wound, and Trevor hissed with a sharp intake of breath as he tried to move away from the red-hot pain.

Kristen had to put all her weight on his body, attempting to keep him still, and yet she could feel him quiver with every probe of the knife. She couldn't imagine the pain he must be in.

"Just a little bit deeper, and I'll have the ball. Any normal man would have been unconscious by now," the doctor said, more to himself than to anyone.

When Dr. Harrison reached the metal piece, Trevor let out a roar and bucked against Kristen's restraining hands. She was going to need more help, but before she could ask Trevor to quit moving, he suddenly lay still. Too still.

"What's happened?" Fearing the worst, Kristen looked down at Trevor's closed eyes, the sweat beaded on his brow. "Is he all right?" She realized, for the first time, that she had tears streaming down her face, and she had to remind herself that she didn't cry. Crying showed weakness. She must be strong.

"Yes, ma'am. Here's the slug." The doctor held up the dark piece of metal with his forceps. "He's just passed out as most mortal men should, which will make it a little easier when I start stitching him up." The doctor patted Kristen's hand. "Now, now. Let's not have any tears. We're not finished yet, and I still need your assistance."

Kristen felt Trevor's forehead. It was clammy. "But he'll be fine?"

"I promise he will not miss your wedding if that's what you're worried about." Harrison chuckled. "I'll wager that the next time I'm summoned here, it will be for your firstborn child.''

"I can't imagine having children," she admitted. As a matter of fact, she'd never considered the possibility that she might have a baby. She could have Trevor's baby. The thought frightened her. How would she leave if that happened? There were so many things she'd never considered. As usual, she only took care of each immediate situation.

"Young lady, can you hold his wound together so that I can stitch?"

"I'm sorry. My mind must have wandered." Kristen quickly did as instructed.

"What's your name?" he asked as he expertly placed tiny sutures, closing up the wound.

"Kristen."

"Kristen, don't let childbearing bother you. Believe me, I've delivered scores of babies during my day, and it's a natural part of a woman's nature. You'll do just fine," he said, trying to reassure her.

" 'Tisn't childbearing that frightens me as much as Trevor."

The doctor had been taking neat little stitches, but he stopped and chuckled at that comment. "If you can ever get beneath that hard shell that he's put up around himself, then you'll have no problems. But you will be the first young woman to do so."

"Why?"

"I really should not be telling you this." Dr. Harrison leaned back, having finished his task. "But in this family, I'm sure no one else will, if I don't. You really don't know much about the man you're going to marry, do you?"

"Nay. He's never said much."

"Didn't think he would."

Kristen looked at him, imploring. "Can you tell me something that will help me understand him?"

Dr. Harrison looked up and studied her a long moment before he spoke. "Trevor's mother didn't want him. When he was two, she left him and never came back."

"How could she do something like that?" Kristen gasped. "He was her own flesh and blood."

"I've often wondered that myself." Dr. Harrison shook his head sadly. "Trevor was such a beautiful child. Always laughing. Always happy. But she simply didn't want children, so she brought him to Chatsworth and left him with Constance to raise."

"What about his father?"

"He wanted no part of Trevor after that. Seems Trevor was the image of his mother, and that reminded Claremont of his unfaithful wife. So what I'm saying to you is that this boy has never known much love. And he doesn't trust easily." The doctor reached over and took her hand. "I hope you can provide what he needs. I delivered this boy, and I've watched him grow into a lonely, driven man."

Now, Kristen felt really guilty. She wanted to confess that their marriage would be nothing more than a sham. They were not marrying for love . . .

Then she realized that was just what Trevor wanted.

A cold marriage . . .

And who better than a stranger to have it with?

With an agreement such as theirs he didn't have to worry about wooing a woman, he didn't have to worry about love. His marriage would be just like his life . . . empty . . . safe.

Kristen stared down at this man who had given her so much. He had so much to give. Somehow, she sensed that. But would the wall be too thick?

What could she give him that he truly needed? And

could she teach him to love, when she'd had so little of that commodity of her own?

And that was when Kristen realized how much they were both alike.

Alone and unloved.

CHAPTER SEVEN

At the doctor's insistence, Kristen followed him downstairs to let Constance know how her grandson was doing. Kristen needed to check on Hagan and change her clothes before returning to sit with Trevor, but she knew it could wait a few minutes. After all, she knew that if she were in Constance's shoes, she would want to know immediately how Trevor was doing.

The duchess got to her feet as soon as they entered the sitting room. She looked pale and worried.

"How is my grandson?"

"With a little rest, he will be fine." Harrison rubbed the back of his neck, his weariness showing just a little. "He needs a good night's sleep to shake off the whiskey, but Trevor is as strong as a horse, and he'll be on his feet by tomorrow, if I'm any judge." He rubbed the back of his neck again. "You could try keeping him confined to bed for a day, but I doubt you'll be successful." Harrison chuckled, then added, "Your new daughter-in-law was a big help to me." He turned to Kristen. "Thank you very much."

"She isn't my daughter-in-law yet!" the duchess blurted out. Her vehemence made Kristen wonder if the woman would do something to prevent the marriage.

"Now, Constance." Harrison shook his head. "I'm used to your being rude to me, but I'm sure Kristen doesn't realize you have a heart buried in there somewhere."

"I don't know why I put up with your insolence, Harrison." The duchess looked like an angry dog when its hair stands on end.

"Probably because you have little choice. Another physician wouldn't put up with you." He actually winked at Constance, then got his hat and started for the door.

"Kristen, you need to get some rest yourself," he said. "I'll check on Trevor tomorrow. Good night."

"Good-bye," Kristen replied automatically, then decided to leave, not wanting to be in the same room with the old bat. How could she have felt sorry for the woman? But she stopped dead in her tracks when the duchess called her.

"I want to know what you are up to, young woman. I'm telling you now that it will not work!"

Kristen turned slowly. "I beg yer pardon?"

"I find it strange that my grandson suddenly appears with a *Scotswoman,* whom I've never heard of, telling me he intends to marry her."

Kristen was determined that the woman wasn't going to get under her skin. "Was it not yer wish that Trevor marry?"

"Of course it was, but—"

"But not to a Scot," Kristen said, finishing the sentence for her.

"Precisely."

" 'Tis sorry I am that ye feel that way. However, yer grandson seems to think differently and practically begged me to marry him. I guess ye never know when true love is around the corner." Kristen smiled at the speechless woman. "Now, can ye show me where they sent my brother?"

"Certainly not," Constance huffed, folding her arms across her chest. "One of the servants will show you to the second floor. At least my mind is relieved that the lad isn't yours." She turned and called for a servant.

Kristen's eyes flared. "I'd be very careful how ye speak of my brother. He's ten times better than ye'll ever be. 'Tis a shame our relationship will be painful. I was hoping for something more."

"If it's money you are after, you'll never get a farthing!"

"I dinna think that ye instructed Trevor on how he can and canna spend his money. 'Tis funny, he struck me as being his own man." Seeing the startled look on the duchess's face gave Kristen a small victory, but she knew that battling with this woman every day would be difficult. She followed the servant who appeared in the door, leaving the old woman by herself.

Upon reaching the second floor, Kristen resisted the urge to look in on Trevor, but instead went seven doors down to Hagan's room and peeked in on him.

"Hello, Kristen." Hagan glanced up from where he sat in a chair looking at a large book. "Isn't this the biggest place you've ever seen? Never been in a house this big before."

" 'Tis grand. I hope we'll like it."

"I think we will." Hagan sounded like a grown man. He put his book down. "How's Trevor?"

"The doctor removed the bullet, and said he'll be fine after a few days."

Hagan looked very somber. He paused before he finally said, "I was worried."

"That's sweet." She reached over and ruffled his hair. "Ye'll talk to him tomorrow, but right now ye need to be in bed."

"Oh, Kristen."

She held up a hand. " 'Tis been a bit trying today, so do as I say."

After getting Hagan to bed, Kristen went out and found her own room was just as somber as the rest of the house. Rebecca had wasted little time in putting away her clothes, and was just now turning back the bed.

"How is His Grace?" Rebecca straightened.

"I'm getting ready to go back and check on him. But I think he'll be fine tomorrow, though maybe a bit sore." Kristen started unbuttoning her dress. "Ye know, I thought he was dead back there. When I think about it, we were all lucky to still be alive."

"Yes, mum," Rebecca agreed as she helped Kristen into a comfortable day dress of dove gray.

"That feels much better."

Rebecca sat down on a chair. "Have you had a chance to meet the duchess?"

"Unfortunately, yes. She's a grumpy old bat."

Rebecca laughed. "That's an appropriate description."

Before Kristen knew it, she had joined in Rebecca's laughter too. All the tension Kristen had built up was slowly ebbing away.

"I probably should have warned you about the duchess. My mum said she has never seen the woman smile, and that she's constantly complaining about something." Rebecca blushed at her boldness. "I really shouldn't be talking about my employer."

"Ye know I'd never tell anyone," Kristen assured her.

"Besides, if ye don't tell me, who will? I'm a stranger here. I don't see what the woman has to complain about. She has a beautiful home, people who wait on her hand and foot." Kristen shook her head. "I don't understand. She should try living down on the docks; then she'd appreciate what she has."

"Docks?" Rebecca questioned. "I never did understand why you went down to the docks. Trevor said you came from a convent."

"I know." Kristen couldn't make up her mind whether to tell Rebecca the whole truth. She decided against divulging her background just yet. "It really is a long story that I canna comment on because I promised Trevor."

"I understand. I'm just glad you're here."

"Thank ye."

"As far as the duchess appreciating her wealth, I don't think she ever will. Some people never find the good in anything."

Kristen smiled ruefully. Rebecca was wise for her years. "Yer right, but I bet if we look hard enough we'll find some good in her."

"I'll leave it to you to find," Rebecca said. "The staff will appreciate it."

Kristen looked at Rebecca with amusement. "Get some sleep. I'm going to stay with Trevor for a while."

Kristen carried an oil lamp to Trevor's room. Just before she got there, she noticed the door was halfway open. Carefully, she peeked through the doorway and frowned. Constance was leaning over her grandson speaking to him.

"What has that woman done to you?" she murmured to him.

Great! Kristen thought. She could see it now. She would be blamed for everything that happened around here, whether she did it or not. She would take credit for the first wound, but not the second. Kristen bit the side of her mouth to keep from saying something she'd regret.

"Don't worry, Trevor." Constance patted his hand as she bent over the bed. "I'll help you see the right thing to do. I can't believe you brought a Johnstone under our roof." She sighed. "I do wish you'd wake up, Trevor, and talk to me." She sighed again.

"You remember Charity Fullbright? Well, she'll be here in two days for a visit. You remember how pretty you always thought she was? She would make you the perfect wife, Trevor, and she is English, not a bloody Scot!" Constance pulled the cover up and folded it back across Trevor's chest. "I do wish you'd wake up. We have so much to discuss." There was a moment of silence. "Well, I guess I shall have to wait until tomorrow. Rest now." She leaned down and kissed him on the cheek. "We'll talk in the morning."

Kristen moved back around the corner so Constance would not realize that she'd been eavesdropping, and waited. The old bat was determined to cause trouble, Kristen realized. Just what she didn't need. She could find trouble on her own. She didn't need any help. She'd been hoping to find a family, yet she'd only found more problems.

But then, Kristen was used to trouble. It seemed to follow her, no matter where she went.

Trevor clenched his teeth as suffocating sleep kept pulling him back under. Every muscle in his body felt as if it were on fire, and an odd sort of coldness made him shiver as he huddled down under the blankets. He hoped Dr. Harrison had worked his magic one more time. He'd taken care of all Trevor's aches and pains over the years. He'd smile if the effort wasn't so great.

Kristen?

Somewhere, Trevor remembered her soft touch as the doctor worked on him. She had stayed to assist Harrison when most women would have fainted dead away. There seemed to be so much more to Kristen than just a common thief. Every day, he could feel her stealing closer to him, and he wasn't sure how he felt about that. He wanted to share his thoughts . . . his feelings, but he didn't know how.

And then he remembered how painful love could be. Kristen would probably leave him too. He'd have to be careful.

Damn, his head hurt as he tossed and turned. Much better to let the darkness claim him again. Sleep. That was what he needed. Peaceful sleep.

When the hallway was free, Kristen moved quietly back to Trevor's room. She set the lamp on the dresser, then moved over to his bed and placed her hand on his forehead. She found it warm, but not hot. Her fingers trailed down the side of his face, and she marveled at how strong his features were. His square jaw was rough where he needed to shave, but he was beautiful just the same. Especially when he slept. His chestnut hair gave a warmth to his face, and she resisted the urge to run her fingers through it.

He appeared to be slumbering like a baby and not in any need of her attention. But something kept her there. Some unknown drawing force made her want to shield this man, and that brought a smile. How could she protect him? The protectee trying to protect the protector. In a funny sort of way, Kristen knew she could save him from himself.

Trevor stirred slightly, catching her hand in his. Kristen watched his face as he slowly opened his eyes, trying to figure out exactly where he was.

"Kristen," he whispered.

"I'm here," she said hoarsely. "How do you feel?"

"Not worth a fig," he rasped.

"Are you in pain?" She smoothed the hair from his forehead. "Is there something I can get you?"

"Maybe a sip of water."

Kristen leaned over and poured a glass of water from the pitcher on the stand. She slid her arm under his head and helped him sit up as she held the glass to his lips.

When she put the glass back, she wondered if Trevor had ever been this helpless before. She couldn't imagine so. She sensed he was a man used to doing everything for himself.

He was a man who needed no one.

A man who probably would never need her.

Trevor stared at her so intently that Kristen couldn't figure out what he was thinking.

"You know, Kristen, we are a lot alike." His speech was slurred by the whiskey he'd been given earlier.

As usual, the whiskey brought back unpleasant memories to Kristen, and she had to will herself not to panic. She had to stay by his bed. As she watched him, she realized that just because she could smell the liquor, it didn't mean that he would become violent.

That had been in another world. One she needed to forget. Actually, Trevor looked so calm and peaceful she couldn't help but smile at him. "I dinna think so," she said. "We come from very different worlds, and are nothing alike."

"That's true, but we are still very similar, you and I. We both use people to get what we want. Our present arrangement is a perfect example."

She nodded. "Aye, I guess it is."

"Maybe that's why I understand you so well." He absently rubbed the back of her hand with his thumb.

"I think it's best ye get some sleep." She lifted her hand and let it drift down the side of Trevor's face. She wondered why she had this strong urge to touch him . . . to be close to him.

"Would you like to kiss me good night?"

"Nay."

One of his eyes opened a little wider. "Why not?"

" 'Cause ye are sick, and ye smell of liquor." Every time his gaze met hers, her heart fluttered. "Ye know I have a strong dislike for the drink."

"Kristen." Her name was a caress upon his lips. "I'm not your stepfather. I will never abuse you."

"Just the same, liquor has a strange way of making one forget who they are."

Trevor studied her intently as sleep threatened to pull him back to its silent world. He fought it a little longer. He could sense her nervousness, and he wondered how many bad memories she had. He never wanted to see fear in her eyes.

Sleep seemed to be calling him more strongly this time and he struggled to keep his eyes open. Yet he didn't want Kristen to go. He wanted her to stay with him while he slept. He knew that was being very selfish, but still . . .

"Why don't you get some sleep, sweetheart. I will be fine and you need some rest."

"But what if ye be needin' something?"

"Go." He squeezed her hand. "This house is overrun with servants. I'll be fine, and I will rest better knowing that you are resting too. You know you could sleep here beside me. That would make me feel much better." He grinned.

"I'm sure it would." She tried to look stern, but a smile overrode her best intentions. "Ye really are a rake." She stood.

"Now, you have insulted a sick man. Rodney is the rake, not I." Trevor shut his eyes because the effort to keep them open was too great.

"Really." She looked at him doubtfully. "Good night," she said as she left the room, leaving Trevor to wonder just what this woman meant to him.

This business arrangement would be a sound one. Kristen wasn't one of those females who required a lot of attention. So he'd be free to come and go, and he knew she'd be waiting for him when he came home. Yes, he'd have the best of both worlds ... a lovely wife and his freedom to do as he pleased.

Trevor frowned. At the moment, he couldn't imagine not seeing Kristen every day. Then he reminded himself that it was just because she was new to him. Once they were married, and he'd made love to her, she'd lose all her novelty, and he'd be back to normal.

Damn, he was giving himself a huge headache. He began to toss and turn again, searching for sleep. Of course, the whiskey wasn't helping. One thing was sure. He'd done a hell of a lot of thinking since that woman came into his life, and he needed to stop. He was the ruler of what he did and said, and thought. He'd make a mental note to stay away from liquor, so he wouldn't upset Kristen.

Sighing, he finally let the welcome sleep pull him into a dream world. But there, in its mist, was a woman with hair the color of the sun on an early morning sunrise, and eyes the color of the forest, and lips that tasted of strawberries.

Trevor Claremont, Duke of Chatsworth, knew he was a doomed man.

CHAPTER EIGHT

Streamers of light drifted across the covers and warmed Kristen's face, waking her much later than she'd intended.

Quickly, she threw back the covers, slid out of bed, and hurried over to the wardrobe.

The wardrobe was filled with gowns of blue, lavender, and rose. Everything was beautiful, Kristen admitted to herself, but life had been so much simpler when she'd had only two dresses and little choice.

Deciding on a dark blue morning dress, she slipped off her gown and grabbed the lacy undergarment she loved to feel next to her skin. Silk and lace were luxuries she really enjoyed, she thought as she stepped into her chemise and began to dress.

She had wanted to see how Trevor was feeling this morning, and she'd hoped to see him alone before his grandmother started complaining about her again.

Kristen really resented that the dowager duchess had

judged her because of her nationality when the woman knew absolutely nothing at all about her. If she'd known that Kristen had lived in the streets and picked a few pockets every now and then so they could eat, that would be a different story. However, she didn't think Trevor would divulge that small bit of information. He had too much to lose himself.

Kristen wondered where Rebecca was this morning as she brushed her hair to remove the tangles from the night before. She assumed her maid had taken Hagan down for breakfast, and she was thankful. It must be near noon if the bright sun was any indication.

Pinching her cheeks, Kristen glanced at her reflection in the mirror. She was still not accustomed to having the privilege to do so, but enjoyed the luxury. She hurried down the hall to Trevor's room.

"Good morning," she said upon entering, then stopped short. There was no reply, because Trevor wasn't in the bed. The room was completely empty.

Surely, he was too sick to be up, she thought, glancing frantically around the room. Perhaps something had happened to him during the night while she'd slept. No, that couldn't be. Someone would have let her know. Maybe she could find her answer downstairs, she decided as she left the room.

Kristen barely remembered flying down the stairs in a panic. She paused only long enough for a deep breath before she barreled into the formal dining room and found Constance and Trevor sitting at one end of the table, with Hagan seated one chair down from Trevor. Kristen's stomach plummeted, and she took another deep breath, trying to calm her nerves.

Trevor looked up and smiled. "There's my future bride now."

Constance's gaze was glued to Kristen. "You need to teach *her* how to enter a room like a proper young lady," Constance snapped as she dabbed her mouth with a napkin. The look on her face gave one the impression she'd just eaten something sour.

"Boy, Kristen you sure are a sleepyhead. It's almost noon. We had breakfast a long time ago," Hagan informed her as he placed his fork on his plate rather noisily. "And lunch."

"I must have been tired." She frowned at her brother. Must he always state the obvious? She needed his support, not someone pointing out her flaws. She looked back to Trevor, who had now risen and was walking toward her. "Why are ye out of bed?" she asked. The tenderness in his expression amazed her, but she kept talking. "And dressed! I'm sure the doctor meant for ye to stay in bed today."

Trevor took her elbow and escorted her to a chair beside him. "As you can see, I'm just fine," he said calmly. "I must admit, I am a tad sore, but that's to be expected." He moved around the table, reclaiming his spot. "You have my shoulder bandaged so thoroughly I can scarcely move, but the rest of my body is fine."

"Yeah, Kristen." Hagan sat his glass down, just missing his plate. "He ain't no dandy. We're going riding—on horses."

Kristen couldn't help smiling at her brother. Nothing ever bothered Hagan. Then she frowned as his words sank in. Going horseback riding? "I think ye should wait," she told both of them.

"But Trevor said—" Hagan persisted.

"Children should be seen and not heard!" Constance's voice echoed around the cold dining room.

"What does that mean, Grandmère?" Hagan looked at the woman with a quizzical stare. "Can't you see me?"

"I am not your grandmère, young man." Her words were as cold as ice water.

"That's what Trevor calls you," Hagan persisted.

Constance's eyebrows shot up and her face turned a pinkish color. "Trevor, speak to the child!"

"What she meant, Hagan, is that ye are talking too much," Kristen explained without saying *old bat*.

"I'm not talking too much." He shook his head and his eyes brightened. "I just got started."

"No, ye are not talking too much, but since ye have finished yer lunch, why don't ye find Rebecca and ask her to get ye ready for the ride." Kristen gave him a little nudge toward the door.

"Ye really shouldn't be riding," Kristen reminded Trevor. "Do I have to remind ye, ye were shot?"

"I must agree with her." Constance nodded in Kristen's direction, though she didn't bother to look at her.

"I hear your concerns, but I assure you both that I am fine," Trevor replied. He turned toward his grandmother. His profile spoke of strength. "Did you arrange for the dressmaker to come and fit Kristen?"

"Yes, I have." Her expression was a mask of stone. "I have also sent out the invitations at your insistence. You are to exchange vows a week from Saturday." Constance gave Kristen a piercing look. "That is, if you don't change your mind."

"Grandmère." Trevor sighed as if he'd gone over this many times before. "I know this is sudden, but if you remember it was at your suggestion," he reminded her. "I had no intention of getting married."

"But this woman is a Scot!" Constance waved a hand toward Kristen.

That did it! Kristen stood so fast she nearly knocked the chair over. "And yer a bloody Englishwoman, but ye don't hear me constantly harping on the fact!"

"Don't raise your voice at me, young lady." Constance's gray eyebrows shot together. "I will not have it!" She threw down her napkin and stood too.

The whole scene reminded Kristen of two roosters getting ready to fight, but she wasn't about to back down now. "I'll do as I damn well please, Yer Highness. Ye need to get yer nose out of the air and see how people really live!"

"Why, I never! You ill-bred Scot! Trevor, speak to her at once," Constance demanded in a shrill voice.

"Don't bother." Kristen glared at Trevor, her annoyance increasing when she found that her hands were trembling. "I'm leaving." Kristen left the room without saying another word.

Trevor turned to his grandmother, unsuccessfully trying to hide his smile. "Did I fail to mention that Kristen has a slight temper?"

"I will not tolerate her speaking to me like that!" Constance said firmly. "Just this short outburst has set my heart to fluttering." Constance placed a hand over her heart and sank back down in the chair.

"Calm yourself." Trevor reached over and patted her hand. "Kristen is just a little nervous. After all, she is in a new home surrounded by strangers. You would probably feel the same way if you were in her place, surrounded by Scots," he added.

"Precisely my point, Trevor," Constance shot back. "She is an interloper that we know nothing about."

"Believe me, Grandmère, I know all that I need to." Trevor clenched his jaw and told himself to stay calm. "Should I remind you again that marriage was your idea, not mine? Besides, if I remember correctly, you didn't know Grandfather very long before you married him."

"But she is a Johnstone!"

"I was taken aback when I heard the name too. But Kristen was raised in London, so she could only be a distant relative at most. Furthermore, she told me herself that her father died a long time ago."

"All Johnstones are related," Constance persisted in a grudging voice. "Have you not forgotten what they did to your poor grandfather?"

"No, I haven't." Trevor slid his chair back. "I want you to promise that you'll try to get along with Kristen."

His grandmother ignored him. "Did I tell you that Charity Fullbright is coming to stay for a few days?" she said.

Trevor tried to look into her crafty eyes even though she turned her head quickly. "What are you up to?"

"I don't know what you mean." Constance glanced down quickly under Trevor's sharp gaze. "Her mother wanted to visit, and I suggested that they both come. I knew you'd enjoy the company. Charity is such a lovely girl."

Trevor stood and looked at his grandmother. "It won't work, Grandmère. I *am* marrying Kristen a week from Saturday." He'd had his fill of being nice, and his shoulder was beginning to throb, which didn't help his mood in the least. "I suggest you accept the fact, and be happy for us."

Constance merely stared at her grandson in stony silence. Just when he was getting ready to leave, she said, completely out of nowhere, "Do you love her?"

Trevor swung around and stopped, looking as if he'd been turned to stone. He was surprised by the question. After all, what did love have to do with anything? How could he love somebody he'd just met?

"Love her?" he repeated as hundreds of thoughts ran through his mind. "I care a great deal for Kristen. More than I have for any other woman. But love? Do any of us really know what love is?"

Constance looked at Trevor, studying him. She caught a strange look in his eyes. One she hadn't seen before. There was also a calmness she sensed in Trevor instead of that restlessness that always seemed to plague him. She knew she'd surprised him with talk of love, but she didn't want Trevor to make a mistake. She had seen too many marriages suffer from lack of love.

"Love is truly a gift that few of us get to experience," she said in a voice that seemed to come from a long way off. "And believe me, son, you will know when you're in love."

"How is that, Grandmère?"

His dark eyes showed the tortured dullness of disbelief. What else could she expect? Trevor hadn't had a normal childhood. When he had come to her, he had been fully grown at ten years old, and she could vividly remember the lackluster expression in his eyes back then. He'd wanted his parents' love so badly he'd tried to be the perfect child. Of course, he had never succeeded, but that hadn't been his fault. How she wished she'd realized what was going on, and that she'd rescued Trevor sooner.

"Love is special and hard to explain, but I shall try," Constance said, taking a deep breath. "When you can think of nothing but that one person. When they block all others from your mind so that when you're not with them, you find a part of yourself missing. When the first thing you do is look for them as you enter a crowded room, and think of them when you are eating, and dream of them when you are sleeping. When you forget about pleasing yourself and think only of pleasing them. And suddenly the moon and stars are brighter when they are standing beside you, and turn dull when they are gone . . .

"That's when you'll know a love so powerful that it will bring you to your knees," Constance finished in a whisper, wiping a tear that had slipped down her wrinkled cheek.

Trevor looked at his grandmother. He'd never heard her speak like this before. She usually never showed her emotions, and he really couldn't picture her and his grandfather in an intimate embrace, but evidently she had another side he'd never seen.

"You loved Grandfather very much, didn't you?"

"I did love," she said sadly and looked away. Someone, she thought to herself.

Trevor reached over and pulled the older woman into his arms, giving her a hug the way he used to do when he was a child.

"I know you miss Grandfather." Trevor sighed and moved away. "Perhaps, one day, I can tell you I've experienced all the things you have just said. But I doubt that kind of love will exist for me." He held her away from him. "For now, I can tell you that I want Kristen for my wife." He didn't add that he wasn't sure why, other than the reason he'd told Kristen. "I pray that we will be as happy as you and Grandfather were," Trevor added, though he doubted that statement. After they were married he'd probably see Kristen every couple of months to check on her. After all, he had a business to run and work to do. He couldn't be tied down in one place for very long.

"I wish that for you too." Her voice had a compassionate tone. "But she is a Johnstone."

"Yes, but in a week she'll be a Claremont." Trevor smiled at his speechless grandmother.

* * *

Kristen had left in such a hurry and with such a full head of steam, she hadn't paid attention to where she was going. When she did slow down, she had no earthly idea where she was or what part of the house she was in. The place was so big she needed a map!

She spotted a doorway to the right. If she was lucky, it would lead to a vacant room. Kristen hadn't made a good impression on the dowager duchess, who could very well make Kristen's life miserable. At the moment, she really didn't give a fig as she tested the doorknob to see if it opened.

Luckily, the knob twisted, and she didn't see any reason why she shouldn't wander inside and look around, if only for a little while. The worst that could happen was someone would start yelling at her all over again.

The room was of medium size and in the back part of the house. It had windows across one wall with little seats under each one. A plush yellow cushion perched on each seat. Kristen stepped closer to look out. She couldn't control the small gasp that slipped out as she marveled at how beautiful the view in the back of the house appeared.

To her left lay a garden of bright red and yellow tulips, and there were green shrubs everywhere. Surely, this must be paradise. She'd be sure to take a walk later and enjoy the beauty she'd seen only in books. There was nothing about the docks in London that were pretty and the only thing colorful had been the language. She now had the ability to swear in several languages. A giggle escaped her before she could stop it as she wondered whether the duchess would care to hear a few of the words she'd learned.

Looking around the room, she found the decor of yellow and green cheerful indeed. It was very comforting. This room seemed more like a home and didn't have the formality of the rest of the house.

There were pictures everywhere. One especially caught her attention. Kristen moved over to take a closer look at the child's portrait.

The artist had been good, for he'd caught the rare mixture of color that made up Trevor's unusual eyes. She bent closer. She could even see the small brown fleck near the center of his eyes.

"Amazing," she murmured.

"Do you like my portrait?" A voice came from the door, catching her attention.

She glanced over her shoulder. "Very much," she admitted. "You were a handsome child."

"Thank you." Trevor smiled at her praise. "There is something special about this painting." He moved up behind her. "Stand here." He pointed. "And look at the child's eyes. What do you see?"

"Green. Very vivid at that."

"Good." He nodded his approval. "Now, stand over here." He took her by the arms and positioned her on the other side of the painting. "What do you see now?"

"Why, the eyes are blue!" She turned and looked at him with her astonishment clearly showing. "How did he do that?"

"I'm not sure." Trevor smiled and inclined his head. "I was around ten years old, and I remember the artist complaining about painting my eyes. The first time he painted them green, and then he rubbed that out and painted them blue." Trevor's smile widened as he told the story. "To tell you the truth, I believe he'd wished he never

taken the commission." He chuckled. "Grandmère said
he couldn't leave until he got the painting exactly right."

"Of course everything would have to be perfect," Kristen
said before she thought. "That sounds like her." She
frowned. "This time, I must admit, her persistence paid
off."

"Listen." Trevor rubbed his chin as he decided how to
explain his grandmother's behavior. "It's going to take
Grandmère a while to adjust. But she will come around.
I'm sure of it. She'll accept everything when you stand
beside me next week."

Kristen twisted her lips into a cynical smile. "Ye wanna
bet money on that?"

"I see you gamble too." He grinned. "Let's just say
under that hard crust the woman loves me, and she'll come
to love you if given time."

"As in a hundred years."

He moved closer. "Who couldn't love my little thief?"

"Yer a bit too close." She took a step back.

"Not as close as I'll be a week from now." He shortened
the distance.

"But that's in a week." She placed a hand on his chest.
"Ye could be disappointed 'cause I—I dinna—"

Trevor caressed her cheek with his fingers. "I will not
be disappointed." His voice softened. "You have been full
of surprises so far. I can't imagine you changing in a week."

Kristen felt the warmth spread through her like melting
butter on hot bread. But she wasn't comfortable in this
house, and she didn't want him to think that every time
he touched her, she would fall into his arms. She needed
to show him some resistance instead of melting at his feet.
But he didn't need to know that.

She pulled away. "I thought you were going to take
Hagan riding." She tried not looking at him, knowing

she'd go straight back into his arms with very little encouragement. She was addicted to this man for sure.

She was doomed.

Trevor went from deliciously warm to ice cold. In less than two seconds. What was the matter with him? Normally, he couldn't keep his hands off her.

"Yes, I was," he answered, his tone a little irritated. "And I believe the seamstress has arrived to start fitting you for your dress."

"Then ye'll have to show me the way." She started for the door. "Do ye have a map of this place?"

Trevor chuckled. "No, you'll find your way around in due time."

"I wouldn't bet on it."

CHAPTER NINE

After three days of fittings, Kristen grew tired of standing on the small stool while three women pinned and poked her. Every time she moved, a pin stuck her somewhere, and she felt that she'd been patient long enough.

Kristen looked down at the yards and yards of beautiful white, pearl-drenched satin and French lace that draped across a solid white skirt, then swept up in the back and blended with a long train down the back. She ran her hand across the smooth material.

The satin felt cool.

She felt numb.

The women chattered around her, talking about how fine the material felt and how much the tiny pearls had cost, but they were not speaking directly to Kristen. It was as if she didn't exist except as someone to hold the garment off the floor. That was one of the problems. Since she'd come to Chatsworth, she'd felt absolutely useless. Before, she'd had to provide food for Hagan, and take care of him, and had always been on the move. Now all that was done by someone else.

She had no purpose in her days. And Trevor most certainly didn't need her. He seemed to be always busy, and the dowager duchess wanted no part of her, which left Kristen alone most of the time.

"If you'll hold your arm out," one of the girls said, bringing Kristen back to the moment. She looked down at them, but they were too busy pulling more pins out of boxes to talk to her.

Mainly they issued instructions, to turn this way and that, but after days of standing perfectly straight Kristen's patience had worn thin. She didn't want to hold her arms out anymore. She wanted to sit down and rest.

"Stand up straight!" A sharp voice snapped out from somewhere behind Kristen. "A Claremont always stands tall."

Kristen turned, causing the three seamstresses to grumble. She looked at Trevor's grandmother, who stood in the doorway with her arms folded, eyeing her down her aristocratic nose. Kristen would bet that ice water ran in the *old bat's* veins.

"Then I have a week to rest till then," she said flippantly.

"I suggest you start now," Constance bit out again. A shadow of annoyance crossed her face. "You have much to learn about your new station in life, young lady, and in a very short time. So I suggest you try harder."

A lesson in manners wouldn't hurt you either, Kristen thought, but she politely didn't voice her thoughts this time. She did stand a little straighter just to prove to the old bat that she could. "Are ye about through?" she asked the women scurrying around her. "I need to sit for a while before I fall down."

The youngest seamstress looked at Kristen. "I think we have it." She stood and for the first time smiled. "You will make a lovely bride, mum."

"Thank you," Kristen said as she stepped out of her satin gown. Immediately, she started scratching all the places where the pins had pricked her tender skin. What a relief, she thought with a sigh. Kristen pulled on her yellow jaconet muslin dress. The skirt was neatly trimmed with fine double tucks. One of the seamstresses helped fasten the corded band around Kristen's waist. She turned to leave, but found that Constance still lingered in the doorway.

Constance addressed the seamstresses in her most haughty voice. "Please put your best effort into this gown. My grandson deserves only the best."

The oldest seamstress, who had an armful of wedding dress, gave her an indulgent smile. "This will be the loveliest gown I have ever created, Your Grace." The woman handed the gown to her assistants, then gathered her scissors and pins while the other two packed up the garment. "I will have it ready three days hence."

"Good. I will look for it then." Constance dismissed the seamstresses by turning to Kristen. "I would like to speak with you—"

"Kristen," Kristen said supplying the missing name, knowing she needed to get along with this woman. If the saints were willing, she'd try. "Are ye able to walk in the garden?"

"I haven't been in the garden in ages," the dowager duchess said as a look of longing crossed her face. "Yes, I would like to go outside today."

For a brief moment, Kristen saw a human element in the woman. "If ye'll lead the way, I believe sunshine awaits us." Kristen swept her hand toward the door, then followed

Constance, keeping with the woman's slow pace. "Why haven't ye been out to yer lovely gardens? I saw them from the window earlier and they are very beautiful."

Walking leisurely, Kristen could see how feeble the woman really was, though she hid it well most of the time. Maybe that had a lot to do with her gruff exterior.

They moved through the glass doors at the rear of the house out onto the terrace. Kristen held Constance's arm as they went down the flight of stairs that led out onto the lawn, and surprisingly, the woman let her.

"The past winter has been so miserable with these bitter Scotland winds that I took to my bed for months," Constance complained, her eyes hard and filled with regret.

Kristen's steps slowed as she tried to figure out this woman. "Why do ye stay here when London might be more suitable?"

"Because this is my home," Constance explained as she walked with a stiff dignity, her heels clicking on the flagstone steps.

"I'm sorry that ye haven't been feeling well. Ye are feeling better now?"

"Yes, a little. I must admit that Trevor's news was a bit of a surprise, as I am sure you can imagine." Constance stopped and picked a blood-red rose, then held it to her nose as she studied Kristen.

" 'Twas a wee bit of a shock to me too."

A thin white eyebrow rose a fraction. "Oh, really?"

Kristen studied the lady. Her skin was wrinkled and thin, and she looked very tired. But she'd probably been pretty in her youth. "Trevor hasn't explained how we met?"

She shook her head. "No, he hasn't."

"Then I will let him tell ye, but I can say 'twas a bit of a rescue."

"I see. He felt responsible."

"Something like that." Kristen reached down and picked a rose for herself.

"Where is your family from?"

The woman might have a few wrinkles, but her mind was sharp. Kristen was trying to be careful and not say the wrong thing. She could imagine the woman having a stroke if she heard the real story. "Hagan is the only family I have. My parents are dead."

"Such a shame." Constance handed Kristen the rose she had picked, then reached for another. "I guess, in that way, you and Trevor are alike. He didn't get to know his parents very well. I hate to admit it, but my daughter-in-law wasn't the best mother." Constance seemed to catch herself before she revealed too much. "I will not have anyone hurting Trevor. Do you understand? He has a bright future, and deserves the best."

"I agree," Kristen admitted. "And I have pointed that fact to him. He could do much better than me."

"I quite agree. But he sees things differently, so I expect you to live up to his standards." Constance spoke with cool authority.

He saw things differently? Kristen wondered what he'd said to his grandmother. "I'll do my best as long as he lives up to mine." She would meet the woman halfway, but she would stand her ground. Actually, Kristen could see a different woman hidden just beneath the surface. She had caught a glimpse of that person just a minute ago. Maybe this crusty exterior was the duchess's way of protecting herself.

"Your Grace," a maid called as she hurried toward them.

As soon as the maid got close enough, she continued. "We have guests, mum."

"Who?"

"Miss Charity Fullbright and her maid, mum."

Constance immediately smiled. "Good. Tell her I'll be there in a moment." She slowly turned back toward the house. "Come, Kristen, and I will introduce you to a very lovely young lady."

Kristen complied, but she had misgivings at meeting anyone who was a ravishing beauty. Especially since she considered herself very plain.

In a few minutes they were in the drawing room, and Kristen stood face-to-face with the lovely Charity. Kristen watched as the dowager duchess hugged the girl. Constance was right. Charity was beautiful. She had black hair that hung in ringlets, and vivid blue eyes. Her cheekbones were high and refined and her lips a soft pink.

Kristen hated her! And then she realized how unfair she was being. Hadn't she resented the way the duchess had judged *her*?

"Where is Catherine?" Constance asked. "I thought she was coming with you."

"Mother wasn't feeling well and decided to stay home. She sends her regards." Charity smiled.

"I'm sorry to hear such. However, bed is the best place when one isn't feeling chipper." Constance turned and motioned for Kristen to come beside her. "I would like you to meet Kristen Johnstone."

Charity nodded. "Charmed."

" 'Tis nice to meet ye." Kristen managed to smile.

"Thank you," Charity murmured politely. "I'm sorry Mother couldn't come."

Charity was very feminine. Yet another reason to hate her.

"You must be Trevor's fiancée," Charity said.

Kristen nodded.

"I've known Trevor since we were children. It will be

nice to know you're living here." Charity's smile seemed sincere.

Confusion settled on Kristen's shoulders as she found herself softening to someone she'd expected to hate. "And why is that?"

"Because we will be neighbors. Living this far out, it's very nice to have friends."

"Come, let's find Trevor." Constance ushered Charity out of the room, leaving Kristen behind. "I know he will want to see you immediately."

Kristen really wasn't surprised by Constance's rude behavior. It actually put Kristen on guard when the woman was nice to her. She shook her head and went to find Hagan.

As she walked down the hallway, her mind kept wandering to Charity and Trevor. Would Trevor really be glad to see the lovely lady? What man wouldn't? Kristen shook herself. Why did she care?

"Oh, no!" she gasped as she made her way to Hagan's room. Somewhere along the line, she'd come to care for Trevor. The one thing she'd wanted to avoid had somehow sneaked up and bitten her.

Now what? The sides of her mouth turned down in a frown. She couldn't let Trevor know how she felt. Surely, he would laugh at the foolish notion. He didn't believe in love . . . and she wasn't sure she did either. The only love she could really vouch for was what she'd felt for Hagan.

She'd never experienced any other kind.

Trevor had just finished going over Chatsworth's books, and he was pleased with the figures he'd found, but irritated that he'd had such a hard time keeping his mind on the task at hand. He'd never had trouble concentrating before, and he usually looked forward to sitting behind his desk, but not today. Somehow he felt different.

Just as he looked up, his grandmother entered, followed by Charity Fullbright. He automatically stood to greet them. What was his grandmother up to? He was afraid he knew. He took Charity's hand in his. "Charity, it's good to see you."

She blushed. He'd forgotten how pretty she was.

"It has been a while, Trevor." She squeezed his hand. "Congratulations on your upcoming marriage."

"Thank you," Trevor said. Charity was as beautiful as always, but she didn't compare to Kristen. He'd known Charity since childhood, and though his grandmother would like to see them together, he saw Charity as no more than a friend.

"Dinner will be ready in an hour, so you two will have plenty of time to catch up." Constance turned to leave, but Charity's next statement stopped her.

"I really would like to freshen up before we eat."

"Of course, how thoughtless," Constance said. "We'll see you at dinner, Trevor."

Trevor smiled cynically. It was impossible to please his grandmother. She wanted him to get married, and that was what he was trying to do, but she still wasn't happy. She'd only be satisfied if she made the choice for him.

And that wasn't about to happen.

Kristen didn't find Hagan when she arrived at his room, so she went to her own suite to dress for dinner. She really couldn't believe people changed clothes so often, but since it seemed to be the custom, she was trying to fit in, and she was learning to love the luxury of so many gowns from which to chose.

This time she picked a plain velvet dress of deep green. The neckline fitted low on her shoulders and the material was finished with gold embroidered lace around the top. A solid embroidered ceinture fastened in front with an antique gem. Rebecca quickly pulled Kristen's hair up and pinned it so it would tumble down her back in soft curls.

As Kristen headed down the stairs, Hagan came barreling out of his room. "Whatcha been doing all day?"

"Slow down." Kristen reached out and grabbed him by the arm in midstride. "I've been trying on my wedding gown."

"All day?"

"Afraid so," Kristen said, starting down the steps.

"I'm glad I'm not a girl."

"Me too. 'Tis no fun," she admitted. "What did ye do today?"

"Went riding. And guess what?" Hagan didn't wait for her to answer, but went on. "There are some boys that live downstairs and they let me play with them. We had lots of fun."

Kristen stopped at the foot of the stairs and stared at her brother. "I just realized ye never had playmates before." She placed a finger under his chin and tilted it up. "Do ye like it here, Hagan?"

"Sure. It's a lot better than where we used to live. And you know what else?"

"What?"

"There's so much to eat." His eyes grew wide as he took her hand. "I'm hungry. Come on."

Kristen was still laughing when they entered the dining room, and she received an arched brow from the dowager duchess for her behavior. Trevor was seated at the head of the table with the duchess to his right.

"I see you're in a jolly mood," Trevor commented as he stood and helped Kristen take her seat.

"You didn't pull the chair out for me." Hagan giggled.

"Hasn't anyone taught that child that children are to be seen and not heard!" Constance thundered.

"That's the same thing you said last time," Hagan pointed out. "Do you have trouble hearing, Grandmère?" Hagan asked.

"Certainly not!"

Hagan's brows drew together in a puzzled frown. "Well, why would you only want to look at me, and not hear what I'm saying?"

The dowager's eyes widened. "Trevor, do something!"

Trevor managed to stop laughing long enough to say to Kristen, "I'd like you to meet an old friend. Charity Fullbright."

"I met Kristen earlier." Charity smiled.

"Oh, really," Trevor commented, a little surprised.

"She didn't meet me, though," Hagan butted in, and Constance cleared her throat.

"No, I didn't," Charity commented.

"There is no hope," Constance grumbled, and raised her eyes skyward.

Kristen gave Hagan the evil eye to calm him down before he gave the dowager duchess a stroke. "This is my very talkative brother, Hagan."

Charity's laughter tinkled like little bells, soft and feminine. Everything about the woman was perfect.

Charity smiled. "I have a brother too. I bet you're five years old?"

"I'm this many." Hagan held up five chubby fingers.

"So is my brother," Charity said.

The food started arriving and the conversation halted temporarily. It was a feast of roasted turkey and small potatoes, followed by macaroni, mutton casserole, and mince pies.

Dinner ended up being pleasant, and Kristen found Charity was easy to engage in conversation. Kristen couldn't help noticing that Constance was frowning. Evidently, things were not going as she'd planned.

After dinner, Trevor excused himself. A half hour later, Kristen left Constance and Charity talking, and strolled out onto the terrace to get some fresh air. The crickets seemed to be serenading her as she looked out into the dark night.

"Is this a private moment? Or would you like some company?" Trevor asked.

Kristen could see the orange glow of his cheroot. "I just needed some fresh air. Thought ye'd want some time to renew your acquaintance with Charity." She watched him as he propped his hip on the railing and faced her.

Featherlike laugh lines crinkled around his eyes. "Now, why would I want to do that when I can come out here to be with you?"

"Ye can save the silver tongue." Kristen laughed, knowing he was playing with her. He sent her pulse spinning when he was in this kind of mood.

"You can see through me already." Trevor smiled. "How are you adjusting to life here at Chatsworth, Kristen?"

"Everything is so different 'tis hard, I do admit, but I guess it isn't too bad." She managed to shrug and say offhandedly, "Hagan really likes it here. I want to thank ye for giving him a home and taking so much time with him." She bent her head and studied her hands. " 'Twasn't part of the bargain, but thank ye."

"I like Hagan," Trevor admitted, throwing the cheroot on the ground. "He's a bright little boy, and he shouldn't be in the streets."

"I agree," she murmured, looking deep into his eyes. They spoke to her with a language all their own. And when he looked at her the way he was looking at her now, it made her very nervous. She forgot everything . . . except him.

He seemed to control every sense she had. No longer could she hear the crickets or feel the breeze. She had to remind herself to breathe as a vaguely sensuous flicker passed between them.

He reached up and brushed her cheek. The smoldering flame she saw in his eyes startled her. "Do you realize when you talk about Hagan your eyes absolutely glitter? Do you think they will ever light up like that for me?"

Her body ached for his touch. "Would ye like that?" she asked huskily. She turned her head and kissed the palm of his hand.

"I think I would." His mouth brushed hers, and she melted easily into his arms. Something intense flared through her and her heart thumped erratically.

Trevor held her for a moment, letting his head rest upon her silky hair. Strange, he felt content just to hold her. She shivered. "Are you cold, love?" he whispered, his breath hot against her ear.

" 'Tis the weather that makes me shiver."

"I think it's more than that, Kristen." He took her mouth with a tenderness that he didn't know he possessed as he slipped his hand around the nape of her neck. His hands slid down and locked against her spine while he coaxed her lips to part so he could taste all of her. The kiss was as tender and light as a summer breeze.

She was so wonderful, Trevor thought as he lost himself in her kisses. Desire rose in him and the only thing he could think of was how to remove her clothes. Blood pounded in his brain.

She pulled back. "I dinna want to feel like this."

"Why?"

"Because ye dinna love me."

Her statement definitely cooled the driving force churning within him. "Ours will not be a normal marriage, but it's what we agreed on," he answered coldly. He stepped back away from the source of his temptation.

"That's right," she remarked, pleased at how nonchalant she sounded. "I remember now."

Trevor felt incredibly low and guilty, but it had been their agreement. "Listen. I do feel something for you, and that might be more than most people have." He could sense she was drawing away from him, and he didn't want that. "How are you and Grandmère getting along?"

"We had a few good moments this afternoon."

"That's more than what I had hoped for." He sighed with exasperation. "Sometimes her good moments are rare."

" 'Tis yer grandmother yer taking about." Kristen giggled, putting her hand over her mouth.

"I know." He took her hand. "We better go back in since we're unchaperoned."

Kristen paused and glanced at him. "I did enjoy this quiet moment."

"I did too." He leaned down and kissed her. There was a dreamy intimacy to their kiss now. "I like kissing you. You kiss very well."

"I had a good teacher." Kristen winked, then turned and disappeared through the doors.

Trevor turned and looked out into the night. Somehow the night seemed just a little colder . . . just a little lonelier.

CHAPTER TEN

Trevor paced in a small room off the side of the white chapel while Rodney adjusted his coat in front of the full-length mirror.

"Still find it hard to believe that in less than a hour you'll be a married man." Rodney shook his head in utter disbelief. "Always thought I'd be the one."

"I figured you'd be the one too," Trevor replied with a grin. He continued to move restlessly around the room.

Rodney turned from admiring himself, leaned against the wall, then folded his arms across his chest. "You seem a bit nervous. What's bothering you?"

"Nothing!" Trevor snapped, but after a few moments he added, "Do you realize that a month ago I didn't even know Kristen?"

"I believe I pointed out that small fact to you a few weeks ago. Yet you refused to listen."

"There are a few things I've not told you." Trevor

stopped his restless pacing and looked at his friend. Maybe he should have listened. Trevor was surprised at how nervous he'd become about the entire situation. Perhaps, talking with Rodney would ease these pre-wedding jitters he was experiencing.

Trevor watched Rodney with keenly observant eyes as he confessed, "I met Kristen when she tried to pick my pocket."

"Good God!"

"I know." Trevor shook his head, but couldn't help smiling as he remembered that particular day. "My intentions were to punish the girl once I caught her. However, after I apprehended her, there was an attraction so strong that the next thing I knew I was offering her a proposition. I wouldn't turn her over to the authorities if she'd marry me. It seemed like a simple solution at the time."

Rodney laughed. "You're not that hard up. You could have any woman you choose. But no, you have to make a bargain with a street urchin." He held up his hand to prevent Trevor from interrupting. "Not that I blame you. She is beautiful and seems to have a good disposition. Never thought she was a thief, though. Now that you've mentioned it, I lost my watch at the Cranford bash and had to purchase a new one." He rubbed his chin, looking at Trevor curiously. "You don't suppose?"

"Of course I suppose." Trevor laughed, in spite of himself. "Kristen is good. She could steal the eyes out of a dead man."

Rodney shook his head, truly amazed. "Then why are you marrying her?"

"Because I need a wife."

"Well, you're getting one." Rodney pulled out his pocket watch. "In about fifteen minutes."

"I know that. It's what to do with her afterward that's the problem."

Rodney let out a loud chuckle. "After all these years I was certain you knew precisely what to do with a woman once you got her into your bed."

Trevor glared at him. "That isn't what I meant. Kristen will never fit in with the people with whom we socialize, and I'll constantly have to be away on business. I'll have to leave her here in the country. At least here she'll be out of the streets and won't have that much social contact with others. She doesn't belong with those reprobates."

"I, for one, hope she'll never be like the *ton*. She's so genuine and refreshing to be around." Rodney nudged Trevor, then said in a low amused voice, "Haven't I always heard you say you wanted a wife who you could leave and then visit when you chose?"

Trevor nodded with a taut jerk of his head. "Yes, but—"

"Now you have just that," Rodney pointed out. "Kristen has no money so she can't leave you. You'll have everything you've ever wanted." Rodney slapped Trevor on the shoulder.

"That's true. I'll never have to worry about her leaving me."

A loud knock rattled the door. It was time.

Trevor stiffened. Everything he ever wanted. He'd done some mad things in his life, but this one had to top the others. . . for he was preparing to marry a thief.

Kristen waited patiently as the last hook was slipped into place. Turning, she stared into the mirror at the woman who stood before her. Funny how she had always thought of herself as a girl until now.

But today she looked like a woman.

The gown had turned out beautifully. The long skirt with eyelet lace across the bottom of her dress floated around her.

She smiled as she took in the details. The snow-white satin overskirt was longer in the front and tied up in the back with a sash. The cap sleeves and bodice were the same eyelet lace studded with tiny pearls and small diamonds. The top fitted off the shoulders and plunged between her breasts to show off her creamy skin.

Rebecca had left her hair loose after being brushed a hundred strokes. Now, she pulled the sides up and fastened Kristen's hair with ivory combs on each side. Then a lace veil was placed on her head with the netting flowing down her back. There was little need for cheek and lip color because her color was a gloriously high pink.

A noise sounded at the door. Kristen turned to see Charity enter dressed in a soft burgundy gown. She looked extremely pretty, as always. Actually, Charity should probably be the bride, Kristen thought sadly. Trevor deserved better than *her*. However, Kristen was glad Charity had agreed to be her friend, because she was very nice. And Kristen certainly needed a friend.

"You are simply beautiful," Charity gushed after she'd walked all around Kristen and assessed every angle.

"I dinna like any of this." Kristen threw up her hands. "I'm so nervous."

"You'll be just fine. Every bride is nervous before her wedding. What you're feeling is natural." Charity reached for Kristen's hand. "I've come to get you. It's time to go. Everyone is waiting for you."

Kristen cleared her throat nervously. "Has Trevor made an appearance?"

"Of course he has, and he looks extremely handsome.

You're very lucky.'' Charity gestured with her hands again. "Come along. It's not going to be as horrid as you think. The way you're frowning, one would think you are going to a funeral instead of your wedding.'' Charity chuckled.

Kristen stared at her friend. How could she tell Charity that she felt doomed? If she and Trevor were marrying for love, she would feel much better. This was a sham, and Kristen couldn't see anything good coming out of the situation.

"Give me a smile, Kristen,'' Charity commanded.

This time Kristen did as instructed, and forced her numb legs to step forward. Before she knew what was happening, she found herself standing in the vestibule of the dimly lit church.

The church was filled with Trevor's friends, who all turned to look at her. As she waited for the music to begin, her eyes automatically searched for Trevor. There were so many people that it was hard to see past them, but she persevered until she finally saw him. He stood at the foot of the altar, looking extremely elegant in a dark-blue frock coat and light-gray breeches. His skin looked dark next to his white waistcoat. Next to him, Rodney had taken his place, and of course Hagan, who had a finger in his collar, tugging on the neck.

Her gaze drifted back to Trevor, and she felt her bottom lip quiver. What was the strange feeling she had for him? It was as if she was happy and scared at the same time. Her finger touched her bottom lip to stop the quiver, but before she could turn and run, the music started, and someone nudged her from behind. She took her first step toward her new life.

Kristen felt the hundred pairs of eyes looking at her, but the only ones that really mattered were Trevor's, and his gaze never left her face. He was drawing her with that strange power he seemed to have over her. Suddenly, she was beside him, and he was taking her cold hands, giving them a squeeze for reassurance. She looked into his eyes and saw the same doubt and nervousness that she felt. His uncertainty made her feel better.

The minister began his prayers, blessing their union, and the rest of the service became a blur. Kristen's mouth moved, the proper words came out, but she couldn't hear anything for the blood pounding through her ears. She heard the words "till death divide," and the next thing she knew, Trevor had pulled her into his arms and cupped her chin tenderly in his warm hand.

She looked into his soft eyes, and her turbulent heart-beat raced just that much harder. Trevor's arms tightened, and he lowered his head to possess her mouth. He took it in a hot, searing kiss that was very different from the other kisses they had shared. An undeniable magnetism had developed between them, leaving her to wonder what would happen next.

As suddenly as it began, the kiss was over, leaving Kristen dazed and wanting more.

The minister had them turn, and announced, "I present to you the Duke and Duchess of Chatsworth."

The minister swept them into a side room where he produced a register and held a quill out for Trevor, who signed his name with a sure and quick stroke.

"What's this?" Kristen asked when Trevor handed her the quill.

"We have to record our marriage, love." He smiled at her.

With wide eyes Kristen stared at the parchment. Every-thing was legal, but somehow it wasn't right—not what she'd dreamed. She looked up at her new husband, and then signed her name next to Trevor's.

Slowly they moved back out into the church and down the aisle. Once they were at the back of the church, everyone rushed up to congratulate Trevor on his new marriage.

Then they were whisked to the waiting carriages that would take them back to Chatsworth. Once the conveyance started to move, Trevor surprised Kristen by turning her until she lay across his lap, her head pressed against his shoulder.

"We can't do this now," Kristen said.

"I think we can," he replied before his lips found hers. His mouth was scalding, devouring, searching for something more from her. A warmth spread all over her, and she responded, clutching him close to her and returning his kiss.

Her hands slid around his neck and she welcomed his tongue. She heard him moan just before he broke the kiss.

"We will continue this later, love." Trevor looked her over seductively. "But for now we will have to entertain our guests." He helped her sit up and straightened her skirts, just as the carriage came to a stop.

Once they entered the house, they were again surrounded by guests. Kristen politely smiled and made light conversation, but she felt lost with all these strangers.

She found her mind going more and more to Trevor and his promise that they would continue later. Just the thought of what they would do made her quiver inside as she looked at him across the room. He had awakened in her many new emotions that she didn't know how to handle, and that left her reeling. She simply had to get her mind off the man.

"You look pretty, Kristen," Hagan said as he tugged on her skirt from beside her.

"Ye look mighty smart yerself." She smiled at him, thinking how glad she was that she could give Hagan a better life. He grinned back, then darted away. She watched as he went straight to the dowager duchess. Kristen prayed Constance wouldn't cause a scene. Not today.

"Are you all right, Grandmère?"

Constance looked down at the sandy-haired child looking up at her with such concern in his eyes, and something within her heart twisted just a little. She saw Trevor at that age. "I feel a little weak, Hagan."

"Here, take my hand." He held up his chubby little hand, and she reached out and accepted it. "I'll take you over to get some punch."

"I would like that." And for the first time Constance smiled at the child, and felt a huge burden lifting off her shoulders. Perhaps this daft marriage of Trevor's would work after all.

Kristen couldn't believe what she'd just seen and heard. This was truly a day for miracles! Then she remembered the jewels they had not yet returned to Constance. They had planned to give the necklace to her on the day they married. She hoped Trevor had remembered to bring it. Kristen squeezed Trevor's hand. "It's time to give your grandmother her necklace."

"Thank you for reminding me. Come with me." Trevor escorted Kristen by the elbow over to his grandmother.

"Grandmère, could you join us for a moment?"

When they were by themselves in a sitting room off to the side, Trevor reached into his pocket and grasped the necklace. "Kristen helped me return something that I believe belongs to you." He held up his hand and let the chain slip through his fingers until the jewels dangled from his fingers.

"Gracious!" Constance exclaimed. For a moment she stood there without moving and stared at the necklace. Finally, she moved forward and took it from Trevor. "I never thought to see this again. Someone very special gave this to me a long time ago.''

"Grandfather?"

"No, dear. It was someone else."

Trevor wondered who she could be referring to, but decided now wasn't the time to have such a discussion. He did notice a certain glow in her eyes. One he'd not seen there before. The necklace must have meant a great deal to her.

"Thank you both." Tears brimmed in Constance's eyes.

Kristen smiled. "Here, let me help you put this on." Kristen hung it around the woman's neck and fastened the clasp. This is novel, Kristen thought. Putting jewelry on someone instead of taking it off. Maybe she had changed her ways.

The rest of the day was filled with feasting and dancing. Finally, it was time to leave the guests and head for their room.

Trevor thought his bride looked very nervous as she started up the stairs ahead of him. To give her as much time as she needed, he didn't follow. He'd have to find a way to calm her down. He'd waited much too long to have anything spoil this night. He wanted Kristen more than he could recall ever wanting a woman before. Tonight, everything had to be perfect.

When he thought she'd had enough time to herself, Trevor went upstairs. He watched his lovely bride from the doorway of his chamber. Her white satin gown looked as delicate as she did, and it left absolutely nothing to his imagination as it clung to her every little curve. He had to curb the desire to lick his lips.

His body sprang to life with desires he'd not felt in a long, long time, or maybe it had just been too long, but he definitely wanted the woman standing in front of him . . . and in the worst way.

However, his little bride didn't look like an adoring wife eager to jump into his arms and smother him with kisses. Her eyes were enormous as she stood hesitantly staring at him, and desire wasn't what he saw in her eyes. It was more like stark terror.

She finally cleared her throat. "Are ye sure ye want to do this?"

Trevor took a step closer and smiled at her ridiculous question. "Very certain indeed."

She shook her head. "What if I dinna care for this?"

"You will," he assured her confidently. He lifted his hand and slipped her strap off her shoulder.

"How can ye be sure?" She tugged the strap back in place. "Have ye ever done this before?"

Not to be undone, he slipped the strap down again and this time, drew her to him before she could readjust her gown. "I've done this many, many times."

Kristen shivered. "Then why do ye want to do it again?"

He chuckled. He really didn't know how to tell her his blood boiled at the sight of her, that he wanted to completely possess her and make her his. "Do not be afraid, sweetheart." He enfolded her in his arms. "You'll understand in a short while," he whispered, then kissed the end of her nose.

Her eyes fluttered closed as his lips moved across her cheek. She trembled in his arms, making Trevor feel like a king.

"I want you," Trevor rasped. He tugged on her soft earlobe with his lips, and was pleased to hear her soft groan. "And I think you feel the same."

Picking her up in his arms, he carried her over to the bed and laid her down. He returned to the chair and slipped off his shirt, which he'd unbuttoned earlier, and then took off his breeches and turned to face Kristen. She looked so beautiful to him, he'd never let another man have her. Never.

"Oh, my God," Kristen exclaimed.

Trevor saw where her eyes had drifted. Evidently, she was as innocent as she'd claimed. He now knew he'd have to be very gentle. How could he manage when his blood simmered for her so? "You really don't know about this, do you?" He asked as he lowered himself to the bed beside her.

"Nay."

"Then I shall teach you." He pulled her to him, his fingers slipping through her hair and finally resting on the back of her head as he hovered just above her. He looked deep into her eyes, eyes that had suddenly changed from an expression of uncertainty to one of anticipation and desire that even she didn't yet realize.

Her lips parted slightly, and he took what he wanted. What he needed. She slid her arms around his neck and pressed her body into his.

Trevor Claremont was a doomed man.

Their kisses grew intense. Their breathing became labored as they were caught up in a ritual as old as time. "I need you, Kristen," he whispered tenderly as his tongue touched her earlobe.

"I need ye too." Kristen replied. "I've tried hard not to." She didn't know anything could feel so wonderful and torturous all at the same time. What was this crazy burning that had spread from her stomach and had managed to engulf her body and drive everything else out? Except for the touch and feel of Trevor.

His tongue touched her ear and she went limp as shivers

of desire ran through her. His lips slid down the side of her neck and then pressed lower.

The saints above! This man can kiss! Kristen couldn't seem to get enough of him. She wanted more. Her satin gown slid down her body as Trevor expertly removed the garment. Now she lay completely naked beneath him. The warmth of his body engulfed her.

"Beautiful." He gazed at her body and then followed with his mouth, lower and lower until he found the soft mound of her breast.

"No," she gasped, but her body betrayed her objections as she arched against him.

What was he doing to her? This couldn't be decent, but it felt so wonderful, she admitted to herself. She was no longer afraid. Her burning need had to be satisfied, and Trevor seemed to be the only one who could give her what she needed. He'd said he knew what he was doing . . .

So far he hadn't lied.

The next thing she knew he was nibbling the lobe of her ear, making her shiver. Then ever so slowly his lips moved down her neck and back to her mouth, where his tongue plunged into hers. He caressed her tongue with bold kisses that held nothing back. His hands wandered down her back as he pressed his hips against her.

She began to match his desire with her own. She gasped for air when he tore his mouth from hers. The pleasure that ran through her was so intense she could hardly believe anything felt so wonderful or that it could get any better.

He lowered his head and took one nipple into his mouth and began to suckle. Kristen clung to his shoulders. Lord, she was going to die right there.

Trevor's hands seemed to be burning everywhere they touched, and Kristen didn't know how much longer she could stand this torture. When his fingers moved between her legs, though, she immediately clamped them together. "Ye cannot do this!" she exclaimed, her eyes wide.

"It is part of it, sweetheart. You must trust me."

She wasn't too sure about that, but she needed something more than kisses. She needed Trevor as she'd never needed anyone before. Finally, she relaxed and, for once in her life, trusted someone else.

He shoved his fingers into her warmth and started to move while he kissed her over and over again. Her nipples were taut, pressing into his chest, and she was arching into him with a sensual desire that was matching his.

Somehow she'd found heaven, she thought as raw pleasure soared through her.

"Are you ready, Kristen?"

"I dinna know. I just know that I want ye closer somehow."

A growl of satisfaction rumbled from Trevor as he separated her thighs. He needed to go slow, he reminded himself, but the blood pounding in his head pushed him on. In one swift move, he became one with his bride.

God! She was tight and warm and he didn't want to stop, but he did when he felt her tense. Kristen hadn't lied to him, he thought with pride. She was no more a common thief than he was. He felt a big piece of the puzzle was still missing from his knowledge of this girl, and he hoped one day to find that piece, but right now he only wanted to make her completely his.

He lifted up and looked down at her. "Are you all right?"

She looked at him with accusing eyes. "Ye never said anything about pain."

He watched her for a long moment. Thank God, the desire was still in her eyes. "It will only hurt that one time, I promise." He began to move again.

She felt passion rising in her like the hottest fire. The

way he held her betrayed his hunger and she opened her mouth further. She needed to taste all of him.

After several minutes she began to move with him. An odd sort of pressure began to build as she matched his every move, faster and faster until, without warning, everything exploded. She could feel herself being washed away into a sea of oblivion. From somewhere, she heard Trevor cry out her name in triumph; then he became very still and collapsed, sated. He still held her within his arms, and she savored the feeling of satisfaction he'd given her.

Neither said a word as they let sleep claim them. But just before Trevor fell asleep, he murmured the words he'd spoken to Kristen the first time he'd met her.

"You are a wicked lady, Kristen Johnstone . . . make that Claremont."

"Aye, I am," she whispered. Then she leaned over and kissed his chin.

Somehow life would never be the same again.

CHAPTER ELEVEN

The next two weeks passed in a blur for Kristen. She and Trevor made passionate love at night, but in the daylight she hardly saw him. He stayed behind closed doors working, or so the servants told her. She began to wonder if he was going to great lengths to avoid her.

Yet at night she'd tell herself she was being silly because Trevor was so warm and loving, taking her to heights she'd never imagined. Then, the next day he would stay away from her again. Kristen was beginning to think she was daft.

One thing was for certain. She was bored! Kristen had been active all her life, and sitting around doing nothing wasn't her cup of tea.

And today she'd decided she'd had enough, so she summoned Rebecca. After dressing in what Rebecca called a riding habit, Kristen decided to take a ride and enjoy the outdoors. It didn't matter that she'd never been on a horse before. Riding couldn't be that hard. Even children could do it.

Looking at her reflection in the dressing room mirror, she admired the light-green riding habit made of soft linen. It would be perfect for the gorgeous spring weather they were experiencing. She tied back her hair with a lime-green ribbon and let her unruly strawberry-blond curls cascade down her back. There. She smiled. She felt better all ready.

Kristen encountered only a couple of the upstairs maids as she went downstairs. She didn't waste any time heading out the back door.

So far, so good. She smiled.

As soon as the door shut behind her, she noticed something moving to her left. Turning, she spotted Hagan and a couple of the servants' children playing in the corner of the terrace under one of the many trellises that stood at each end of the brick veranda.

"Hello, Hagan," Kristen said as she strolled over to where the children played.

Hagan looked up. "Hello, Kristen. Where are you going?"

"I thought I would go riding."

Hagan giggled. "But you don't know how."

"It canna be so hard. After all, ye learned." She pointed out. "Would ye like to come?"

"Sure," Hagan said, and immediately stood, but didn't follow his sister right away. He waited until she'd moved away from them. "Sorry," he whispered to his playmates behind his hand. "I need to protect my sister. She gets into all sorts of trouble." His statement produced several giggles from the children.

Kristen held out her hand, and Hagan ran to catch up with her. She wondered what he'd said to make the other boys giggle. Probably some deep secret. She was glad he was coming so she'd have some company.

"Where is Trevor?" Hagan asked innocently as he skipped along beside her while they made their way through the sunken path with clipped yews on either side.

"Working, I guess." Her voice sounded tired even to her own ears. "That's all he seems to do." She finally sighed.

"Maybe he doesn't know how to do anything else."

Kristen glanced sideways at her brother. He sounded so wise. Far beyond his five years. "Ye could be right. We'll have to teach him other things besides work. Won't we?"

"Sure. I like him." Hagan thought for a moment. "He might not like us riding without him."

Kristen gazed out over the velvet lawns and parterres. This place looks like paradise, she thought. "I think he's too busy to care," Kristen said as her earlier irritation returned. How could anybody live in a place like this and not enjoy it? They went on across the lawns until they reached the stables.

Upon entering, Kristen could smell the leather saddles and horses. She hadn't realized that Chatsworth's stables were so large. Eight stalls lined each side. Several horses peered over the half-doors, watching the stable hands as they mucked out the stalls and put fresh straw on the floors.

A stocky man with a receding hairline and a pipe hanging out of the corner of his mouth came shuffling down the center of the stable. "What can I do for you, miss?"

"We would like to go riding if ye don't mind fixing two horses for us?"

"It's called saddling," Hagan whispered behind his hand.

"Just give me a minute." The man chuckled at Hagan's

comment. "And I'll have a horse and a pony saddled for you." He bowed curtly. "Name's Baxter, mum." He reached out and ruffled Hagan's hair. "This little scamp is taking a real likin' to that pony."

"Thank you, Baxter. My name is Kristen," she said to the man's back, as he'd already started on his way to do her bidding.

"See this big red horse?" Hagan pointed up to a horse who looked curiously at them over the door. He had a white blaze going down the center of his face and was much larger than the rest of the animals.

"He's beautiful." Kristen moved over so she could rub his muzzle. "Feels like velvet."

"Let me." Hagan held up his hand, but he didn't quite reach, so Kristen picked him up and he stroked the horse.

"This is Trevor's horse." Hagan ran his hand over the horse's soft nose. "He's fast!"

" 'Twould take a big man to control this one," she murmured her thoughts as she lowered Hagan back to the ground. Trevor definitely fit that description.

"Ready, miss?"

Kristen followed Baxter to the paddock where the horses were tethered. Hagan wasted little time climbing onto his pony; however, Kristen hesitated as she stared at the odd seat.

"Let me help you, miss." Baxter cupped his hands so she could put her foot in them.

Placing her hands on the saddle, she managed, somehow, to land in the right place, but decided she'd much prefer the pony that Hagan was riding than this tall beast.

Baxter scratched his head, his eyes sharp and assessing. "Are you sure you know how to ride, miss?"

"Of course. I'm just a little rusty," Kristen lied, and tried not to look him straight in the face.

THE WICKED LADY 163

"Well, keep a firm grip on the reins. Like this." He positioned the leather straps between her fingers. "Take it slow at first and then it will come back to you."

"Thank you." Kristen turned her mount so they could head for the arched doorway. "What's her name?"

"Paznell."

"All right, Paznell. We're going to be good friends." Kristen patted the animal's neck.

"Come on, Kristen," a merry voice called. Hagan had already left the paddock.

"Go, Paznell," Kristen commanded, but the horse showed no inclination toward budging.

"Kick her with your heel," Baxter instructed.

She did. Thankfully, the horse paid attention this time, and soon Kristen had caught up with Hagan.

"Murphy," Baxter called to one of his men who was pitching hay. "Run to the house and inform His Grace that his little lady is going for a ride." He shook his head. "Just hope she doesn't break her fool neck. I'm not too sure she's ever seen a horse, much less ridden one."

Kristen and Hagan rode out away from the house. Hagan told her it was the way that he and Trevor always rode, so she followed Hagan's lead.

Streams of light peeked from behind puffy white clouds scattered across a light blue sky. The sun's rising had warmed the crisp air, and the sunlight soothed her body like a soft caress. The countryside was so beautiful and fresh that Kristen decided this was just what she'd needed. She'd been cooped up for too long. There was a certain feeling of freedom she found in riding, and she liked it.

They had ridden for over an hour, and Kristen was feeling very confident that she'd master such a simple task. She knew this would be easy, she thought as she released her death grip on the saddle and reins.

That was when Hagan's pony took off, jumping a small stone wall. Evidently, her mount didn't want to be outdone because Paznell took off after Hagan's pony, jerking the leather straps from her fingers. Kristen screamed and clutched the saddle. Surely, the horse would stop when it got to the wall.

It did not.

Kristen went one way and the horse the other. The next thing she knew she was no longer on the animal but flying through the air. She heard herself scream again as she landed in a heap on the other side of the wall.

She lay on the ground, gasping for air. Unable to breathe, she took a few minutes before she finally caught her breath. Sitting up, she straightened her clothing. The world still seemed to be spinning before her eyes.

Blast, did she ache. The ground was much too hard. Next time she'd ask for a shorter horse. Shoving her hair out of her face, she looked around for Hagan, but didn't see him.

Kristen decided she wouldn't move for a few minutes until her head stopped this crazy spinning. Looking out on the rolling hills in front of her, she noticed for the first time a large estate in the distance. It was every bit as impressive as Chatsworth, and she wondered who lived there.

A rider cut across the field and seemed to be coming from the house, but stopped at the second stone wall. This land is very funny, she thought. In the middle of this huge field were two stone walls no more than thirty feet apart.

Kristen realized the rider was a woman, but she couldn't see the lady's face very well. She had long black hair and seemed about the same size as Kristen. She only paused a moment as she called out, "Are ye all right?"

Kristen couldn't help noticing the lady sounded just like

herself. "Just a wee bit shaken, but my brother should be along shortly, thanks."

The lady looked directly at Kristen, smiled for a brief moment, then rode away.

Kristen sat there, dumbfounded. Maybe she had hit her head harder than she'd thought, because she could have sworn that she'd just seen herself on that horse. Impossible.

Horse's hooves sounded from behind her. The ground shook. Before she knew what was happening, the hooves came flying over the top of her head. She screamed and ducked.

"Christ!" Trevor swore as he dismounted and knelt down beside her. "If you wanted to go riding, I would have taken you." His hands moved along her legs, checking for broken bones.

She slapped his hands away. "Oh, would ye now? That would mean ye'd have to leave yer desk." She attempted to stand, but her head was still spinning.

Trevor grabbed her as she swayed. "Are you hurt?"

"I seem to have hit my head. I'll be all right, though." However, her words didn't match her actions as she leaned against Trevor for support. "Who lives on that hill?"

"Johnstone," he spat. "This is the tract of land that's in dispute."

"Why don't one of ye buy it from the other?"

"It belongs to my family," Trevor stated firmly. "I'll not buy something I already own."

Even with her head whirling, Kristen could see one thing clearly. "Ye know something?"

He gave her a questioning look, but didn't say anything.

"I dinna think ye really know what the feud is about."

Trevor gave her a half laugh. "You are absolutely right."

"Then why—"

Trevor held up a hand. "I do not want to discuss the matter."

All right, she could see this was a touchy subject with him, but this feud seemed ridiculous to her. There had to be more to the story than she'd heard so far. Maybe one day she'd find out.

Hagan trotted up on his pony with Kristen's horse in tow. "Did you lose something, Kristen?"

Kristen glared at her brother. "I was doing just fine until that pony of yers took off."

"I didn't think your horse would follow mine." For just a moment, Hagan did manage to look a little guilty. "You should hang on better next time," he said.

"Do you think you can ride back?" Trevor asked.

Kristen straightened. "I think so."

Trevor escorted her over to the horse and helped her mount. Then he mounted, and they started for home.

"This is beautiful land," she said. "Funny, I feel as if I've been here before."

"Really?" Trevor said. "I would think that was impossible. I do agree, however, the land is lovely. It's good English soil." He twisted in the saddle to look at her. "We'll have to ride more often. I didn't know you could ride."

"I didna know I could ride either," Kristen admitted with a nervous laugh.

"Are you serious?" Trevor grinned. "Well, you ride very well for the first time. Maybe you learn *everything* quickly." His grin grew wicked.

Kristen liked it when Trevor teased her. He seemed so much younger and carefree when he was in this kind of mood, one she sensed he wasn't in often. And that was a shame, she thought as she fought the desire to reach out and touch him.

"I would race ye," Kristen challenged, "but I better wait

until my second lesson. I remember how hard that ground felt.''

Trevor nodded in agreement. "I think that is a very good idea."

Kristen regarded him with a speculative gaze. "I suppose ye need to get back to work." Her voice dropped a notch, and she realized she didn't want him to leave her just yet.

"Well—" His hazel eyes lit up with a golden glow, as if he were toying with his decision. "I don't think it will hurt to take a little time off. Let's ride to the lake." He turned to look for Hagan. "Hagan, come on and stay with us. We're riding back."

Hagan came galloping up on his pony. "But we haven't been out here that long," he complained.

"We are going to stop by the lake for a few minutes on the way back. I guess I can spare a little time. Will that make you happy?"

Kristen laughed at him. "You don't know what do with yerself when you're not working."

"Of course I do," he scoffed, then rode off, not waiting for her.

The lake shimmered a gray-blue. Rocks clung to the edge of the shore and sprigs of lavender bobbed in a gentle breeze. The gray rocks sprinkled with lavender led from the edge almost to the middle. She noticed that the black swans she had seen that first day were on the far side of the lake.

Trevor bent down and picked up a small, flat stone. He threw it across the water, making the stone skim just across the top.

"Splendid. Teach me," Hagan called out.

"You have to find a flat rock," Trevor told him.

"Kristen, you look too," Hagan instructed.

Kristen walked along the edge of the pond until she found several good throwing rocks.

"How about this one?" Hagan asked.

She looked at Hagan and laughed. He had a rock the size of an egg in his hand."

" 'Tis a wee bit big."

"Yes, it is," Trevor agreed. "It will make a big splash, then sink. However, your sister seems to have found a nice supply for us."

Kristen watched as Trevor patiently showed Hagan how to hold the stone so he could get the greatest distance. She could picture him showing his own children someday. However, she didn't think that she'd be their mother. The agreement hadn't called for wee ones. Besides, Trevor would want children with someone he loved, and that didn't mean herself. He would make a good father, she thought regretfully.

Trevor straightened and shoved his hands back into his pockets while he watched Hagan, and Kristen watched Trevor.

She liked watching the man far too much. He was so handsome that at times it simply took her breath away. At the moment, he looked the most relaxed she'd ever seen him. She realized he must keep all his emotions bottled up inside him, and that couldn't be good for him.

"Would you like to toss a couple of stones?" Trevor asked her. "Come over here and I'll show you." He motioned for her to join him on the rocks.

Carefully, Kristen made her way to the end of the protruding rocks. Trevor wrapped his arms around her, taking her throwing arm and positioning the stone between her thumb and forefinger.

To hell with the rock, Kristen thought as she enjoyed the closeness of her husband. Usually, the only time she was this close to him was at night when they were in bed. This little time felt like a real treat. Reluctantly, she dragged her mind back to the small stone that had brought them together.

"All right now, give it a try," he said, and stepped away from her. She reared back and hurled the stone, watching as it barely hit the water at least ten times before sinking.

"I'm impressed," Trevor admitted.

"Beginner's luck," Hagan called from the bank.

Kristen laughed until she turned to walk back and saw a huge snake. Horror seized her. Immediately, she let out a bloodcurdling scream.

"Stand very still," Trevor warned as he eyed the coiled-up snake.

" 'Tis easy for ye to say," Kristen barely choked out.

Trevor pulled a pistol from inside his jacket and, taking careful aim, fired at the snake just as it slithered toward Kristen.

Kristen screamed, stepped back, and caught her heel on the edge of her skirt, sending her tumbling into the water.

Trevor scrambled over and fished her out of the cold water. She was half laughing and half crying as he enfolded her into his arms.

"It's all right," he murmured. "I took care of the snake. It can't hurt you."

"I wasn't frightened, just surprised." Kristen clung, trembling, to her pillar of strength.

Trevor clutched Kristen tightly until she quit shaking. Finally, he bent and brushed his lips on her wet hair, and once again assured her, "You're out of danger now, love.

I think we need to get back, so you can remove these wet clothes." He plucked at one of her wet sleeves to illustrate his point.

"All right," Kristen said. She bent down and picked up her skirt to wring some of the water out of the material. Then she let Trevor lead her toward the shore. His arm still rested around her waist.

Hagan waited for them. He couldn't, however, hold his giggles back when he saw his half-drowned sister.

"Drat, Kristen. I guess you've had a pretty rotten day. First, the horse throws you, then you fall into the lake." He shook his head. "I told my friends that somebody had to watch after you."

"Ye didn't do too good a job then." Kristen frowned at him. Did the child ever worry about her? He seemed to always assume she would land on her feet.

Hagan held the bridle of her horse while Trevor helped her mount.

"I think you did a good job for your age," Trevor told Hagan. "Even *I* couldn't keep your sister out of trouble. It just seems to find her." Amusement played clearly on his face.

"If ye two are through discussing me, I'd like to go to the house." She gathered the reins and left them both staring at her.

Later that night, Kristen awoke with a sore throat and a stuffy head. She tossed and turned until she finally woke Trevor.

"What's wrong, love?"

"I dinna feel good," she whined.

"Come here." Trevor pulled her body next to his and threw his arm over her. She fitted perfectly with his curves, as if they were made for each other. Soon, his warmth relaxed her, and she drifted off to sleep . . . miserable, yet contented.

The next morning her head felt three times its normal size, and her eyes ran water every time she tried to open them. She was just plain suffering.

Trevor insisted that she stay in bed, and she didn't argue since holding her head up seemed to be a real chore. He even brought her some hot tea and toast, then sat with her while she ate. She realized he was trying to take care of her, and she thought that was sweet.

At midmorning, Hagan climbed up on her bed and started to read her children's stories. She was glad for the company, and she was really pleased at how fast and well Hagan had learned to read.

Trevor stuck his head through the open door. "How is our patient?"

Kristen moaned and pulled the covers over her head.

"She's a bit grumpy," Hagan informed him.

"Perhaps she has a right to feel out of sorts." Trevor moved over to the bed, and pulled the covers back to reveal his patient. "Kristen." She didn't bother to answer. "Come on and just peek at me."

This time she barely opened one eye. "Have you been drinking the warm tea?" he asked, trying to be patient. She nodded her head. Her nose had turned a very prominent red, and she looked absolutely miserable, Trevor thought. He wished she would feel better before he had to go, but it didn't look like that would be the case.

Trevor sighed. "I know you're sick, but I have to leave."

"Leave?" she croaked, cracking open both eyes this time.

"I must go to London. Something unexpected has come

up and Miller is packing my bags as we speak. I shouldn't be gone long."

"I didna leave ye when ye were sick," she accused.

"I was shot. Not sick. And you were one of the ones who put a bullet in me, or should I remind you of that?" He squeezed her hand. "Besides which, I have a whole staff to wait on you hand and foot."

Her bottom lip poked out. She knew she was being childish, but she didn't feel well, and she didn't want Trevor to go. After all, he was warm to snuggle up to, and he was a dear, sweet man most of the time. And unfortunately for her, she loved him. He didn't need to know that yet; it would give him too much power over her. After a few minutes, she said, "Go take care of yer business. I'll just lie here and die." At least he could feel guilty while he was gone.

He chuckled. "I think you'll be fine." He placed a finger under her chin and tilted her head up. "Are you going to give me a hug good-bye?" Kristen jerked away.

"*I* am." Hagan leapt into his arms and wrapped his small arms around Trevor's neck.

"Well, I'm glad someone will." Trevor set Hagan on his feet and patted his bottom. "Run along and see if Miller has my bags packed."

Trevor turned back to Kristen. "Well . . ."

She frowned while she pushed back the covers and got to her knees on the bed. Trevor hugged her to him. He held her so tightly that she could forget everything, even how bad she felt. He hugged her as if he loved her. Maybe he really didn't want to go. Finally, he leaned back and kissed her forehead.

"I won't be gone long." Trevor started for the door, but looked back at her. "You stay in bed and get well. And don't go riding alone." For a moment, he thought she looked a little sad that he was leaving, but her next words shot that thought out of his mind.

"Yer a nag."

"You heard what I said." Trevor chuckled, then shut the door.

CHAPTER TWELVE

Trevor told himself for at least the twentieth time that he didn't feel guilty about leaving Kristen. However, his mood didn't change as he tried to find a different position in the carriage so he could stretch out his legs.

Hadn't he said this was what he wanted? His freedom to come and go? He'd stayed much longer than he'd expected to. So why did he feel so damned guilty?

Besides, his business was urgent. He'd lost two ships in a bad storm, and he'd have to commission the shipbuilders to construct replacements. The only problem was that he needed them immediately.

If he shut his eyes, he could picture Kristen curled up in bed. For one brief moment, he thought she'd looked a little sad that he was leaving, and he almost turned around and went back for one more kiss. But when he looked at her again, the sadness had left her eyes. So he'd gone.

He was getting soft, he thought as he shut his eyes, took

a deep breath, and waited for the sleep he needed to take his mind off the many questions for which he had no answers. His life used to be very uncomplicated before Kristen, and, he thought, with a wry grin, *dull*.

It was midafternoon the next day when Trevor's carriage stopped in front of the little brown building that held his office. He got out and stretched every aching muscle in his body. Damn, it felt good to be out of the carriage. He inhaled a deep breath of salt-tinged air. Oh, how he loved that smell.

The clerk sat up quickly when Trevor opened the door of the little office. "Hello, Your Grace."

"James, are you ever going to purchase some new spectacles so you don't have to get so close to your work?"

"Someday, when I get the time." James rubbed his glasses with a soft cloth. "Did you hear the bad news?"

"Unfortunately, bad news travels fast."

"I think it's a bit odd myself," James commented as he replaced his spectacles. "Two ships going down at the same time. Not bloody likely. This hasn't been the first time you've had mishaps."

"I've thought the same thing." Trevor marched past him and headed for his office.

Rodney came out of Trevor's office and leaned casually against the doorjamb. "So, I see you've left that pretty wife." He shook his head. "Damn fool, if you ask me."

"Well, nobody asked you." Trevor said as he brushed past Rodney, frowning when his friend chuckled. "Have you found out anything?"

"I talked to some of the crew members and they said both ships went down before they knew what was happening. As if they'd suddenly sprung a leak."

"A big leak, wouldn't you say?" Trevor said sarcastically.

"I have a feeling someone is out to put Claremont Shipping out of business."

"But who?" Rodney asked.

"That, my friend, we are going to have to find out. You keep searching, and I'll do some looking myself. But right now, I must get replacement ships, and they don't come cheap."

"I'm glad it's you and not I." Rodney stood. "I'll go with you."

Trevor stared up at the familiar tall wooden building that stood next to the water. He listened to the hammering and swearing as the craftsmen went about their daily jobs. He breathed in the scent of sawdust, new wood, and tar as he and Rodney entered the building and looked for the manager.

Jervis smiled as he spotted Trevor. He put down his drawings and hurried toward Trevor and Rodney. "Ah, my favorite customer."

Trevor skipped the pleasantries. "I think you have been providing me with faulty merchandise."

"I think not." Jervis's smile quickly disappeared.

"Then how do you explain that I'm in need of two frigates?"

"That's not good news, but it was not the fault of my workmanship." Jervis shook his head. "We are behind with our work. Looking at nine months, and that's working night and day."

"That will not do," Trevor stated. "I need at least one ship in six months," he insisted. "I have cargo booked that I don't want to cancel." Turning around, he looked at a huge ship down near the dock. "Who is that frigate being made for?"

"Isn't she a beauty? Measures one hundred fifty-one feet along the keel and she sets thirty-one sails," Jervis bragged as he folded his arms and gazed proudly at the ship.

"Who's buying it?" Trevor asked again.

"I am trying to sell her to Admiral Neils of the Royal Navy."

"Forget it. I'll pay ten percent more."

"She is expensive and big. Much larger than your other ships. Why, the mainmast, with topsail and topgallant, rises one hundred seventy-five feet above the deck."

"I can see that with my own eyes." Trevor shrugged impatiently. "However, you just stated that you were looking for a buyer—now you have one. And one who has agreed to pay more, so don't try and talk me out it."

Jervis rocked back on his heels. "Very expensive."

"No doubt." Trevor frowned. "But she'll hold twice the cargo."

"Sold!" Jervis smiled, evidently very pleased with the deal. "I'll go write up the necessary papers," he said, and went to his office.

"What a ship," Rodney finally said.

"I agree. And she's sturdy enough to mount guns. We'll have plenty of protection in the future."

Rodney nodded his agreement. Then they turned and followed Jervis to his office.

Trevor was quite pleased with his business, and his step was jaunty as he and Rodney made their way back to Trevor's office.

As soon as they entered the front door, James informed Trevor he had a visitor in his inner office.

He stared a moment at James. "Who is it?" Trevor demanded. It was too soon for Jervis to come running with second thoughts. And if he did have them, it was too bloody bad. Trevor had the bill of sale.

"Don't know, sir." James shrugged. "Wouldn't say."

Trevor's brow arched. He didn't like this at all.

"Appears as if you're going to be busy. Perhaps I should be going." Rodney turned to leave.

"No." Trevor stopped him. "Stay. Let's see who my mysterious visitor is."

When they entered Trevor's office, he didn't have to ask the man who he was, or what he wanted. Every muscle in Trevor had tightened. "What are you doing here?"

"Just a friendly visit, mate."

"I told you quite clearly that there would be no more money!" Trevor bit out as he moved around his desk toward Ned, who had the audacity to have his feet propped up on the desk.

Ned jumped up and moved around to the opposite end of the desk, to a chair in the corner. "Who's this?" Ned Blume asked, cutting his eyes toward Rodney.

Trevor didn't bother to answer. He took one look at Ned's dirty jacket and knew he had probably spent the money he'd gotten before on liquor. The liquor smell was still on the man.

"Well, this here's private business," Ned insisted as he sat in the chair still eyeing Rodney.

"Rodney, this is Hagan's father." Trevor gestured toward Ned, then addressed him directly. "Whatever you have to say to me can be said in front of Rodney." Trevor sat behind his desk.

"Suit yourself." Ned shrugged. "How's my boy?"

Trevor leaned forward in his chair, his arms placed upon the desk. "He's far better than when he lived with you."

"And Kristen?"

"Kristen is no concern of yours," Trevor ground out the words catching between his teeth. "She is now my wife."

"Fine little piece you got there." Ned grinned.

Trevor reached over the desk and grabbed Ned's jacket hard enough to jerk him out of his chair.

Rodney came to his feet, also ready to fight. "Want me to throw him out?"

"Hold on, hold on," Ned blustered. "Didn't mean no harm." He held his hands up in defense. "I need more money."

Trevor released Ned, and Rodney relaxed, taking his seat again. "You evidently did not hear me the first time," Trevor said, his voice hardening. "There will be no more money."

"Well," the man whined, "you just might change your mind." Ned rubbed the back of his hand across his mouth as if he needed a drink. "Kristen ain't who you think she is."

Trevor's left eyebrow rose a fraction. "What do you mean by that?"

"The information will cost you." Blume rubbed his fingers together in a gesture that indicated he wanted money.

Trevor hesitated before reaching into his pocket and tossing Ned a couple of gold coins.

Ned bit down on one of the gold coins to make sure it was gold. He then pocketed them. "That ain't much. Bet you'll pay more when you hear what I've got to say." He grinned, showing his missing front tooth.

"You are pushing my temper, Blume. Either spit out what you've got to say or get out!"

"Kristen was kidnapped. Happened when she was just a small child. That's why she grew up in the streets."

Trevor leaned forward, his eyes cold. "Kidnapped from whom?"

"Ian Johnstone. His wife had twins, ye see. Two girls,

like peas in a pod, except their hair. One had black hair, and the other that reddish mess of Kristen's.''

Trevor's stomach tightened. "Go on."

"Well, they always doted on the raven-haired baby, according to Myra, the woman Kristen thinks was her ma. So one day, Myra just up and took Kristen and run off, she did." Ned leaned back on his elbows and looked smug. "She did love that girl, I'll give that to her. But she deprived her of her heritage. Knew it all along. Now, I figure old Ian would pay a good sum to reclaim his missing daughter."

"So why haven't you told him?" Trevor asked calmly, even though he did not feel calm at all.

Ned chuckled. "I heard that you and Ian don't get along none, so I thought it just might be worth a few coins if I kept what I know to myself."

Trevor slid his chair back so fast that it tilted over backward. "You're a slimy bastard."

Ned sprang out of his chair and darted behind it just in case he needed to make a quick escape. "Bastards have to eat, Your Grace," he sneered. "And I'm sure the *ton* would love to hear how your little wife used to live with the scum and swindle people so that she could eat."

"Is he telling the truth?" Rodney asked.

Rage blinded Trevor as he moved around the desk. "I should choke you with my bare hands and rid the world of your presence."

"Now, wait a minute." Ned stiffened. "They even put yer high-and-mighty kind in jail for murder . . . now don't they?"

Rodney put out his hand and grabbed Trevor's arm just as he reached for Ned. "Think about it," Rodney cautioned, having the cooler head at the moment.

Trevor took a deep breath and willed himself to calm down. "I'm not going to kill you this time, because you are Hagan's father.'' He pushed the man with the flat of his hand against his chest so hard that he thudded against the wall. Trevor jerked his head around. "James!" Trevor shouted, then waited.

James rushed into the office.

"Give the man two hundred pounds and then escort him out of here," Trevor announced coldly.

James nodded and turned to leave. Ned started after him, but not fast enough. Trevor snatched Ned's arm and held him so tightly that Ned actually squealed with fright.

In the most deadly voice Trevor could manage, he said, "If I ever so much as hear of you again, you're a dead man."

Rodney pulled Trevor back, and Ned scurried like a rat from the room.

"How about a drink?" Rodney patted Trevor's shoulder before letting him go.

Too angry to speak, Trevor jerked his head in assent.

Rodney went to the liquor cabinet and poured them both a generous portion of Scotch, then came back and shoved a glass at Trevor. "Would you like to explain? Or is this none of my business?"

"Sit down," Trevor said tiredly. He forced himself to tell Rodney the complete story of what he knew about Kristen and her past.

"I'll be damned. I always knew there was something you were perhaps not telling me. But this? I'd never have known."

"That's because Kristen really is a lady. I just didn't know it. All the time I thought I'd turned her into a lady, but she had it in her blood the whole time."

"You know, I remember how confident you were that Kristen would never leave you because she had no money," Rodney pointed out. "Suddenly, she could possibly be quite wealthy. That puts an entirely different slant on the situation. What are you going to do?"

"I don't know. You would know that she had to be related to that bastard Johnstone."

"Has the man ever done anything to you?"

"No, not really. I have never even met him, but to listen to my grandmother, the man should be hanged. I knew nothing about the man's children."

"The dowager thinks everyone should be hanged."

"That's true." Trevor smiled and chuckled wryly. "I was taught to hate the Johnstones from an early age, and I've never questioned it." Trevor rubbed the back of his neck. "I don't know what I'm going to do."

"Do you realize that this means Hagan really isn't Kristen's brother? And everything she ever thought was true suddenly isn't. And what if Ian doesn't welcome her back?" Rodney pointed out.

"This won't be easy. Do you think Kristen will leave you for her family if she has to choose?" Rodney had asked the very question that tumbled around Trevor's head.

"I honest to God don't know."

"You love her, don't you?"

"I don't believe in love," Trevor snapped before he thought. "I enjoy being with her, and I desire her, but—" He ran his hand through his hair. "I don't know."

Kristen made friends with all the servants and spent more time with them than the duchess, but she and Constance did have moments when they got along. Kristen assumed that she was growing on the woman—maybe like a wart.

She had been looking for Hagan all morning when she

found herself wandering down the hall to the sunroom. She heard voices, so she paused before entering.

The door was ajar. Kristen peeked in and got the surprise of her life. Constance was sitting on a settee with her head bent down, Hagan snuggled up next to her.

Kristen listened shamelessly to their conversation.

"What's that word?" Hagan pointed.

"Foreboding," Constance answered.

"What does it mean?"

Constance answered him patiently, then said, "Would you like me to finish reading the story?"

"Yes, Grandmère. You do the voices of the people real good. I can picture them all."

"Good." She smiled. "Are you going to take a walk with me after the story?"

"Oh, yes. Can we go down to that big lake and throw stones like we did yesterday?"

Kristen didn't realize her eyes were full of tears until she couldn't see through them. She turned and went back down the hall. The scene she'd witnessed was so touching. She was so happy that Hagan was getting all the things she'd never had. What would it have been like to grow up in a loving family? She supposed she'd never know.

After witnessing the scene between Hagan and Constance, Kristen was so restless that she couldn't concentrate. She decided she would ride and see her new friend.

She rode across the meadows, giving her horse its head, and in no time she arrived at the Fullbright estate.

The Fullbright estate wasn't as big as Chatsworth, but it was affluent nonetheless. A groom quickly took her horse, and she mounted the steps and knocked. An elderly butler answered the door, and Kristen couldn't help wondering if all butlers were elderly.

She was shown to the drawing room to wait. She looked

around her, taking in the warm mauve colors in the furniture and rugs. Much different than Chatsworth.

Charity swept into the room, wearing a beautiful, mauve-colored gown. "Kristen, I'm so glad you've come. Have you finally settled into life at Chatsworth?"

"I'm surviving. But there is so little to do. The duchess directs the staff, of which I'm glad, since I've never done that sort of thing, but it leaves me with too much idle time," Kristen admitted. It hadn't been easy making ends meet in her old life, but she'd never been bored.

"Have you tried embroidering?" Charity asked.

Kristen frowned. "Afraid that isn't for me. I'm all thumbs." Except for picking pockets, she thought.

Charity nodded. "I agree. I'll teach you my favorite hobby. Archery."

"Is it difficult?"

"Come on, I'll show you," Charity said, taking Kristen's hand and pulling her along.

They hurried across the lawn toward the stables.

"How are the duchess and Hagan getting along?" Charity asked.

"Ye wouldn't believe it. Before I came over here, I found Constance reading stories to Hagan. I never thought the old girl had a heart, but in that brief moment, when she thought no one was looking, I saw a very loving woman."

"I would have to see that for myself before I could believe it," Charity said. "She was strict even when she raised Trevor. She was constantly telling Trevor how he should behave. He must do this, and he must do that, because he would become the next Duke of Chatsworth. He had so little childhood, I'm afraid."

When they passed the stables, Kristen grew concerned. She'd never been this far from the main house. "Where are we going?"

"Right here." Charity picked up a bow and arrow propped against the barn wall, then moved a good twenty-five feet away from the structure.

"What do ye do with that?"

"See that big circle?" A brightly colored target decorated the side of the barn.

"Aye."

"Well, we shoot these arrows and try to hit the small circle in the middle of the big circle."

"Why?"

"Just for fun." Charity laughed. "And it is much better than sewing."

Kristen watched her friend place the arrow onto the string of the bow.

Charity shot, and her arrow whizzed through the air. It landed next to the line of the big circle.

Kristen look doubtful as she picked up the strange object and mimicked what she'd just seen her friend do. She tugged the string and sent the arrow flying through the air, but it landed five feet away from the circle, catching the corner of the barn. "Oops."

"Well done for your first time." Charity giggled. "It will take lots of practice."

They took turns shooting as they passed the afternoon away.

"Let's sit a while," Charity suggested as their arms began to tire. She sank to the grass and patted the ground beside her. "I'm surprised Trevor let you come alone."

"He isn't here. I've not seen him in near four weeks."

Charity looked at her. "Where has he gone?"

"He said something had come up in London."

"That sounds just like him," Charity admitted. "He's always kept things to himself. It makes him a hard man to know."

"I dinna know how to break though that shell."

Charity shook her head. "I can't advise you there. I'm not sure anyone can get him to raise the castle gates."

Kristen sighed. She wasn't sure she'd ever find the answer either.

Ned Blume was feeling very pleased with himself. He had gotten money from the duke, and he now knew better than to try that road again, so he'd devised this new plan. And if it worked, he'd have a nice little income going again.

For now, he'd just have to sit and wait.

She always came this way, so his informants had told him, but he'd have a surprise for the ungrateful wench this time.

His patience finally paid off. His prey had just ridden into sight. She was a pretty one, he thought, but she always had been. Blume kicked his horse in the side and his mount bolted forward.

CHAPTER THIRTEEN

Kristen relished her ride as she returned from Charity's. Today she had ventured off without a groom so she could have a little freedom. She'd enjoyed her afternoon with Charity. At least it had made her forget about Trevor for a while.

He had been gone four weeks, and she hated to admit she missed the man, but she did. He'd become a part of her life in such a short time.

The pounding of hooves sounded much too close behind her, and for a brief moment she thought maybe Trevor had returned to surprise her. So she slowed her mount and turned in the saddle, her smile bright.

It wasn't Trevor.

The rider was coming too fast and seemed to be moving straight toward her. Had something happened at the house?

As the man drew closer, she saw who it was. Someone

she never wanted to see again. Her stepfather had found her! Kristen gathered her reins to make her escape; however, Ned was faster. He reach out and grabbed her horse's bridle.

"Not so fast, girl."

"What are ye doing here?" Kristen noticed Ned's clothing had changed, and that he was fairly clean. Where had he gotten the money for clothes and a horse?

"I kind of missed me little family around me, and I wanted to see them."

"Yer a bloody liar. What is it ye really want?"

"Kristen, Kristen, Kristen." He leered at her, his yellow teeth turning her stomach. "You should be nicer to your old man. I could arrange for your little brother to disappear very quickly, you know."

"What do ye mean by that?"

"Don't ya worry about it."

"I am worried." Fright shook her, confusing her thoughts.

"Hagan could make me a good little thief," Ned went on as if Kristen weren't there. "I've been thinking I could teach the boy a few things, and he'd come in right handy."

Kristen swallowed hard, trying not to reveal her anger. "Ye had better leave Hagan alone."

"Now, that's where ya should be real nice to me, if ya don't want me catching the baggage and taking him back to London."

Kristen's annoyance increased when she found that her hands were shaking. "Trevor would kill ye."

"He might, and then again he might not." Ned shrugged. "He'd have to find me first. And I can think of plenty of places to hide." Sarcasm laced his voice.

"I hate ye," she spat.

Ned reached to touch the side of her face, and Kristen

jerked away. She didn't want his filthy hands on her. His
touch turned her stomach.

"Is that any way to talk to me?" Annoyance crossed
Ned's face. "I should give ya the back of me hand right
now for speaking to me all disrespectful like that. It would
pay for ya to listen."

"What do ye want?"

"I want ya to fetch me some valuables from your new
house, so I can keep myself up."

"What did ye do with the money Trevor gave ye?"

Ned shrugged matter-of-factly. "That didn't last long.
Had a terrible thirst, and I needed some things. But I'm
thinking one or two pieces of jewelry can make things a
little easier for me."

"I don't steal anymore. Especially not for the likes of
ye," she said.

"I'd think twice about that if I were ya. Or maybe you
don't give a damn about that brother of yours."

"Leave Hagan alone!"

"I will as long as you cooperate. I expect ya to bring me
something valuable in two days."

"And if I don't?"

"Then you can kiss Hagan good riddance." He gave
her a twisted smile. "Don't think the high-and-mighty
wouldn't be very interested in knowing where you came
from. It would sure bring the mighty duke down a couple
of notches. It might even put the dowager in her grave
where she belongs."

"I hope ye rot in Hell."

Ned bent over her until he was close to her face, foul
breath and all. "If I do, rest assured I'll take ya with me."
He kissed her on the lips, pinching her cheek painfully as
she tried to get away.

Kristen slapped him and turned away to spit on the

ground. It was all she could to keep from retching. Nudging her mount, she took off racing across the countryside.

Just when she thought she had found a little bit of happiness, her past came back to haunt her. Would it always be like this?

What was she going to do? She could go into her little stash and give Ned some of that, Kristen thought. Then what would she have to fall back on?

She would have to start stealing from the household. She hated that, and if she started, would there ever be a stop to it? She was damned, for sure.

Tears streamed down her face as she neared the stables. She dashed them away, then dismounted.

"Are you all right, miss?" Baxter asked.

"No, but don't worry. I'll think of something," she said, leaving Baxter scratching his head.

Kristen had scarcely gotten control of herself when she entered the house and ran into her missing husband. She bumped his shoulder, and the connection forced her to back up. She rubbed her nose as she stared at him. If it were possible, he was even better-looking than she remembered. Dressed in a chocolate-brown coat and cream-colored pants with gleaming Hessian boots, he was dashing and extremely regal in his stance. Evidently she'd surprised him too, because he'd yet to say anything—he just stared.

"Ye've returned," she said as she tried to gather her wits. She had wanted him to come home, but when three weeks had turned to four, her hopes had faded. Then here he was without a word that he was coming or that he'd missed her.

She smiled at him; however, Trevor didn't return the smile.

"Why were you out without a groom?"

"I missed ye too," she quipped sarcastically.

"Answer me, Kristen."

Her nerves were stretched to the limit. First Ned had threatened her, and now she was faced with an irritated Trevor! "Because I felt like it," she snapped.

"Do not go riding again unless you are accompanied by someone!"

Kristen ignored him.

It took a moment, but finally Trevor's face softened. "It's good to be back. I was gone so long. I missed you."

"Did ye now?"

Trevor stared at her. He couldn't believe he'd said that to her. His intentions all along had been to come and go. But the time away hadn't diminished his desire for her. Evidently, it had for Kristen, because she was treating him with ice-coldness. He wanted to touch her, hold her. Despite all his vows, desire burned deep within him. He placed his hands on her arms. She stiffened, but didn't shake them off. He didn't want her, he told himself.

He didn't need her . . .

But he most assuredly wanted to kiss her and hold her more than anything else.

He pulled her close and Kristen turned her frowning face up to him. "I did miss you," he whispered before his mouth covered hers.

Pleased with her response, he deepened his kiss, and soon his tongue was mating with hers. He'd missed her more than just a little, he realized.

"I see you are home," Constance said from behind them. Reluctantly, Trevor let Kristen go.

"Good to see you, Grandmère." Trevor stepped closer and embraced the older woman. "I hope you are feeling well."

"As good as an old woman can feel. Did you get your ships ordered?"

"I did. But it will be six months before I can get both ships. I managed to attain one vessel, but I had to cancel several shipments I had booked."

"Ye've had trouble?" Kristen realized that Trevor hadn't told her anything about his business. Of course, she hadn't bothered to ask either.

"You could say that." Trevor frowned. "I lost two ships with very expensive cargo."

"I'm sorry," Kristen said because she didn't know what else to say. Trevor turned back to speak with his grandmother, and Kristen was glad because she didn't know how to discuss his business. There was so much she didn't know, but she made herself a promise to find out so they'd have something to talk about next time.

Her thoughts shifted to her other problem: her stepfather. If ever she wished someone dead, it was that man. She knew he wouldn't stop with just a few trinkets; he'd always wanted more.

She had no choice but to steal for him, though. Because she didn't doubt he'd get to Hagan somehow. And Ned would probably carry through with his threat to ruin Trevor.

If only she could tell Trevor. But none of this was his fault. They had made a bargain, and Trevor had kept his part. Perhaps, if he loved her, things would be different.

But he didn't.

She knew she could hold Ned off for a little while with the things she had already gotten, and then she knew what she would have to do—take Hagan and run. It was that or keep meeting Ned's demands forever.

Later that night Trevor had Kristen very much on his mind as he opened the door to her room. Should he tell her about her parents? What would she do? And his grandmother—that was another matter. She would have a royal fit when she found out Kristen belonged to the man Constance hated.

Kristen sat on a sateen stool in front of her mirror, brushing her hair. Just the sight of her made Trevor's loins tighten. He stepped behind her, picked up a strand of auburn hair, and rubbed it between his fingers. Silk, he thought. Just like her body. "It's been a long time," he told her.

"Aye, it has." She nodded her head, and her eyes locked with his. "I was beginning to think you'd forgotten where home was."

"Never." He finally smiled. "Kristen, have you ever noticed that Hagan doesn't have the same accent as yourself?"

She shrugged and stood. "Never thought much about it, but I don't remember my mother having my accent either. Perhaps, I took after me da. Why do ye ask?"

Now was the time to tell her. She had every right to know, but when he opened his mouth, something entirely different came out. "No reason. Come here."

Deciding he would tell her later, he pulled her against him. Right now, he wanted the woman he held so much that it overruled every other thought in his head.

Hunger ignited in him as he kissed her. The feeling was so overpowering that his arm tightened, pulling her closer as his tongue tasted her sweet mouth.

Evidently, she'd missed him too, because she didn't resist him in the least. Her arms slid up his chest and wrapped around him as she pressed herself against his arousal.

"Did you miss me?" Trevor whispered against her throat. For some odd reason, he had to hear it from her.

"Aye," she said breathlessly.

Her admittance pushed him over the edge. He swept her up in his arms and pushed through the connecting door, then shoved it closed with his foot. He laid her on the coverlet of his bed, and her hair spread out across the bed like hot coals spraying in a grate. God, she was a beauty.

She slipped her hands behind his neck and drew him down to her. "I want you," she whispered.

Trevor dragged her against him with a groan. His mouth eagerly took hers and raw passion exploded. His tongue explored her mouth with tender strokes as he deepened the kiss. She clung to him as though she couldn't get enough, which pleased him very much.

In very little time they had disposed of their clothes, tossing them carelessly on the floor, their eyes never leaving each other. Finally they were holding each other again.

Kristen couldn't get over how Trevor made her feel when he kissed her. He'd actually robbed her breath until she was talking in ragged gasps. She was withering within his arms, wanting more. Now she began to explore his mouth. The minute she did that, his arms tightened around her.

Every time Kristen was with this man, it was a completely different experience. When she thought she could feel no more, he would awaken a new sensation within her. She marveled at the taste and feel of him.

His lips were hot and insistent as Kristen lowered her hand ever so slowly and marveled at the texture of his skin beneath her fingertips. His skin trembled everywhere she touched, until her fingers found his arousal, and then he gasped. She closed her hand around him, and felt the warmth of him. She realized he'd suddenly gone very still. "I'm not hurting ye, am I?" she asked.

"N—no, love."

She thought he sounded funny as she rubbed and stroked him, and she found she liked having control over him. Usually, he was doing things to her body.

Finally, he moaned, brought her hand up to his lips and kissed her fingers. "I cannot endure any more of that, love. Now it's my turn," he whispered.

He kissed a path down her throat until he found a taut nipple. His lips closed tightly, and he began the sweet torture. Her hands twisted in his hair. She enjoyed the strange sensation running through her body. His hand slipped between her legs, and she gasped when his fingers slipped between her curls and began to stroke her, making her wild with need. Her hips moved restlessly. She could hear her own whimpers as she clung to him.

She couldn't stand any more, she thought as she tugged on him to kiss her again. He captured her lips with his and the hunger inside her begged for fulfillment. "I want you to make love to me now," she pleaded.

Trevor had waited as long as he could. He plunged inside her, and Kristen wrapped her legs and arms around him. She belonged to him, and he claimed her as he poured himself into her and they became one.

The demons that plagued each of them dissolved and, for a little while, they knew peace and contentment.

Kristen felt gloriously happy when she woke up in Trevor's arms. She felt so warm and protected as she lay in the morning light.

Then her stepfather's warning came barging back into her head, and she tensed at the thought of having to do what he wanted. She really had been trying to be good since she'd promised Trevor she would. Now the sorry business would start again. Somehow she would have to find a way to honor both promises. A way out of the house was what she needed, and without being noticed. She remembered all too well Trevor's warning yesterday about her riding alone.

"What are you thinking about, love?" Trevor's deep voice startled her, and she flinched.

Feeling silly, she realized he couldn't possibly read her thoughts. "Oh, nothing really." She hoped her voice didn't betray her distress.

He brushed a finger up and down her arm in a leisurely manner, teasing her newly sensitive skin. "I think it's about time you learned how to run the household. It is, after all, your responsibility."

"I thought it was yer grandmother's."

"Only until I wed."

Mixed feelings surged through her. " 'Tis perfectly fine with me if she continues. After all, she's been doing it for so many years."

"But it's your job."

" 'Tis a job I dinna know how to do." The admission stung, but it was the truth.

"Then you will learn."

Kristen rose up and leaned back on her elbow. She could see Trevor wasn't going to take no for an answer, so she reluctantly agreed with a sigh. "As you wish."

He chuckled. "It's about time you learned to be obedient."

Kristen punched him in the side with her hand, then scooted out of bed before he could catch her.

She didn't want to run the house. Most of the servants were her friends. How could she order them about?

*   *   *

Kristen tried to keep her mind on Constance's instructions while she followed the duchess around the house. She noticed that Constance was moving more slowly than normal, and wondered if the woman was feeling ill. The duchess would never admit she was sick.

Kristen learned that everyone in the house had a special job they were supposed to do. There was a head cook and her staff, and that was just the beginning. There were so many maids that she lost count. The butler seemed to carry the most weight, and even though Frederick was old, he commanded respect when he spoke to the other servants.

She was instructed on the proper way for the servants to serve dinner and tea.

When they went into the kitchen, Kristen noticed a young woman scrubbing a spot on a tablecloth. Kristen thought it impossible to get that purple stain out, but after a few minutes the stain was gone.

"How did ye do that?"

The girl's eyes grew large as she stared up at Kristen and said, "It's water mixed with alkaline salt, black soap, and bullock's gall." She gave Kristen a quick smile. "It's never failed, mum."

"Really?"

"Yes, mum."

"Kristen!" Constance snapped, and Kristen jumped. The woman didn't sound sick anymore, and as usual, she'd once again made Kristen feel like a child.

Constance said nothing else until they were out of the kitchen. Then she turned and said, "It isn't proper to mingle with the help. Remember your station."

Kristen knew better than to argue. She was losing precious time, and she needed to finish this ridiculous training and leave the house.

The sun was slowly sinking behind the trees when Constance finally grew tired and decided that Kristen had learned enough for one day. She dismissed Kristen.

Kristen breathed a sigh of relief and headed straight for her room. Yanking open the bottom drawer, she grabbed the red silk scarf and untied the knot. She selected a brooch and a ring, and slipped them into her pocket. Then, deciding she was in too big a hurry to refold the scarf properly, she laid it loosely in the drawer and shut it. A little too late, she noticed that part of the scarf had caught in the drawer, but she'd fix that later. For now she had to hurry.

Kristen hurried down the stairs, wondering where Hagan was. She couldn't remember seeing him all day. She hoped he hadn't gone out riding; she hadn't had the chance to warn him about Ned's presence yet.

She ran to the stable. "Hello, Baxter," Kristen called as she opened Paznell's stall. "Have you seen Hagan?"

"No, mum. He hasn't been to the stables today."

"Good. Will ye saddle Paznell for me?"

"Certainly, mum." He took the mare's halter. "I'll find a groom to accompany you."

"No!" When Baxter's eyebrows shot up, Kristen realized how sharp she sounded.

"But His Grace said—"

Kristen waved her hand. "I know. But I'm only going down to the lake today instead of a long ride. It would be senseless to take up someone's time. I don't think he meant for ye to waste your time unless I was leaving the grounds." She hoped God wouldn't strike her down for her lie.

"Well, in that case . . ." Baxter agreed reluctantly as he tightened the cinch.

Kristen didn't wait a moment once she was in the saddle. She spurred the horse and raced toward the lake. However, once there, she veered left and raced to where she was supposed to meet Ned.

When she arrived at the spot, she looked for Ned. She didn't see him anywhere, and her heart plummeted. She was too late. He'd be hungry for revenge.

"About damn time ya showed up," Ned said as he rode out of a clump of trees. "Do ya have something for me?"

Kristen didn't answer with words, but reached into her pocket. "Here." She shoved the jewelry at him.

He looked at the lovely items, turning each one over in his hand. The dying light caught in the gems and seemed to make them glow. Grinning, he licked his lips. "A few more of these and I'll be set."

"Wait a minute," Kristen cried. That was not what she'd agreed to. "What I gave ye is enough."

"Not hardly," Ned said, casting a contemptuous glance over her. "I want to make sure my future is safe. I'm not getting any younger, ya know."

Kristen wanted to say that dead would be a preferable state for him, but she held her tongue. She was going to have to do something; she couldn't let him control her future. He would always come up with an excuse to want more valuables. It would never be enough, and she'd be just as much under his thumb as she had been on the streets. She'd have to think of something to stop him, but for the moment, she'd just play his game.

"Get me some more and meet me here tomorrow."

Kristen glared at him, then turned her horse to leave. How in the world was she going to get out of this muddle? She remembered how Trevor had reacted the last time he'd met Ned. If she told Trevor, he might kill Ned. She didn't want Trevor to go to jail.

No. This was her problem. She'd solve it somehow herself.

CHAPTER FOURTEEN

As Kristen lay in bed, she experienced something she never had before . . . guilt. She lay beside Trevor regretting that she'd broken her word to him. She thought about confessing and asking him to help her, but she couldn't. She couldn't burden him with her problems, and she would never let Trevor hurt Ned. Not because she cared about Ned, but because she cared about Trevor. After what seemed like hours, she finally fell asleep.

Late in the night the sound of footsteps in the hall, immediately followed by someone pounding on the bedroom door, woke her.

Kristen gasped, then raised up on her elbows as Trevor slid from the bed.

"Just a minute," Trevor called out. He went to open the door. "What is it, Frederick?"

"The dowager duchess, sir. She—she's had a seizure." Frederick's eyes showed the tortured dullness of disbelief as he twisted his hands together in dismay. "You had better come quickly."

"Send for the doctor. I'll be right there." Trevor came back to the bed to fetch his robe.

"What is it?" Kristen said sleepily, peeking out from the covers.

"It's Grandmère."

"What?"

"She's had a seizure. I'm going to her."

"I'll be there in just a minute." Kristen threw off the covers.

Trevor hurried down the hall unsure of how many more attacks his grandmother could survive. She became frailer every time she fell ill.

Trevor shoved open the door. The room was bathed in a dim yellow light from the candles beside the bed. He could see her still form, and immediately went to her bedside. Her eyes were closed. He propped a hip on the side of the bed and picked up her hand so he could hold it in his. Her skin felt cold and dry.

"Grandmère," Trevor said softly, and waited for Constance to look at him.

Finally, her eyelids fluttered open, and a weak smile touched her lips, "Trevor."

"This is a fine way to get attention," he teased, though he wanted to weep. "The last time you did this, I ended up with a wife. Now I'll wager you'll demand a baby."

"Yes, you have been a good grandson." She gave him a weak smile. "Although Kristen wouldn't have been the wife I'd have chosen for you." Constance clutched at her chest.

"Calm down, Grandmère. Take a deep breath." A sense of inadequacy swept over Trevor. "The doctor will be here shortly."

She looked him straight in the eyes. "I don't think I can wait for him."

Trevor felt an uncertainty as it crept into his expression, but he tried to keep his voice calm. "Nonsense."

"As I was saying," Constance added with a slight smile of defiance, "I wouldn't have picked Kristen, but now that I've gotten to know her, I see something special in her. She is so full of life that she has a sparkle in her. I just hope you'll be lucky enough to discover it." Constance spoke with quiet but desperate firmness. A light flush stained her cheeks.

"I can see now what you first saw in her," Constance continued. "It's something very special and rare."

"I'm not sure what you're saying," Trevor said, trying to conceal his confusion. "What do you see?"

Constance wished she could have taught Trevor more about love. On that subject he seemed to be completely in the dark. But she knew he couldn't go through life keeping everyone at arm's length. If he was truly going to be happy, he would have to trust someone with his heart and be open to her. She knew he associated love with hurt.

"That, Trevor, you'll have to find out for yourself."

"You're not making any sense." His eyes narrowed as he held her gaze. "I married the girl, and I like her."

"Yes, I can see that." Her tongue was heavy with sarcasm. "These eyes are not that old." She gripped his hand. "If you're not careful, you'll lose her. I watched Kristen while you were gone. She is just as lost as you are. You need to tell her that you love her."

"But I don't," he muttered uneasily.

"Do you not?" Constance answered weakly.

The door opened, and Kristen came in and moved toward the bed. "Is there something I can do?"

"Just hold an old woman's hand." Constance held her

hand up. "Trevor, go get Hagan." She watched her grandson leave, and she said a small prayer that he would find his way. She'd done all she could.

Once Trevor had gone, Constance squeezed Kristen's hand. "I know I've not been easy on you, but I only had Trevor's interests at heart. I want you to have something." She reached over and opened the drawer next to the bed. Pulling out a black velvet pouch, she handed it to Kristen.

"What's this?"

"Something that is very dear to me."

Kristen opened the pouch and shook the contents in her hand. The necklace that Kristen had stolen for Constance lay glittering up at her.

"I canna accept—this is yers."

"It will do me no good where I am going and I want you to have the necklace and think of me when you wear it."

"I canna accept something so nice."

Constance didn't push the necklace on Kristen. There would be another way to give the child the gift she most cherished. "Hear me," Constance said with a sigh, her breathing labored. "My time is growing short. You must get Trevor to open up if you ever want to keep him."

"I've tried."

"Try harder. Remember, everyone he has ever given his love to has let him down. After a while he just grew cold inside."

Kristen gave a choked, desperate laugh. "But I dinna know what to do."

Constance reach up and pointed to Kristen's chest. "Look deep inside yourself, and you'll find out what to do."

When Constance's hand dropped limply to her chest, Kristen gasped.

"Are ye all right?"

The door flew open, and Hagan scrambled into the room followed by Trevor.

"Grandmère!" Hagan climbed up on the stool beside the bed until he was at Constance's elbow. "What's wrong, Grandmère?"

She turned her head and smiled. "There's my big boy."

"What's wrong?"

"I'm tired, Hagan." She cupped his chin. "Sometimes people just wear out, but I do love you. Come closer and let me whisper in your ear."

Hagan straightened, then nodded. "I love you too, Grandmère." He reached over and hugged her. "You need to go to sleep. You've got to finish my story." When she didn't say anything, Hagan shook her hand, but received no response. He looked at Kristen. "I think she's sleeping. We'd better be quiet." He slipped down from the stool and looked up at Kristen. "Why are you crying, Kristen?"

Kristen took his hand. "Come on, I'll put ye to bed." She just couldn't tell Hagan tonight that Constance had died.

Kristen glanced at Trevor, her heart going out to him. The stricken look on his face tore at her heart, but she had no earthly idea how to comfort him. She touched his arm and squeezed. "I'm sorry."

As she said the words, a mask dropped into place on Trevor's face, covering the hurt and pain she'd seen only a moment ago. How would she ever get past that wall he'd erected between them?

She felt completely helpless.

Trevor went through the motions of dressing. He wanted so much to see Kristen, but he didn't have time. He'd been so unorganized since the death that he'd completely ignored his wife. It seemed like days, but it had only been a day.

He stepped through the connecting doors between their rooms to find Kristen's room empty. Disappointment flooded him. Perhaps she had already gone downstairs.

He shrugged. There was nothing left to do but join her. As he turned to leave, a red scarf caught his attention. It was hanging out of a closed drawer. He smiled for the first time in several days. The one thing he hadn't managed to teach his wife was tidiness.

Moving over to the dresser, he bent to adjust the drawer, and pulled on the knob. It seemed to be stuck, so he pulled a little harder, only to successfully land the drawer and its contents on the floor at his feet.

"Damn," he muttered as he stooped to retrieve the scattered contents.

As he replaced everything, he reached for the red scarf, which he realized was tied around an object. Carefully, he unloosened the knot. Before his eyes lay a vast array of jewelry, which he couldn't recall giving his wife.

Kristen hadn't kept her promise!

Trevor frowned. His little thief had been stealing all the while and hiding her valuables. For what? He didn't like the thought that came to mind.

Kristen was stealing so she could leave him.

Kristen searched for the right words to tell Hagan that Constance had died. When she finally found them, he wept like she'd never seen him weep before.

She held Hagan tightly in her arms and let him cry knowing he needed to get everything out.

" 'Tis time to stop crying, Hagan," Kristen said gently

"Trevor will be down in a moment, and then we'll go to the burial plot. Do ye understand?"

"But why did she have to die?"

" 'Tis God's way. She'd been sick for a long time, and her body had simply grown tired of the battle. I'll wager she is feeling much better now. She's probably dancing a jig with the angels."

"Do you really think so?" Hagan gave a teary-eyed grin.

"Aye, I do."

"I like that."

"I want ye to be strong for Trevor." She looked at Hagan. "This will be a hard day for him."

"He's going to miss her too."

Trevor's footsteps announced his arrival, and they both turned. "Are you ready?" he said from the doorway.

Kristen stared at Trevor, and an odd sensation crept up the back of her neck . . . an odd feeling she didn't particularly like. There was a coldness in his eyes she'd never seen before. Perhaps she was being overly sensitive. After all, neither of them had slept after . . .

She smiled at Trevor, hoping to reassure him. He nodded, and turned. Again Kristen felt cold. She took Hagan's hand and followed Trevor, unsure of these strange warning feelings that ran through her body.

The air felt cold today, Kristen thought as the drizzle came down in a fine mist that coated everything it touched, clinging to the mourners like a shroud as they stood beside the empty, dark hole.

Kristen stood between Trevor and Hagan. Her brother's soft sobs made Kristen ache inside, but not half as much as she ached for Trevor.

He stood like a stone statue, never showing any emotion.

She tried to hold his hand, and he let her for a few moments before pulling away.

Pulling away . . . that was exactly what Trevor was doing to her. What little ground she'd gained since they were married was rapidly slipping away, and she didn't know what to do. To be truthful, she was scared to death.

After the small wooden coffin was lowered, Hagan clutched her hand tighter. She leaned down to whisper in his ear, "It will be all right, Hagan. The duchess has gone to a far better place. Now she'll be an angel, and she can look down and watch ye."

He looked up at her with tears swimming in his huge brown eyes. "Do you really think so?"

Kristen could feel her eyes burning, but she held back the tears as she nodded her head. "Aye, I do." Kristen had seen such a change in Constance since they'd come to live there. Maybe they had made a difference and Constance had finally been happy before she died. "Now she's yer guardian angel, sent to heaven to watch over ye."

Trevor placed a hand on Kristen's waist and murmured in a toneless voice, "It's time to go back."

They made their way from the family cemetery, across the back lawns to the house. All three walked in silence until they reached the house.

Once inside, Trevor stopped and addressed her. "I have something to take care of. I'll see you later." Trevor excused himself and went into his study, leaving Kristen and Hagan standing in the hallway . . . alone.

Kristen never had a chance to say anything. She was trying to understand. She was trying to help. He just needed time to be alone, she convinced herself, and she needed time with Hagan. So for now, she wouldn't worry about Trevor. Hagan was her problem. Maybe things would work out.

Time. That was all Trevor needed.

Alone in his study, Trevor went to the windows and leaned against the windowsill. He watched the raindrops as they slid down the lead-glass panes like giant tears.

His grandmother had been a part of his life for as long as he could remember. When he was a child, she had been his pillar of strength. She'd always been demanding and quarrelsome, but he knew her love was a constant thing he could count on.

He had wanted so much to have his mother's love, but he'd learned much too young that he wasn't allowed to touch her. He might disturb her clothes or her hair. Trevor couldn't remember ever hugging his mother, and the only thing his father had done was shake Trevor's hand, saying, "You have to be a man, son. Not a bit of fluff."

For a brief moment today, he'd considered hugging Kristen to him. He wanted so badly to bury his face in her soft hair and forget . . . forget about everything . . . all his responsibilities . . . everything.

But that wasn't the way life worked. Life was for responsible, hardworking people. They were the ones who got ahead in life . . . ahead to what? Well, he had no answers for himself, he thought as he turned from the window and moved to the liquor cabinet. He wanted to make this dull hurt go away.

"Kristen," he said to the empty room as he took the stopper off the decanter and splashed Scotch into a glass. He had married her as a business arrangement to please his grandmother. It was a firm deal. He had gotten a wife with no strings attached, and she'd gotten a roof over her head. But now . . .

Now, he knew Kristen was a true Johnstone robbed of her birthright. She was a very wealthy young woman on her own. She didn't need his money, and she could walk out on him anytime. "Which she was evidently planning to do anyway," he murmured as he brought the glass to his lips.

He should tell her the truth. Of course she had the right to know. If she knew, would she leave him? He took another swallow of the golden liquid. Probably. Anyone he'd ever cared about had left him.

He placed the glass down, and it bumped into the crystal decanter with a loud clink. The noise echoed around the room.

"Care for her?"

All right, he'd admit he did care for Kristen. And he didn't want her to leave him. What was he going to do? He wasn't sure, he decided as he slipped down into the overstuffed chair with a bottle in one hand and a glass in the other.

Right now he just wanted the pain in his chest to go away.

Kristen was worried sick.

Trevor had stayed in his study all last night and most of today. Well, he'd have to come out sooner or later, she thought as she went downstairs to find him. He'd have to eat.

She rapped on the door. There was no answer. This time she knocked a little louder. Still no answer. She twisted the knob and barged inside. Enough was enough.

Kristen hadn't taken more than a few steps when she

smelled the liquor. Her stomach tightened at the sour smell that filled the room. She almost heaved.

Not this.

Not Trevor. Please, God. Don't do this.

She stared at him, her hand to her lips to keep from screaming.

Trevor slowly lifted his head off the desk. His eyes were bloodshot and a day's worth of stubble clung to his face. "It's you," he managed, slurring out the words.

She felt sick. She gagged. She was reliving a nightmare, and all the buried memories of abuse came flooding back to her. Why Trevor, of all people?

"Here ye sit drunk!" Kristen waved her hand. "While I was worried to death about ye!"

"You were worried about me?" Trevor's head lolled as he tried to focus. "And why was that? You afraid I'd break our little agreement now that Grandmère has passed on?" He sneered.

The question stopped her. "Nay, I'd not thought about that," she admitted. "I was worried about yer sorry hide because I hadn't seen ye since yesterday. 'Tisn't good to keep all yer emotions bottled up inside ye."

Trevor staggered to his feet. "That is so touching, love." He started for her. If she was going to leave him, he'd make it easy for her to go. And deep down he knew that was what she wanted.

"Is it that hard to believe that someone should care for ye?" she asked.

"Now that you mention it . . . yes." He managed a sarcastic smile. "The only thing most people want from me is money."

Kristen held up her hand in front of her. "Don't ye come near me. Yer drunk."

He bumped into a chair. "So I am."

"Do ye do this often?" Kristen asked, her voice shaking.

"Hardly ever," he admitted as he stopped in front of her, swaying as he searched for balance. "Kristen, I've found out you are related to that damned Johnstone."

That notion stopped her colder than the liquor. "What are ye talking about?"

"Your stepfather paid me a visit and told me a very interesting story about you. Seems you were taken from Johnstone's son and his wife when ye were a wee babe," he said, imitating her accent. "The woman you think was your mother was the maid."

"What?" Kristen's eyes grew wide with disbelief. "You're making this up. Why are ye lying to me?"

"I only wish to God I were," Trevor said. "You are a very wealthy lady. You don't need me anymore." He gave a cynical laugh. "You probably never did."

"I dinna ken any of this."

Trevor grabbed her arm. "What's not to understand, Kristen. You *are* a bloody Johnstone. You shouldn't have been brought up in the streets. It was a grave injustice to you, and I'm simply giving you back your life."

"Ye knew I was a Johnstone when ye met me."

"There are many Johnstones, but if you recall, you told me yourself your father was dead and couldn't possibly be related to my neighbors."

"So what am I to do?"

"That's up to you, Kristen." He reached for her. He could feel the heat of her body beneath his fingertips. He needed to hold her one last time, but she jerked away from him as if his touch repulsed her.

She went very still. "Yer drunk. Don't touch me!"

"Now I see." His jaw was clenched, his eyes slightly narrowed. "You've no need for me now that you know you have a family and money. I suppose you won't be needing these." He reached in his pocket and pulled out a handkerchief full of jewels. "You were planning to leave me all along. As soon as you had enough stashed away," he accused her.

Kristen gasped. He'd somehow found the stolen jewels, and he must have thought she'd been stealing all along. But she hadn't. She had kept her promise since coming to Chatsworth.

" 'Tis not what ye think," Kristen said.

"Isn't it? You promised not to steal! Didn't I give you everything you would need? And yet you still chose to steal from me."

"If ye'd let me explain—"

He held up a hand to stop her. "Why? So you could tell me more lies? Just when I thought we had something special, you managed to destroy what little belief I had." He shoved her away. "I don't want to see you anymore."

"Please." She reached for his arm.

Without thinking Trevor pulled her to him, his lips crushing down on hers in a punishing kiss. He would get free of her one way or the other.

He told himself to let her go, but he was already dragging her firmly against his hard body, his mouth savoring her sweetness. He wanted her just as badly now as he had the first time he'd laid eyes on her. Yet he couldn't fathom why she could evoke such strong emotions in him when no other woman had. There seemed to be no logical explanation.

Her lips tasted so sweet, he didn't want to stop kissing her. He wanted to forget she'd deceived him, he wanted to forget who she really was, and he wanted, for once in his life, to be able to trust someone.

Kristen knew this kiss had begun with Trevor trying to punish her. For some strange reason Trevor was trying to push her away from him. But somewhere along the line, the kiss had turned from hurting to softness. However, the smell of liquor once again brought back dreaded memories of beatings, her stepfather's sloppy kisses . . . his awful groping . . .

She didn't want Trevor like this. She put her hands on his chest and pushed him away.

Trevor looked down at her kiss-swollen lips. He wanted to say something sweet, but the demons in his head brought out his doubts stronger than ever. "Why don't you go ahead and leave too? Everyone else has," he snarled at her.

She stared at him, her eyes large and liquid. Trevor could see the hurt he'd caused. But it was better this way. Now they'd both have their freedom.

"What are you waiting for? Get out."

Tears streaked down her cheeks as she turned and ran from the room.

Why hadn't she argued?

Why hadn't she begged to stay with him? Trevor ran a hand through his hair, and then looked at the door in front of him. The door that Kristen had just passed through.

"It could have been so good, Kristen. It could have been—" Trevor slurred out the words. His legs seemed to melt beneath him. He saw the floor rushing up to meet him.

Then he saw nothing as he passed out and hit the floor.

CHAPTER FIFTEEN

Too numb to cry, Kristen fled to her room.

She quickly changed into a dark brown riding habit. She should have known everything was too good to be true. Just when she thought her life was changing and she'd begun to trust Trevor, he'd let her down. He'd turned toward the bottle to drown his problems instead of sharing them with her. She wanted no part of drinking.

She had to get out of this place before he became violent. She'd seen it happen too many times in the past, and she knew what would come next. And hadn't he told her to get out?

Grabbing a few dresses out of her wardrobe, she stuffed them into a valise, then hurried to Hagan's room and packed his clothes. She picked up the valise, looked around the room sadly, then hurried downstairs to look for Hagan. She checked several places before she finally found him in the servants' quarters playing with his friends.

"Come on, Hagan!" she said, sounding gruffer than she intended.

He scrambled to his feet and stumbled toward her. "What's wrong?"

"Dinna ask right now." She shoved a bag a him. "Hurry now," she urged, tugging on his hand as they hurried toward the stables.

"You're walking too fast, Kristen!"

Kristen realized she was practically dragging the child, and slowed down. "I'm sorry."

"What's wrong? Where are we going?"

"We're leaving Chatsworth," Kristen stated firmly.

"I don't want to go. I like it here."

"I like it here too, but Trevor no longer wants us."

"Why?"

" 'Tis hard to explain. We are going to meet my family. Hopefully, we can stay with them."

"We're going back to Pa?"

"No." She frowned at him. "I'll explain it all to ye as soon as we're riding."

When they reached the stables, Baxter was quick in saddling the horses. "I will get a groom to accompany you, mum."

Kristen didn't bother to argue. She knew Ned was lurking out there somewhere, and there was no time to waste on words. Besides, she could send the horses back with the groom once she and Hagan reached their destination.

After they started riding, Kristen slowed her horse so she could talk to Hagan. She began explaining what she'd been told, and he listened patiently until she finished.

"I don't care what they say. You'll always be my sister."

"I know that, Hagan." She reached down and he reached up until their fingers touched. "I love you," she said. And at the same time, she realized how she would have loved to hear Trevor say those words to her.

Hagan grinned. "Yeah, I know."

With that, they urged the horses forward and galloped until Scotgrow, the Scottish house of her grandfather, came into sight. Kristen pulled up on her horse and gazed at the house in front of her. The building was long under a span roof with crowstepped gables and many chimneys. The most unusual things were the windows of all shapes and sizes, in all kinds of odd positions.

Kristen waited for the groom to catch up with her. "Ye can go back now. We'll not be returning."

"Are you sure, ma'am?"

She nodded. "Yes." She climbed down from her mount and motioned for Hagan to do the same.

She watched as the groom rode away, taking with him her last contact with Trevor.

Once they reached the huge house, Kristen stood a moment until her legs, which had suddenly grown weak, could support her. She realized she was shaking and more than a little scared. However, she had come this far. She squared her shoulders and marched up to an archway that housed the main door.

She knocked.

The huge black oak door opened slowly, and a medium-sized man dressed in a kilt stared at them. "What do ye be wantin'?" he said. Then he looked her over from head to toe.

"Look, Kristen, he has on a skirt." Hagan pointed, then giggled.

" 'Tis a kilt," the man said, looking at Hagan from beneath bushy eyebrows. His gaze shifted to Kristen again; then his eyes widened.

"Saints above," he muttered. Turning, he shouted. "Ian, come quickly!"

Kristen had yet to utter a word, but she was beginning to think he was going to leave her on the doorstep forever. What would happen to them if they were sent away? They would be back on the streets, and all of this would have been as real as a dream.

" 'Tis rude to leave us standin' here," Kristen pointed out. "Are ye going to invite us in?"

"Aye." He stepped back and swept his hand to bid them enter.

They moved past him and stood in a huge hallway. Kristen and Hagan stared up at the banners hanging on every wall. The furniture seemed to be oversized, but there was color everywhere . . . bright reds and oranges. It was warm and inviting—a big difference from Chatsworth.

"What's all the bloody fuss, Darroch?" came a bellow from the far end of the great hall. The sound was followed by one of the largest men Kristen had ever seen.

When the man drew near, she could make out his features. His hair was gray, yet she could still see signs of its former red, giving her a glimpse of what his hair must have been like in his youth. His eyebrows were bushy, his features harsh, but his eyes were exactly like her own.

As he stared at Kristen, a variety of emotions filtered across his face. Then his eyes sharpened, and he murmured in a voice hushed with disbelief, "Kristen?"

"Aye," she managed to squeak.

He scrutinized her a moment longer, then swept her into a bearlike hug and swung her around. "The saints above!" He roared. "My prayers have been answered!"

Kristen squealed with surprise.

"Don't hurt her!" Hagan shouted, trying bravely to protect her.

Raising a bushy eyebrow, Ian put her down and looked at Hagan. "And who is this little scamp?"

" 'Tis, Hagan," Kristen explained as she put a hand on Hagan's shoulder. "He's my brother."

"I dinna think so," Ian said. "Since yer mother and da are both dead."

"Kristen is too my sister! Who are you?" Hagan demanded.

Ian started at the young scamp. There wasn't any way on God's green earth that the boy could be related to Kristen. But this lad seemed to think differently, and Ian could see it was a very important matter with the child. Perhaps Kristen was all the child had.

"Well, now, if ye insist that Kristen is yer sister, then that would make me yer grandpa," Ian informed him.

"Really?" Hagan's brows knitted together. "I had a grandmère for a while, but I've never had a grandfather."

Ian reached down and scooped Hagan up into his arms. "Well, ye have one now." He put Hagan down. "Come on." Ian placed his hands on both their backs and urged them down the hall. " 'Tis time to meet the rest of yer family. And I want to hear all about what happened while ye were gone."

They were escorted into a huge room that held several settees and three big fireplaces. A girl with long black hair sat before the fire doing needlepoint. Putting down her work, she stood and turned to face them. She gasped, putting her hand over her mouth. " 'Tis she," she barely whispered.

Kristen stared at what easily could have been her own image, and realized this was the girl she'd seen the day she'd fallen off her horse. She hadn't been dreaming. It was if she were looking in a mirror. The only difference was that her sister's hair was as black as soot.

The girl walked over to Kristen. "My lost sister," the girl said, sweeping Kristen into a hug.

"Kristen, this is yer twin, Keely," Ian said, his voice thick with emotion.

"Look, Kristen. She looks just like you," Hagan exclaimed. " 'Cept her hair is the wrong color."

Kristen couldn't believe what she was seeing. She felt as if she were in a fog, watching everything around her, but none of it seemed real.

" 'Tis what they mean by twins," Kristen explained, looking at her brother. "Keely, this is my brother, Hagan."

"Brother?" Keely looked at Kristen as if she were daft.

" 'Tis a long story," Kristen said.

"Hello, Hagan." Keely bent down and squeezed his arm affectionately. "Come, let's sit down so ye can tell us where ye've been all these years."

"I dinna know where to start. I lived with my mother and stepfather. We had very little money and when Myra died, I became more or less a thief." Kristen had to smile at Keely's gasp. Kristen went on telling them what she knew, and they were quiet until she mentioned Trevor.

"Ye married a cursed Englishman!" Ian shouted. He jumped to his feet, his face as red as a rose.

"Aye, I did. He's the one who told me about ye."

"I'll wager he had nothin' good to say about us. And Constance can be an angry old bat."

Kristen smiled when Ian used her own description of Constance. "I discovered that she only pretended to be gruff. She could be quite nice when she let down her defenses. I will miss her." Kristen swallowed a lump of emotion and said no more. When she looked at Ian, she found him watching her intently as she talked about Constance. "Have ye ever met Trevor?" Kristen asked.

"Haven't spoken to a Chatsworth since I met Edward

that day on the glen," Ian said stubbornly, folding his arms
across his broad chest.

This one was as stubborn as Trevor, Kristen realized.
"Then ye dinna know a thing about him."

"He's still a Claremont."

" 'Tis the same thing he says about ye," Kristen said,
trying to suppress a giggle. "Perhaps one day ye can tell
me what the argument was about."

"Perhaps," Ian replied grudgingly. "Let's get ye both
settled into yer home. We'll have plenty of time for getting
acquainted now that ye've come home."

God, his head hurt!

Trevor's head felt three times its normal size as he rolled
over and tried to remember exactly where he was, and
exactly what had happened.

The floor?

How in the hell had he wound up on the floor?

Struggling for balance, he managed to sit upright. Pain
shot through his eyes as he wrapped his arms around his
knees and rested his head on folded arms. It took many
long minutes before the spinning subsided.

Now he remembered.

The liquor still seeped from the pores of his body, foul-
ing the air with its sour stench. He smelled like one of the
seamen he'd passed so many times lying on the docks. Did
they all feel this bloody awful? How in the hell had he
gotten so drunk? It wasn't something he usually did.

And definitely something he intended never to do again.

Wondering just how long he'd been on the floor, he
struggled to get to his feet. How was he going to get rid
of this pounding headache?

Ever so slowly, he made his way out of his study. He used

the walls to support him, but when he reached the stairs, they loomed like a steep mountain above him. He thought about getting on his hands and knees and crawling up the stairs, but with great effort he managed to slowly climb them.

He paused at the top, sweating and gasping for breath. He instructed the first maid who came to him to prepare his bath.

Maybe drowning was the answer.

When the water had been delivered to his room and he was alone again, Trevor sank into the steamy water and rested his throbbing head on the back of the tub. He'd have to get better just to die, he thought miserably.

Half an hour later, his headache started to abate, and flashes of yesterday's events began to gallop through his mind like a stampeding herd of horses. Trevor flinched. He didn't like what he was remembering.

He knew that Kristen was afraid of drunks. Was that why he'd overindulged? Had be been trying to send her away from him?

He would have to explain as soon as he dressed. Perhaps an apology would help.

When he finished bathing, he felt a little more human, but just a little. He groped his way over to the connecting door and let himself into Kristen's dressing room.

She wasn't there.

Trevor glanced around the room. The wardrobe door stood half open and clothes were strewn across the bed. He stumbled over to the wardrobe doors. There were still clothes hanging! He dared hope that she was elsewhere in the house.

However, when he went to Hagan's bedroom, he found it just as empty. All the boy's clothes were in place, yet there was a deserted air about it.

She must be here somewhere.

He started down the hall, opening every door and checking in every room.

Nothing!

Next, he started questioning the servants. When he turned up nothing, he decided to go to the stables.

It had occurred to him that he hadn't seen Hagan either. Cold dread spread over Trevor like frost on a blade of grass.

He sprinted to the stable. "Baxter!" Trevor called out crisply upon entering the building.

The small man came quickly from the back of the stable. "Yes, Your Grace?"

"Have you seen my wife?"

"Not today, sir." Baxter hesitated. Two deep lines of worry appeared between his eyes.

"What are you not telling me?"

"They rode off yesterday."

"They?"

Baxter's expression grew serious. "Lady Kristen and Hagan."

"And they have not returned?" Trevor snapped, though he already knew the answer.

"No, Your Grace. I sent David with them, and he said they went to Johnstone's. She told him to return to Chatsworth with the horses because they wouldn't be returning."

"I see." Trevor rubbed the back of his neck. His head felt as though it would burst, if that were possible.

So she'd gone to her family. What else could he have expected? That she would stay because she loved him? Had he hoped that she did care enough? Surely, he hadn't grown that soft.

Then he remembered the jewels she'd hidden from him. Evidently, she had planned to leave him anyway, so it was better that it had happened now. From this moment on, Kristen would be dead to him. He would have all reminders of her removed from his home before the sun went down.

He knew then that love didn't exist, except in his grandmother's mind.

He'd been foolish to think— He broke off the thought and ran a hand through his hair.

He wouldn't be so foolish again.

Three weeks had passed, and Kristen still felt strange with her new family. The fact that she missed Trevor didn't help, but she tried not to think of him.

Scotgrow, her grandfather's manor, didn't feel like home, though she'd been born to it, but she was trying to adjust. All her childhood dreams now made sense to her. She hadn't been dreaming, but remembering bits of her childhood all this time. Her life could have been so different had she not been stolen away, she thought sadly. It could have been full of flowers, silks, and all of the finer things.

As the weeks dragged by, she and Keely grew close. Like most sisters, they talked and giggled, except they were closer since they were twins. However, Keely was vastly different from Kristen. Keely was a proper lady with genteel manners. She'd never seen life beyond the walls of Scotgrow. She had had everything Kristen hadn't.

Kristen couldn't imagine living a life so confined. It was true that she hadn't been raised in the life of luxury, but she had truly tasted life on the other side. The things she had learned could never come from books. Looking back, she probably wouldn't have traded those experiences, no matter how bad they were, because she knew she had grown from each one.

But having experienced that life, she now felt suspended between both worlds. She didn't feel as if she belonged in either one.

After days of drizzling rain, the weather finally grew mild with a gentle breeze. The climate was never very warm, she'd learn.

Kristen and Keely decided to go for a picnic lunch. Along with Hagan, they rode away from the house on their horses with a basket packed with a feast. They settled on a nice grassy hill, where they spread their blankets and laid out the food on top. Hagan didn't have to be asked twice to eat. His exuberance showed how much he was enjoying his lunch.

After they ate, Kristen noticed Hagan was sitting in a corner playing with a blade of grass. He should be up running around, she thought.

"Are ye all right, Hagan?" Kristen asked.

"I guess so." He sighed, and Kristen could see that same sadness she'd seen in him for the past three weeks, and she wasn't sure what to do about it.

Hagan had been polite to Ian and Keely, but he wasn't his usually happy self. He'd been so withdrawn. She had a hunch that Hagan missed Trevor, and she knew she missed the man—so much it hurt. Yet Trevor had not come after her. Obviously, he wanted nothing more to do with them. He was probably very happy to have them out of his hair.

"Why don't ye ride yer pony for a while so Keely and I can sit here and talk?"

"All right." Hagan scrambled to his feet and wiped his hands on the back of his breeches. Kristen shook her head. When would he remember to use his napkin?

"Dinna go far."

Hagan gave her a grin that reminded her of his old self, then mounted his pony.

"He's a bonny lad," Keely said.

"Aye, he is," Kristen agreed, watching him mount. "But ye've not seen the real Hagan. He's been much too quiet since we've been here. I hope he comes out of this mood soon."

"I bet he misses yer husband."

Kristen looked at Keely and frowned. "I think he does."

"Ye've not told me much about this man ye married. Tell me what he's like."

" 'Tis a hard question ye ask. I dinna know how to describe a man who's bigger than life. He's nice to look at and his shoulders are this big." Kristen held her hands out wide. "There are times when he looks at me and I just melt into a puddle. He can be tender and kind. I canna help myself when I'm near him. Yet he can also be cold and withdrawn. I dinna like him much at those times because I dinna know what he's thinking or how he feels . . . It's all so confusing," Kristen admitted.

Keely's eyes widened, and Kristen laughed.

"And his eyes . . . they can be as blue as a morning sky or as green as the new grass."

" 'Tis a pretty picture ye painted." Keely gave her sister a puzzled look. "Why did ye leave him?"

" 'Tis a long story. Maybe I should begin with how we met." Kristen started telling her sister everything that had happened to her since she'd met Trevor. When she finished, Keely said nothing.

Kristen waited for her sister's reaction. She knew the story sounded farfetched, but it was all true. "Well?"

" 'Tis the most romantic thing I've ever heard," Keely said, a faraway look on her face.

"Nay, I dinna say he loved me. 'Twas just a simple agreement."

Keely opened the hamper lid so she could put everything back. "Perhaps that's the way it started out, but I'll wager the man loves ye."

"If that's true, then why hasn't he come after me? Ye've not seen him breaking the door down to get us back."

Keely thought for a moment, nibbling at her bottom lip. "Perhaps it is pride. Ye left him. Maybe he is waitin' for ye to come back. Perhaps he thinks that since ye left, that ye dinna love him."

"I dinna love him," Kristen stated firmly.

"I believe ye do."

"Why would ye say that?"

"Because when ye talk about him, like ye were just doing, yer face lights up and yer eyes turn all dreamy." Keely laughed. "Yer voice changes too."

"I dinna believe that." Kristen pressed both hands over her eyes as if they burned with weariness.

"Well, ye should," Keely persisted. " 'Tis true."

Kristen felt empty and drained. "He told me to go."

"He was also drunk, and probably hurting somethin' fierce, I believe ye said, and probably doesn't remember anything he uttered."

"The liquor, 'tis a problem." Kristen sighed and shook her head.

"But he'd never done it before," Keely reminded her. "Remember, his grandmother had just died. He just slipped—'tis possible. Haven't ye ever made a mistake before?"

Lord, she was sweet, Kristen thought. Mistake? Kristen had made so many, she'd quit counting long ago.

Kristen considered what her sister said. "This must be a first: a Johnstone taking up for a Claremont."

"I dinna see the point in the feud. I've never gotten Grandfather to tell me what it's about. Therefore, I can't judge people I dinna know."

"Well, I canna tell ye either, because Trevor doesn't know."

They both laughed at the ridiculous situation. Suddenly, Keely stopped and asked, "Tell me what it's like to be kissed."

Kristen blushed, her cheeks feeling like fire. " 'Tis very nice, but I dinna know if I can explain it in words."

"Try. Please." Keely begged like a child wanting to hear a story.

"It is wonderful. He holds me tightly like he's afraid someone will take me away. And then there's his kisses—his lips are soft and warm. They are so demanding that it takes my breath from me, and I cease to remember anything else but him . . . the feeling . . . the taste . . . it's all him."

"Oh, Kristen." Keely clapped her hands together. "That sounds so wonderful. I only hope that one day I can experience such feelings."

"You will," Kristen assured her. Then, realizing she hadn't seen Hagan, she looked around for him. "One day ye'll be able to tell me how it feels for ye."

Kristen clambered to her feet. "I wonder where Hagan has gotten himself off to," she murmured, scanning the area for any sign of him.

"Hagan! Hagan!" Kristen shouted, but received no response.

"Ah, well. He must have found an interesting puddle to play in." She shrugged, and set about packing up the remains of their picnic.

Hagan still hadn't returned. Kristen turned to her sister.

"I should go and look for him. Ye go back to the house so that they dinna worry about us."

Kristen rode all over the grounds looking for her brother, but there was no sign of him. She pulled up, trying to decide what to do next.

Trevor. That had to be the answer. Hagan had gone to see Trevor.

CHAPTER SIXTEEN

Without a second thought, Kristen turned her horse and headed home.

Home. Strange how she could think of Chatsworth as home after such a short time, but she did. Unfortunately, she'd never be at home with her family. She just didn't belong. Would she always feel like an outsider, no matter where she went?

The beautiful rolling hills were covered with purple and yellow wildflowers, and the trees were lush and green. A cool breeze teased Kristen's loose strands of hair and tickled her nose as she neared Chatsworth. She reached up and brushed the tresses out of her face, and that was when she caught a glimpse of the shimmering lake where she, Trevor, and Hagan had tossed stones. She realized that Chatsworth was the closest thing to home she'd ever known.

The ride across the estate seemed to take forever, but

finally, she spotted the familiar long barn and the horses out in the pens beside the building. However, she didn't see Hagan's pony.

Kristen couldn't take time to sort out her jumbled emotions. Hagan was the most important thing to her right now. She had to find him.

She didn't stop at the stables, but rode across the back lawns. If she could locate Trevor, surely Hagan would be close by. She was preparing to dismount when a harsh voice stopped her.

"What are you doing here?" Trevor demanded, his expression wretched. "I thought you preferred your new home."

Kristen stared at him for a moment, then lifted her chin a tad.

Trevor's face was much too pale, and circles darkened his eyes, as if he hadn't had enough sleep. She wondered how much he'd been working.

Had he thought of her? She most certainly had thought of him more than she cared to admit. It was hard to forget his broad shoulders and sculpted mouth. Today his eyes were blue and cynical, and held not a trace of warmth. He was dressed impeccably in a hunter-green jacket and tan breeches as normal, but his usual dapper air was missing as he watched her.

"Are you through with your inspection?" he inquired in a bored voice.

Trevor narrowed his eyes, showing his angry disgust, and Kristen realized that *he* blamed *her* for leaving him. When *he* was the one who had practically thrown her out!

Of all the nerve!

Tears burned the back of her eyes, but she wouldn't give the man the satisfaction of seeing her cry. However, she needed his help, so there was nothing she could do but swallow her pride and ask, "I can't find Hagan. Is he here?"

"Of course not. He left with you."

Kristen slid from her horse and luckily landed on her feet. "But he's not with me!" She advanced in his direction. "Earlier today, he was telling me how much he missed ye, and then he up and disappeared. He went for a ride, and didn't come back." She stopped in front of Trevor. "I thought maybe—"

"I miss Hagan as well," Trevor said softly, his expression softening for a moment. Then he straightened and the coldness returned. "As you can see, he isn't with me."

The blood drained from Kristen's head. She swayed. The next thing she knew, Trevor had wrapped his arms around her, and he pulled her to his side.

"What's wrong?" she heard him say.

At least he'd caught her, Kristen thought ruefully, her head still swimming. Maybe that was concern she thought she'd heard in his voice. "If Hagan isn't here . . ." She took a deep worried breath. "Then I'm afraid that Ned has taken him."

"Your stepfather?" Trevor stared at her with disbelief. "How could he get him?" Trevor must have realized he was touching her, for he immediately dropped his arms as if he'd been burned. "The last time I saw the man, he was in London."

"Well, Ned isn't in London anymore. Three weeks ago he accosted me while I was riding and swore that, if I didn't provide him with valuables, he would take Hagan and teach him to steal."

"So you were stealing from me all along." Trevor concluded with disgust.

To her annoyance, she found herself blushing. "Nay!" she almost shouted. "I dinna do that. What ye found was taken before I ever came to Chatsworth.'' She seethed with anger and humiliation, but ironically, she knew she would need Trevor's help, so she swallowed her pride. ''But then ye never wanted to hear any explanations, as I recall.''

''I know the reason.'' He spat out the words contemptuously. ''You promised you would not steal!''

Kristen clenched her fists at her side. Oh, how she'd love to give him the bloody nose he deserved. ''Yer as thickheaded as ever! I will not argue with ye. Ye already have me tried and convicted, so what's the point?'' She threw up her hands and let them fall. ''For now, I just want to find Hagan, and then we'll be gone . . . out of yer life.'' She clapped her hands together. ''Just like that!''

A muscle twitched in Trevor's rigid jaw, and Kristen held her breath while she waited for him to speak.

''How long has Hagan been missing?''

''At least three hours now.''

''Go to the house, and I will go after him.''

''Nay.'' She set her mouth in a stubborn line.

''Don't argue with me, Kristen.'' He clenched his jaw, and his eyes narrowed slightly. ''We're losing precious time.''

''I agree.'' She took a deep, unsteady breath and stepped back. ''He's my brother, and I'll not stay behind.''

Trevor shook his head. ''I can go faster without you.''

''I will not stay behind. I'll follow ye.''

''Christ, but you are stubborn,'' he said curtly. ''Somehow I'd forgotten that small flaw.''

Kristen lifted her chin until she could look him in the eye. ''How can ye be forgetting my flaws when ye are constantly pointing them out to me?'' She knew she should be quiet, but the words came out before she could stop them.

''Kristen!'' he snarled with warning. ''We can argue our differences later. Hagan is more important right now.''

"At least we agree on that point," she said grudgingly.

He took her horse's reins. "Go inside and gather your things. As I recall you left most of them in your haste to get away." He waited for her to say something. When she didn't, he added, "We are heading for London." He started toward the stables. "I'll have the carriage readied." Then, as if an afterthought hit him, he said, "You do remember where your room is located?"

"Aye, unless ye've moved it."

Trevor strode briskly to the stable, where he issued instructions like a general. "Baxter, ready my carriage and my guard. I will be going to London for several days."

Baxter propped his pitchfork next to a stall. "Consider it done, Your Grace," Baxter said as he turned and marched down the stalls issuing orders to the stable boys.

Trevor started back to the house. A rumble in the distance drew his attention, and he looked upward at the blackened clouds.

Rain. Just what he needed to make this day worse. He should have his bloody head examined for letting that female back into his life. He massaged the muscles in the back of his neck as he walked up the back steps onto the terrace.

He had expected that Kristen would come back to him of her own free will, not because she needed his help. He'd hoped that she cared for him, at least a little. Of course, that was his mistake. Trevor stiffened.

He'd realized after the second week that he'd been wrong. At the first sign of trouble, Kristen had run and deserted him, just like everyone else in his life. She should have given him the benefit of the doubt and waited until he'd sobered up. But no, she had run away. If she had loved him, she would have believed in him. She would have stayed.

When he reached Kristen's room, he told her to pack a few things and meet him out front in precisely ten minutes—no arguments!

The sun was low in the sky when, accompanied by four guards, they finally left Chatsworth. Thunder boomed, rolling across the landscape, a foreboding sound as the sky darkened and rain began to pelt down. Trevor knew they were in for a downpour.

The carriage was much too small, he thought. At least when they each were in their present gloomy moods, it felt way too confined. He made sure that he sat on one side, Kristen on the other . . . with an imaginary line drawn between them.

She stared out the window, and had yet to look at him. He knew she couldn't see anything but the raindrops sliding down the window. Yes, this would be a long journey, he was sure.

"I had a messenger sent to Johnstone, telling him where you were," Trevor finally said, wondering why he didn't keep his mouth shut. She was not in the mood to talk.

"Thank you," Kristen murmured. She turned and leveled a cold stare at him. "I didn't even think about them," she admitted, a little shamefaced.

Trevor couldn't seem to help himself, but the next question slipped out before he could stop it. "How do you like your new family?"

Kristen was startled by the question. She darted her gaze to him to see if he was going to make fun of her. She decided that this time he seemed sincere in asking. "They're fine. I have a twin sister who looks like me, and

I've enjoyed getting to know her. But they're still strangers. I dinna feel like I belong.''

"There are two of you?" Trevor chuckled.

Kristen arched an eyebrow. "Ye find that amusing, do ye?"

"Unfortunately, I do." He looked at her, and then burst out laughing. "One of you is enough trouble. God help us all now that there are two of you."

Kristen tried to keep a straight face, but failed miserably. At least, Trevor seemed to be out of the angry mood he'd been in earlier. "My sister is sweet."

"Really." Trevor's brow rose a fraction. "Then you're not *exactly* alike."

Kristen picked up a book that was lying in the corner of the seat and threw it at him.

Trevor caught the volume before it could hit him. "See, you have proven my point. And quite nicely, I might add." He chuckled again.

"Yer impossible."

"Look, it's going to be a long ride." He held up his hands in a truce. "Maybe we'd better get some sleep," Trevor suggested as he stretched out his long legs in front of him, folded his arms across his chest, and shut his eyes.

Kristen looked at her husband and sighed. Why did just the sight of the man start her blood racing? Why couldn't she ignore him as he could her? What she wouldn't give to be held in those strong arms and feel his strength as he held her. However, things had changed between them. They both blamed each other for what had happened, she realized, and until he realized the whole thing was his fault, they'd never be able to talk.

Every night she'd been gone, she had dreamed of being with Trevor, and every night he had held her in her dreams and kissed her as if he truly loved her. What she wouldn't give for that love. She sighed again. The familiar tightness in her throat made her swallow hard. She wouldn't cry in front of him. She'd cried herself to sleep most nights with wanting him. It was painful enough wanting something she knew she could never have without humiliating herself too. They didn't trust each other, and without trust and love, they didn't have anything.

She rested her hands in her lap and leaned her head against the back of the velvet seat. Just as she drifted off to sleep, she decided she was miserable with Trevor and miserable without him. Some way, somehow, she was going to have to convince him that he needed her.

But how?

Always, the same question plagued her.

The sound of the pelting rain finally lulled her to sleep. She'd just dozed off when the carriage hit something hard, jarring her fully awake again. Her first thoughts were that they were being robbed again, and she didn't want another bullet hole in Trevor.

Her gaze flew to her husband. "Is it bandits?"

The carriage lurched to a stop, and Trevor glanced at her, but didn't comment. He slid across the seat and twisted the knob on the door. "I don't think so," he finally said.

He opened the door and stuck his head out. "What's the trouble, Herbert?"

"I fear it's the wheel, Your Grace."

Trevor slipped on his greatcoat before stepping out of the carriage. He pulled up the collar, then went to examine the wheel with his driver. "Can it be fixed?"

Herbert ran his hands over the spokes. "Believe so. But it will take a while with it being dark and all. And this infernal rain won't help." Herbert stood, shaking the water from his sleeves.

"I see," Trevor said as he straightened. "How far is it to the inn?"

" 'Bout a mile."

Trevor's head guard rode up beside the carriage. "John," Trevor said to him. "Give me your horse, so I can take my wife to Wayweather's Inn. We'll spend the night, and you can come for us in the morning."

"Yes, Your Grace." John dismounted and held the horse for Trevor.

Trevor didn't have to open the door for Kristen because she was just putting her feet on the ground. She frowned as the mud sucked at her shoes. "What's wrong?"

"We have a broken wheel," Trevor explained as he led the chestnut horse over to her, then swung up into the saddle. He extended his hand to Kristen. "We're going to the local inn. Give me your hand."

Kristen looked at him, hesitantly pulling her cape close around her. Was the man crazy? She'd just spent the last two hours trying not to touch him, and now he wanted her to ride a horse with him. "Only one horse?"

"Yes," he replied stiffly. "Now give me your hand, or you can walk."

She was definitely too tired to walk in this miserable weather, and she had a feeling that if she refused, Trevor would make her walk just to spite her. So she grabbed his arm and in one swift motion, he lifted her in front of him into the saddle with his arms around her. Immediately, she straightened, trying not to touch him anymore than she had to. She couldn't let him know how much she had longed to feel his arms around her, even if it was by necessity, not desire.

Trevor chuckled. "You should lean against me so you don't fall off."

He was much too arrogant. "I'm just fine," she replied stubbornly.

"Suit yourself," he said before he kicked the horse in the sides and they lunged forward.

Twenty minutes later Kristen's back was aching from sitting stiffly upright, arms folded in front of her, but she was determined. The temptation to relax against him was growing more appealing with each jarring step the horse made. Suddenly, the horse stumbled and she had to grab Trevor to keep from falling.

"You shouldn't be so obstinate," he whispered close to her ear, and draped his cape around her.

She decided to ignore the barb, and let her head rest on his firm chest. He immediately tightened his arms around her, and she felt safe.

God, she loved it when he held her!

Kristen could hear his heart beating softly beneath her ear, and found it comforting while they rode toward the inn.

The lights shone softly from Wayweather's Inn when they arrived. Trevor dismounted first, then reached up to help Kristen dismount. She felt every inch of her body slide down his muscular form, and it took her breath away. She almost forgot about the rain as she stared up at him.

Thank God, a fat raindrop hit her in the eye, bringing her back to her senses. Why did she always have to respond to him this way? The bloody man was a curse.

Trevor didn't say a word. And she couldn't read his thoughts. Did he feel anything? Hadn't he missed her just a little? Evidently not, because he dropped his arms and went into the inn, leaving her to follow him. She would be sure to treat him with the same indifference in the future, she thought, more than a little irritated.

Just as Kristen stepped into the building, she heard him say, "That will be fine. We would like to have dinner too."

After they removed their cloaks, they were shown to a table in a corner that had a low-burning oil lamp. Several other couples sat around a long table and were already eating. Kristen's stomach rumbled, and she was thankful Trevor had thought about food. It had been a long time since the picnic, and that made her think of Hagan. Was he having dinner or was he going to bed hungry?

"Good thing I ordered some food, by the sound of your stomach," Trevor commented as he sat down.

"A gentleman wouldn't comment about such things."

"Perhaps." He grinned and leaned forward. "I'm not a gentleman."

She blushed, but ignored him. She was too tired to battle him with words at the moment. "I am hungry and tired," she admitted as she placed a napkin in her lap. " 'Tis been a trying day."

"For once, we agree on something, madam."

Kristen smiled at Trevor's lighter mood. They grew quiet when they were served a warm stew, fresh bread, and ale. Kristen ate, but her mind was on Trevor, as usual. She wished things were back the way they used to be, but she didn't know how to fix their problems, and she didn't want to be hurt again.

She peeked at Trevor, when she thought he wasn't paying attention, and marveled at how handsome he was. The light made the front of his hair a lighter color and softened his features. Yet there was always that dangerous ruggedness about him, tugging on her and daring her to take a chance.

"If you're finished with your meal, we can go upstairs," Trevor said, breaking into her thoughts . . . thank goodness, because she didn't need to be drooling over him.

"I am so tired," Kristen said. She stifled a yawn with her hand, then stood and placed her napkin on the table.

"Then I imagine a bed will feel much better than my carriage," Trevor said as he guided her to the stairs.

They climbed the stairs, Trevor's hand resting on the small of her back. They stopped at the first door on the right. Trevor inserted the key and opened the door, then stood back so Kristen could enter.

The room was cozy, Kristen observed. There was a bed and a washstand and the covers had been turned back and looked very inviting. A chair sat in one corner and a screen for undressing stood in the other corner.

" 'Tis nice," Kristen said, looking around the room for a second time. She heard a click as the door shut, and whirled around and looked at Trevor. "Where will ye be staying?"

Trevor took off his coat and hung it on a peg by the door. "Right here."

"Nay, ye cannot," Kristen protested, furious at her vulnerability to him.

"Since I'm paying for the room and you are my wife, I believe I can," he stated as he removed his waistcoat.

"But—"

"Kristen." Trevor swung around to look at her. "I don't like this any better than you do, but we are man and wife and they only had one bed available. The hour is late, and I'm not arguing anymore tonight."

He unbuttoned his shirt. "I suggest you take off your clothes and get into bed if you want to get some sleep. Or you are free to sleep on the floor." His gaze shifted from her eyes to her breasts. "I assure you your virtue is safe with me tonight," he said, looking very disgusted.

He finished removing his fine linen shirt and followed it with his trousers. Kristen couldn't do anything but stare.

Her anger cooled while she watched. She'd forgotten how much she liked looking at the man. And she knew if he touched her, she'd willingly fall into his arms. But she didn't want that until he could admit how he felt about her.

This time she wanted his love or nothing at all.

Trevor climbed into bed and blew out the candle, leaving Kristen staring into the darkness, wondering if it would be safe to climb into bed with the enemy.

"You're going to get cold standing there in the dark, Kristen."

"Yer impossible."

"So you've said before. But no, just practical." Trevor yawned. "Good night."

Kristen didn't budge. She waited what seemed like forever before she heard Trevor's deep breathing and knew he had fallen asleep. Then very quietly, she slipped out of her clothes all the way down to her chemise and sneaked into her side of the bed.

The sheets, warmed by Trevor's body, caressed her chilly skin. It felt good to stretch out and rest, but she made sure she stayed as far away from Trevor as she could. Not that she didn't trust him . . .

He evidently didn't care what she did. How else could he have fallen asleep so quickly? It was herself she didn't trust.

"Damned man," she mumbled, not knowing how she felt about him at this very moment. Every time she closed her eyes, she could remember the feel and warmth of his lips on hers as his arms tightened around her. He made her feel as if she were the only woman who mattered to him. She remembered the eager touch of his tongue on her lips just before she opened her mouth to match his passion. And then she remembered the pure lust that always overcame her like the heat of a roaring fire when they came together. She rolled and tumbled and tossed until she finally became so exhausted that she couldn't think anymore.

Blissfully, sleep claimed her and she drifted off to that dream world where she made all the rules. And in that world Trevor reached out and pulled her to him. In that world, he held her and kept her safe from everything . . . even herself.

Beautiful dreams, Kristen thought. At least she had her dreams.

The next morning, Kristen awoke feeling tired from tossing and turning through the night. She tried to move, but found Trevor's arm draped across her chest, preventing escape. When she twisted to face him, it was all she could do not to lean over and kiss him. Instead she shook him. "Trevor, 'tis morning."

Slowly his eyes opened, and he gazed at her in a most peculiar way. She held her breath as a lazy smile spread across his lips. She thought, for just a moment, that he was going to kiss her, but instead he rolled over and slipped out of the bed.

She let her breath out in slow disappointment, all the while telling herself it was for the best. He'd shown her he didn't care, and she had to protect her heart.

"Go ahead and get dressed," he ordered. "We need to get an early start."

"And a good morning to ye too," she snapped. She gathered the sheet around herself and slipped out of the bed.

Trevor crossed over to the window and looked out. "Yes, I believe it will be a good morning."

Kristen wouldn't give him the satisfaction of a reply. She dressed quickly, but struggled with the last two hooks on the back of her gown. She had little choice but to ask Trevor for help. "Can ye fasten the hooks for me?" She presented her back to him and waited.

He brushed her hair to the side and placed a kiss on her neck. Shivers of delight trembled through her and she squealed, causing Trevor to chuckle.

Why had he done that when he'd been so cold just a few minutes before? He had an annoying habit of keeping her totally confused about his feelings and intentions.

"Hold still," he said as he fumbled with the tiny hooks.

"Then dinna be fooling around," she warned.

His warm fingers continued to make her skin tingle until he successfully fastened her gown.

"Thank ye," she said, pushing her hair back in place. She promptly stepped away, putting some distance between them.

"That's what husbands are for," he told her, opening the door.

She couldn't help the half smile she gave him. "I knew they were good for something," she murmured as she scurried past him and hurried downstairs.

The rain had stopped. A bright morning sun shone with a radiant orange glow as they made their way outside. The carriage stood waiting for them, the horses prancing as they impatiently waited to be going. Once in the carriage, they wasted little time getting under way.

Since Kristen had gotten very little sleep, the swaying of the carriage quickly lulled her to sleep. However, when she dozed off, her leg would brush Trevor's and she'd jar herself awake, then doze off again.

The next thing she realized, Trevor was shaking her

awake. "We're here. Do you want to stay in the carriage or come into my office?"

Kristen rubbed her eyes as she gazed out the window at a small brick building. "I'll go with ye. My legs are cramped and stiff, and it will do me good to stretch them out."

Kristen was surprised at how small the office was compared to all the other places that Trevor owned. When she commented on the fact, Trevor explained that they didn't need much room.

A small gentleman sat behind a desk. He was bent over a large book, which he was writing in as they entered. He looked up. "Good day, Your Grace. I did not expect you."

"This is an unplanned trip, I'm afraid," Trevor said, then motioned to Kristen. "James, this is my wife."

"Nice to meet you, mum." He nodded his head toward her, his spectacles sliding further down his nose.

Trevor stopped in front of James's desk. "Have you seen the man who came here the last time I was in London?"

"No, Your Grace. I believe the bloke was too scared to show his face around here again."

Trevor muttered a curse. "Now I will have to track the scoundrel down!" He nodded to James, then turned to Kristen and said, "I'll be only a moment, Kristen." Trevor strode past her and ducked into one of the back rooms.

James squirmed in his chair as if he felt he needed to talk to her. Finally, he laid down his quill and folded his hands on the table before he said, "The man His Grace spoke of had some nerve asking him for money." James shook his head and looked over his spectacles at her. "I don't think I have ever seen His Grace so angry."

"What did this man look like?"

As soon as James described the person, Kristen knew it had been her stepfather. So Ned had gone to Trevor for more money! And Trevor had paid him. She wondered why. He'd said before that he would never give Ned any more money. Could Trevor possibly have done it for her?

"That's a fine husband you have, mum."

"Thank you," Kristen said, wanting to ask a few more questions, but Trevor returned and prevented her from doing so.

"We'll go to my town house," Trevor said.

She felt momentary panic as her mind jumped. "But Hagan!" She had not come so far to be left at home.

"I'm sending a dispatch out for help," Trevor said, his response holding a sour note of impatience. "We'll find him. But first I want to get you safely home." Not waiting for her to comment, he took her by the elbow and escorted her out of the office.

Kristen didn't bother to argue. It was kind that he wanted to protect her. Did that mean he cared for her and didn't want to admit it? No matter. She was not going to sit at home while her brother was out on the streets. She would find Hagan herself if Trevor couldn't.

Because Kristen Johnstone Claremont knew these streets better than anyone.

CHAPTER SEVENTEEN

Over the next several days, Kristen stayed behind while Trevor went out to search for Hagan. She felt much like a caged animal, and it killed her to be so passive and wait, but for once she was trying to listen to her husband.

On the fifth day, Trevor came home extremely tired. There were shadows under his eyes, which hadn't been there before, and she knew then that he loved Hagan just as much as she did. Her heart tightened at the realization.

That night, they ate dinner in silence. Kristen didn't like the uneasiness she sensed. What was Trevor thinking? Did he know something, but wasn't telling her?

Soon dinner was over, and they retired to the library, where tea was served. She noticed Trevor hadn't indulged in spirits since she'd returned, and she hoped he wouldn't. But when he withdrew like this, she became nervous. She still remembered the last time he'd become drunk much too well.

Trevor sat in a chair, his shoulders slightly slumped. He stared down at the brown liquid as if it held some dark secrets. He didn't seem to notice that she was even in the room.

When Kristen couldn't stand the silence any longer, she demanded, "Tell me what's wrong!"

He looked up at her and blinked a couple of times before he spoke. "I thought we'd have turned up something by now," he admitted as he shook his head with regret. "I hate to think of Hagan out on those streets with that leech."

"I do too." She shuddered inwardly at the thought. "He's so young."

"I know." Trevor stood, then went to the window, and stared out into the darkness as if he were searching for answers. His shoulders were rounded and his head bent.

Kristen had never seen him so helpless and sad. Without thinking, she got up and went to him, placing her hand on his arm. "We'll find Hagan," she assured Trevor in a choked voice, wanting to ease his hurt. "Ye just haven't looked in the right places." She hesitated. "I appreciate ye helping me," she added softly next to his ear.

Trevor turned, capturing her within his arms. He hugged her fiercely and for the longest time. Then his hands began exploring the soft lines of her back down to her waist, before he squeezed her tightly. He looked at her again. "Don't you know? I would do anything for you," he admitted honestly as he gathered her back to him, letting her soft curves fit into his body. Slowly, his seductive gaze slid over her face, and she saw the longing in his eyes.

She melted right on the spot.

He examined her in a way that made her knees buckle. His hands held her head captive while he lowered his mouth inch by inch until she wanted to scream to please hurry.

God, she couldn't breathe. Nor did she want to.

After a few agonizing minutes, his lips touched hers. Softly at first. Inviting her . . . enticing her to give into her swirling emotions . . . and become his.

Trevor's mouth moved in such a mesmerizing way, she automatically opened her lips. She wanted to be a part of him so badly it hurt. Wrapping her arms around his neck, she shaped her body into his. She felt his arousal pressing against her. There wasn't any mistaking that he wanted her, but she needed more. How could she make him love her?

She drew his tongue into her mouth, marveling at how seductive it felt. His arms tightened in response.

"Kristen, I want you," Trevor whispered in her ear. He heard her soft whimper of assent, and it took every ounce of control not to take her over to the couch and cool his burning need for her. Time away from Kristen hadn't eased his desire for her one bit. He wanted her just as badly now as he had the first time he'd met her. Her fingers slid into his hair, and she kissed him back with a hunger he hadn't expected.

He explored every corner of her mouth. He couldn't get enough. He adored the taste of her . . . the feel of her. She was more like opium to his system. No matter how much he obtained, he needed more. Somehow this woman managed to always be in his thoughts, no matter what he was doing. When they were not together, he felt as though something was missing. Kristen was a part of him, whether he wanted her to be or not.

As Trevor pulled away and looked at Kristen's slightly swollen lips, he heard his grandmother's words.

When you can think of nothing but that one person. When they block all others from your mind so that when you're not with them, you find a part of yourself missing. When the first thing you do

*is look for them as you enter a crowded room, and think of them
when you are eating, and dream of them when you are sleeping.
When you forget about pleasing yourself and think only of pleasing
them. And suddenly the moon and stars are brighter when they
are standing beside you, and turn dull when they are gone. That's
when you'll know a love so powerful that it will bring you to your
knees.*

His grandmother had been right, Trevor thought. But
what was he going to do? He had no idea how Kristen felt
about him. He couldn't trust her. But he wanted her just
the same. He wouldn't lie to himself on that point.

"My beautiful temptress, I want you. Just as much now
as I did the first time we met. And I believe you feel the
same things I do."

Kristen wanted so much to deny his statement, but she
made the mistake of looking deep into his eyes. She knew
the lust she saw there matched her own, and she couldn't
lie because she too burned with need. "Aye," she murmured.

He kissed her forehead. "At the moment, I don't have
the answers to our problems," he said, brushing his lips
across her cheek. "I may not have the answers tomorrow
either, but tonight I'd like to forget everything but us."
He stepped back and looked at her. His gaze bored into
hers in silent expectation.

Kristen's blood raced through her veins like a raging,
boiling river. She wanted to say something, but couldn't
find the words. With a moan of desperation, she slipped
her arms around him and squeezed. She just wanted to
be close . . . to be able to have some small part of him. If
only for tonight, with no thoughts of tomorrow.

Without another word, Trevor swept Kristen up in his
arms and carried her upstairs to his bedroom. Kristen

barely noticed the upstairs maid, who opened the door for them as they brushed through the door.

All Kristen could see was Trevor. He was the most important thing to her tonight . . . tomorrow . . . forever. Somehow she knew she'd never have feelings like this about anyone else.

Her mind tried to tell her that she needed to know how Trevor felt about her, but her body wouldn't let it. Did he love her? She needed his love as much as she needed to breathe.

He stopped beside the bed, where he let her slide out of his arms. He fumbled with the fastenings of her gown, then removed the layers of her clothes until there was nothing left between them. Warm fingers brushed her skin.

Kristen tried to resist the sensuous onslaught his fingers brought to her needy body. She trembled as all the questions she had asked herself slipped easily into an abyss. She loved this man, whether she wanted to or not.

Trevor noticed her flushed face, and liked what he saw. The pink of her cheeks accented the emerald green of her eyes. He started to remove his clothes as he stared at her magnificent body. He liked the way she didn't try to hide herself from him. Her nipples were erect, her waist narrow, her hips voluptuous, and he intended to explore every inch. He saw the hungry look in her eyes when she boldly returned his gaze. The slow-burning ache deep inside him grew to an inferno.

He cupped her breasts, marveling at the weight and smoothness of each one. He massaged each mound as his thumb teased the ends of her nipples into tight little buds. Bending down, he placed a soft kiss on her lips, then nibbled his way down her neck and across her cheek. He couldn't stop there, and moved lower. He ran a tongue around her nipple before closing his lips over the tiny bud.

Sliding her fingers through his hair, Kristen gasped. She held on to him so she wouldn't fall down. He might threaten her soul, but she couldn't think when Trevor's lips seared everywhere they touched.

Hot . . . she was too hot.

Urging her down on the bed, he placed featherlike kisses on her forehead, then down her cheeks, and finally, after agonizing teasing, he took her mouth.

His lips sucked the very life out of her. Her fingers held the back of his head as she opened her mouth to let his thrusting tongue enter once again.

God, this was good.

He was good. How could he not love her?

Instinctively, she pressed her body into his. His firm muscles felt splendid against her softness.

And to think only a short time ago, she'd never been kissed. Her tongue met Trevor's as she pushed her way into his mouth. She wanted to give as much pleasure as he gave her.

Pulling back slightly, she placed small kisses on his face and down his neck, loving his manly smell. She moved lower. The hair on his chest tickled her nose.

But Trevor needed her now. He pulled her back to him and rolled over her, pinning her beneath him. His fingers sought a path down her stomach until he found the warmth between her thighs. Gently, he stroked. She responded, withering beneath him as he kissed her.

He had to have her now. He positioned himself over her, and with a powerful thrust he entered her warmth. He found heaven as she wrapped her legs around him, pulling him closer.

Kristen gasped with pleasure. Her hands caressed the

muscles and planes of his back. She trembled as he began to move within her.

Something was different this time. She felt a desperate tenderness. Pleasure soared within her, and she wanted to shout out how much she loved him.

Instead, she held back. Kristen knew he might laugh at her softly spoken words, so she showed him with her caresses and kisses until she drove them both to the brink of insanity.

"Kristen, my love." The words sounded weak as Trevor drove into her one final time. Waves of pleasure washed over her, and she tightened her arms, never wanting to let him go. She held him close until his breathing returned to normal.

He slid to the side, pulling her with him. She cuddled next to Trevor as he drifted into an exhausted sleep.

"I love ye," she murmured, but knew her voice landed on deaf ears. Maybe it was for the best that he not know, she thought as sleep called to her, because she didn't know how to handle these strange new feelings.

And she didn't know if she could trust him.

Kristen stretched leisurely and opened her eyes to the soft morning light. She rolled over to wish Trevor a good morning, but found herself alone in bed.

Frowning, she felt a sharp stab of disappointment. She had wanted to snuggle and enjoy Trevor holding her close.

Evidently, he'd had other ideas.

She sat up in bed. Last night Trevor had been so loving, so tender, and simply wonderful. She'd hoped they had, perhaps, made a fragile beginning. She gnawed on her bottom lip, and wondered how he felt this morning when he'd first awoke.

Had he been happy?

Did he have regrets?

Kristen climbed out of the high old bed and pulled the bell cord for the maid.

It wasn't long before the door opened, and the maid came through the door. "Yes, mum."

"Do you know where Trevor has gone?"

"Not exactly, mum. I heard him tell the butler he was going to search for Hagan."

Kristen sighed. She didn't know whether to consider that good news or bad. Kristen moved over to the wardrobe.

"Let me get your dress, mum."

"I want to look a moment," Kristen said. "Will you style my hair this morning?"

"Of course, mum. I'll fetch my things."

Kristen glanced over the gowns hanging in the wardrobe while she thought. Hagan had been gone for two weeks, and every day he was gone made it just that much more difficult to find him. She knew her crafty stepfather could cover his tracks well.

Kristen decided she wasn't going to sit and wait one minute longer. While the maid was out of the room, Kristen snatched a plain brown dress off a hook, and she threw it on the bed.

The maid returned and placed her combs and hairpins on the dresser.

"Please style my hair in a tight bun in the back," Kristen told the maid as she sat down in front of the dressing table.

"Hadn't you rather have something prettier?" the maid asked as she brushed Kristen's long red hair.

"Not today. I've an errand to do and I dinna want to be bothered with a lot of curls."

"As you wish," the maid replied as she expertly pulled

Kristen's long hair together and started wrapping it around the center. She secured the hair with hairpins.

"Put an extra pin at the very top," Kristen instructed.

"Is that to yer likin', mum?" The maid patted Kristen's curls and moved to the side while she watched her mistress and waited for approval.

"Fine, thank ye." Kristen stood. "Ye did a good job."

The maid helped Kristen dress, and in no time she was ready. Giving herself a final glance in the mirror, she was satisfied she wouldn't draw much attention in her old neighborhood. She turned to leave, and that was when she noticed the maid staring at her in a most peculiar way.

"What?" Kristen asked.

"If you don't mind me saying, mum, you are acting a bit strange. Is there something I can help you with?"

Kristen smiled. "I wish you could, but this is something I need to do by myself."

"You should not go out alone," the maid reminded her. "If you give me a minute, I can get ready and go with you."

"I do many things I shouldn't," Kristen said, and smiled. "I'll be back soon," she added on her way out the door.

Soon Kristen was on her way. She had the driver of her carriage drop her off at Grafton House, the dress shop where she'd bought her wardrobe, with instructions to pick her up in the afternoon. She'd thought of everything. No one would question a lady visiting her dressmaker's shop.

As soon as the carriage left, she weaved through the streets until she was once again in her old neighborhood.

She paused to look at her rat-infested street. It was so much worse than she remembered. Somehow she had forgotten.

Vendors were crying out what they had to sell on their carts as they moved up and down the docks. Kristen glanced out at the Thames. It was low tide and the Mudlarks were busy, she noted, as they scrounged for coal, copper nails, anything they could sell that would buy a little food for an empty stomach. And they were all children.

Kristen had never tried scrounging herself because she couldn't stand the mud covering her bare feet, but there were many children who became Mudlarks. She vowed that Hagan wouldn't be one of them, providing she found him in time.

An orange girl held a bright orange up to her as she passed. Kristen couldn't help stopping to buy one. How often had she longed to do so when she lived on this street.

Further on down the street, several barrels were turned over with debris strewn on the streets. The usual tabby and black cats stood on top of the barrels, reaching their paws into the openings in hopes of finding a morsel of food someone had thrown out. She shook her head at the dirt she'd lived in for so long.

Kristen hurried past a couple of taverns, then made a left on Waters Street. Dirty Sally glanced up as Kristen went by, but said nothing. Evidently the woman didn't recognize her, or didn't care, because she continued searching through a pile of trash. Further down the street, Kristen observed Two-Fisted Joe stalking his next unsuspecting victim. She couldn't help but smile at what once was her life—a life she didn't intend to go back to.

Finally, she spotted the one person she thought could help her. "Sam!" she called to a small man wearing a faded brown coat.

He whirled around and stared warily at her as if he were trying to decide whether to run or stay in recognition. "Whatcha want, lady?"

" 'Tis Kristen." She held out her arms.

Sam squinted and peered a little closer at her. "Kristen, girl," he said, and finally grinned in recognition. "Look at ya. Somebody has gone and cleaned ya up real nice."

"Yes, they have," she admitted with a wry smile. "How are ye doing?" she asked.

"Not too bad for an old man. Still trying to dodge the Bow Street police. Ya know what a pain in the arse they can be. What brings ya back?"

Kristen took a deep breath and prayed he would be able to help her. "Ned has stolen Hagan. Have ye seen them?"

"I did. Hagan was with your pa." Sam rubbed his chin as he remembered. "Ned said pickings were slim round here, and he and the boy were going to head north."

"He's not my da!" It was impossible to steady her rapid pulse. "When did ye see him?"

"Last night."

"Oh, dear!" she blurted out. " 'Twould mean they'd be leaving today or tomorrow." Kristen felt a scorching heat spread through her body. An inner torment began to gnaw at her. "Where are they staying?"

"Ya wouldn't believe it—"

"Where, Sam?" Kristen said, cutting him off.

"They're staying at the Dirty Lady. Actually sleeping in a bed they are." Sam rocked back and forth, nodding his head. "Seems Ned's getting too good for the rest of us."

"Thanks, Sam." Kristen placed a gold coin in his hand, then turned and headed for the tavern. The Dirty Lady had to be one of the worst taverns on the wharf, and she didn't want Hagan to stay there one minute longer than he had to.

But how was she going to get him out? She couldn't go in the tavern dressed as she was. She'd draw too much attention. Even if her gown was plain, it was still better than most of the clothing seen in this area.

The sky had turned a dusky hue by the time Kristen reached the Dirty Lady. She stood in the shadows across the street, watching the red front door. Now what? She had come this far. She wasn't leaving without her brother.

There wasn't any way she could get in through the front without Ned seeing her; chances were he was at the bar. Where there was liquor . . . Ned lurked close by.

That meant she needed to find another way into the building. She stepped from the shadows and bumped into a seaman passing by.

He grabbed her arms. "Lookin' for some fun?" he asked, pulling her next to his body.

He was drunk, of course. Everyone in this part of town stayed drunk, but he was way too strong for her to pull away. She decided to try another approach. "I'm looking for my husband. I think he's in there." Kristen batted her eyelids prettily. "I could make it worth yer while if ye'd go into the pub and confirm the fact."

He grinned at her. "How much?"

Kristen dug down in her reticule and produced a gold coin, which she placed in his hand. "I'll give ye four more upon yer return."

His eyes widened as he stared at the gold piece. "Ya got a deal," he said. Letting her arm go, he placed the coin in his pocket.

"Be back." He winked and started across the street.

Just as soon as he disappeared through the door, Kristen hurried across the street, this time watching to make sure she didn't bump into anyone else. She didn't have an abundance of coins left to bribe people.

Moving between the buildings, she looked up at the Dirty Lady. There were three windows across the top. She silently prayed that Hagan was behind one of them. However, the windows were much too high for her to get to from the street, so she maneuvered around to the back of the place.

Her luck held out. There was a back door, and no one was around.

She twisted the knob, but the door wouldn't budge. "This is why I needed the extra hairpin," Kristen murmured as she reached up, removed a hairpin from her hair, and jimmied the lock until she heard a click. Carefully, she peeked in the room, and seeing it was safe, she entered.

A dim light let her see only a small part of the room, which appeared to be some sort of storage area. Fearing discovery, she glanced quickly around and found what she wanted: a set of stairs, leading to the next floor.

Kristen took the stairs two at the time, being careful not to make any noise. A man was just coming out of the first room, and Kristen held her breath as he looked up and spotted her. However, he merely nodded in her direction and moved toward the other set of stairs, which led to the front of the building. She released a pent-up breath.

She listened behind the next door, then whispered, "Hagan." When she didn't receive an answer, she walked to the next door. "Hagan?"

"K-Kristen," came a soft cry.

She tried the door, and surprisingly this one opened. She saw why the minute she entered. Her hand flew up, and she covered her mouth to keep from making any more noise.

Hagan was tied to a chair, his little head bent over. He looked up when she came in.

Kristen gasped. One of his eyes was black and swollen, and dried blood crusted his lower lip. Tears burned her eyes as she hurried toward him, and anger scorched her stomach.

"What in the saints has the man done to ye?" Kristen whispered furiously. She ran a hand down the side of his face. She was shaking with rage at what Ned had done. Bending down, she tried to loosen the ropes, but her fingers were clumsy as she untied the bindings. Finally, after several tries, she freed him.

Hagan threw his arms around her neck, squeezing her tight. "I'm sorry, Kristen," he sobbed.

"Sorry for what?" She patted his back.

"That I rode too far. I wanted to see Trevor, but Pa caught me before I could get there."

She held Hagan away from her. " 'Tis not yer fault. But promise me ye won't go off again without telling me first. Can ye walk?"

He nodded. "Aye."

Kristen took Hagan's hand and reached for the doorknob. "Come on." The door flew open, and she shrieked and jumped back. Ned filled the doorway, a near-empty bottle dangling from his fingers.

"See ya finally showed up," Ned snarled. "Where do ya think you're takin' my boy?"

"Away from ye," Kristen retorted defiantly. She heard Hagan weeping, so she shoved him behind her. The sour stench of liquor made her want to retch. The man was a pig.

"Ya ain't going nowhere, girl." Ned took a step forward.

Kristen tried to push past him, but he grabbed her shoulders and shook her hard. He slapped her, knocking her backward. She landed on Hagan, but she didn't stay there long as she quickly scrambled to her feet. She had begun to shake again. Terrified, she was determined not to break down.

Ned swayed toward her, raising his hand to inflict another blow. Quickly, she held up her arm to deflect the next punch. Hagan ran from behind her and grabbed Ned's leg, trying to stop him.

"Leave her alone!" Hagan yelled.

"Watch it, Hagan!" Kristen warned, glancing down at him, and in so doing, not seeing the fist that suddenly connected with her left eye.

Again she hit the floor. This time she didn't get up so quickly. She took a deep breath, trying to stop the panic that threatened to engulf her. Bile rose in her throat. She swallowed hard. Her eye had already begun to swell, blurring her vision. Her head swam.

She had to get up. She couldn't stay there. Ned would start kicking her if she did. She tried to shake the fog away. Desperately, she held on to the side of the bed as she shoved herself off the floor.

Someone was screaming.

Kristen blinked several times, trying to focus. Hagan was screaming. Ned was shaking him. Then, as if a miracle had occurred, she saw the dull metal of a gun barrel sticking out from under the pillow.

She didn't stop to wonder what Ned was doing with a gun. She just slid her hand under the pillow and grasped the weapon. Quickly, she turned and pointed the gun at Ned. "Let Hagan go!"

Ned cuffed Hagan again and sent him tumbling against the wall. The boy screamed at the top of his lungs.

"I said to leave Hagan be!" Kristen cocked the gun.

Ned grinned at her. He didn't think she had the nerve to shoot. She could see it in his eyes. He swung his leg to kick Hagan.

Without thinking, Kristen shut her eyes and pulled the

trigger. A loud explosion shattered the air. Gunpowder burned her nose.

Her eyes flew open.

Ned was still standing. Oh, God, she had missed him!

"You bitch!" Ned cursed. He let go of Hagan and grabbed at his chest. That was when she saw the red stain. Ned stumbled backward and fell out into the hallway.

Kristen slumped to the floor. Hagan scrambled over and threw his arms around her. She should feel something. Sadness? Regret? But she felt nothing—nothing at all.

Suddenly, everything happened much too quickly. Footsteps sounded on the stairs. There were people in the hallway, staring at Ned and then at Kristen and Hagan.

"What's happened here?" someone asked.

The bartender said, "Look. It's Ned."

"Is he dead, mate?" a sailor asked.

Another man leaned over him. "Dead as a stone."

The sailor pointed. "The girl killed him. See, she still has the gun."

Kristen looked down at the gun she held in her hand. Then she realized what she'd done. She'd killed a man!

"Somebody get her!"

A couple of men started through the door.

Kristen raised the gun and leveled it at them, automatically halting their progress. She didn't know who these men were, but they definitely didn't look friendly, and they were not going to touch her if she had anything to say about it.

"Who is she?"

"The lady is my wife. Step aside," said the firm voice that Kristen knew so well.

Trevor moved between the two men and started for his wife. But he stopped suddenly at the sight before him.

He couldn't do anything but stare. Kristen and Hagan

looked as if they'd been through Hell. Hagan was black and blue, and the side of his face was bloody. And Kristen's beautiful green eyes . . . One was swollen and already turning purple. Trevor's blood ran cold.

Hagan jumped up and ran to Trevor, throwing his arms around Trevor's leg. "He was mean," Hagan whimpered.

Trevor scooped the child up in his arms and hugged him to him. "You're safe now, son. He will not be hurting anyone again."

Putting Hagan back down, Trevor noticed that Kristen hadn't moved. She still held the gun pointed at the other men.

Trevor held out his hand. "Give me the gun."

"Arrest that woman," the bartender said to a petty constable who'd just arrived on the scene.

"She still has a gun," the officer said, stating the obvious. He backed away, pulling his pistol and aiming it at Kristen.

"There is no need for a weapon," Trevor said, looking at the constable.

"Are you crazy? She has a weapon, I tell you. Who are you anyway?"

"I am Trevor Claremont, the Third Duke of Chatsworth," Trevor bit out. "And that woman is my wife."

"A duchess?" The constable looked startled, and lowered his weapon a tad before he snapped it back into place. "I don't care if she's the bloody queen herself. She has shot a man, and she will have to stand trial."

Trevor glared at the man dressed in his blue coat, blue trousers, and drab waistcoat. "I suggest you watch your language in front of my wife!" He didn't give the surprised officer a chance to say anything before he turned his attention back to Kristen.

She had an odd, blank expression in her eyes. He wasn't

even sure if she saw him as he made Hagan sit on the bed. Trevor stepped closer to Kristen.

Stooping down, he held out his hand. "Give me the gun."

Finally, she looked at him. Her eye was starting to turn an ugly color and her cheek was bruised.

"Kristen, give me the gun," Trevor said a little more firmly. He didn't want her shot, even though he could shake her for not staying at home where she should be now.

She blinked a couple of times, but finally handed him the gun.

Trevor placed the gun behind him and took Kristen by the shoulders, bringing her to her feet. "It will be all right," he said soothingly, realizing she must be in shock.

"I killed him," she whispered, her eyes never leaving Trevor's.

"I know. But it was in self-defense." Trevor hugged her to him. Slowly, her arms came around him and she lay her head on his chest.

Kristen trembled. She was cold. So cold. She felt safe in Trevor's arms, though. Every time she was in trouble, he seemed to be nearby.

"Come on, lady." The constable came up behind Trevor and reached for her. "I have to take you in."

Trevor turned. "Do you have a name?" he asked as he glared at the constable.

"Yes, Your Grace, the name is Henry Holborn," he said as he stood at attention.

"I will escort my wife. Lead the way," Trevor said in a voice that meant no further discussion.

The constable didn't bother to argue. Instead he dropped his hand and left.

"Come on, Hagan." Trevor helped the child off the bed and they followed the petty constable.

When they were in the carriage, Hagan asked, "What are they going to do with Kristen?"

"I hope they will see reason, and she will go home with us."

Kristen didn't bother to say anything because she didn't have the same optimism, and when the carriage came to a halt in front of a familiar brown building, what little hope she had died instantly.

They entered the building, and Henry showed them to a desk where Frederick Hendrickson, the Superintendent of Police, sat with his hands resting on his big belly. He wore a scarlet tunic with gold epaulettes and a military cocked hat with plumes.

Upon seeing Kristen, the superintendent straightened, raised a gray brow slightly in question, and stared at her.

His was a face, unfortunately, Kristen had seen before.

"Well, if it isn't Kristen Johnstone," Frederick Hendrickson said. He smiled and reared back in his chair. "What have you stolen this time, girl? Appears your victim put up a real struggle by the looks of your eye."

"You know her?" the escorting constable asked.

"You could say that, Henry. I must say, she does look some different from the last time she was dragged in here. What has she done?"

Trevor looked at Kristen. "You know this man?"

"Afraid so." She nodded and frowned.

Trevor wondered why he should be surprised. He didn't, after all, have an ordinary wife.

Hendrickson looked at Henry. "Well, Henry?"

"She murdered a man."

"It was self-defense," Trevor injected quickly.

Hendrickson glanced at Trevor, his bushy gray brows

arching as he noticed the cut of Trevor's clothing. "And who, pray tell, are you? I thought you were probably the poor victim Kristen had robbed, but I see you're still alive."

Kristen had to choke back a laugh. She knew how serious the whole situation was, but at the same time it was also amusing. And totally unbelievable—even for her. Trevor had to wonder what he'd gotten himself into. He probably wished he'd never laid eyes on her, she thought, all her amusement leaving her.

"I am Trevor Claremont, Duke of Chatsworth."

"Well, Your Grace. Since you're not the victim, how do you figure in this situation?"

"Kristen is my wife."

"You poor man." Frederick shook his head slowly. "Probably takes a saint to live with the woman."

"It has been an adventure," Trevor admitted dryly.

"So you're a duchess," Frederick said to Kristen. "All the more reason you shouldn't be here. Someone tell me what happened. And slowly this time."

Henry gave him a short summary on what had transpired. It wasn't even close to what had really happened, but Kristen remained quiet. She figured they wouldn't believe her anyway.

Frederick considered her a moment. "Kristen, I've known you the last few years. However, this surprises me. What do you have to say?"

"The man deserved to die," she told him, her chin raised stubbornly.

Trevor squeezed her arm, and she realized that wasn't the smartest thing to say.

"You can see what the man has done to her." Trevor pointed out. "I would like you to release my wife to my custody."

"Your Grace, under normal circumstances, I probably

would do as you request. However, murder is a serious charge, and your wife does have a *slightly* tarnished background, which I can't ignore. Therefore, she will have to remain in jail until she goes to trial."

"No! Kristen!" Hagan shouted as he wrapped his arms around her waist.

Kristen bent down to Hagan. "I'll be fine. Ye go with Trevor and take care of yerself."

"But I don't want to leave you," Hagan protested, looking at her with tear-filled eyes. "What's jail?"

" 'Tis a place where people who have done something wrong have to stay."

"But he was hurting us," Hagan pointed out.

"I know. Everything will be all right." She gave Hagan a quick kiss and a hug before turning back to Trevor. "I'm sorry I have caused so much trouble."

Trevor gave her a grim smile. "If you had stayed home and let me handle everything, you wouldn't be in this situation," he pointed out needlessly.

"I've never been good at listening."

"Among other things." Trevor grabbed her arms and made her look at him. "I will get you out of this as soon as I can." He hugged her to him, then drew slowly away. Taking Hagan's hand, he left.

Kristen watched them walk out. She had never felt so alone in all her life.

CHAPTER EIGHTEEN

Kristen didn't think her day could get much worse, but she was wrong . . .

The minute Trevor left, she found herself slapped with manacles that pinched her wrists. She waited for a chain to go around her neck, but thankfully that hadn't occurred—yet.

"Why are ye doing this?" Kristen asked, holding up her hands and staring at the horrible irons they had imprisoned her with.

Hendrickson gave her a half smile. "I do believe you just murdered a man, Your Grace. What did you expect? Tea?"

Kristen lifted her chin, but didn't bother to give the superintendent an answer as he shoved her out toward an open cart in the alley behind the building. In Hendrickson's eyes, she'd already been tried and convicted. She just hoped a jury would feel differently. Ned had caused much suffering to many people.

Hendrickson ordered her to get into the vehicle, but offered no help as she struggled to climb inside. Kristen was barely seated before Henry clucked the horse and the cart lurched forward. The ride was rough, and she was tossed from side to side. She was certain she'd added a few more bruises to her already battered body.

Finally, Newgate loomed in front of them, looking menacing with its drab stone walls. Two towers stood on each side of the main gate. The door was only about four feet high, perhaps a little more, and a man like Trevor would have to stoop to enter. She had heard stories about this notorious prison. One story was that in ancient times London had been a walled city with four gates, and Newgate was one of the original four gates. She wondered about that because the structure looked threatening, not welcoming.

Across the top, it had menacing spikes that would impale any human who tried to climb over.

She'd definitely not try that form of escape. There had to be another way, she thought.

"Let's go," Henry ordered as she stood by the cart.

Kristen looked down to the street and realized it was a good distance to the ground. To make matters worse, her swollen eye obscured part of her vision. She didn't know if she could climb down without falling.

Henry must have seen her dilemma, for he offered his hand. Not wanting to fall flat on her face and add to the bruises she already had, she took the assistance Henry offered. To her surprise, he was a gentleman, setting her down gently and backing away.

She followed him into the dark hole reminiscent of Hell. The heavy door groaned as if in pain as it slowly opened.

Once inside, Kristen noticed a room with windows over

the doorway. She didn't have time to figure out what that room was, because Henry didn't stop there. They moved forward until they came to a second oak door braced with iron, which led to the interior of the prison.

Why did she have the sinking feeling that she'd never get out of there alive?

She didn't get time to come to an answer before she was shoved through a second door. Once inside, she hesitated, and Henry grabbed her elbow. "Come on. We need to go to the lodge room where they receive incoming prisoners," Henry said as he pulled her into a small room on the left.

"Watcha got tonight, Henry?" A heavyset man with faded red hair asked him.

"How the hell are you, Grady?" Henry smiled his question.

The man placed his hands on the small of his back and stretched. "Back's been hurting a mite."

Henry must have remembered why he was there, because he pulled Kristen in front of him. "This here's a special guest. She needs a special room."

Grady took Kristen's face in his pudgy hand and turned it back and forth. "Looks like she's been in a bit of a scrap."

"This here's a duchess," Henry said proudly.

Grady's eyebrows arched almost to his hairline. "And why, pray tell, is she here?"

"Murder."

Grady shook his head. "I hope you got the fellow that gave you that fat eye," he told Kristen. He chuckled and reached for her again. "Well, Your Highness, let's get this over with."

Kristen tried to move back, but couldn't because Henry stood behind her. "I dinna understand."

"I have to search you, sweetie. Don't want you slitting someone's throat." The man jerked Kristen to him and started running his meaty hands over Kristen's body, stopping every now and then on certain parts of her body.

Kristen wasn't sure she could be any more humiliated. However, a blessed coldness settled over her body and she withdrew into her own shell—a shell where she felt nothing. Nothing at all.

"I'll take her on in, she's clean," Grady grunted as he slowly maneuvered across the room.

Once again they headed deeper into the dark hallways. Grady picked up a lantern and turned up the wick until it cast a brittle glow over the pewter-colored walls. When they came to the cells, men pressed their faces against the iron bars to see the new prisoner.

"Put her in with us, Grady. We'll take care of her real nicelike," one called out, followed by other rude remarks from other prisoners.

"This ain't your lucky day," Grady told them, and kept on moving.

Water trickled down the walls, and the foul stench of human waste almost made her retch. A little further along, another smell—a mixture of damp and musty—let her know that things would only get worse. Then she heard an eerie noise. Was it human or animal? She wasn't certain she wanted the answer to her question.

Finally, they came to a cell and stopped. Grady set the lantern down and opened the heavy wooden door, then shoved Kristen inside. Weak light filtered in through a barred window high on the wall.

Kristen sighed with relief when she didn't spot another occupant in the room. She didn't want another fight or argument tonight. She was bloody tired, and if she couldn't go home, at least she could sleep.

Taking in her surroundings, she found a low table on a mat on the floor against the wall. She wondered what kind of vermin lived in this cell as she glanced at the other corner and saw a beaten-up chamber pot.

All the other times Kristen had been arrested, they had set her free. This was the first time she'd actually been locked up. There was no way she could get the key to slip out, because it was on a metal ring with the other keys.

"There's a blanket in the corner, and someone will bring you water shortly," Grady announced. "Probably not what you're used to, sweetie, but it's better than most of these pens. His Grace did send enough money to get you a cell by yourself."

Kristen wanted to laugh. The cell was no worse than where she used to live. She'd gotten too soft and used to nice things, and that had been her mistake. What a fool she'd been. Hadn't she known her time at Chatsworth would never last?

The thick door swung shut with a heavy, final thud that echoed around the cell. There was silence. Standing in the middle of the dark cell, Kristen stared at the door, not knowing what to do.

She heard a cough from down the hall, and faint sounds of men swearing and fighting among themselves. At least the noises reminded her that she wasn't alone. But they offered her very little comfort indeed.

Kristen began to pace. She'd never been caged in her life, and she didn't like it at all. She had to get out of there. There had to be a way. She would keep her eyes open and wait for her opportunity, and when the time came she'd escape.

As the night progressed, Kristen had too much time to think. Why hadn't she stayed behind as Trevor had advised? She wouldn't be in this mess if she had only listened. But no, she had to be headstrong and try to do something herself.

Could she ever be an obedient wife to Trevor? Probably not. That word didn't seem to go with her nature. She laughed ruefully. Of course, she would have to live long enough to get out of this place to be a wife. She could end up dangling from the end of a rope.

Unconsciously, her hands came up and touched her throat. She shut her eyes and pictured herself dangling in midair. Her eyes flew open, and she paced some more. She didn't want to shut her eyes again and see the same vision.

She had killed a man.

That was hard enough to think about.

She should feel bad about Ned, but she felt nothing. Ned had never been any good, and she couldn't stand by and let him mistreat Hagan. It bothered her that she had been responsible for a death, but she couldn't feel sorry for removing Ned from the world.

How was she going to get out of this mess? She reached up and touched her puffy eye. At the moment she was very thankful not to have a mirror. She probably looked like she *belonged* in jail.

Finally, Kristen could no longer put one foot in front of another, and she sank down to the hard mat. Reaching for the blanket, she found it surprisingly clean. Trevor's money had probably gotten her that small favor. She wrapped herself up and stretched out, trying to forget where she was.

At least in her dreams, she was free.

Trevor could not sleep. The thought of Kristen in jail ate at him.

He had to get her out. Even though Kristen had broken the law, he knew it could sometimes take a year or more to come to trial. He would have to pull a few favors to make sure Kristen would get on the next quarter sessions.

He wasted little time dressing the next morning, and he didn't even bother to eat his breakfast in his haste to be on his way.

The carriage had been brought about, and Trevor gave the address of the Justice of the Peace to his driver and settled down in the plush interior of his coach.

While Trevor rode, he thought of Kristen. He could think of nothing else. Her pale face and black eye had haunted him all night. She'd been a pitiful sight. If Ned were not already dead, Trevor would have shot him himself.

There had been no weeping. No tears. Kristen had stood proudly without begging. He couldn't have been prouder of her or her courage. His grandmother would have been proud—on second thought, she'd have probably fainted dead away at the news that Kristen had shot someone.

Kristen was a problem . . .

And had been since he'd met her. He looked out the carriage window, picturing her petite face. That glorious red hair that framed those emerald eyes could bring any man to his knees. But there was something else about her that kept him intrigued. Her spirit. True, it usually kept her in trouble, but he wouldn't have her any other way.

He sighed at all his mixed emotions. He could walk away. He could go back to his quiet life with its endless balls and faces that couldn't wait for him to glance their way. Or he could fight to free Kristen, knowing that the trial would cause a scandal. He didn't know whether Kristen would stay with him or return to the Johnstones.

He could choose a life that was dull and boring.

Or constant chaos.

Trevor laughed for the first time in two days. There was no contest. The fiery, saucy wench had twisted him around her finger, and he loved every minute of it. And every inch of her. Of course, that was something he'd never tell her.

The carriage slowed to a stop, bringing Trevor back to his problem. He got out and hurried to the front door of an old family friend, then knocked.

A butler appeared in minutes, one Trevor didn't recognize. "I would like to see John."

The butler looked down his nose. "Who may I say is calling?"

"The Duke of Chatsworth." Trevor articulated each word, and raised a brow a fraction.

The man in front of him blinked several times and became flustered. "Begging your pardon, Your Grace. Please enter. I will go and get Mr. Briggs immediately." The butler bowed twice, backing away from the door. "This way, if you please." The butler led the way to a sitting area.

Trevor didn't laugh until the man was out of the room, and then he chuckled at the man's bowing. It had been much too long since he'd seen John. But the Justice of the Peace had been a friend of his grandmother's for years.

Someone cleared his throat, and Trevor turned around and smiled. "John, it has been a long time." Trevor extended his hand.

"Much too long, Trevor," John said when he took Trevor's hand.

"I quite agree. I wish I could say this was just a visit, but I am in need of your help."

"You sound serious. Please have a seat and tell me what's bothering you." John held his hand out and motioned in the direction of a chair. "But first, how is Constance?"

"I take it you've not heard," Trevor said quietly. "I'm

sorry to tell you this way, but Grandmère passed away a month ago."

John frowned. His shock showed and he remained silent for several moments. "I'm so sorry. I knew she'd been sick, but I expected she would have many years ahead of her."

"I did too."

"Tell me, how I can help you?"

"I don't know how to state this, except to be very blunt. My wife is being held in Newgate, and I want her out! Also, I need her trial placed on the docket for the upcoming quarter sessions."

"A duchess in prison? I have never heard of such a thing. I will have her released immediately. How did this happen?"

"She killed her stepfather."

John frowned. "That puts a different light on things, I'm afraid. Even I can't grant bail for a murder case. Can you tell me what happened?"

Trevor explained Kristen's background, leaving nothing out.

John rubbed his chin. "I can see that this is not a normal case. I will do what I can to make sure she makes the quarter sessions. A friend of mine by the name of Dickens Fagin is the Assize Judge. I will speak with him. But I do think you have a problem."

"And that is?"

"Your wife had a very unsavory background before she married you. I think you will add a lot of credit to her, but you also need her grandfather in court with you."

"You really think that I need Ian Johnstone?"

"I do. And you need a barrister. The word 'murder' will be heard again and again in court. Your lady is going to need as much help as she can get."

"You do realize that my family and the Johnstones have never gotten along?"

"Perhaps it is time to reevaluate your relationship. The feud was between your grandmother and the Johnstones, not you and them. Besides, you married a Johnstone," John pointed out. "Think long and hard about it, Trevor."

Trevor stood. "I appreciate your time, John."

"Sorry I couldn't help more. But think about what I said."

Trevor could think of nothing else as he rode to Newgate. He didn't like having Kristen in that place. He also didn't like the fact that he was going to have to beg her family for help. But what else could he do?

Stepping out of his carriage, Trevor stared at the cold-looking building. Prior to yesterday, he'd never given a second thought to who could be behind its walls. Now as he entered the prison, he realized he had never felt so helpless in his life. He would have to concentrate on Kristen's defense or she'd never get out of prison.

He waited while the warden was summoned.

"Your Grace." A tall thin man moved into the room. "I am Adam Williams."

"I would like to see my wife."

Williams rubbed his chin before he spoke. "With a master felon, visits are only allowed in the hall with the prisoner behind—"

"But for a price you can make arrangements," Trevor said, cutting the warden off.

Williams smiled. "Come with me," he said without further comment as he turned and went back out the door he'd come through. "I heard we had a special guest, and

I made sure we found an empty cell for her. Knew a ward would never do."

"What is that appalling smell?"

"It's the stench of Newgate, I'm afraid. After a while one gets used to the odor."

"I, quite frankly, don't see how," Trevor muttered as he followed the willowy man through the hallways until they came to a big oak door.

Williams set his lantern down and pulled out his keys. He opened the door and stepped back so Trevor could enter.

Trevor ducked down and entered the dark pit. "There is no light."

Williams followed him with the lantern. "It is a dark day."

The weak light from the lantern reached into the room, casting long shadows across the filthy floor and shabby interior. Kristen sat huddled in the corner with her arms wrapped around her legs, her head resting on her knees.

She slowly lifted her gaze, squinting from the light. A slow recognition finally registered in the green eyes he knew so well, and she came off the bed to throw herself in his arms. "I dinna like it here. You must free me."

"I know, sweetheart." Trevor hugged her.

After he let her go, he turned to Williams. "Are there no better accommodations? This cell is deplorable."

"This is, after all, a jail."

Trevor arched a brow. "Yes, but I presume there are better rooms for a price. Am I right?"

Williams grinned. "You're a very smart man, Your Grace. For a small deposit, I could put her into the press yard, and for a few more shillings she'd have clean sheets and blankets," he said with supreme confidence. "When Lord Grodon was incarcerated, he had his servants here also."

Trevor remembered the stories of the parties Lord Grodon had thrown in prison. Trevor realized that Williams
intended to get every gold coin he could get his hands on.

"And how much thereafter?"

"A small payment each week. We can discuss that pres-
ently, Your Grace."

"Very well," Trevor stated, then took his wife's arm.
That was when he noticed the handcuffs. "I would like
these fittings removed also."

"When we are at the other cell, I will give her easement
of irons for a mere three shillings."

"Let's go," Trevor stated, thinking he would like to take
this man out back and beat him to a pulp.

As they followed Williams, Kristen whispered, "I dinna
want to stay here."

"I know." Trevor slipped an arm around her and
squeezed her shoulder, wishing he could take her with
him. "Unfortunately, because of the seriousness of the
crime, I can't set you free."

"But he deserved to die."

"I know. Now we'll have to convince a jury of that fact."

They reached the new cell, which was a vast improve-
ment. It was clean and had plenty of light. It had two beds
and the floor was made of oak plank, and it was large
enough for any prisoners to move about comfortably.

Williams drew Trevor aside, and the two men haggled
over money. Once again, Trevor felt like beating Williams
to a pulp. Finally, reluctantly, Trevor handed over several
gold coins.

Once the transaction was complete, Kristen was allowed
in the cell, and Trevor followed behind her.

"Listen to me, Kristen," he said. "Don't do anything
foolish."

She looked at him. Her eyes widened in surprise. "Such as?"

"Swiping the keys and letting yourself out."

Awkwardly, she cleared her throat. "But, I dinna—"

"Kristen!"

"All right," she muttered hastily.

"I have to go. I will send for Rebecca. She can bring over some of your things, and she can stay with you."

"She doesn't have to stay," Kristen said.

"Rebecca will want to stay with you."

Tears filled Kristen's eyes as she watched Trevor leave. That man was forever making her promise one thing or another. Now she was stuck with no chance of escaping. She just hoped Trevor had a firm plan to get her out of there. This time she would have to trust him. She just hoped she wasn't being bloody stupid. At least, she'd have some company when Rebecca arrived.

However, deep down she wished Trevor would be the one staying with her. She could stand captivity a little better being held in his arms.

CHAPTER NINETEEN

Trevor went to see John Winthrop, a highly recommended barrister. Trevor explained his situation and all of Kristen's background, then sat back and waited as John and his partner, Edward Gates, discussed the case in the next room. Finally, Winthrop came back into the office and sat behind his desk.

"This is a most interesting case," Winthrop said, then cleared his throat. "My one worry is your wife's background before you married her. By your own admission, she was a thief and quite capable of murder."

"Kristen didn't murder the man. It was self-defense," Trevor was quick to remind Winthrop.

"I'm sure it was." Winthrop nodded his head in agreement. "However, the prosecutor might decide to dwell on Kristen's background and further damage her reputation. Does she not have a family who could vouch for her?"

"She does have a grandfather and a sister," Trevor reluctantly admitted.

"Then I suggest you have them at court. We will need their help."

Trevor stood, thanked Winthrop, then left. He had tried everything he could think of to avoid a meeting with Ian Johnstone. But now it was obvious that Ian was his last resort, and he had no choice but to return to Chatsworth, and then to visit Scotgrow.

Reining in his horse, Trevor looked across the green fields at the gray stone manor. He had to admit the home was impressive and nearly as large as Chatsworth. *Nearly.* He smiled to himself. Chatsworth was still more impressive. But Kristen's relatives had done well for themselves.

Trevor drew in a long, deep breath. Nothing would happen if he continued to sit there. He nudged his horse, and they cleared the final distance to his first meeting with the enemy.

Trevor was glad he'd sent word of his arrival ahead. He wouldn't have to do any explaining at the door. A rather large brute met him at the door, and showed him to a sitting room, where he waited for Ian to make his appearance. Trevor wasn't too sure how to handle this meeting, but he bloody well wouldn't beg the man for his help.

"And to what do I owe the honor of this visit?" a Scottish voice boomed out behind Trevor.

Trevor swung around. He wasn't sure what he expected—maybe some small, feeble old man stooped over from the years. Certainly not this hulk of a man who was just as tall as himself, and reasonably fit for his age. Trevor saw the resemblance to Kristen in Ian's sharp green eyes and his faded reddish-gray hair.

"I must speak with you. It's a matter of great importance," Trevor said, deciding it was better to come straight to the problem at hand.

"I dinna believe we have a thin' to discuss except for Kristen." Ian raised a bushy gray brow. "What have ye done with my granddaughter?"

"Kristen is exactly what I need to discuss with you." Trevor tried to remain patient, but he feared his anxiety showed in his voice.

"What have ye done to her?" Ian grabbed Trevor's coat. "If ye have hurt the lass, I'll kill ye here and now."

Trevor shoved the man's hands away from him, and narrowed his eyes. "I haven't done anything with Kristen, but she is in trouble and needs our help. So keep your bloody temper in check. Shall we sit down?" Trevor pointed to a set of tall black chairs that were opposite each other in front of a huge stone fireplace. "And I'll explain what has happened the best I can."

Ian grunted and grumbled, muttering under his breath. Finally, after a tense moment, he sat down in one chair and motioned for Trevor to take the other. The perfect place for two opponents.

"Kristen is in prison," Trevor said bluntly. It wasn't the best place to start, but he wanted Ian to understand the seriousness of the matter.

"What!" Ian shouted, and jumped out of his chair. His face had turned as red as an apple. "By the saints above, what happened?" He threw his hands up in the air as if he expected an answer from the heavens.

Trevor watched the old man's reaction with observant eyes. The Scot was too damn excitable. He wondered how much help he would be. "If you don't remain calm, you'll be no bloody help to Kristen," Trevor said between clenched teeth, trying to keep his temper under control.

"Let's get one thing straight. I don't like you any more than you like me. However, if we are going to free Kristen, we will have to work together."

"Not bloody likely!" Ian's eyes blazed with a sudden anger. "Never could trust a Claremont."

"Then I suggest you start now, or Kristen will hang."

That statement knocked the wind out of the old man and he slowly sank back down in his chair.

Good, Trevor thought. Maybe he could get through this without any more outbursts. "Kristen killed her stepfather."

"He wasn't her stepfather!"

"Precisely. And that's exactly what we need to tell the court. You know how Kristen grew up."

"No, I dinna know. We've never spoken about it. Always thought there would be time later."

"Then I shall tell you." Trevor drew in a deep breath and shifted in the chair, impatiently wanting to get down to the heart of the matter. "Kristen grew up in the streets. She was underfed and basically had to pick pockets in order to survive. From what I can gather, Ned, her stepfather, beat her every time he started drinking."

"Saints above!" Ian shook his head sadly. "I'd probably have killed that man myself. And the woman if I'd got my hands on her. She stole my granddaughter and robbed my little girl of her childhood."

"I agree. The situation is sad," Trevor said. "We can't do anything about her past, but I hope we can do something about the future."

"What do I need to do?"

Trevor finally felt as if he was getting through the man's thick head. He leaned forward, propping his elbow on his knees. "Kristen's trial is in three days. We need to pull together and show that she was a victim of the man. We must convince the jury that she is a good person who ended up in a bad situation.''

"Aye," Ian said, then grew quiet. "After she's acquitted, then what?''

"Kristen will be free, of course.''

"That's not what I meant.''

Trevor eyed the crafty old buzzard. "Then what do you mean?''

"Are ye smelling a trap now?" Ian grinned. "I will help ye, but I'll be wantin' something in return.''

Trevor should have known this wouldn't be easy. What did the old buzzard have in mind? "And what may that be?''

"I've been deprived of Kristen for all these years. Ye can't imagine what it has done to me." Ian looked Trevor dead in the eye. "The Claremonts have robbed me once before.''

"And what's that supposed to mean?" Trevor snapped, barely controlling his own temper. "I stole nothing from you!''

"I think ye know, but now is not the time to discuss such matters. I want ye to promise me that when Kristen is free ye'll send her to me, so I can spend some time with her.'' One corner of his mouth twisted upward. "Besides, ye don't love her.''

"You don't know a damned thing about me!" Trevor exploded as he rose and looked down at Ian. "Kristen is my wife.''

"Aye, and ye wed her when she had little choice in the matter, if I recall the story correctly.''

"True, we had an arrangement.''

"Then why don't ye give her a chance to make a choice of her own free will?" Ian demanded. "Or are ye afraid she won't choose ye?''

Trevor resented being backed into a corner, and he particularly didn't like having his fears thrown back at him. However, he did need to present a strong front, with Ian's help, so he could free Kristen.

He would agree to anything as long as it would help Kristen. Trevor clenched his fists tightly and said with a vague hint of disapproval, "I will agree to send Kristen with you when she is set free as long as you agree to let her come home to me if she so chooses."

"Done!" Ian stood and offered his hand.

Trevor noted the pleased look on the man's face and wondered just what Johnstone thought he'd won. Trevor frowned and didn't bother to take his hand.

As they sized each other up, the door opened and a young woman breezed through. Trevor glanced around Ian at her, then stopped and looked again, speechless. Kristen had told him about her sister, but he was completely unprepared to see another woman who looked so much like his wife.

Ian turned and looked in the same direction. "Keely, girl. Come meet Kristen's husband." He gestured toward her. Keely approached shyly and offered her hand.

"I'm glad to meet ye," she said, smiling demurely. "Kristen spoke of ye often."

"She did?" Trevor couldn't help the note of surprise in his voice.

"Aye, she did. I must say her description of ye was very accurate."

Trevor laughed. "I don't think I will ask you to explain that remark."

Keely laughed. "She spoke quite fondly of ye."

Keely's similarity to Kristen made him think of his wife, and where she was spending her nights. He felt once again that all this was his fault. If he had not gotten drunk and driven Kristen away, Ned wouldn't have gotten his hands on Hagan, and Kristen wouldn't be in jail. Trevor had to get her out of prison one way or the other. He owed her that much. And if she chose to return to Johnstone, he would do whatever it took to change her mind, he vowed.

He turned back to Ian. "We should ride to London together. I can arrange for my coach to take us."

"And what's wrong with my coach? Are ye insinuating my carriage isn't good enough?" Johnstone bristled.

"I didn't say there was anything wrong with it," Trevor bit out. Did the man have to be obstinate about everything? "But my coach has already been readied to travel."

"That being the case, I'll use yers." Johnstone turned and called to his man.

"Where are ye going?" Keely asked, then added, "And where is Kristen?"

Trevor glanced at Keely, and an idea came to him in a rush. "Perhaps we should take Keely. No one can doubt that Kristen is a Johnstone if they see Keely. And we'll stop by Chatsworth and pick up Hagan. The more family we have there, the better it will appear."

"For once, we agree on something, Englishman."

"Take me where?" Keely asked, confused.

"Go make ready to travel to London, girl," Ian declared. "We'll be explaining everything on the way."

Kristen gazed around the cell. She had to admit this cell was better than the one she'd move from, but she still felt caged. She sat on the bed, impatiently brushing her hair.

"Let me get that for you, mum," Rebecca said from across the room.

Kristen smiled at her. "Thank you, Rebecca, but I need something to do. This confinement is driving me crazy,"

Kristen complained. Thank God Trevor had sent Rebecca with some decent food. At least, the girl could keep her company.

Rebecca perched on the other bed and carefully pulled a needle through a tapestry. "Would you like for me to teach you how to sew?" Rebecca looked up, piercing her finger as she did so. "Ouch!" She immediately held her finger to her mouth. "It will help to pass the time."

"I dinna think so." Kristen smiled. "Looks painful."

What she wanted was to see Trevor. It had been a week since she'd last seen him. And she didn't understand why he stayed away.

Kristen had asked Rebecca, but the maid hadn't been a bit of help on that subject. The only thing she'd said was that Trevor had given her instructions to pack some of Kristen's things and to keep her company.

Was that so he wouldn't have to come see her himself? Kristen couldn't help wondering.

Kristen did manage to find out from one of the guards that her trial would be the next morning. As the time drew closer, she grew worried. What was she going to say in her defense?

"Why are you frowning so?" Rebecca asked.

Kristen looked up at her maid, and tried to mask her turmoil. "Was I frowning?"

Rebecca nodded.

"I was thinking about the trial tomorrow. What if the jury doesn't believe my side of the story and finds me guilty?" she said with a long, exhausted sigh. She stood. "I could hang."

"No, mum. You mustn't say such things," Rebecca protested, and put down her sewing. "Surely, they'll see how good you are."

"But I've not always been good," Kristen admitted as

she paced back and forth. She really wasn't sure she was good, but it was nice to know someone thought so. " 'Tis sorry that I am. I've stolen a few things and I've lied—not that I didn't have a good reason, ye ken?'' Kristen tried to judge Rebecca's reaction.

"Oh, dear." Rebecca's eyes widened.

Kristen swallowed hard. She could see the fear in her maid's eyes.

God, she was doomed.

Kristen looked to heaven. If ye get me out of this one, I swear I won't steal again, she silently prayed. And I really do mean it this time.

She didn't want to die. Now that she had a chance for happiness, she wanted to live. She had Hagan to take care of, and she had Trevor. At least, she hoped he still wanted her. Somehow, some way, she'd have to make the judge see that she had killed Ned to protect Hagan. She was not the criminal she was presumed to be.

"You're very lucky, mum," Rebecca said, finally coming out of her shocked silence.

"Are ye crazy! How can I be lucky?" Kristen tossed her head and gave an irritable tug at her sleeve. "We are sitting in the middle of a prison, or had ye forgotten that small fact? The only luck I seem to have is all bad."

"I disagree." Rebecca blushed, but persisted.

"Perhaps I should have yer thoughts."

"Now that you have shared your background with me, I think it was a stroke of luck that you found a man like His Grace."

"Actually, I didn't exactly find the man." Kristen smiled as she remembered their very first meeting. "I robbed him."

"Oh, no," Rebecca gasped, hugging her arms to herself.

Kristen frowned. "Aye, I did."

"But he married you. I don't understand."

Kristen sat back down on the bed. " 'Tis a long story, but we seemed to need each other, and we kind of struck a bargain."

"Then I will go back and say you are very lucky. You have a fine husband who loves you."

"I dinna think so. I had hoped so, but how can he love me after what I've done?"

"Oh, but he does. True love isn't conditional. It doesn't depend on what you do, but who you are." Rebecca smiled wistfully. "He looked real worried when he sent me here."

"So worried that he hasn't bothered to show himself in a week!"

Rebecca shrugged. "I'm sure he has his reasons."

Trevor almost laughed at the absurdity of the situation. Here he sat in a carriage with people he barely knew, riding to the rescue of a wife he'd never planned to have.

And what was worse, they had to pretend to be a cheerful family.

With the look on Ian's grumpy face, it would take a small miracle to convince the jury they were family at all . . . much less a happy one.

Keely seemed to be the only happy one because she was sound asleep next to Ian.

"Are we going to bring Kristen home?" Hagan asked.

"Aye," Ian said.

"Yes," Trevor and Ian answered together, then glared at each other.

"We hope so, Hagan," Trevor added. "Kristen will have to be tried. You must remember to be very quiet during the trial."

"What's a trial?" Hagan asked.

"By the saints, the chap can be asking some questions," Ian grumbled.

"A trial is what people get when they have been accused of doing something wrong." Trevor spoke to Hagan, but glared at Ian. "The trial decides if they are guilty or innocent."

"Kristen didn't do nothing wrong," Hagan insisted.

"I agree, she didn't."

" 'Tis a bloody English court," Ian snapped. "Ye probably can't trust any of them."

"Well, it's all we have." Trevor sharpened his voice. "I have obtained the best barristers money can buy."

"That's yer answer to everything. Money!" Ian grunted.

"You're grumpy, Grandda," Hagan said as he looked up at the man. "Didn't you sleep well?"

"I canna sleep with all the bloody racket," Ian informed Hagan. Ian shifted and tried to make himself comfortable in his seat.

Hagan smiled at Ian. "You remind me so much of Grandmère."

Ian raised a bushy white brow as he studied the child. "And how is that?"

"She was always grumpy too. Did you know her?"

Trevor noted the strange look that entered Ian's eyes, and he wondered. Trevor could almost swear that Ian's eyes looked misty.

"Aye, I knew her."

"She's gone, you know," Hagan replied sadly.

"I heard." Ian's words seemed worn and thin. "Why don't we get some sleep?" Ian folded his arms across his chest and shut his eyes, putting an end to the conversation.

"I'm not sleepy," Hagan protested, looking at Trevor.

"Ian's right," Trevor said. "We'll be traveling all night.

You must try to rest. As you can see, Keely has already gone to sleep.''

Hagan got up on his knees so he could whisper in Trevor's ear. "It's queer how much she looks like Kristen."

Trevor chuckled and nodded his agreement. "Lie down and put your head in my lap. No arguments."

"Ah, Trevor," Hagan grumbled, but did as he was told.

Trevor leaned back, resting his head on the coach's plush bolster. "Good night."

"Night," the child said, then added, "Don't forget to pray for Kristen."

"I will. Go to sleep." Trevor rubbed the child's head, and then he did something—something he hadn't done in a long time.

Trevor shut his eyes and prayed for a small miracle.

CHAPTER TWENTY

Kristen would rather sleep . . .

Maybe if she slept all day, someone could tell her what the jury decided when she woke up. But that wouldn't happen. The jailer had already told her they would be leaving in half an hour.

Rebecca had been her usual efficient self and had packed their few belongings. Evidently she didn't expect they wouldn't be returning.

If only Kristen could share her optimism. She looked into the small hand mirror and noticed how her hand shook. Her eye had turned an ugly purple and yellow color. Maybe the lingering evidence of what Ned had done would help her case. At least, she hoped it would.

Kristen heard the keys jingling before the door opened and the jailer—one she'd not seen before—stepped inside.

"It's time, miss," he informed her.

Kristen drew in a long, slow breath. Her time had come.

"I'm glad ye stayed with me," Kristen whispered to Rebecca as she hugged her.

"I didn't mind. It's my job, mum. I'll just take your things home and wait for you there. I know everything will turn out all right." Rebecca squeezed Kristen's arm reassuringly.

"Ye have more confidence than I do."

The jailer shuffled his feet. "I said it's time to go, miss," the big, burly man repeated. He slapped the manacles onto Kristen's wrists impatiently.

He shoved her out the door, then led her through several long hallways until they entered what they called Old Bailey, where he placed her in another cell under the courtroom.

The room was nothing but four walls and a door. There was no place to sit, and this time Kristen wasn't alone. Seven men and three women were already in the small cell, and the men had the same shifty appearance as Ned. At least they were not making rude comments. Kristen assumed they were too worried about their own necks to bother with her.

Kristen leaned against a far wall so she could keep her eyes on her new roommates. And she waited.

The wall felt damp against her back and she wondered if this room ever had any light in it. After an hour passed, the bailiff came and took two of the prisoners upstairs. They left in pairs until finally she was the only one left in the cell.

"You're next," the jailer said as he opened the door to fetch her.

Kristen straightened her spine. She lifted her chin, determined she wouldn't be a coward. She stepped forward and asked, "Do you know anything about this court?"

He nodded and explained that the Old Bailey was divided into four courts. He was taking her to the fourth court, where she would be tried by the Assize Judge.

Kristen swallowed hard at that tidbit of information. Even she knew that the Assize Judge only tried the most serious cases, and usually his sentences were severe.

She didn't know whether she hoped it was a long way to the court or whether she wanted to get there and get the trial over with quickly. She followed the bailiff.

When she entered the courtroom, Kristen was overwhelmed by the size of the room and the many long tables. She was taken to the center and told to stand on a small platform. Glancing to her left, Kristen saw Trevor, Hagan, and her new family all sitting together. She almost looked a second time to make sure she wasn't seeing things. *A Claremont and a Johnstone shoulder to shoulder.* At least one miracle had occurred today. She smiled a little at the irony.

She faced the judge, who sat in the middle of a semicircle. He wore a scarlet robe and a white powdered wig. Below him, another group of men sat dressed exactly the same. She had no idea who they were, but they looked like judges also.

Everywhere she looked she saw red. The seats were crimson, and the walls had a faded hanging cloth that she was sure had been red at one time. She hoped the scarlet color everywhere did not symbolize what was to come: her death, bloody and cruel. Over the center of the judge's bench, a sword of justice with a gold handle and ornamented scabbard was displayed.

Her small enclosure was directly across from the Assize Judge.

The man who brought her in pulled on her arm. "Stand here and face the Clerk of the Arraign," he instructed.

"Who?"

"The man over there." The jailer pointed. "The desk beneath the judge."

Kristen leaned over the rail so she could keep her voice low. "Who is sitting at the long table with the green cloth?"

"One is the prosecution and the others would be your barristers," he said, then left her alone.

Kristen straightened and glanced to her right at the jury box, which consisted of two long seats. Every man seemed to be staring at her, and she shuddered. She just hoped she looked innocent to them.

A tall, thin man came toward her and stopped. "I am your barrister, Your Grace. Mr. Winthrop at your service." He bowed, and she felt ridiculous, seeing that she had handcuffs on her wrists. Her cheeks warmed with her embarrassment.

" 'Tis nice to meet ye, Mr. Winthrop."

"Is there anything you would like to tell me? You will not be permitted to testify on your own behalf, but I have been granted the right to cross-examine, which, I assure you, is rare."

Kristen stared at the stranger who knew absolutely nothing about her. How could he know what she'd lived in or how she had endured over the years? He couldn't. But he seemed to be all she had at the moment. "I did pull the trigger, but only out of fear for myself and my brother. Ye have only to look at our black eyes to see what the man inflicted on us."

Winthrop nodded. "I do see that. Did he do this often?"

"Every chance he got."

"Let us begin," a clerk announced as he stood. He waited a moment for everyone to quit talking.

Her barrister hurried back to the table with the green cloth where the two other men sat staring at her.

The clerk started reading the names of the Members of

the Commission. When the clerk had finished, he sat down and silence crackled across the room.

"What is the prisoner's name?" the judge asked in a booming voice, looking not at Kristen but her barrister.

Mr. Winthrop stood and cleared his throat. "Kristen Johnstone Claremont, the Duchess of Chatsworth, Your Honor."

"So this is the one," the judge muttered more to himself than to anyone. Then he continued. "She is charged with murder?"

"She is, Your Honor."

"Does she understand the charge?"

"She does, Your Honor."

"Then let us begin."

Kristen watched as the prosecution called some of the men she'd seen in the hallway the night of the shooting. They each pointed to her as the woman who had held the gun when they'd arrived. She listened as they painted a grim picture of what they'd seen. She sounded guilty, even to her own ears.

Then her barrister questioned the same men, asking if they knew what had happened before the fatal shot was fired. Each man replied no.

Next the prosecution questioned Trevor, who gave all the correct answers. However, when asked about the gun, he had to tell the court that his wife had been holding the weapon when he'd arrived.

The prosecution rested. It was apparent in the man's face that he didn't think there was a need to call anyone else.

Just as Kristen thought her fate was doomed, Winthrop turned and called Ian Johnstone.

"Can you tell us your relationship to Kristen Claremont?" Winthrop asked.

"Her name is Kristen Johnstone ... Claremont," Ian declared, then added, "The lass is my granddaughter."

"But we just heard testimony that she was raised in the streets," Winthrop interjected.

" 'Twas no fault of her own," Ian snapped. "Kristen was kidnapped by my housekeeper when she was just a wee bairn."

"Then you don't think she is capable of killing anyone?"

"Nay, I do not. Just look at her eye. If she were a murderer, she'd have killed the man before he struck her."

Her barrister seemed pleased with the last remark. "No further questions," Winthrop said, then sat down.

The prosecution stood up for cross-examination. "You just testified that your granddaughter was taken from you at a tender age. How can you possibly know what she would do?"

"Kristen came to spend some time with me. She is exactly like her sister, and could never do anything that would purposely hurt someone."

The prosecutor placed an arm on the rail. "How do you know Kristen is your granddaughter?"

"If ye'll have Keely, her sister, stand, ye'll find yer answer."

The prosecutor turned and said, "Keely Johnstone, please stand so that we may see you."

Keely slowly stood, and everyone gasped.

The prosector frowned, having been caught in his own folly.

"You have heard testimony that your granddaughter was an accomplished thief," he said. "What do have to say about that, sir?"

Ian thought for a moment. "If I were hungry enough, I suppose I could be a thief too. But 'tis not the same as murder."

"Then, you think what she did is right?"

"I didna say that. I am old, and I have seen many men in every situation imaginable. I believe we would do most anything in our power to survive, even yourself, sir."

The prosecutor, seeing that he wasn't getting anywhere, dismissed Ian.

Winthrop stood. "I would like to call one final witness," he stated. "Hagan, will you please come forward?"

Hagan made his way to the front of the courtroom, but as soon as he neared Kristen, he darted over and, standing on tiptoe, he reached up a hand to her.

Kristen leaned over and squeezed the child's hand.

"I've missed you," Hagan whispered.

"I've missed ye too," she said, then gently pushed him in the direction he should be going.

As soon as Winthrop helped Hagan into the stand, the judge asked, "What happened to your eye?"

Hagan stared at the judge a moment before he said in a very small voice, "My father hit me."

The judge didn't bother to say anything else, so Mr. Winthrop spoke. "Did he do this often?"

"Every time he got liquored up, he usually beat Kristen."

"And why not yourself?"

" 'Cause Kristen would hide me until he sobered up."

Winthrop placed his hand on the rail and leaned toward Hagan. "Do you think that he would have killed Kristen?"

"He'd have killed anybody who got in his way. He was hitting me when Kristen pointed the gun and told him to stop."

"Thank you, young man. You may step down," the judge said as a surprised Winthrop looked on.

The prosecutor stood. "We would like to question the child."

"The child has been through enough, and so have I,"

the judge stated. The prosecutor sat down, his mouth still open.

"You have heard all the evidence. What do you have to say for yourself?" The judge looked straight at Kristen.

Kristen tried to remain calm, but her knees shook as she racked her brain for the right words. "I have done things in my past that I'm not very proud of, Your Honor, but the only thing I am guilty of now is protecting my brother."

"So be it." The judge looked to the jury and nodded. The jury gathered together to discuss her fate. She could see their heads bobbing and heard their murmurs. Every once in a while a member of the jury would look in her direction and frown.

Kristen's knees grew that much weaker. If the jury didn't make a decision soon, they would be picking her up off the floor.

Finally, one of the jurors approached the judge and whispered something in his ear.

The judge looked at Kristen solemnly. "Kristen Johnstone Claremont, you have been judged by your peers and found . . ."

The judge didn't finish his sentence. He frowned intently down at her.

Saints above! Kristen thought frantically. She was doomed!

Glancing down at her hands, she found her knuckles had turned white from gripping the rail.

"Not guilty," the judge's voice rang out.

Kristen didn't move. Did he say not guilty? Did that mean it was all over? Her legs gave way, and she had to cling to the railing to keep from falling to the floor.

The jailer approached her and removed the handcuffs.

Kristen started to follow him out of habit. She wasn't sure what she was supposed to do.

"No, mum. You are free to go and be with your family." He pointed to the happy group of people waiting for her.

Kristen felt as if she were in a fog. Was it really over? Could she really go home with Trevor and Hagan? She stumbled toward them. Ian was the first one she reached. He grabbed her and hugged her. Then Hagan rushed into her arms.

How wonderful it felt to have that little boy in her arms. She brushed his unruly hair with her hand and breathed in the wonderful little-boy smell.

Finally, Trevor took her arm. "Let's get out of this court-room."

When they were outside, Kristen had to shade her eyes from the light even on such a cloudy day. It had been over a week since she'd been outside and the light overwhelmed her.

Trevor immediately wrapped his arms around her. "Are you all right?" he asked, leaning over, holding her next to his side.

" 'Tis the light. It's so bright."

"I didn't think about it," Trevor admitted. "Try and open your eyes slowly."

She followed his instructions until she could keep her eyes open without them watering.

"That's my girl. Now, turn around and look at me," Trevor said tenderly.

She did as he asked, and tilted her head back until she could see his eyes. What she saw made her pulse quicken. They were definitely blue and smoldering today as he gazed down at her. A promise lingered in their depths.

Heat spread through her like a wildfire. She didn't hesitate, throwing her arms around his neck, hugging him to her until his arms tightened around her like a steel band.

Then his lips were on hers, parting them and taking her breath as his tongue drove deep into her mouth. She tried to show him how much she loved him by returning the urgency of his kiss.

She touched her tongue to his and tightened her hold around his neck. She felt as if she was holding on for dear life because she didn't want to let him go ever again. The desire to shower him with love and affection overwhelmed her.

They were both heedless of their surroundings until Ian said from somewhere behind them, "I kept my part of the bargain, Englishman."

Trevor pulled back. He hugged Kristen one final time before stepping away from her.

Kristen stood a moment, trying to regain her balance. She was embarrassed that she'd forgotten about the rest of her family, who were standing outside Old Bailey. She turned to them. "I want to thank ye for coming today."

Keely stepped closer and hugged her. "We're family."

When Keely stood back, Kristen noticed for the first time that there were two black coaches that seemed to be waiting for them. She recognized Trevor's, and she assumed the other one belonged to her grandfather.

"Are we ready to go home?" Kristen asked, when no one moved.

Trevor frowned as he took her elbow and pulled her aside. "Kristen, I think you should go home with your family, so you can have time to get to know them."

Hagan shoved between them. "No, I want Kristen to come home with us."

"If you want, you can go with your sister," Trevor said, looking down at the child.

"But I want to stay with you at Chatsworth."

Kristen felt completely numb.

She had gone from gloriously happy to miserable in the matter of a minute.

She had thought all this confusion was behind her, but Trevor had just made it clear that he wanted her to go with her grandfather.

Trevor didn't want her.

Had he just felt guilty about her being in jail? Now that she was free, so was he?

But the kiss . . .

How could he kiss her like that and not feel anything? Kristen stepped away from him and pasted a determined look on her face. Well, she most certainly wouldn't make a fool out of herself twice in one day. She should face the fact that her life would never be simple, much less normal.

"Hagan, 'tis all right if ye want to stay with Trevor. I understand." It took all of Kristen's power to stay focused on her brother and not look at her husband. She'd never let him see the rejection she felt.

"Ah, Kristen," Hagan groaned, and hugged her. "Will you come and visit me?"

"Of course I will. And I expect to have ye visit me too," she said, giving him a final hug.

She looked at Trevor, careful to keep all emotion out of her expression. "I appreciate everything ye have done." She didn't wait for his reply. Instead, she turned and made her way quickly to Ian's carriage before she broke down in tears.

Trevor watched Kristen leave. He felt helpless to stop her. The old man had gotten his way, and now Trevor finally had his own reason to hate the old buzzard.

The carriage pulled out, and Trevor followed the vehicle

with his gaze. She could have at least put up some kind
of a fight. She could have said she wanted to stay with him.

That was all it would have taken for him to break his
agreement with Ian.

Instead she had said nothing . . . nothing at all.

Evidently, he had his answer. She'd been waiting for a
way out of their marriage, and he'd just given it to her.

"Do you think she'll come back, Trevor?" Hagan asked
tremulously, and slipped his small hand into Trevor's.

"I don't know, Hagan. I honest to God do not know."

CHAPTER
TWENTY-ONE

How many weeks had gone by since Kristen had come to Scotgrow? Too many, she thought as she watched the meadow and waited for Hagan.

Hagan galloped across the rolling meadow on his brown pony. He was accompanied by a groom, but Kristen had looked for Trevor anyway, hoping he would come with Hagan. She moved down the back porch steps and across the yard.

The minute Hagan saw her, he slipped agilely from the pony and ran toward her. He threw himself in her arms and squeezed her tight.

"Look at ye." Kristen laughed and swung Hagan around. "Ye've grown at least an inch in the last month," she said as she placed him back on the ground.

"A half inch." He grinned devilishly. "Trevor measures me every week and makes a mark on the side of the barn if I've grown any," Hagan explained. Then, completely out of the blue, he asked, "Why haven't you come to visit?"

Tears welled in Kristen's eyes, but she blinked them away. "I thought it better if I stayed here. I dinna think Trevor wants me at Chatsworth," she said huskily.

"Why do you say that?" Hagan frowned at her. "Has he said not to come?"

In so many words, Kristen thought. She shook her head. How could she explain so a small boy could understand? She swallowed.

"Come with me," she said, taking his hand. The child sounded too much like a grown-up. "We'll have cookies and milk in the gazebo." She decided it would be better to get his mind off Trevor, and better for herself as well.

"I like cookies."

Kristen smiled down at him. "I remember."

Once they were settled in the gazebo, Kristen said, "Tell me what ye've been doing. And dinna leave anything out."

"Well." Hagan grinned as if he had a big secret that he was dying to tell. "I've been helping Trevor train a colt," Hagan blurted out. "He's real pretty."

"What does he look like?"

Hagan stuffed a cookie in his mouth. "He—he's—"

"Dinna talk with yer mouth full," she scolded, and handed him a glass of milk.

"He is black with four white feet and a white streak running down his nose," Hagan said proudly, not bothering to wipe the milk mustache from his lip.

"He does sounds pretty." Kristen reached over and wiped his mouth with a cloth. "Have ye named him?"

"Trevor let me name him," Hagan said proudly. "Said he will be all mine, but he's still too young to ride 'cording to Trevor."

"So what did you name him?" Kristen prodded.

Hagan grinned. "Flash."

She watched Hagan's eyes brighten with pleasure. " 'Tis an odd name," Kristen said.

"The white down his nose reminds me of lightning, and Trevor suggested Flash 'cause it means quick."

Every time the child mentioned Trevor, Kristen hurt a little more inside, and now she was going to have to ask the question she swore she wouldn't. But she was dying to know. "How is Trevor?"

Hagan rolled his eyes. "He works all the time. I heard one of the maids say he gets up before dawn and goes into his office. Then, in the afternoon, he spends time with me around the barn. I like that. But I think it makes all the workers nervous 'cause Trevor never did anything like that before. But he does now."

"I see." Kristen bit her lip. "Does he ever say anything about me?"

Hagan thought for a moment. "No. Once I was talking about you and he walked away. I think he had something else to do," Hagan said with childlike innocence.

Something else indeed.

The revelation hurt, but Kristen struggled not to let it show. So Trevor didn't give a damn about her. It must be bad when he couldn't bear to hear her name. Where had she gone so wrong?

Not wanting to dwell on anything so painful, she made herself clean up the table. It helped to keep busy. "Let's get up and stretch our legs."

They whiled away the rest of the afternoon walking and playing games, but all too soon it was time for Hagan to leave. She hugged him to her, then helped him mount his pony and instructed the groom to take good care of him.

Blinking back the tears, Kristen turned toward the house. Then Hagan called to her.

"Kristen."

She turned and looked at him.

He rode up on his pony. "I almost forget something," he said as he dug deep into his pocket and pulled out Constance's necklace. He smiled sheepishly. "I'm supposed to give this to you."

Kristen held out her hand, and Hagan dropped the lovely necklace into her open palm. "Did Trevor send this to me?" she asked, her hopes soaring.

Hagan shook his head. "Grandmère told me before she died that if anything happened to her she wanted me to give you this necklace. She said you would need it and"— Hagan looked up to the sky and drew a deep breath as he tried to remember—"and she hoped you would treasure it as much as she always did."

Kristen recalled the time when Constance had tried to give the necklace to her. She could picture Constance's pale face . . .

"I want you to have something." Constance had reached over and opened the drawer next to the bed. *"Something that is very dear to me."*

"I canna accept something so nice."

"Hear me!" Constance said with a sigh, her breathing labored. *"My time is growing short. You must get Trevor to open up if you ever want to keep him."*

Constance had reached up and pointed to Kristen's chest. *"Look deep inside yourself, and you'll find out what to do . . ."*

Shaking herself from her reverie, Kristen smiled. Constance hadn't taken no for an answer. Even in death she still got her way. Kristen folded the necklace in her hand. She would treasure the gift, but how would she ever convince Trevor that she hadn't stolen the jewelry? It would be the first thing he would think. But she would be damned if she'd take the necklace back to him.

She dared hoped he would notice it missing. Just maybe he would get angry, and then he'd have to come to see her. If only to take it back.

Kristen sat on the top porch step, her chin propped on her hands as her elbows rested on her knees, and looked out at the lush green grass of Scotgrow.

Why couldn't she be happy here? She'd always wanted a family. Now she had one, but something was missing, and she knew what that *something* was. Unfortunately, she lacked the answers about how to solve her problem. Her whole body was engulfed in tides of indifference and despair. She sighed, weary of the arguments in her head.

She had enjoyed seeing Hagan this afternoon. She shut her eyes and recalled the pleasant afternoon.

A breeze blew her long hair across her face, bringing her back to the present and her loneliness.

She had hoped Trevor would come with Hagan. She had not seen Trevor once in two months, and she'd stubbornly not gone to Chatsworth. If the man wanted no part of her, then so be it. Let him grow old and weary without ever again experiencing any fun or love. Let him work himself to death.

She could remember when she had asked him if he knew the meaning of the word "fun," and of course he hadn't. Hard work was all he knew. It wasn't good for him, and she had thought she'd changed him a little and brought some pleasure to his life. Trevor had seemed to grow more carefree when he was with her, but according to Hagan, now Trevor was working harder than ever.

This was one situation she had no answers for, and she

felt completely helpless, not knowing what to do. Would she ever see him again?

Ian glanced across the porch and spotted the redhead he'd been looking for all morning.

He paused to watch her. She sat on the top step, her arms folded around her knees, staring out in the direction of Chatsworth. He'd hoped she had forgotten about the Englishman by now.

Maybe he'd been wrong. He had only wanted to give the girl some time to find herself. Ian had not wanted that bloody Englishman forcing Kristen into something she might not want. Now, thanks to her newfound family wealth, she had the opportunity to make her own choices.

"Bargain," Ian huffed. The Englishman knew that Kristen had had no choice but to marry him. Trevor needed to suffer a little. Let him find out what it was like to have something precious taken away from him.

However, Ian's plan did not appear to be working. Instead of Kristen blossoming into a beautiful woman, she had quickly become withdrawn. And the bloody Englishman had made no attempt to see her. None that Ian knew about.

Perhaps he'd just have a talk with the girl. He shoved away from the wall. "Are ye not feeling well, lass? I thought with Hagan coming, ye'd be a bit more cheerful," Ian said as he sat down with a groan. "I fear the bones are not what they used to be."

Kristen looked up at him with those vivid green eyes so much like his own. However, something was missing . . . they lacked a spark . . . they lacked life. She did manage a brief smile that somehow didn't quite reach her eyes. "I'm a little tired."

"Tired, is it?" Ian gave her a knowing look. "Are ye not sleeping well?"

"Aye. I sleep fine."

"Then why, pray tell, are ye tired? I'm the one who should be tired, with my ancient, old bones."

"Ye're not that old, Grandfather," Kristen said as she lifted her gaze to study his face. "Sometimes I forget ye are my grandfather, and I think of you as my da."

"Unfortunately, I canna forget, since I have to live in this body," he joked. "Tell me what's wrong, lass. We're family. Ye can tell me anything."

"I know," she said. "I—I thought Trevor would have come to see me by now."

"That bloody Englishman." Ian's voice rose. He forgot he was trying to be understanding. "Ye can do better, by far, for yerself."

"But I love him," Kristen stated simply.

Now it was Ian's turn to sigh. "I was afraid of that. Are ye sure, lass?"

Kristen nodded, and the tears she had tried not to shed crept slowly down her cheeks.

Ian slipped his arm around Kristen and pulled her close. " 'Tisn't easy to love a Claremont," he confessed.

Kristen nodded her head in agreement, then mumbled, "How would ye know?"

" 'Cause I've loved one myself," Ian admitted as he looked down at Kristen's small hands. Something gold tangled between her fingers caught his attention. "What's that in yer hand, lass?"

Kristen opened her hand, and Ian recognized the necklace.

"Hagan brought this to me today. It once belonged to Trevor's grandmother. She told Hagan before she died that she would like me to have it, but I fear Trevor will think I have stolen it."

"I've not seen that necklace in some fifty years," Ian said in a hushed voice as he reached for it. An emerald the size of a walnut hung at the end of a gold rope and caught the afternoon light.

He turned it over and examined every detail. The pain that had haunted him for so many years came rushing back. Memories of what could have been flooded his mind. He pictured Constance's beautiful face and glowing eyes when she told him the emerald would always remind her of his eyes.

"When did ye see this necklace?" Kristen asked.

"Around Constance's neck," Ian replied. "I gave it to her the first time I told her that I loved her. And she said the emerald would always remind her of my eyes." That had been many years ago, Ian thought, and still the pain felt fresh.

"I've probably done ye a grave injustice, lass. I asked Trevor to keep away to give ye some time to yerself. Made him promise."

Kristen's brow lifted in surprise. "I'll wager he readily agreed to get rid of me."

"Nay."

"He didn't?" she asked in surprise. Then she realized that her grandfather had really interfered with her life. Maybe she *would* have gone home with Trevor after she'd gotten out of prison. Maybe things would have been different.

"Why did ye do such a thing?" Kristen asked with a vague hint of disapproval. She watched his expressive face as it grew somber.

"I knew ye had little choice in marrying the man, and I simply wanted to give ye a chance to change yer mind."

She sighed, held her hands together, and stared at them. "I dinna want to change my mind. I love the man."

"Aye, I can see that now," Ian admitted. "Does he know?"

She shook her head. "Nay."

"Why have ye not told him?"

"Because he doesn't love me."

"And are ye sure of that, lass?"

Kristen glanced at him. "He has never told me that he does."

Ian snorted. The lass was as stubborn as he. He clasped his hands around a knee and looked at her. "Doesn't mean a thing. He has shown you in many ways."

"I canna believe ye are taking up for him."

Ian chuckled.

"Why do ye not like Trevor?"

"Goes way back, lass."

"Then tell me. I think I deserve to understand." Kristen watched her grandfather as he drew in his breath.

"Many years ago," Ian began as he stared out over the lawn, his eyes focusing not on the grounds, but something long ago, "I fell in love with a beautiful young girl. Her name was Constance."

Kristen stared at him sharply, but he didn't seem to notice, for he was lost in his thoughts. Kristen could sense his dazed state, and she didn't want him to stop now that he'd started. She had to hear the story.

"And she loved me," Ian continued. "But she had been promised to Claremont, and there was nothing she could do to convince her parents to break the marriage agreement."

"Did they know about ye?" Kristen asked softly.

"Nay. Constance tried to convince me to talk to them, but I was too stubborn. Wouldn't have done any good with me being a bloody Scot. I wasn't a laird at that time, so I had verra little to offer a wife except my love."

"So what happened?"

"She married Claremont. And I married Maggie."

That was the first time Kristen had ever heard her grandmother's name. "Did ye love Grandmother?"

"Aye, but not in the same way. Maggie died at childbirth. We only had a year together.

"Over the years Claremont and I became friends and business partners. I had a twofold purpose, ye see, business and being close to Constance. I could see her from time to time.

"Ye might not believe me, but every time I looked at that woman, I saw love in her eyes. Over the years, it never died. Once in a while, she'd hold my hand or glance at me across the room, and my heart would race out of control.

"We never did anything about our love," he said thickly. "Not until—"

Ian stopped abruptly. Kristen perceived he was having to collect himself before he went on. She felt his pain, and she could only imagine how he'd suffered over the years. Much as she was suffering herself.

"Until Constance's son died. I tried to comfort and console her." Ian's voice caught, and Kristen could see that his eyes had grown as misty as her own.

"That's when it happened." He ran a hand through his gray hair, then leaned over to place both arms on his legs. "All those years when we had denied our love finally burst loose, and I dinna think I need to tell ye what happened. But 'twas love, lass, pure and simple. 'Twas nothing sordid. Just two people giving comfort and solace. I can tell ye, I worshiped the ground that woman walked on."

"I can see that." Kristen squeezed his hand. "So what happened?"

"For a while we went on as before, but 'twas difficult. Then I found out that Claremont was keeping a paramour in London, and I confronted him."

"So that's what ye were arguing about when he died."

"Aye. 'Twas not my place, but I told him he couldn't do that to Constance. I would not stand for it."

"What did he say?"

"The bloody bastard told me he would do as he pleased. Said he'd never loved Constance, and it was his right to have another woman. Rage took over my body, and I told him he didn't deserve Constance. I told him I loved her, and intended to make her my own, by God!" Ian said forcefully.

"And?"

"He swore he would kill me first. He might not love her, but he'd never give her up. We struggled. And that's when Claremont dropped dead at my feet."

"I dinna understand." Kristen shook her head. "With Claremont gone, ye never married Constance."

"Fate has a cruel way with one," Ian whispered in a voice that seemed to come from a long way off. "Constance blamed me for killing her husband, and she never spoke to me after the funeral."

"Dinna ye tell her what he'd told ye?"

"Nay. She dinna need to know such. I just told her that I'd told him about our love, and she thought that's what pushed Claremont over the edge."

"Are ye sure she blamed ye? She could have blamed herself."

Her grandfather looked at her sharply. "What do ye mean?"

"I got to know Constance before she died. She was not a happy woman. Bitter is how I'd describe her. Now I know why. I think she blamed herself for her husband's death.

She probably felt guilty that she'd never loved him and had always loved ye, and since ye didn't tell her the real truth, she never knew what her husband was really like."

"Never thought of that, lass, but no matter, 'tis too late for us."

Kristen reached over and hugged her grandfather. "I'm sorry. But ye shouldn't hold what happened in the past against Trevor. Your quarrel was with his grandfather."

"I always felt I might have a chance after the death, but then Trevor came to live with Constance, and she poured all her love into him."

"But Trevor was a child."

"Aye, a Claremont child."

"Just listen at how ridiculous ye sound. Ye always possessed something Claremont could never have, and that was Constance's love. The hating and the anger must end now."

Ian opened his mouth to say something, then stopped. He sighed, then smiled sadly. " 'Tis a fool I've been over the years. Ye must learn from my mistakes, lass. Go after what you want in life and hold onto it as hard as you can, so ye don't lose it."

"What do ye suggest I do? Trevor wants nothing to do with me."

Ian smiled down at her, his emerald eyes bright again. "We'll think of something . . . 'Cause a Johnstone can outsmart a Claremont any day."

CHAPTER
TWENTY-TWO

"Where is Kristen?" Rodney Brownwell inquired as he leaned against a post, watching Trevor trot a colt around a ring on a long tether.

"Why do you ask?" Trevor responded dryly, not bothering to look at his friend.

"I've been here half the day and haven't seen your lovely bride yet. After her narrow escape from the hangman, I assumed you wouldn't let her out of your sight."

Trevor wasn't sure he even remembered seeing Kristen after the trial. Everything had happen so fast. The one thing he did remember was watching the coach as it rolled away from the prison. "Kristen is with her grandfather," he said in a gruff voice.

"Oh, I see." Rodney propped his arms on top of the fence. "She is visiting."

"No," Trevor said flatly as he handed the colt over to a groom. Slowly, Trevor walked over to where Rodney

324 Brenda K. Jernigan

stood. He wished Rodney would drop the matter, but he knew his friend well enough to realize he wouldn't. "Kristen is living with her grandfather."

"What!" Rodney shouted. "Why?"

"It was an agreement I made with Johnstone to get his complete cooperation at the trial. He said he deserved Kristen since he'd missed her all these years."

Rodney's eyebrows snapped together. "And what did Kristen have to say about the subject?"

"We didn't ask her," Trevor replied.

"Don't you think she should have a say in the matter?"

"She could have said something at the time. But she didn't say a damn thing," Trevor snapped.

Rodney wasn't in the least perturbed at Trevor's abruptness. "So how long are you going to leave her there?"

"That, my friend, is completely up to the lady in question."

"Wait a minute." Rodney grabbed his arm. "You take a thief, clean her up, make her suitable to be your wife, marry her, pay off her stepfather, then hire the best lawyers to get her acquitted when she kills a man. And you're going to let her walk completely out of your life after she's turned it upside down?" Rodney stopped, but only because he needed to take a breath. "Well, are you?"

Trevor frowned. Rodney had summed up the last few months of his life in a simple statement. "Something like that."

Rodney straightened and glared at Trevor. "Are you bloody stupid?"

"Careful, Rodney," Trevor warned. Then, a little exasperated, he asked, "What would you have me do?"

Rodney gave him an incredulous look. "Well, doing nothing most certainly isn't working. Go after the woman you love and bring her home."

"Rodney, my friend," Trevor said. "You make everything sound so simple. Have you thought that she might not want me?"

"Rubbish! I have seen the way Kristen looks at you, and, I might add, I've also noticed the way you look at her," Rodney pointed out. He crossed his arms over his chest.

Trevor didn't want to admit that Rodney was right. But Trevor felt an acute sense of loss. The pain in his heart had become a fiery gnawing, impossible to ignore. "Have you ever wanted something so badly that you hurt inside?" Trevor asked.

"Can't say that I have. And I'm not sure I want to if it makes me as miserable as you are," Rodney said, smiling. "What do you want, Trevor?"

"Kristen." The word seemed torn from Trevor's throat as he surprised himself by finally admitting the truth.

"Then, by God, go after her. Make peace with her family if you have to, but claim what is yours."

"What if she doesn't want me?"

Rodney patted Trevor on the back. "You'll never know unless you ask."

Trevor wasn't certain what he should do. He had never been in this kind of position before. He'd always known exactly what he wanted, and to be thrown into this uncertainty dug like a thorn in his side. He didn't like it.

Rodney made everything sound so simple. That he and Ian hated each other was an enormous obstacle. Trevor didn't want Kristen to have to choose between him and her family. "I've never been in this situation before," Trevor said. "I don't know what to do."

Before Rodney could respond, Hagan and his groom came galloping up to the stables, and Trevor forced himself to calm down.

"Slow down, young man," Trevor said in a teasing manner. He reached for the pony's bridle.

"I had a wonderful time," Hagan said, sliding from his pony into Trevor's arms. He wrapped his arms around Trevor and squeezed.

Rodney cleared his throat.

"Who's this?" Hagan asked, peering around Trevor.

"A friend of mine," Trevor said, then put Hagan on the ground in front of him. "Rodney Norman Brownwell, Marquess of Middleton. Rodney, I would like you to meet Master Hagan Blume."

Hagan tilted his head to the side. "How do you remember a name that long?" he asked with typical childish innocence.

Rodney laughed. "I agree it is a bit much, and difficult to remember at first. You may call me Rodney."

"That's much easier," Hagan said, then turned back to Trevor as if that were the end of it. "Aren't you going to ask me about Kristen?"

Rodney chuckled and arched an eyebrow.

Trevor glared at Rodney, but he stooped to look at Hagan.

"How is your sister?" Trevor finally asked.

"She wanted to know what you were doing," Hagan said. He smiled, his face brightening. "I told her about Flash." Then Hagan's smile faded. "Trevor, when is Kristen coming home?"

Trevor studied the child, reluctant to admit he'd been wondering the same thing, and hating to acknowledge that he didn't have the answer. He cleared his throat and tried to formulate a reply.

"Trevor and I were discussing that very subject when you rode up, Master Hagan," Rodney said. "I think your sister is coming home very soon."

"Good." Hagan's smile returned. "I want to have you both in the same place. I'm hungry," he informed Trevor.

"Go dress for dinner. We'll follow soon."

Hagan scampered toward the house, then stopped suddenly and came back. "Grandfather said they're going to have some Scottish games five days hence." Hagan held up five fingers. "He said lots of big Scottish lads will come to Scotgrow and compete. Can we go?"

Trevor smiled grimly. "I wouldn't miss it."

"Do you suppose they'll all wear those skirts?" Hagan asked, making a face.

"Those skirts are called kilts, and yes, they will wear them."

Hagan giggled, then turned and ran off toward the house.

"Trevor," Rodney said, drawing Trevor's attention away from the boy. "I think there is something else you should know."

"I'm not sure I like the sound of that."

"Your uncanny sense is as good as always." Rodney chuckled. "But this is news you will not find amusing, I assure you. I learned that the two men who sabotaged the *Alastair* and sent it to the ocean bottom worked for Ian."

"That filthy bastard!" Trevor felt the blood surge to his face. "Are you sure?"

"Evidently, Ian's grudge ran deep," Rodney replied grimly. He watched Trevor, but other than the tightening of Trevor's hand on the fence post, there wasn't any visible reaction to the startling news.

"He most certainly will not get away with it," Trevor said with determination. "I'll press charges."

"And put the old man in jail?"

"Of course. What would you have me do?"

Rodney shrugged. "Ian is technically related to you by

marriage. That would make him a relative whether you like it or not. I don't think your wife would understand."

Trevor slammed his closed fist against the stable wall. "You're bloody right."

A lone rider galloped across the meadow, drawing Rodney's attention. "Are you expecting a guest?"

"No."

He nodded toward the advancing rider. "Well, I think you're getting ready not only to have company, but also to confront your enemy." Rodney bowed, then headed for the main house. "If you'll excuse me, I'll see you inside."

Trevor turned back as Ian Johnstone galloped up on a magnificent white stallion. He must have seen Trevor, for he headed straight toward him. Ian pulled his mount to a halt in front of Trevor.

Ian didn't dismount at first. He sat upon the stallion and looked down at Trevor with a critical eye. Ian could see more of Constance than her husband in Trevor. Perhaps there was some good in the man. However, Ian had yet to discover what it was.

"So, have ye been missing me, lad?" Ian taunted as he dismounted and tied off his mount.

"Like a bloody stomachache." Trevor folded his arms across his chest. "Why have you come?"

"I've come for Kristen."

Instantly, Trevor forgot his anger. "What's wrong?"

"Kristen isn't verra happy. Somehow, Lord knows why, she seems to be missing ye," Ian said, though it pained him to do so. "I think ye should pay her a visit."

"Did she send you?"

"Nay. However, since I'm the one who insisted she needed time to herself, I wagered it was my place to fix the problem."

"Then you are ready to let Kristen go?" Trevor showed very little emotion.

"If that's what she wants," Ian said.

"Strange that you should appear," Trevor said. "I was just informed that you had one of my ships sunk. Do you deny the fact?"

"Nay, I do not," Ian replied, looking Trevor straight in the eye.

"I cannot believe that you freely admit your deed. Perhaps you're more of a man than I first thought." Trevor shifted his stance. "Why did you do such a thing?"

Ian shrugged. " 'Twas before I met ye."

Trevor glanced impatiently toward heaven. "What does that have to do with anything?"

"Ye're family now," he acknowledged grudgingly. "I can see much of Constance in ye, so ye canna be all bad."

"It's so good of you to approve of me," Trevor said sarcastically. "Especially when one of my best ships is at the bottom of the sea."

"Did ye know that half the shipping business was once mine?"

"Really?" Trevor arched an eyebrow.

"Yer grandfather cheated me out of my half after I sank all my savings into the ships. I thought ye were just like him, so a few setbacks seemed in order. I figured ye were some dandy who had inherited his wealth and . . ." Ian paused and shrugged. "Ye see the picture. Perhaps I was mistaken. I will pay for yer lost ship."

"You're damned right you will!" Did the old buzzard think he could waltz in here and confess and Trevor would forget everything?

"Watch it, lad. I'm not used to this generous mood."

"What made you change your mind?"

"Despite the fact that ye are a Claremont, I believe ye

to be an honest man. And as I said, I see much of yer grandmother in ye. You canna be all bad.''

"Thank you, I think," Trevor said, frowning. "You have mentioned my grandmother several times. What was the feud about? Grandmère would never explain.''

"I've just finished recounting the entire story to Kristen. She will tell ye, providing ye are man enough to go after what's yers.''

Trevor's expression became a mask of stone. "What do you mean by that?''

"In order to be accepted by the Johnstones, I think ye need to prove yerself worthy of my granddaughter. 'Twould be the way of it if she'd been living with me all along.''

Trevor chuckled. A sound that came out dry and cynical. "You want me to win back what is already mine?''

Ian leaned back against the fence, his tension relaxing. "If ye think ye can," he taunted.

"And how do you suggest I win her back?''

Good, the lad was interested. Ian smiled. "By participating in the games we're having. There will be many brawny lads there, and Kristen has been long without a husband. She could decide that some of those Scottish lads look much better than ye do.''

Trevor stiffened immediately. "I need to play games in order to impress my wife?''

Ian threw his head back and roared with laughter. "Are ye afraid, lad?''

"Of course not," Trevor snapped. "I will participate in your bloody games. If for no other reason than to wipe that damned smile off your face when I do win!''

"I'm warning ye, the games are verra hard. It takes a brawny man to hurl those cabers." Ian moved back toward his horse.

"Thank you for your lack of confidence." Trevor propped both arms on the top rail. "I'll be there."

Ian mounted his horse, then looked back at the man. "I'm glad we had this little chat. I won't tell Kristen that ye are coming. Just in case ye change ye mind."

"I won't change my mind, you old buzzard," Trevor said. "Now be off with you before it's dark and I have to invite you to stay with me." This time the warmth of his smile echoed in his voice.

"Heaven forbid." Ian laughed. Then, kicking his horse into action, he rode off. Everything had gone as planned. The Englishman was easy to get riled.

Maybe now Trevor would prove how much he wanted Kristen. If he didn't kill himself first. The man wasn't as brawny as the Scottish lads, though more hardheaded. And, perhaps, a wee bit more determined.

Claremont just might be worthy of wearing the Johnstone colors after all.

One thing was certain . . . they would soon find out.

CHAPTER
TWENTY-THREE

The music had already begun.

A haunting melody surrounded Kristen, filling her with awe. She hadn't realized what a festive event these games would be. Glancing out the window, she saw the men gathering in groups talking. The bagpipes played behind them. Such a sweet sound, she thought. Somewhere in her vague memory she remembered hearing bagpipes as a child.

Today, she truly felt like a Scot, dressed in her blue plaid. Her finger traced the fine yellow line that darted through the plaid, proclaiming for all who saw that she was a Johnstone.

Taking the long drape of plaid material, she tossed it over her shoulder and secured it, then announced herself ready.

Her hair hung loose down her back, and she was trying to decide whether to tie it or let it hang free when Keely marched through the door.

"Are ye ready?" Keely asked.

"I think so." Kristen smiled. "Should I tie my hair back?"

"I didn't."

Kristen held her hands out and twirled, showing the swirl of her skirt. "How do I look?"

"Like a Johnstone." Keely grinned. "And exactly like me."

" 'Tis true. 'Tis like looking in a mirror."

Once outside, Kristen confessed to her sister, "I've never seen anything like this. Look at the colorful flags, and there are so many tents. They remind me of wild mushrooms."

Keely laughed. "I never thought of it like that, but ye're right." Arm in arm, the twins strolled to the top of the hill.

"Just look at those brawny men," Kristen said. They were much bigger than the men she was accustomed to seeing when she had lived near the docks.

" 'Tis the same every year. There is one in particular that is so big." Keely held out her hands. "He reminds me of a barbarian."

"Does he frighten ye?"

"Nay."

Kristen looked sharply at her sister, and she detected a special light in her twin's eyes. "I believe ye like this barbarian."

"Aye," Keely admitted with a blush. "He's almost as good-looking as yer Trevor."

Kristen frowned. "I'm not so sure he is my Trevor anymore. He hasn't been to see me or sent any word. Probably doesn't think about me at all."

"Perhaps he thinks ye dinna want to see him."

"Why would he think such a thing?"

"Because ye dinna say a thing about going with him after the trial. Ye just meekly came with us."

"He told me to go!"

"He might have said one thing, but felt another," Keely said wisely. "I know he was very concerned when he came here to get our help. He was determined to get ye out of jail."

"Well, he accomplished that, then politely sent me on my way," Kristen huffed.

"Kristen," a youthful voice called from behind them, and they both turned.

"Look, 'tis Hagan and a groom," Keely said.

Kristen gasped. " 'Tis no groom. 'Tis Trevor."

"Well, now ye have ye answer. He's come for ye," Keely whispered.

Trevor and Hagan dismounted and handed their horses over to a groom, then proceeded to the top of the hill, where the women stood. Hagan seemed eager to scamper ahead, but Trevor held him back.

Unable to move, Kristen could only watch. She had wanted to see Trevor so badly and now he was here. She held her breath. Trevor was dressed casually in a white linen shirt and black breeches, and, of course, shiny Hessian boots. He looked wonderful, even more so than she remembered.

Lord, how could a man look so good? she thought. And why did she have to be in love with him?

Hagan ran up and hugged her. "Have the games begun?"

"I dinna know. 'Tis where we are headed now."

Trevor stood before her. Kristen found herself remembering the time when she had asked him to teach her how to kiss. They had certainly mastered that. She wondered what he would say if she asked for another lesson.

He hadn't reached out to touch her, nor had he turned from her.

He looked so handsome. His hair was a little longer than the last time she had seen him, his stubborn jaw a little more prominent. Then there were his eyes . . . those wonderful eyes with their mixture of blue and green, a grayish turquoise. Today they were stormy, being neither blue nor green.

Her heart began to hammer in her chest as he gazed at her. Why didn't he say something . . . anything? Why didn't he take her into his arms?

Trevor had gone over what he would say to Kristen when he saw her at least a hundred times in his mind. Unfortunately, he couldn't remember a word of that speech. God, she was beautiful. That glorious red hair hung in disarray around her shoulders and the sun seemed to catch each strand, making it sparkle like hot gold. Her emerald eyes seemed to trap his gaze. They glittered with uncertainty, and he realized she felt the same things he did. However, this time they were going to get a few things straight between them first.

He reached out and pulled her to him. Thank God, she responded, wrapping her arms around him. It had been too long . . . much too long. "I've missed you," he whispered.

"I've missed ye too." Kristen's heart soared.

Ian walked briskly toward them. "So, you've decided to come," Ian said.

"I told you I would be here," Trevor replied, stepping away from Kristen.

"What is this about?" Kristen asked, confusion made her frown.

"Today, yer husband is going to prove he's man enough for ye," Ian said as he looked at her.

"I dinna understand." Kristen looked at her grandfather with surprise.

"Since Trevor never asked me properly for yer hand, I've challenged him to compete against these fine Scottish lads."

"He doesn't have to," Kristen protested.

Trevor glared at Ian. "Yes, I do."

Ian chuckled. "Then I suggest ye go and get dressed, or have ye not noticed ye are dressed differently from the rest?"

"Are you going to wear one of those skirts?" Hagan asked.

Trevor frowned. "It appears so."

Hagan laughed.

Trevor took him by the hand. "Come on, young man." Trevor pulled Hagan along with him. "If I can wear a dress so can you."

Ian showed them to a tent where he had clothes laid out for them.

Kristen wasn't sure how she felt about any of this until Trevor emerged from the tent. She stared at him, feeling very proud to have him in the Johnstone colors. For some reason, Trevor looked so much bigger in the tartan. And Hagan was adorable, even though he was frowning and brushing his kilt with his hand.

Trevor took Hagan over to where the other children were playing, and Kristen and Keely followed their grandfather.

Some fifty yards in front of them, the first game had begun. Two big men nodded to Ian, then moved over to speak with him.

One had to be the barbarian Keely had spoken of. Kristen found she agreed with her sister's description. He had brown hair that hung way past his shoulders and very dark brown eyes. He was as tall as a mountain and his body was just as wide, and he certainly had a glimmer in his eye as he looked at her twin.

" 'Tis a fine day for the games, Ian," the second man said. He had blond hair and eyes as green as the grass they stood upon. He was no small man either.

"I'm glad ye could come, Malcolm." Ian swatted Malcolm on the arm.

Malcolm peered around Ian, then straightened, his expression startled. "What have we here? Ye have two of the same," Malcolm remarked, his eyes never leaving Kristen.

"Malcolm Scott and Gillionan McDougald, I'd like ye to meet my granddaughter Kristen."

Malcolm immediately stepped in front of Kristen. "Where has Ian been hiding ye, lass?" He took her hand. "I do believe I've lost me heart."

"Then I suggest you find it quickly," Trevor said, moving beside her and glaring at Malcolm.

"And who might ye be, Englishman?" Malcolm asked with a frown.

"Her husband."

Malcolm swung around to Ian. " 'Tis unfair, Ian. Ye been promisin' the winner of the games could have a kiss from yer granddaughter."

"Kristen has been without a husband for a while. We were not too sure Trevor was coming. But being that he has agreed to participate in our games, the offer still stands. The winner of all still gets a kiss from either of my granddaughters." Ian's smile widened as he watched Trevor. "Ye havena changed yer mind, have ye?"

"I haven't," Trevor assured him. "Let's get on with it."

"Wait." Kristen tugged on her grandfather's sleeve. "Trevor doesn't have to prove anything to me."

"Aye, but he does to me," Ian stated with his hands on

his hips, looking very much like the laird that he was. " 'Tis been three months since ye've last see him." Ian looked pointedly at Kristen, his brow arched. "And if he'd asked me properly before he wed you, he would have had to prove himself to me."

"But—"

"Stay out of this, Kristen," Trevor snapped. "It's time that I demonstrate to your grandfather that I can beat any of these Scottish lads."

"We'll see about that, Englishman," Malcolm stated, then stalked over to where the game was being played.

Ian and Trevor followed Malcolm and Gillionan. No one had ever been jealous over Kristen, and the thought filled her with wonder. Trevor had most certainly acted jealous. Did that mean he did care for her, or was it just that she was his possession? Perhaps he'd come to tell her he wanted a divorce. Somehow the day didn't seem as bright as it had before.

Keely punched her sister in the side. "What did ye think of Gillionan?" she whispered.

"He's a fine one," Kristen admitted, trying to shake off her gloominess for her family's sake. "I think he likes you."

"I hope so. He makes my knees go weak," Keely admitted with a giggle.

"Aye, I know the feeling," Kristen confessed as they followed the men to the playing field. "What is this game they are playing?"

" 'Tis the stone toss."

"That doesn't look like a stone to me."

" 'Tis a big stone," Keely said, but Kristen noticed her twin's gaze had settled firmly on Gillionan. "About sixteen pounds, I believe Grandfather said."

"What do they do with it?" Kristen asked with a wry

smile, knowing her sister would rather watch Gillionan flexing his muscles than tell her about the game.

"That board there is a toe board," Keely finally said, her eyes still on Gillionan. "They canna go past it. They take the stone, place it on their shoulder and under their chin. Then they whirl around and throw the stone. They get three throws, but only the longest counts."

Kristen watched as Malcolm picked up the huge round stone. "This one's for ye, lass." He nodded toward Kristen, and winked.

Kristen couldn't help but smile. He really was being brash. But the minute she smiled, Trevor frowned.

Malcolm's throws were good. Each one further than the last.

The next five men came nowhere close to Malcolm's distance. Finally, it was Trevor's turn.

Malcolm looked at Trevor. "I believe ye'll have a tough time, Englishman. I'll be enjoying the kiss I'm to receive from yer wife."

"Like hell you will," Trevor ground out as he picked up the stone with very little effort and placed it on his shoulder.

Kristen was surprised at the muscles she saw in Trevor's arms when he lifted the stone. Then she remembered she'd first seen Trevor aboard a ship where he must have done some heavy work. He was just as brawny as the other men.

Trevor's first shot fell half the distance of Malcolm's shortest toss.

"Got to do better than that, Englishman," Malcolm taunted.

Trevor didn't bother to respond. His second shot was disqualified because his toe went over the line. This time he swore and Malcolm laughed.

The muscles tightened in Trevor's jaw as he picked up the stone again. He paused before he threw, making sure he had the stone positioned just right. Kristen held her breath as he concentrated very hard. Suddenly, he spun around and heaved the stone and sent it soaring through the air. The crowd hushed as the rock sailed by them to land six inches further than Malcolm's.

Kristen applauded and cheered, which produced a big smile from her husband. Maybe the day would turn out well after all.

The games went on all afternoon. Some Trevor won and some Malcolm won. It was as if they were the only competitors.

During a break in the men's competition, Kristen and Keely decided to check on Hagan. On the way, they passed a group of ladies playing a game.

"What are they doing?" Kristen asked, pointing to the laughing women.

"They're tossing the wellie."

"It looks like a boot to me."

Keely laughed. "It is. I was told the game started when the men would come home from the fields, and would enter the house with muddy boots, tracking mud onto the freshly washed floor. As ye can imagine, the women who had been hard at work all day scrubbing the floors were so angry that they grabbed up the boots, chased the men out of the house, and threw the offending boots at them."

Kristen laughed. "So now 'tis a game to see who can throw the boot the farthest?"

Keely nodded. "That's right. Would ye like to play?"

"Nay. I've had no experience thus far throwing anything," Kristen admitted. "The truth be told, I dinna feel much like a wife."

"Ye've not had a normal marriage thus far." Keely squeezed Kristen's arm. "It will get better."

They found Hagan playing with about ten other children.

Hagan looked up and, spotting his sister, ran to her. "I don't have to go, do I?"

"Nay, I was just checking to see what ye were up to."

"They have all kinds of games," Hagan said, the excitement showing in his eyes. "They're going to teach me to hurl the haggis. They like to throw everything." Hagan looked around. "Where is Trevor?"

"He is still competing with the other men. Right now they are resting."

"Is he winning?"

"Aye."

Hagan giggled.

"What's so funny?"

Hagan motioned for his sister to bend down so he could whisper. "Trevor said Hell would freeze over before he lost to a Scot," Hagan informed her, then ran back to his friends.

Kristen shook her head and then wandered over to where Keely stood. The music played, and they watched the Scottish dancers dancing around the swords. But no matter where she went in the crowd, her mind was on Trevor.

Soon it was time to eat. They spread out blankets and some food and were joined by Trevor, Ian, and Gillionan. They feasted on roasted chicken and crusty bread prepared by the cooks.

"Ye've proven yerself well," Ian said to Trevor. "However, Malcolm got the best of ye the last game. Are ye worried?"

"Has anyone ever told you that you're a crafty old buzzard?"

"I believe I've heard that from ye." Ian chuckled.

Kristen marveled at what she was seeing and hearing. Her grandfather and Trevor were actually joking with one another. Maybe after the talk she had with her grandfather he had softened, but that still didn't explain Trevor's change. Before she'd only heard him say bad things about the Johnstones. What was going on that she didn't understand?

Trevor leaned back on his elbows. "What is the next event?"

" 'Tis the caber toss. The hardest game of all. It carries twice the points."

Trevor had an odd expression on his face as he asked, "When?"

"Half an hour. We'll give everyone's meal a chance to settle a wee bit," Ian said as he got to his feet and stretched his back. "If ye'll excuse me, I'd best check on the rest of our guests."

After Ian left, Trevor leaned over and whispered something to Keely. She nodded her head in answer. Then he looked at Kristen. "I'll see you at the next game," he said, then got to his feet.

Kristen watched him go. She didn't understand her husband at all. She wanted to ask Keely what Trevor had said to her, but her twin got up and left with Gillionan.

Kristen put away the food and folded the blankets, then made her way to where they would have the caber toss. She stared at several long poles and shook her head.

"What's wrong?" Keely asked.

"I dinna see what they are going to do with those logs. They look heavy."

"Aye, about one hundred and twenty pounds. I dinna

see how they throw them either, but they do. Look, the first man's ready.''

They watched him throw his caber. It hit the ground and fell backward. He swore and moved off.

''What's wrong?'' Kristen whispered.

''They must toss the caber end over end so that it lands with the bottom or small end pointed directly away from the contestant.''

''I dinna see the point. How did they come up with such a silly game?''

'' 'Tis the same thing I asked. Grandfather told me it started when the men were clearing the forest to make fields. There were so many streams to be crossed that the men would toss trees across the streams so that one end was on each bank. Those who couldn't toss the trees correctly ended up with wet feet all day.''

Kristen laughed. ''Let's hope Trevor can keep his feet dry.''

He was next.

She couldn't believe how easily Trevor lifted the caber, his muscles straining with the weight of the thing. His toss was perfect. But so was Malcolm's. They went back and forth several times, until Ian finally declared a tie.

She hurried to congratulate her husband, but Trevor turned briskly in the other direction and disappeared, leaving her filled with disappointment.

Tears stung her eyes as everyone gathered round so that Ian could present the awards. Everyone except Trevor. Was he angry that she would have to kiss Malcolm too? Maybe he didn't care and had returned home.

Malcolm eyed her from across the field as the men cheered him.

Kristen swallowed hard. She'd simply kiss him on the cheek and it would be over with . . . she hoped.

She scanned the crowd. Where was Trevor?

Ian stepped up on a small platform. "I'm proud to announce that our overall winners are two. Malcolm Scott and Trevor Claremont." Ian turned to Malcolm. "Seeing as I dinna see Trevor at the moment, ye can collect yer reward first. Which of my lovely granddaughters do yer choose for yer kiss?"

Malcolm moved up beside Ian. "I prefer the redheaded lass."

The cheers of the other men roared around her. Kristen's face heated with embarrassment as Ian looked at her too.

"Kristen, lass, would ye come up here?"

She maneuvered through the crowd and across the field. She must get this over with, and it didn't appear that Trevor wanted his prize at all, which was a severe blow to her ego.

She'd just reached the top of the platform when she looked up. Malcolm advanced toward her with lust in his eyes.

From out of nowhere, she heard the pounding of a horse's hooves. She turned. A rider raced across the field at a breakneck pace. The crowd turned to see who approached.

The rider didn't slow as he approached the group, and they had to scatter like ants to get out of the way.

Kristen gasped when she recognized the rider. He galloped straight toward her. He had no intention of stopping. Was he going to run her down?

She hadn't meant to make him *that* angry.

The next thing she knew, she'd been swept off her feet and pulled in front of Trevor. His arms tightened around her as they sped off. Shouts from the crowd followed until they became a soft whisper on the wind.

Kristen felt so contented to be held by Trevor that several minutes went by before she asked, "Where are we going?"

"I wanted to speak with you," Trevor said tersely.

"Ye could have spoken with me back there."

"No, I could not."

Kristen was surprised that she wasn't worried about their talk as she'd been earlier. She decided to test his mood. "I dinna get the chance to give Malcolm his prize."

"Nor will you," Trevor snapped.

He sounded jealous. Good, she thought, and pressed for more. "He did tie with ye, after all."

"He's a bloody pain in the ass. If he wants his kiss, he'll have to choose Keely."

Kristen smiled, but Trevor couldn't see it. "But he didn't want Keely."

Trevor jerked his mount to a stop, grasped Kristen by the shoulders, and glared at her. "I'll not have you kissing another man. You're my wife."

And to prove the point, he pulled her to him, crushing her within her arms. With the swiftness of a bird of prey, his mouth swooped down on hers in the most breathtaking kiss she'd ever experienced.

Trevor tasted heavenly. After the initial shock, his mouth softened and he began to place soft kisses over her face, tender kisses down her throat until she shivered within his arms.

Looking down at her, he whispered, "We'll continue this later."

Once again, he enfolded her in his arms. He kneed his mount, and they galloped off toward Chatsworth.

Trevor reined in his sweating steed and dismounted at the front door. He said nothing, but took her upstairs to his room.

Once inside, she turned to face him. Hoping for the

best, fearing the worst, yet knowing they had to talk, she could not go on. She had to know how he felt.

"Kristen." Trevor paused. "I don't know where to begin."

She watched him, afraid to say anything for fear that it might be wrong.

"I can see you're not going to help me." He didn't look happy. "Kristen, I think . . ."

Oh my God, he wanted a divorce. No, Kristen prayed. Please don't take him from me. Not the only thing I've ever wanted.

"Kristen, I—I . . ."

CHAPTER TWENTY-FOUR

"Kristen, I want to start again."

"Ye want a divorce?" Kristen asked, not knowing what he meant. From somewhere far off, she heard Constance's voice as if she were still standing beside Kristen.

You must get Trevor to open up if you ever want to keep him. Remember, everyone he has ever given his love to has let him down. He has grown cold inside.

"No," Trevor stated flatly. "Not unless you do."

Kristen closed her eyes and shook her head. "Nay, I do not." Finally, she opened her eyes and asked, "What do you want?" She held her breath as she waited for the answer.

Trevor laughed wryly. "Do you know how many times I've asked myself the same thing?" He saw the anticipation in Kristen's wide emerald eyes as she waited for him to say more. A voice he thought never to hear again sounded in his ear.

You can't go through life keeping everyone at arm's length. You must open your heart and trust. For if you're not careful, you'll lose her.

Trevor looked around as if he expected to see his grand-mother behind him. But no one was there.

"What is it?"

"I thought I heard—never mind," Trevor said, looking back to Kristen. "I want you to stay here and be my wife," he finally said, and then in a softer voice, "I need you."

Kristen couldn't move. She wanted to leap into his arms, yet she held back. She needed more, but found she was unsure how to ask for it.

Look deep inside yourself, and you'll find out what to do.

Kristen smiled as Constance gave her the final shove. "I *canna* promise that I'll never be any trouble."

Trevor laughed. "I must admit you have kept me in a whirlwind. The funny part is that I've come to like it." He took a step toward her.

"I *can* promise that I will never leave ye. If ye get tired of me, ye'll have to send me away."

"That will never happen," Trevor admitted. His gaze never left her. He took another step toward her. "Remem-ber, until death do us part."

"I plan on living a long, long time." Kristen blushed. Her heart raced faster the closer he got to her. For once, she was letting him make the first move.

"As do I, providing I can keep all weapons out of your hands."

She blushed. "I really didna mean to shoot ye."

"Oh, really?" He stopped in front of her.

"Had I not, we never would have met," she pointed out.

"Well, your plan worked." His breath brushed across her face.

"Aye," she said with a sigh, and looked into his eyes. "Say the words."

"What words?"

"The ones ye have avoided saying since the moment we met."

He lifted a finger and brushed her cheek softly with a gentle touch. "It took me a little while to figure everything out."

"And what did ye find?"

"I found that the sun and the stars were much duller when you were not around."

"And?"

"And my life was empty without you." He cupped her chin and tilted her face up.

"And?" she prodded.

His thumb traced her bottom lip. "And I could think of no others, but you."

"And?"

"And . . . I love you, Kristen Johnstone Claremont. From the moment you taught me there was more to life than just going through the motions. You are the stars . . . the moon . . . you are my life."

Kristen began to tremble as Trevor's mouth descended to hers. But instead of kissing her, he just brushed her lips and moved to place warm kisses across her ear. When his tongue touched her soft lobe, she had to grasp his arms to keep from falling. He whispered how much he loved her over and over again.

Gathering her courage, she murmured, "Trevor, ye have taught me many things. Can ye teach me how to have a baby?"

His mouth covered hers in a heart-stopping kiss that robbed her of her breath. After a long moment, he lifted his mouth and she saw the dark passion that burned in his eyes.

"I think that can be arranged," he murmured. He caressed her lips again. Then drawing in a steadying breath, he whispered huskily, "If you catch on as quickly as you did to kissing, we shall have a house full of children."

"I love ye, Trevor." Kristen gazed up at the one thing she had wanted all her life. She just hadn't known that it was Trevor. "I'm ready for my first lesson."

Trevor chuckled as he lifted her off her feet and carried her to the bed. "Kristen, *you are a wicked lady.*"

"Aye," Kristen murmured as she finally found her little bit of heaven . . .

"And yer a wicked man."